Over the Rainbow

KATIE FLYNN

Over the Rainbow

CENTURY

1 3 5 7 9 10 8 6 4 2

Century
20 Vauxhall Bridge Road
London SW1V 2SA

Century is part of the Penguin Random House group of companies whose
addresses can be found at global.penguinrandomhouse.com.

First published in Great Britain by Century in 2021

www.penguin.co.uk

A CIP catalogue record for this book is available from the British Library.

ISBN 9781529123890

Typeset in 13/16.5 pt Palatino LT Pro
by Integra Software Services Pvt. Ltd, Pondicherry

Printed and bound in Great Britain by Clays Ltd, Elcograf S.p.A.

The authorised representative in the EEA is Penguin Random House Ireland,
Morrison Chambers, 32 Nassau Street, Dublin D02 YH68.

Penguin Random House is committed to a sustainable future for
our business, our readers and our planet. This book is made from
Forest Stewardship Council® certified paper.

Acknowledgements

The brave women of the WAAF who carried on despite the danger.

Mum.
For giving me the confidence to believe in myself.

Prologue

1922

Olivia Campbell was watching the dragonflies as they hovered above the surface of the pond when she overheard a boy's voice from the far side of the privet hedge. He appeared to be having a heated discussion with someone. Of course, Olivia knew it was wrong to eavesdrop, but he was being so vocal with his thoughts it was impossible not to overhear.

'The man's an idiot,' he said sullenly, 'a bully and a coward.'

Olivia listened with interest, wondering who it was the boy had such beef with. She waited for the other person's response, hoping that they would shed some light on the matter, but the boy continued to talk before his companion had a chance to respond.

'He thinks he can do what he wants because it's him what pays our measly wages,' he fumed. 'The whole thing's a damned joke if you ask me. The old git gives with one hand and takes with the other, paying us to work for him then taking it back through the rent he charges for his run-down, rat-infested, damp-riddled slums.'

Olivia gently nibbled the inside of her bottom lip. The man he was describing sounded very much like her father. The Campbells were used to disgruntled workers visiting the house to air their grievances, but they normally came on their own. Her father might be a miserable so-and-so, but he was getting on in years, and two against one wasn't fair on any man. She frowned. Whoever the boy was talking to seemed unwilling to make a contribution to the conversation. As he drew nearer to the house, she decided to see for herself just how many of them there were.

She walked along the length of the hedge until she came to a gap where an old gate once stood. Crouching down, she peeped through the sparse branches as she waited for the boy to draw level. Much to her surprise, he appeared to be on his own. Not wishing to be caught spying, she quickly ducked back down out of sight, but she was too late. The boy stopped abruptly and turned to face her, then stepped forward and peered through the gap in the hedge. 'Hello?'

Olivia kept quiet, hoping that he would believe himself to be mistaken and move on, but instead he edged closer to the small gap and looked through. She tried to make herself as small as possible, but in doing so she caught his eye. He pointed at her. 'I can see you!'

Olivia looked up in embarrassment. 'I wasn't spying! I live here,' she said defensively. She stood up and indicated the house just visible through the trees.

He looked past Olivia to the large white house much further up the garden and blew a low whistle. 'Blimey! You must have a penny or two!'

Her cheeks turning pink, she averted her gaze. 'Not me, my dad.'

'Who's he? William Campbell?' He laughed, expecting her to laugh with him, but seeing the stony expression on her face he stopped short, his Adam's apple bobbing nervously in his throat.

'Is it him you're mad at?' Olivia asked tentatively.

He swallowed before turning on his heel. 'I'd best be off.'

Being an only child, and with no friends of her own and she was keen for him not to shoot off before she'd had a chance to talk to him properly. 'What's your name?'

He shook his head, then considered her question. 'Why do you want to know? So that you can run off and tattle-tale to your dad?'

Olivia's cheeks flushed hotly. She knew people talked badly about her father and could fully understand why; the last thing she would do was tell tales on someone for speaking the truth. She drew the sign of the cross over her left breast. 'I promise I won't say a word.'

He regarded her sceptically. 'Why wouldn't you tell your father what I'd been saying?'

Olivia eyed him darkly. 'Because it's not just his employees who he's mean to.'

His brow shot towards his hairline. 'You mean ...'

Olivia nodded. 'Do you want to come in? Only people might think you're a bit strange if they see you talking to a hedge.'

For the first time since they'd met, the boy grinned. He pushed his sandy hair back from his eyes and winked at her. 'Oh, I dunno, I've been talkin' to myself most of the way here.'

Olivia giggled. 'I did hear.'

Stepping back, he glanced the length of the hedge. 'How do I get in?'

Olivia's tummy gave an excited jolt as she pressed closer towards the gap in the hedge and pulled at some of the branches which had grown across the old gateway.

'Thanks!' said the boy as he passed through. He held out a hand. 'My name's Edward Hewitt – my pals call me Ted.'

She shook his hand. 'Hello, Ted, I'm Olivia.' She gazed into his ice-blue eyes which looked back at her with warm intrigue.

'Olivia's a bit of a mouthful. What do your pals call you?'

She looked down at her tan Josie Jane shoes in embarrassment. 'I don't really have any friends.'

He glanced in the direction of the large house. 'If your father treats your school pals the same as his workers, then I can't say I'm surprised.'

Olivia followed his gaze. 'I daresay it'd be like that if he allowed me to go to school, but I have a private tutor – Mrs Bellingham. She's not a bad old stick, but it's not the same as being with people your own age. There again, that's the whole reason why he doesn't want me to go to school, because he doesn't want me mixing with the local children – he thinks they're beneath us.' Her eyes flicked up to meet his. 'Sorry.'

'Doesn't bother me none,' laughed Ted, '''cos I'm not local.'

Olivia could have kicked herself. She had spoken without thinking. Of course Ted wasn't local – he couldn't afford to live somewhere like Aigburth Drive on the wages her father paid. 'Sorry, I didn't think.' She glanced back at the house. 'I know you're angry at my father, and I don't blame you for wanting to give him a piece of your mind, but I think it might be wise to reconsider. He wouldn't think twice about reporting you to the police, and that's if you're lucky. If he's in a really bad mood he won't bother with the police, he'll ...' Her voice faded into silence.

Ted eyed her sharply. 'He'll what?'

Olivia looked miserable. 'He'll take the law into his own hands and deal with you himself.' She rubbed her forearm as the words left her lips.

Ted fixated on her forearm. 'I know he's got a bad temper, but I didn't think he'd raise a hand to a woman, especially not his own daughter!'

Olivia stared at him. He'd referred to her as a woman, yet she was only thirteen. She unconsciously pulled the cuff of her cardigan sleeve down over her wrist. 'Please don't misunderstand, he'd never hit me, but he has got a short fuse, and if things aren't going his way his patience wears thin.'

Ted shook his head. 'My dad doesn't have a lot of time but he'd never hurt me – on purpose or otherwise.'

Olivia knew that she was making excuses for her father and that he shouldn't lose his temper as easily as he did, but he was still her father. Eager to change the subject, she looked in the direction of the pond. 'Would you like to see the koi carp?'

Ted's eyes grew wide. 'Would I ever!'

Glad that her father was no longer the centre of their discussion, Olivia led him over to the pond and knelt down. Ted followed suit and together they peered between the lily pads into the inky water. She quickly pointed to a large white koi with orange spots as its back broke the surface. 'Beautiful, aren't they?'

Ted nodded. 'Worth a bob or two an' all.'

'Of course they are,' sighed Olivia, for no matter what she said, the subject invariably turned back to her father in some form or other. 'My father wouldn't have ordinary goldfish because that wouldn't impress any-one. Everything he owns has to be of value.' She gently stroked the tip of the koi's back with her finger. 'You never told me whether you were here to confront him or not.' She glanced at Ted. 'Were you?'

Ted dipped the tip of his forefinger into the water and waited to see if a fish would come for a nibble as he pondered his response. 'I wanted to,' he said slowly, 'but I don't think I'd have gone through with it, not when push came to shove, because I'm not the only one with something to lose.'

She looked at him curiously. 'Oh?'

He leaned back on his haunches. 'My dad also works for your father, so I'd have been putting his job at risk as well as my own, summat I don't think he'd thank me for.'

Olivia nodded wisely. 'Like I said before, you wouldn't be the first to come round here shouting the odds, and unfortunately you wouldn't be the first he sacked and evicted on the spot.'

'That's pretty much what I thought he'd do,' Ted said sullenly. 'It's not fair, he holds all the cards.'

Olivia shook her head sadly. 'I know, but at least you can get away from him after work. Think about me – I have to live with him.'

'If he treats you like he does us, then you have my sympathy.' Ted glanced in the general direction of the house. 'Mind you, your house is big enough to get away from him.'

Olivia smiled absently. 'Is your house really infested with rats?'

Ted frowned. 'What?'

'Only I heard you mention something about rat-infested …'

Ted gave her a lopsided smile. 'All right, so maybe that was a bit of an exaggeration, but I'm sure it would be if my father didn't keep on top of the repairs.'

'He's good at mending things then?'

Ted nodded. 'He's a mechanic in the factory, so he fixes the machines when they break down and makes new parts when they need him to. He's always been handy like that.'

Olivia thought of her own father, who never got his own hands dirty. 'He shouldn't be doing the repairs himself – my father should be responsible for that.'

Ted's eyebrows rose fleetingly. 'I don't think your father would agree with you on that one. According to him, if we live in it, we should be the ones that keep it in good order.'

Olivia tutted softly. 'Sounds about right.' She hesitated. 'Would you mind awfully if we stopped talking about my father?'

Ted grinned. 'Not at all.'

They spent the rest of the afternoon chatting idly as they watched the koi swim lazily around the pond. Ted told Olivia about the house he and his father shared in Fisher Street, not far from the Campbells' factory where they both worked, his father Craig as a mechanic and Ted as a general dogsbody. When Olivia asked about Ted's mother, his tone changed from light-hearted to serious as he relayed the story of how his mother had died from dysentery when he was a small child.

Olivia's heart plummeted as she heard his sad tale. Her own mother had been suffering from ill health for some time now, and it had crossed Olivia's mind more than once that this could be something her mother might not come back from, and she couldn't imagine what life would be like without her.

When Ted asked about her own life, she spoke only about her mother and grandparents, shying away from any mention of her father.

As the daylight began to fade, Ted got to his feet. 'I'd best be off before my dad wonders where I am.'

Olivia looked back at the house. 'My father couldn't care less where I am,' she said baldly. 'As long as I'm not getting under his feet or making a nuisance of myself.'

Tilting his head to one side, he regarded her through twinkling eyes. 'Can I see you again?'

Olivia's eyes lit up. 'I'd like that very much.'

He grinned. 'Shall we say the same time tomorrow, after I finish work?'

Olivia nodded eagerly. 'I look forward to it.'

She watched as he pushed his sandy hair back with his fingers. Olivia liked the way it flopped over his brow in a roguish fashion. 'Only I can't keep calling you Olivia,' he said. 'It sounds too posh ...' His eyes sparkled as he gazed down at her. 'I know, I'll call you Toff!'

'I'm not a toff!' giggled Olivia, who was secretly pleased to be given a nickname.

'You are compared to me,' Ted said firmly.

True to his word, he came back to see her the next day, and the one after that, and the one after that, and it wasn't long before the two had become firm friends, with Ted visiting most days. Olivia had even accompanied Ted to his house on Fisher Street, much to the disapproval of Ted's father who worried that his employer might have something to say if he learned of his daughter's whereabouts.

'I promise not to tell, Mr Hewitt,' Olivia assured him.

Craig Hewitt wagged a finger at his son, although he smiled as he did so. 'Just you make sure you treat Miss Campbell like a lady!'

Ted gave his father his word that he would do so, and Olivia became a regular at the Hewitts' house. Nearly a year to the day of their first meeting had gone by before things began to go wrong. Olivia was sitting beside the pond one day when a pair of hands gently covered her eyes from behind.

'Guess who?' said Ted.

Olivia laughed. 'Honestly, Ted, I'd know your voice anywhere!'

'Worth a try,' he said, settling down beside her.

Olivia leaned against his shoulder. 'Golly, I'm glad you're here.'

Ted placed a friendly arm around her shoulder. 'I take it your father's had another one of his temper tantrums?'

Olivia nodded. 'He got impatient with Mum because she was so tired. He told her she needed to make more of an effort and said she'd never get better if she didn't try.' A tear trickled down the side of her nose. 'I told him he couldn't bully someone into getting better but he wouldn't listen. In fact, I think I might have made him worse because he started to try and pull Mum out of her chair. I was scared he was going to hurt her by accident, so I pushed him off her, and that's when he lost his balance.' She shook her head. 'He was as mad as fire when he threw his walking stick at me – it's a good thing I'm quick on my feet.'

Ted's jaw tightened. 'The one with the dog's head?'

She nodded. 'It's the only one he's got.'

Pulling her close, Ted absent-mindedly kissed the top of her head. 'Don't blame yourself, you were only trying to look after your mother.' He rubbed her shoulder with the palm of his hand. 'If he ever gets too much you can come and hide at ours for a bit.'

She smiled up at him. 'Thanks, Ted.' As she gazed into his eyes, something seemed to be different. She wasn't certain what it was, but in that instant, her feelings towards him had changed and she was fairly certain that Ted had noticed it too, because he was no longer gazing fixedly at her but his attention was alternating between her eyes and her mouth, until eventually settling on her lips. Leaning forward, he kissed her clumsily on the mouth.

Olivia's heart was racing. She had never been kissed by a boy before, not even on the cheek, yet here she was with her dearest friend, sharing their first kiss. He pulled back, eyeing her with shy uncertainty. 'Do you mind?'

A faint hint of pink tinged her cheeks as she smiled back. Yesterday had been her fourteenth birthday, and

10

today had been her first kiss. 'Not when it's you doing the kissing, Ted Hewitt,' she mumbled, and was pleased when he leaned forward and continued to kiss her softly.

She didn't know what it was about Ted, but whenever he was around, it was as though all her troubles had melted away. His mere presence filled her with a warm certainty that everything was right with the world. As they continued to kiss, Olivia felt as though his lips were making her lighter than air. Just as she wished that this moment would last forever, she was jolted from their magical embrace by an angry explosion erupting through the trees behind them. Turning sharply to see what the commotion was, Olivia saw her father striding towards them, his face blood-red with rage. She squealed in alarm and jumped to her feet. 'Go, Ted!' she ordered, but Ted was reluctant to leave her on her own with her father in such a furious temper, so he half turned to face the other man, his hands held up placatingly. Fearing her father's response, Olivia grabbed Ted by the hand and pulled him out of the garden, and they ran as fast as their legs could carry them, not stopping until they had reached the corner of Livingston Drive.

Panting, Olivia looked at Ted before bursting into laughter.

'It's not funny, Toff,' said Ted, fighting for breath, but then he, too, started to laugh.

When they had both finally calmed down, Ted pulled a rueful face. 'I'm certain he didn't get a good look at me, but I daresay that won't make any difference to how he treats you when you go home.'

Olivia shrugged. 'Not a lot I can do about it now. The way I see it, I may as well get hung for a sheep ...'

Ted raised an eyebrow. 'Do you want to come back to mine for a bit?'

Olivia glanced in the direction of Aigburth Drive. 'Well, I certainly don't want to go back there until he's had a chance to calm down, so we may as well,' she bit her lip, 'only I'd rather you didn't mention any of this to your father.'

Ted nodded. 'Don't worry, I don't intend to. He'd only give us a lecture on how he'd warned us that something like this might happen.' Taking her hand in his, he gave it a reassuring little shake. 'If we're lucky he might've gone fishing with his mates.'

When Olivia returned home later that evening, her father was waiting for her in the library. He had demanded she tell him the name of the boy, but Olivia had refused, so he had proceeded to call her all manner of names, none of them nice, before sending her to her room and forbidding her from seeing the boy again.

Olivia blanched at his last words. 'But he's my only friend!' she wailed.

Her father eyed her testily. 'I'm not blind. I could see him slobbering all over you, so you're a damned sight more than friends!'

Blushing, Olivia left the room without a backward glance. She would be hanged if she would allow her miserable father to ruin her only friendship. She headed up the stairs with grim determination. She would go to the garden tomorrow, and if Ted came to see her – and she was certain he would – they would come up with a new meeting place, somewhere her father couldn't find them.

The next day when Olivia entered the garden she saw that the hole in the hedge had been boarded over. Determined that her father would not stop her from seeing Ted, she decided that if he couldn't come to her, she would go to him. She cut across the lawn only to see her father halfway down the sweeping drive, leaning on his walking stick, clearly waiting for her to turn up. 'And just where do you think you're going?' he challenged.

Olivia ignored him. What was the point in responding when they both knew the answer? Her father stepped into her path and repeated the question, but Olivia sidestepped him. She never normally argued with her father over anything, but Ted was worth fighting for; he had brought her a new freedom, making her feel like she was special. If she was to give in to her father now, she would go back to a lonely and miserable existence. Her heart fluttered in her chest, as she felt his hand encircle her wrist. It was now or never. She yanked her wrist sharply in an effort to free herself from his grip. In that moment a number of things happened. Olivia's father momentarily lost balance, and whether he had meant to strike her or not, she couldn't be certain, but either way the handle of his cane split in two as it connected with her cheek. Whilst her father was not unaccustomed to throwing things in his temper, or gripping hold of her harder than he should, up until now he had never struck her with anything. Olivia stood still in shock, slowly putting a hand up to her cheek which was already beginning to throb.

Her father began to mumble a hasty apology, but Olivia was too upset to listen. Something Ted had often told her rang out in her mind: 'You can always come here if it gets too much.' Without a moment's hesitation, she ran down the gravelled drive.

Hearing someone hammering against the front door, Ted jerked it open, only to see Olivia standing before him, her cheek swollen and her eye beginning to turn purple. He enveloped her in a tight embrace as she sobbed into his chest.

'I'll ruddy well kill him,' Ted whispered as he kissed the top of her head.

Olivia melted into the warmth and safety of his embrace. She wished fervently that she could move in with Ted and his father so that she might never have to go home again, but she knew that wasn't an option, not with her mother being as ill as she was. Sighing heavily, she decided to make the most of the time with Ted, before having to return to her father who would undoubtedly be full of apologies, but also resolute that she had caused him to lose his temper and put measures in place to prevent her from ever leaving the house again.

Chapter One

Spring 1923

Tears streamed down Olivia's cheeks as she raced to warn Ted of her father's imminent arrival. He had been understandably furious when he had heard the news, and even though he had assured her he was only going to talk to Ted, she had heard the gravel flying up as the car tyres spun down the drive.

She chastised herself inwardly. How could she have been so careless? In her naivety she had drawn a large love heart in her diary with her and Ted's names inside. Not only that, but she had written her darkest secrets within the pages, and it was one of those secrets in particular which had caused her father to throw the diary across the room before confronting her. Her defence had been to accuse him of reading her diary without her permission, although even she realised this was a lame excuse given the gravity of the situation.

Unable to run any further, she stopped at the corner of Colebrooke Road. Fighting for breath, she winced as the sharp pain of a stitch formed in her side. She gripped hold of the brick wall bordering someone's garden as everything started to spin. Stumbling, she tried to regain her balance, but it was no use and she sank to her knees. Trying to focus on her route, she began to crawl forward in a desperate bid to complete her journey, but she was exhausted from having run the best part of a mile and her body had run out of strength. Her attempt to try to stop her father had proved futile, although how she had expected to catch up with him when he was in the Daimler, she had no idea. Another thought occurred to her. Her father hadn't bothered calling for Robin, their chauffeur, to drive him, but had taken the wheel himself. For a moment she wondered why he had done so, but she already knew the answer. Her father wouldn't want any of his staff to know his business.

She paused for thought. Today was Saturday, so there was every chance that Ted wasn't at home because he played football with some of the lads from the factory on a Saturday. She wondered if her father knew this. Even if he did, there was no way he would single Ted out in front of a pitch full of witnesses. Her stomach turned as an alternative image entered her mind: Ted opening the door to his house, only to find himself confronted with her father, purple with rage, shouting accusations and threats. Ted would deny the accusations because he truly didn't know any different. He would be caught completely unawares, with no chance to defend his actions, on top of which he would doubtless find himself jobless and homeless. It wasn't just Ted who would suffer but his father also.

She began to relive the dreadful moments which had led to the damning revelation. She had been in her mother's bedroom ... Olivia froze. Her mother! In her haste to save Ted, she had fled the house leaving her mother alone in her room. Her cheeks reddening with shameful guilt, she found the strength to get to her feet. Taking a deep breath, she began to make her way back to her mother, who would doubtless be beside herself with worry.

Olivia cursed softly beneath her breath. As a child, her mother Catherine had been struck down with polio, but thanks to the loving care of her parents, she had made a full recovery and they hadn't given the matter another thought. However, Catherine had now been suffering from ill health for many years, and it seemed that she no sooner got over one cold or chest infection than she would be struck down with another. Recently she had started to display the same symptoms as she had as a child, and they had called for Doctor Palmer, who diagnosed her with post-polio syndrome. Olivia had thought her mother would get over this as she had when she was a child, but it wasn't that simple. Doctor Palmer had gone on to explain that post-polio was incurable with a gradual deterioration of the muscles. Olivia had turned to her father for comfort, but he had refused to listen to the doctor, claiming that her mother had always been of a fragile nature, and she was allowing it to get the better of her.

Olivia couldn't believe what she was hearing. She knew from her grandparents – Nana and Pops – that their daughter had always been a fighter, which was how she had got over the polio in the first place.

Now, as she rounded the entrance to the gravelled drive, she looked at the light in the upstairs window. A

17

wave of guilt swept through her. How could she have left her mother alone, to go on a wild goose chase? Another thought entered her mind, causing her to take the stairs two at a time. What if her mother had tried to come after them, and had an accident? She knocked tentatively on the door to her mother's bedroom.

Her mother's voice called anxiously from the other side of the door. 'Is that you, Liv?'

Olivia entered the room.

A visible wave of relief swept over her mother's face. 'Oh, Liv darling!'

Olivia rushed to her mother who was half in, half out of her chair. 'Mum! What on earth were you thinking of?'

Her mother gave her a wobbly smile of embarrassment. 'You took off like a hare, I was frightened you'd do something silly.'

Olivia gently assisted her mother back into the chair. 'I'm sorry, Mum, I just didn't think. I know what Dad can be like and I was worried he was out for Ted's blood.'

Her mother gave her a chiding look. 'I know he can be a law unto himself and he's quick to react, but you can't blame him for being angry, not after what he'd just read.'

Tears forming in her eyes, Olivia nodded guiltily. 'But he'll take it too far, Mum, he always does, and who knows what he's capable of? Although I'm surprised he cares,' she added bitterly. 'He normally doesn't give two hoots what I get up to as long as I don't get in his way.'

Her mother arched an eyebrow. 'A man with his reputation and you didn't think he'd be bothered?' She shook her head in disbelief. 'Not even you can be that naive, Liv.'

'So, you're saying he's only angry because he's worried what other people might think of him?'

Her mother tutted softly. 'Of course not! But it won't have helped his temper any. People round here respect your father ...'

'You mean they fear him ...' Olivia interjected.

Her mother continued without responding. 'If the truth gets out, his reputation will take a massive blow, and if people lose respect for him, they lose respect for the factory too, and that could prove disastrous.'

'And that's more important than me?' said Olivia.

Catherine heaved a weary sigh. 'That's not what I'm saying at all.'

Olivia folded her arms across her chest. 'You didn't deny that they fear him, because you know it's true.'

'Of course they fear him – he owns their homes and pays their wages. If they get on the wrong side of him, they're out on their ear in more ways than one, but that doesn't mean to say that your father's a bad person.'

Olivia threw her hands up in despair. 'For goodness' sake, Mother, why are you defending him? He is a bad person. I've seen inside Ted's house and it's covered in mould and mildew, just like the one you used to live in when you were a child, and look what happened to you.' Her eyes grew wide as the last words left her lips. She apologised hurriedly. 'I'm so sorry, I didn't mean to bring up your illness, but it's true, Mum, you only got polio because you grew up in the courts ...'

Her mother raised a feeble hand, requesting Olivia to be quiet. 'I rather fear that if you hadn't gone into

Ted's house in the first place, you might not be in the predicament you now find yourself.'

Olivia's cheeks reddened but she continued, 'Doesn't change what I'm saying. You grew up in poor conditions and so has Ted, only in his case, Dad's responsible.'

Catherine nodded. 'The courts were a mistake from the start, they should never have been built in the first place, but needs must when the devil drives ...' She reached up and ran her fingers over Olivia's long ebony locks. 'I take it you never caught up with him?'

Olivia shook her head. 'I'll just have to hope that Ted's out with his pals.'

Her mother's eyes flashed. 'He's got to find out sooner or later.'

'If I can get to Ted before Dad, I can at least warn him.'

Catherine nodded slowly. 'That's true, but it won't change anything.'

Olivia shrugged. 'Forewarned is forearmed.'

Her mother regarded her levelly. 'Say you tell him. What then?'

Olivia paused for thought before answering. 'Ted will stand by me, I have no doubt about that.'

Her mother smiled sympathetically. 'It takes more than good intentions, Liv.'

Olivia looked at her mother through tear-glazed eyes. 'Oh, Mum, it's all such a dreadful mess.'

Leaning forward, her mother beckoned Olivia to come close so that she might embrace her. Olivia did as she was told, her tears disappearing into her mother's blouse as Mrs Campbell stroked the back of her head. 'It'll all come out in the wash, Liv, it always does, and whilst your father's angry at the minute, he'll calm down in time. You might think he's a miserable old goat, and on the face of it you're probably right, but deep down he's only trying to do what's best.'

Tilting her head back, Olivia glanced up at her mother. 'What's going to happen?'

Her mother drew a deep breath. 'The way I see it is this: what's done is done, and you're going to have to live with the consequences. As for Ted?' She shrugged helplessly. 'Your father's dealing with Ted, so that's out of your hands.'

'Why does he have to control everything?' said Olivia wretchedly.

Her mother swept a vague arm around the room. 'Because it's in his nature, and it's also why the factory is so successful.' She closed her fingers over Olivia's and squeezed them gently. 'I'm afraid you're going to learn the hard way that life isn't a fairy tale and there isn't always a happy ending.'

'Did you think that you and Dad would have the fairy-tale ending?'

'I think we might have, had your grandfather not passed away so unexpectedly.' She leaned back in her chair. 'It knocked your father for six – I don't think he's ever recovered from it – and my illness doesn't help.'

'That's hardly your fault!' said Olivia.

Her mother smiled. 'I know, but it doesn't make things any easier, and your father's not good with his emotions, that's why he tries to make light of my illness. If he doesn't acknowledge it, he can pretend it's not happening and that I'm not going to ...'

Olivia interrupted her mother before she could finish the sentence. 'Don't, Mum.' She glanced fleetingly at her mother who nodded her understanding. Olivia's mother had once been the heart and soul of the Campbell household, but the illness was weakening her and she was no longer able to stand for long periods, because her legs, once the envy of many a woman, were beginning to deteriorate.

In a bid to change the subject, Olivia asked her mother to tell her the story of how she and William first met.

A smile twitched on Catherine's lips as she relayed the tale.

'Dad had forgotten his lunch and Mam was late taking the laundry to Mr Wong's, so she asked if I'd take his lunch to him whilst she got on with the washing. Your father saw me from his office which overlooks the factory floor and he asked who I was. When his secretary told him, he came down and asked if he might take me for lunch. I knew he was older than me but he was very charming, and I didn't see the harm, so I said yes.' She looked out of the window into the garden. 'He took me to the Adelphi and treated me to food the like of which I'd never tasted before.' She glanced back at her daughter. 'I know you find it hard to believe, but your father was a different man back then, charming, considerate, endearing, and that's why I found myself falling in love with him.'

'Talk about a turnaround,' said Olivia. 'I can't remember the last time I saw him smile, and he always seems to be in a bad temper for one reason or another.'

Catherine gave a half-shrug. 'After Grandpa Campbell passed away, things got a lot harder for your father. He had to manage the factory and all the houses on his own, and he didn't have time for a family any more, but that doesn't mean to say he doesn't love you, Liv, because he does, he just isn't very good at showing it.'

Olivia eyed her mother doubtfully. 'Are you certain you didn't marry him just to get away from the courts?'

Catherine erupted into spontaneous laughter. 'No, I did not!'

Olivia giggled softly. 'You can't say as you blame me for thinking it. You were so young and beautiful, I can't believe you didn't have a line of suitors from here to Ranelagh Street, all vying for your attention, yet you chose him?'

Catherine wagged her finger in an admonitory fashion. 'There's more to life than money, Liv Campbell, and don't you forget it. I married your father for love – he just happened to be rich.'

'I bet Nana and Pops couldn't believe their luck when Dad asked you to marry him,' said Olivia, a small smirk tweaking the corner of her lips.

'As you already know, they were a little surprised because of the age gap – sixteen years, to be precise – but yes, I think they were pleased once they knew how much I loved him.'

'And the house on Ullet Road had nothing to do with it?' Olivia's smirk turned into a grin.

Catherine rolled her eyes. 'I won't deny they welcomed the chance to get out of the courts, if that's what you're implying ...'

They both started as they heard the front door slam shut.

Catherine clasped Olivia's hand. 'He's back!'

Olivia spun round to look at the closed bedroom door. Half of her wanted to rush downstairs and demand to know what her father had done, but the other half wanted to remain in ignorance, so that she could hope for the best.

'Go to your room, love,' her mother said urgently as they heard his cane hit the first step on the staircase.

'And leave you to face him on your own?' said Olivia indignantly. 'No fear!'

Her mother raised her brow. 'It's not me he's angry with.'

Olivia shook her head. 'If he's angry with anyone it should be with himself, because if anyone's to blame it's him.'

Her mother eyed her incredulously. 'I know you two don't get along, but even you can't seriously blame this on him?'

'It's his fault I was lonely in the first place, not allowing me to have any friends for fear I might ...' Olivia rolled her eyes in a theatrical manner, '... lower my standards. He practically drove me into Ted's arms!'

Her mother clasped a hand to her forehead. 'Now is not the time to go pointing the finger, especially when ...' She placed a slender finger to her lips as the door handle turned.

Olivia's heart was in her mouth as her father entered the room. He glared at the two of them before leaning his walking stick against the dresser and taking off his gloves. 'Looks like your boyfriend got wind of your

24

predicament,' he muttered before flinging an envelope down on to Olivia's lap. 'It seems bad news travels fast.'

Olivia looked at the envelope then her father. 'What's this?'

He nodded towards the envelope. 'Take a look for yourself.'

Olivia looked at her mother who nodded her approval. She pulled out the page from inside the unsealed envelope and read the contents. She looked up at her father, her face a mask of fury. 'Lies!' she snapped. 'Which I daresay you wrote yourself!'

Her father eyed her scathingly. 'Wouldn't you just love to believe that? Only I didn't. The place was empty when I got there, apart from that.'

Olivia handed the letter to her mother so that she could read it. 'Well, I don't believe you, and isn't it convenient that you've no way of proving he wrote it?' She folded her arms across her chest. 'Who did you see? Was his father there?' She gave a short, mirthless laugh. 'You wouldn't dare strike his father, you're too much of a coward for that.'

'Liv!' Catherine cried out in protest, but Olivia didn't care for the consequences of her words. As far as she was concerned, it was high time her father heard the truth.

William shrugged his indifference. 'Whether you want to believe me or not, there wasn't anyone there to strike.' He shot her a withering glance. 'You might think badly of me, but at least I don't run away from my responsibilities. Your boyfriend didn't even stick around to see if the rumours were true.'

Olivia was shaking her head. 'It doesn't make any difference. You can sack him and evict him, but I know Ted, and he'll come for me.'

William Campbell scoffed in disbelief. 'You idiotic child! You really think that?' He was shaking his head when a thought appeared to enter his mind. 'I can't prove he wrote this letter, but I can take you to the house. That way you can see for yourself.'

Olivia threw him a withering glance. 'Oh, I believe he doesn't live there any more, because you'll have turfed him out, but ...' She got no further.

'You could prove his father wrote the letter,' her mother intervened.

'How?' said Olivia, hope rising in her chest that she would be able to prove her father to be a liar.

Catherine looked up at her husband, who was staring at her intently. 'His tenancy agreement. They all have to sign one.'

Olivia began to smile, certain that her father would splutter some excuse for why he couldn't produce the document, but was shocked when her father nodded.

'He certainly did.' He eyed Olivia levelly. 'Care to join me?'

Olivia looked at her mother, who nodded her encouragement as she handed the letter back. 'You can't accuse your father of lying then not give him a chance to prove otherwise, and I don't think you'll believe him unless you see for yourself.'

Olivia followed her father out of the room, down the stairs and into his office. She watched as he sifted through the documents in his filing cabinet. A small smile began to curve her lips. Of course! He had brought her down here as though willing to prove his innocence, only to say at the last minute that he couldn't find it. She tutted inwardly. Her father was meticulous when it came to the agreements, everything got filed. She leaned against the doorframe. If she was to wait whilst her father pretended to search for the document she could be here for some time. Mr Campbell closed the drawer he had been searching through and moved on to the next.

Olivia looked through the office window to the garden outside, wondering what his next move would be, and was surprised when he turned away from the filing cabinet, a clutch of papers in his hand. He beckoned her to join him at the desk. Olivia walked unsteadily towards him. Surely he wasn't foolish enough to show her two different signatures? She knew he was determined, but that would be ludicrous. She placed the letter on the desk next to the lease. Olivia stared. The signatures weren't just similar, they were identical. She shook her head slowly. 'You've forged it.'

He scratched the back of his head. 'How on earth did I manage that?' he asked reasonably. 'I didn't know about any of this until an hour or so ago, yet this lease was signed years back.'

Olivia's heart was breaking. She reread the letter.

Mr Campbell,

Due to rumours which Ted strongly denies, I hereby give you our immediate notice as employees and tenants.

Regards,
Craig Hewitt

27

Olivia stared open-mouthed at her father. 'Why would he leave?'

'Only one reason that I can think of, and like I said, bad news travels fast, because they were gone before I got there,' her father said patiently.

Olivia's eyes sparkled with tears. She'd trusted Ted; he'd said he'd look after her and she'd believed him. She said as much to her father who snorted his contempt.

'I daresay he told you that before he got you pregnant?'

'Yes,' she whispered as the first tear fell.

He nodded. 'Typical.' He heaved a sigh. 'I know you always thought it unfair that I didn't want you associating with people like Ted, but can you see why now?'

Olivia nodded miserably.

He glanced in the direction of the stairs. 'We need to make a plan, but I don't want to involve your mother as I fear it may be too much for her.'

Olivia eyed him sceptically. He normally tried to make out that her mother was being theatrical and that she wasn't as bad as she made herself out to be, so why was he choosing to believe her illness now? Could it really be that William couldn't cope with the thought that he might lose his wife?

William held his hands up in a placating fashion. 'I'm not the enemy, Olivia. I'm not the one who got you pregnant then ran for the hills. I'm the one who tried to stop you getting into trouble in the first place.'

Olivia nodded apologetically. 'Sorry, Dad.'

He eyed her stomach with disapproval. 'If you stay here it won't be long before everyone knows our business.'

'So?' said Olivia. 'I've got nothing to hide.'

He looked at her in astonishment. 'You really want everyone knowing you got pregnant out of wedlock and that your boyfriend legged it as soon as he found out? Not to mention your age!'

Olivia's cheeks bloomed with embarrassment. 'No,' she said, her voice barely above a whisper.

Her father nodded curtly. 'Good, because once people find out, you'd never live it down. You'd be called all sorts of names ...'

Olivia frowned uncertainly. 'Won't they wonder where the baby came from?'

He rubbed his fingers over his bare chin. 'There's lots of different options to consider, but I personally believe it would be best if you gave the baby up for adoption.' Seeing the look of horror on his daughter's face, he continued hastily, 'We'd make sure you'd be able to visit whenever you wanted, and that they were good people, more like fostering than adopting.'

Olivia remained doubtful. 'I've got ages to go yet. Won't people wonder where I've gone?'

He shook his head. 'We'll wait until the last few months, then I'll say you've gone away to a boarding school; they'll not even question it.'

Olivia thought for a moment before shaking her head decidedly. 'I couldn't give Mum's only grandchild to strangers.'

Her father pulled his mouth into a dubious pout. 'Very well, but consider the effect watching her under-age daughter go through childbirth might have, not to mention living with a newborn baby that cries from morning to night. The baby will take a lot of your attention from your mother, and I dread to think of the effect that could have on her health. The stress alone ...'

Olivia covered her ears with her hands. 'All right, all right, I get the picture.'

Her father held his hands up in a reasonable fashion. 'It's your choice. I was merely pointing out ...'

Olivia nodded grimly. 'I'll do it.' She knew full well what her father was trying to do, and even though she hated herself for it, deep down she was worried he might be right.

'I shall set the wheels in motion,' William said authoritatively, placing the documents back in the filing cabinet.

She was about to leave the room, when a thought occurred to her. She turned in the doorway. 'What'll happen to Mum? Who'll look after her and what do we say?'

'We tell her the truth, that you're going to go away for some peace and quiet and that you won't be returning until you've had the baby.'

'And if she asks what we plan to do with the baby?' said Olivia.

'We'll cross that bridge when we come to it. Besides, you're only young – chances are ...' He threw her a shrewd look.

Olivia stared at him, uncomprehending. 'What?'

Her father shrugged. 'You're too young to be carrying a baby. Chances are it might not survive ...'

Olivia left the room before an avalanche of tears descended. She knew her father wouldn't be thrilled, of course she did, but it almost sounded as though he wished the baby wouldn't survive. She turned her thoughts to Ted and his treacherous ways. How could she have got him so wrong? He had made himself out to be her confidant, the one she could always turn to, yet he'd left without checking to see if the rumours were true.

She fished out her handkerchief from the pocket of her dropped-waist dress and blew her nose. She never thought she'd rue the day she met Ted Hewitt, but right now she wished she'd never been in the garden the day he walked past.

Ted's father hefted their suitcases on to the train bound for Southampton. He was still too angry to speak to his son, and not because he believed Mr Campbell's accusations that Ted had stolen the koi carp from his pond – he was certain that this was just a ruse to get Ted out of his daughter's life. He was angry because he had warned Ted of the consequences of getting involved with the boss's daughter, but Ted had refused to listen, and they were now homeless and without work as a result.

'I still don't see why we have to leave,' said Ted, appearing at his father's shoulder.

'Because he's only keeping quiet as long as we leave, but if we stay, he'll spread it round that we're thieves, and just you try getting a job once word's got out!' Craig snapped.

'But I never did anything wrong!' said Ted defensively. 'You shouldn't have let him bully you like that,

Dad. You should've stood your ground, demanded to see proof, because I'm telling you straight, I never did it.'

His father drew a deep breath before continuing. 'What do you propose I do, Ted? Take him to court for unfair dismissal? Or try and prove you never stole his koi carp?' He held up a hand as his son tried to protest. '*I* know you never stole them, and so do you, but how do we *prove* it?'

Ted's jaw flinched as he mulled this over. His father was right: how do you prove you never took something? Or force someone to keep you employed when they don't want or have to? He rubbed a hand across the back of his neck, which was tense. 'I'm sorry, Dad, and I know you think this is summat to do with me and Toff, but I don't see how it can be. I've only seen her a handful of times since her father give her a black eye, and we've been really careful not to be seen.'

Mr Hewitt rolled his eyes. 'When you've only eyes for each other, you can easily miss being spotted by someone passing by.' He relaxed a little. 'I've seen the two of you together and you remind me of your mother and me when we first met. The world could have gone on fire and I doubt we'd have noticed, but like I told you from the start, people like us don't mix with people like them. It's not like the movies, love doesn't conquer all.'

Tom shook his head. 'You're wrong, Dad. Me and Toff were different.'

His father shot his son a condescending look. 'Wake up, son, she's out of your league. There's no way her father would allow your relationship to continue – he probably had a word in her shell-like and got her to see sense. She's only fourteen, after all – far too young to be placing all her eggs in one basket. All he had to do then was find a way of getting you out of the picture so that he could rest easy.'

Ted heaved a sigh. He knew how Olivia looked at him, and you didn't look at someone like that unless you really liked them. He joined his father in the carriage and sat down heavily next to him.

'What did he say exactly?'

Craig stared fixedly out of the window. 'That he knew you and Toff, I mean Olivia, had been seeing each other because he'd caught you in the bottom of his garden by the pond, only you'd run off before he could grab hold of you.'

'That was a year ago!' Ted objected.

His father turned to face him, his face radiating disbelief. 'You didn't tell me he'd caught the two of you together.'

Ted blinked; he'd forgotten he'd kept that quiet from his father. He tried to bring the conversation back to the present. 'But I didn't nick any fish.'

'That's not the point,' said Craig, exasperated. 'Campbell knows who you are because he saw you!'

'Only he didn't,' Ted insisted, 'because I ran off with my cap pulled down over my face. If I didn't see him, he couldn't possibly have seen me.'

Craig drummed his fingers against the window. 'Well, he must have.'

'Did he say anything else?'

His father turned to face him wearily. 'Only that if I didn't want a fuss, I'd do as he asked. Oh, and he gave me a month's wages if I promised we'd not come back.'

Ted frowned. 'That just goes to prove he's lying. If you suspected someone of nickin' your stuff, you'd report them to the scuffers, not buy their silence!'

Craig lowered his voice as a middle-aged man wearing a pinstriped suit entered the carriage. 'We both know that story's a pile of cock and bull, to make sure you and Olivia stopped being friends ...' he shot his son a sideways glance, '... you were *just* friends, weren't you?'

Blushing to his roots, Ted nodded quickly before his father could press him any further. 'You know we were.'

Craig's gaze bored into the side of Ted's head. 'Ted?'

Ted looked up rather sheepishly. 'It was only once, after her father ...'

Craig threw his hands up in exasperation, then hastily put them down again after realising he had gained the attention of the other man. 'Just the once?' he muttered. 'You do know that's all it takes ...' He clasped a hand to his forehead, but Ted quickly intervened.

'Don't worry, Dad, it's not what you think, we weren't that stupid.'

Craig ran his tongue around the inside of his cheek. 'Yes, you were, Ted, because you shouldn't have done it in the first place.' He shot a glance in the other passenger's direction to make sure he wasn't eavesdropping before continuing in hushed tones, 'She's fourteen! You do know that's illegal?'

Ted looked down sullenly. 'I'm only fifteen ...'

'You think that would matter in a court of law?' hissed Craig, desperately trying to keep his temper under control. 'Bloody hell, Ted, no wonder her father was desperate to get shot of us!'

Ted stared out of the window before turning back to his father. 'If she was ...' he too glanced at the other passenger before continuing, '... you know, then don't you think Campbell would've had my guts for garters? He'd not let us leave without consequences – to him that'd be letting us get away with murder!'

Craig mulled this over. He sincerely hoped his son to be right, and the more he thought about it the more he believed he probably was. After all, William Campbell had been relatively composed when he had entered their dwelling on Fisher Street. The man was not renowned for being able to keep a hold of his temper, quite the opposite, so had she been pregnant ... Nodding slowly, he looked at Ted. 'I don't think she's ...' Keeping his eyes on the other passenger, he gave Ted a furtive nod, before continuing, 'I reckon Campbell found out what was going on and wanted to put a stop to it before the inevitable happened.'

'But how did he find out?' Ted asked.

'Does it really matter?' said Craig, gazing out at the platform, which was disappearing from view as the train pulled out of the station. He couldn't shake the niggling thought that if Olivia was expecting, the last thing his boss would want would be for word to get round that his daughter had fallen pregnant to one of his workers, therefore the easiest way to deal with it would be to get rid of the worker quietly, whilst sorting his daughter out behind closed doors. He daren't tell Ted his suspicions, because if he did, he felt certain that his son would pull the emergency lever and run to his belle. His stomach gave a guilty lurch. Was he wrong not to voice his thoughts? Ted and Olivia reminded him very much of his relationship with Ted's mother when they had first got together. How would he have felt if someone had kept something like that from him? On the other hand, their situation was entirely different. Phyllis was working for the Chinese laundry on the Scottie Road, and Craig was working in the factory. They had the same upbringing, same values, same prospects. He nibbled the tip of his thumb. Even if he did tell Ted, what then? If Ted demanded to see Olivia, William would undoubtedly have him arrested and slung in jail for a crime he hadn't committed, whilst getting the unborn child aborted, so it would all be for naught.

Ted's voice cut across his thoughts. 'I suppose not, although it must have come from her, somehow.' He too was staring out of the window. Tired of running the whys and wherefores through his mind, he decided to change the subject. 'Why are we going to Southampton?'

His father brightened. 'You won't remember Rob, he's an old mate of mine from back in the day. He moved to Plymouth with his folks because his father was a seaman working aboard a naval vessel. We've not seen each other for years but we always kept in touch, albeit only by way of Christmas cards. He wrote a few months back asking whether I'd be interested in taking a trip down south because he was after a partner to help him run his business. I'd have jumped at the chance, but I knew Campbell would never allow me to have the time off, so I couldn't afford it.' He gave Ted a grim smile. 'I've got nothing holding me back now, though, so I rang the garage which he runs, to make sure he was still on board, and he was made up to hear we were on our way.'

Ted pulled an uncertain face. 'You're the perfect choice, but what about me? I never did any of the mechanical stuff in the factory, and I doubt he needs a dogsbody.'

'You'll soon catch on. I reckon you'll make a good mechanic. I always told Campbell he should give you a chance but he wouldn't listen.' He nudged Ted playfully. 'At least this way you'll get a proper trade under your belt.'

Ted drummed his fingers against his knee. If his father was right, then this could be the opportunity of a lifetime. Back in the factory the only thing he had to look forward to was a game of footie with his pals on a Saturday; other than that his life was going to be pretty humdrum and uneventful. Being a mechanic could change his life immensely. It would mean better wages for a start, and that would lead to a better lifestyle. A small smile began to tweak his lips. If his father was right, then they would be better off putting Toff, Campbell and the city of Liverpool far behind them. With this thought in mind, he pulled his newsboy cap over his eyes and settled back into his seat to daydream of a better life.

William Campbell took the Hewitts' rental agreement back out of the drawer and tore it in two, before taking

Mr Hewitt's note and placing it in his safe. After all, that was the only thing that stood between him and that dratted boy's return. When he had left Aigburth Drive earlier that morning his intentions had been to turf Craig and Edward Hewitt out on their ears with no notice, and he'd tell them why as well. However, as he neared the house it occurred to him that if Edward was as fond of, or indeed as in love with Olivia as she believed him to be, this could turn out to be a big mistake. If Edward saw this as an opportunity to get his foot in the door then William would never be rid of him, or his father. He crumpled up the two halves of the agreement and threw them into the fire which smouldered in the grate. It would be a very cold day in hell before William allowed the likes of Edward to become his son-in-law, and the very thought of introducing Craig to any guests churned his stomach. An image formed in his mind, of Craig and Edward sitting around his dining table on Christmas Day, drinking his port and eating his food. 'Over my dead body,' William muttered beneath his breath.

He knew from Olivia's diary that the two had been meeting in secret, but he realised, too, that Edward must have been the boy he caught kissing Olivia by the koi pond that time. It had been this thought that had given him the idea of accusing Edward of stealing the carp. It wasn't without precedence – as far as he was concerned, all people on low wages were thieves – and whilst he couldn't prove Edward had taken the koi, Edward couldn't prove he hadn't, and he was damned sure that any reasonable person would believe him over one of his employees. If it went as far as court …

he had dismissed the thought from his mind. How could someone like Edward afford to fight his employer in court? The mere thought was preposterous! Especially as William knew most of the magistrates by their Christian names. He cast his mind back to the moment he had pulled up outside the Hewitts' and rapped a brief tattoo on the front door. He had kept the conversation with Craig brief and to the point. He had been surprised, maybe even a little disappointed that Craig had given in as easily as he had. He turned this thought over for a moment or so. Could the other man have suspected Olivia and Ted's indiscretion? He cast the thought aside. Even if he had his suspicions, the outcome remained the same. Craig had assured William that he and Ted would be out of Liverpool by the end of the day, even writing the note which William dictated.

Now, as he poured himself a generous measure of brandy, he reflected on how neatly the rest of it had fallen into place. When he had returned to Aigburth Drive he had been toying with the idea of showing Olivia the two signatures but was wary of raising her suspicions. When Catherine had made the suggestion for him, he could have kissed her! He knew Olivia trusted her mother more than anyone, so for the idea to come from her lips gave validity to the suggestion. Once Olivia had seen the signatures with her own eyes he knew that as far as Edward was concerned, Olivia would want to have nothing more to do with him.

On reflection everything had worked out beautifully. All he had to do now, was think of a way to make sure that once the baby was born it would be out of their lives forever, because if there was one thing that could put a halt to his plans, it was word getting back to the Hewitts that they were now a father and grandfather, and that would never do.

Olivia was sitting up in bed hugging her knees. After she'd given birth four days earlier, her father had brought her to recuperate in the private cottage which he had rented for the duration of their stay. The nursing staff had tried to insist on Olivia staying in hospital until she had fully recovered from the difficult birth, but her father had been adamant that he wanted her out of hospital as soon as possible, stating that whilst he was happy for the private nurse he had paid to come and check on Olivia, he didn't want her staying on the ward to be gawped at by the other mothers. The matron, a cheery woman with kind eyes, had tried to speak to Olivia on her own to see if she might be able to make him see sense, but with William refusing to leave her side, this had proved impossible.

A solitary tear ran silently down her cheek as she looked out of the deep-set window to the beautiful loch which sparkled in the winter sun. With hindsight, Olivia now realised that she had been incredibly naive when it came to childbirth, thinking that once the baby was born that would be the end of the matter, and she and her father could return home. What she hadn't counted on was the yearning ache she would feel for the baby which had been whisked away before she had a chance to catch a glimpse of it, or the effort which her body would endure in order to expel the afterbirth, something which she'd found nearly as strenuous as having the baby itself. She winced as her arm brushed against her tender breasts. Shame filled her as she recalled the embarrassing moment when the private nurse had bound her breasts tightly in order to stop the milk coming through, telling Olivia it would be much easier, although painful, for her to cope with the loss that way.

Olivia remembered very little about the actual birth. There seemed to be a lot of nurses, all of whom did their best to help and encourage her, although she found it hard to look any of them in the eye, so ashamed was she of her condition. The birth itself had seemed to go on forever, and even when she thought she couldn't go on, they insisted she start again.

When it was all over, Olivia had fought the temptation to ask to hold the baby, because her father had assured her that holding the baby would create a bond, and then she would find the loss that much harder to deal with.

She cast her mind back to the day she had left her mother behind in Aigburth Drive. Catherine had tried to smile encouragingly at her daughter, but her bottom lip trembled as she fought to control her emotions. 'I'm so sorry you're having to go through this, Liv. If there was any other way ...'

Determined that her mother should not see how upset she was, Olivia had put on a brave face. 'Don't worry about me, Mum, I'll be fine.' She gave a sombre chuckle. 'I never thought I'd say this, but Dad'll look after me.'

'I told you he had a heart, he just keeps it well hidden. In fact, I don't know where you'd be without him.'

Catherine tutted beneath her breath. 'If I could get my hands on that Edward ...' she took a deep breath, '... still, there's no point in dwelling on the past.'

'All the things he used to say about Dad, and he's just as bad, if not worse,' Olivia said flatly. 'Dad might be a miserable old so-and-so, but he'd never turn his back on his family.'

Now, as the clouds began to gather, blotting out the brilliance of the sun, she mulled over the things her father had done for her of late, but this time she saw things as they truly were and not through the eyes of a young girl, giddy and naive from the attentions of a handsome boy who had fled the city as soon as the rumours had begun to circulate. It was her father who had tried to put an end to her relationship with Ted, and even though she had thought it unfair at the time, with the benefit of hindsight, she could see now why he had been so overbearing. He had seen Ted for what he was and tried to protect Olivia from him; he had said as much on their drive from the hospital to the cottage. 'I know you believed my intentions were to get rid of Edward, but nothing could be further from the truth. I went round to see him so that I could make sure he took care of his responsibilities. I may not know him personally, but I know what boys are like – they take advantage of girls, then when disaster strikes they deny any involvement, say the baby isn't theirs, accuse the girls of being promiscuous and pinning the blame on them. I just wanted what was best for you, but if you want my opinion it's that boy's fault the baby was stillborn – it's all the stress he put you under by running off the way he did,' he had finished bitterly.

Olivia buried her face in the sheets. How could she have got it so wrong? She had put Ted on a pedestal, and her father in the gutter. Yet in truth it had been her father who had arranged for them to rent the cottage they were presently in, so that Olivia could be away from prying eyes in the latter months of her pregnancy; he'd also arranged for a home help to look after her mother whilst they were away, and taken care of all the expenses. He'd made up an elaborate story to excuse his absence from the factory and had bent over backwards to make sure everything ran as smoothly and with as little upset as possible.

Drying her eyes on the bedsheet, Olivia wished with all her might that she had listened to her father.

A few months after returning from Scotland, it became clear that William's good nature had disappeared and he was no longer the caring father, but the man Olivia had always known him to be, short-tempered, self-absorbed and judgemental.

'How on earth I can ever hope to marry you off now, goodness only knows,' he said as they sat down for breakfast around the dining table. 'I took you away to save tongues from wagging, but anyone with half a brain can see you're damaged goods.'

'William!' protested Catherine. 'That's a dreadful thing to say.'

'Just because it's dreadful doesn't mean to say it's not true,' said William bluntly. He jerked his head in Olivia's direction. 'Look at her.'

Olivia looked down at her figure which was still swollen from the pregnancy. Tears brimmed in her eyes. Her father was right. Her once trim waist had gone, her flat stomach was flabby and covered in stretch marks, and her pert breasts had lost their shape.

Catherine placed her hand over her daughter's. 'Don't listen to him, Liv.'

Olivia shook her head. 'He's right though, Mum, look at me.'

'It's early days yet,' her mother said reassuringly. 'Your body needs time to adjust, you'll soon get your figure back.'

'Only next time you meet a boy full of compliments, make sure you keep your legs shut!' William said, his tone heavy with sarcasm.

'That's enough!' snapped her mother, before breaking into a coughing fit.

Excusing herself from the table, Olivia hurried off to her room where she might be alone. She knew her father shouldn't say those things, but she had eyes in her head; she could see the difference and it was not for the better. Not only that, but she had an enormous appetite. She had kidded herself at first that it was because her body was still 'eating for two', but deep down she knew that she was constantly hungry because she was so unhappy. She hadn't just lost her baby, but the man she had loved most in the world, or at least the man she thought she loved, but she obviously didn't know Ted at all, because the man she had fallen for would never have walked away from his pregnant girlfriend.

Not only that but her mother's mobility had worsened since their departure, and she now needed a wheelchair if she were to do more than cross a room,

44

which meant they had had to move her bedroom downstairs, something which she was sure her father blamed her for, not that she could disagree, because she also thought it was her fault.

'One stupid moment, that's all it took,' she muttered to herself as she opened up a paper bag of Parma Violets and popped a couple into her mouth. On reflection she wondered how she could have been so unlucky. She had only had one intimate encounter – what were the odds that she would fall pregnant the first time? But dwelling on what should have been did you no good; her ever expanding waist was proof of that. She would have to work hard, lose the weight and get her life back so that she could carry on as though none of this had happened.

That had been her plan, but as she well knew, things don't always go according to plan. Many years passed and Olivia's mother's condition had worsened to the point where she became bedridden, and William threw himself into his work, rarely returning home until everyone had gone to bed. In some respects Olivia preferred her father's absence, but she knew it hurt her mother, even if Catherine never actually admitted it. Instead she tried to encourage her daughter to make a life for herself, but Olivia chose to stay at home and care for her mother, despite Catherine's protests.

'Please, Liv, get out there and make something of yourself,' her mother pleaded. 'I can't bear to watch you waste your life away. I know you think he won't look after me if you go, but he'll hire someone to take care of me, like he did when you ...' she hesitated before continuing, '… went away. He knows he can't leave me on my own.'

'But I don't want anyone else to look after you,' sniffed Olivia. 'You're *my* mum.'

'Exactly!' said Catherine. 'I'm your mother, I should be looking after you, and that's what I'm trying to do by releasing you from your burden.'

Olivia stared at her mother, stunned. 'You're not a burden.'

Catherine smiled kindly at her daughter. 'That's very sweet of you to say, love, but I am, and I know I am. You should be out there making a life for yourself, not stuck here looking after me.'

'I don't care, I'm not leaving you on your own with him,' Olivia insisted.

'If the worst should happen …' Catherine began.

'It won't as long as I'm here,' Olivia said obstinately.

Her mother smiled uncertainly. 'You must realise I'm getting worse, Liv.'

''Course I do.'

'My illness will win in the end, and I want you to promise me that you'll leave Aigburth Drive when it does.'

Olivia stared at her in astonishment. 'Don't talk like that!'

Her mother drew as deep a breath as her lungs would allow. 'If the rumours of war are true, then there'll be plenty of opportunities. Promise me you'll grasp them with both hands.'

Olivia nodded reluctantly. 'I promise – not that it'll be necessary, mind you.'

A brief smile of relief swept across Catherine's features. 'Good girl.'

Olivia could see what was happening to her mother, but she believed in her heart that something would come along at the eleventh hour – either a cure for her illness, or her mother would make a miraculous recovery and all would be well, just as long as Olivia stayed by her side.

Chapter Two

March 1940

A slow smile formed on Ted's lips as he read his next posting. He turned the letter to show Reg, a pal from initial training. Reg nodded approvingly. 'RAF Speke – looks like the boy's going home after all.'

Ted nodded hesitantly. 'I never thought I'd go back to Liverpool.'

Reg shrugged. 'It'll give you a chance to catch up with all your old mates.'

'I've not been back in sixteen years,' Ted said. 'I very much doubt whether I'd recognise any of them.'

'What about family? Surely you've got family back home?'

'An aunt by marriage and her kids,' Ted conceded. 'Might be a bit of a shock having me turn up on their doorstep.'

Reg frowned. 'You've never said why you left Liverpool in the first place. Was it a family feud?'

Ted ran a finger around his shirt collar. 'Nothing like that. Dad got an offer to become a partner in his pal's car business.'

'That's right, I remember now, you did say summat about it.' Reg glanced at him. 'Not a close family then?'

Ted shook his head. 'Not particularly. Auntie Bea didn't want nothing to do with me and me dad once her husband died.'

Reg nodded wisely. 'That's families for you.' He turned his attention back to his newspaper.

Ted gazed down at the letter in his hands. For the first time in years he cast his mind back to the reason why he had left Liverpool. He wondered what had become of Olivia. Doubtless she would be married by now with children. He turned his thoughts to her father and what his reaction would be if he saw Ted in uniform. He pulled a face. It was most unlikely that William would recognise Ted after all this time. He folded the letter and placed it in his pocket. He would have to tell Isobel that he was being stationed up north. A vision of his wife formed in his mind. Tall, svelte, with large blue eyes and platinum blonde curls – Ted had been the envy of every man. He rubbed his chin thoughtfully. Every man who didn't know her personally, that was. Not that Ted blamed them, for he had been just as enchanted by her appearance. She had won him over with her dazzling smile and her seemingly doting nature, making him feel as though he was the only man in the world. So captivated was he, that he allowed her to push him into marriage, for fear of losing her otherwise. He remembered miserably how everything had changed the moment he climbed into bed beside her on their wedding night. Isobel had flinched as he laid a hand on her shoulder.

She had pulled the sheets up around her neck. 'I thought you were taking me somewhere special for our honeymoon!'

'What's wrong with it here?' said Ted. 'You've got a beautiful beach and ...'

Isobel kept her back to him. 'When you said you were whisking me away on a surprise honeymoon I thought you'd be taking me somewhere like Paris or Rome, not *Morecambe*.' She heaved a dramatic sigh. 'What's the point in running a successful business if you don't get to enjoy the proceeds?'

'It's not my business,' said Ted reasonably. 'You know it's not.'

'As good as!' said Olivia. 'Your father's a partner in it, isn't he? Or did you just say that to get this on my finger?'

'Of course not!' said Ted. 'But he doesn't own the business.'

She shrugged. 'Maybe not now, but Rob won't be around forever, and seeing as how he hasn't got any children of his own to pass the garage on to, it's only logical ...'

Ted stared at her in disbelief. 'How long have you been thinking about this?'

Isobel turned round to face him, a pout forming on her ruby lips. 'I'm only stating the inevitable. I don't know why you're looking at me like that – it's good to plan ahead!'

Ted stared down at the wedding band which encircled her finger. 'Is that why you agreed to marry me, because you were thinking ahead?'

Isobel covered her face with her hands and began to sob. 'You're making me out to be a monster, yet what woman doesn't plan her future?'

Ted swiftly apologised, but Isobel wasn't up for accepting his apology and had spent the rest of the honeymoon in the darkness of their bedroom claiming to be suffering with a migraine, which she insisted had been brought on by his outrageous accusations.

It was odd, Ted thought now, how she had never suffered with migraines before their marriage, but since their wedding day some five years earlier she succumbed to one at least twice a week, something which had not gone unnoticed by his father.

'Is everything all right with Isobel?' Craig asked at work one day.

Ted nodded. 'Why do you ask?'

'She seems to be suffering with headaches a lot. Do you have any idea what could be causing them?'

Ted stopped himself from replying 'marriage', because he didn't want his father to worry unduly, but if Ted was honest with himself, he felt certain that this was the root of her migraines. When war was announced he had jumped at the opportunity to join up, partly because it would get him away from Isobel and her constant whining.

'An RAF mechanic?' Isobel had said, her tone filled with disgust. 'You have the opportunity to own your own business, and even branch out!' She flung his acceptance papers back at him. 'Yet you chose to throw all that away in favour of becoming a grease monkey!'

Ted had stared at her. 'I'll be doing it for king and country,' he said, his jaw flinching as he tried to keep his temper from rising. 'I'd say that's being a bit more than a grease monkey. I'd have thought you'd have been proud.'

'*Proud*?' echoed Isobel. 'You've thrown away an opportunity of a lifetime for peanuts?'

Ted's brow furrowed. 'It's not forever. I'll come back when the war's over.'

She threw her hands up in despair. 'Goodness only knows how long that will be, and what happens to me if you get killed?'

Ted stifled a shocked laugh behind his fingers. Isobel had spoken the truth at last. He smiled levelly. 'You could always get a job.'

She regarded him through narrowing eyes. 'You don't care about me at all, do you? I knew it from the moment we arrived at our so-called honeymoon, you've never valued me for the person I am. Sometimes I feel as though you don't know me at all.'

'That makes two of us,' Ted muttered beneath his breath.

Isobel eyed him sharply, but Ted no longer cared if she flounced off in a bad mood. He had been right. Isobel was only interested in what he could give her. He feared he was trapped in a loveless marriage with someone who wasn't bothering to hide it any more.

Now, as he sat reading his transfer papers, his thoughts turned to Toff. As soon as he got to Speke he would make a few enquiries, see if anyone knew what had become of his first love. A lot of water had passed under the bridge since he had seen her last. What would be the harm in a quick hello?

By the spring of 1940 much had changed in the Campbell household. The factory had switched production from engine parts for cars to parts for heavy bombers, and with so many being shot down, the demand was high.

Olivia's mother's condition had deteriorated to the point where she was struggling to breathe and it was plain for all to see that she was not long for this world.

Olivia had hoped that her father would make more of an effort to be with his wife around this time, but every time she brought the matter up, he would say he was too busy with work, and that he would if he could. One evening she visited the factory on an errand. She had expected to find her father in the thick of things, telling workers what to do or wading his way through reams of paperwork, but instead he was sitting in his office doing a crossword in the *Echo*. She bit her tongue to stop herself saying that she was glad to see he was keeping himself busy with important war work, because she knew he would weasel his way out of it somehow, probably by saying that it was the first break he had had all day, and of course Olivia couldn't prove otherwise.

Many years had passed since the birth of her baby, and she was no longer a naive and frightened fourteen-year-old, but a thirty-year-old woman who could see things for how they were. Gone were all thoughts that her father was trying to protect her from Ted, because Olivia now knew better. If Ted had been the son of one of his snooty pals, her father would have welcomed him with open arms, especially if the marriage paved the way for a new and lucrative business deal.

She had been proved correct when her father had invited one of his associates around to lunch one day. It was something which happened quite often in the Campbell household, so Olivia had thought nothing of it when her father asked her to make herself presentable for their guests. However, her suspicions had been aroused when they turned up with their son in tow. With much enthusiasm, her father introduced her to Guy, and then kept casting her suggestive looks. Olivia had been polite, taken the young man's rather limp hand and shaken it in a friendly manner. Guy, on the other hand, had been rude and sullen, barely raising a smile and making no effort to hide his feelings, and as the meal wore on, Olivia realised the reason for his frosty attitude. This was no regular business meeting, but an attempt to get her and Guy together. Olivia had been inwardly furious at her father's audacity, but she had been well brought up, so she kept her feelings to herself. Guy, on the other hand was not quite so well mannered, as she discovered when she caught him muttering furiously to his father that he had no desire to court Olivia, and that his father had duped him into coming to lunch by misrepresenting Olivia as a trophy bride, whereas in reality she was more like a booby prize at a very low-key event! She had immediately returned to the dining room and relayed the conversation she'd overheard to her father, but William, far from being outraged by the young man's words, had actually blamed Olivia, saying that it was her own fault for not taking care of herself properly and that had she listened to him all those years ago she would have lost the weight by now, and today's outcome would have been very different. Decent men like Guy had standards, he told her, and you couldn't buy their affection. She knew that her father was referring to Ted, suggesting that he had only wanted Olivia because he had hopes of getting his feet under the table.

Something in her father's tone made Olivia question Ted's reasons for leaving. According to her father, it was because he had discovered that she was pregnant, but how could he have done so? Olivia had made certain she hadn't told a soul, apart from her mother, so unless one of the staff had overheard Olivia and her mother talking, there was no way he could have known. She sighed heavily. There was no point in speculating. She hadn't seen Ted since he left so she would never learn the truth, but neither would she accept her father's words as gospel.

Which was the reason why she was currently waiting for him in his study. Determined that he wouldn't be able to sneak away unnoticed, she was sitting in the chesterfield chair, the back of which was turned to the door, so that she might catch him unawares as he came into the room.

'Hearts alive!' spluttered William. 'What the hell do you think you're doing and why are you hiding in my study?'

'Waiting for you,' said Olivia, 'to tell you that you need to spend some time with Mum before it's too late.

You're her husband and she needs you. I know she's got me for company, but it's not the same …'

'Hasn't she just,' her father snapped irritably, glancing towards the window at the sound of knocking on the front door. Olivia spoke, transferring his attention back to her.

'Well, someone has to be with her, because apparently you're always too busy,' she said, her voice heavy with sarcasm.

He looked at her sharply. 'And what's that supposed to mean?'

Olivia folded her arms across her chest. 'When was the last time you actually sat with her?'

Her father pouted. 'You know what they say, two's company …'

'Don't be so bloody childish!' Olivia burst out. 'You're avoiding her because you can't face up to the truth, but I'm not here about you, I'm here because I care about Mum, and I know she must be hurt that you don't spend time with her, even if she doesn't say so …' She was interrupted by someone ringing the doorbell. Whoever it was that had knocked before was obviously keen to gain their attention. She looked at her father. 'Are you expecting someone?'

William shook his head. 'Of course not! I only dropped in to pick up some files.' He made to walk out of the room, but Olivia was quick to react, leaping out of her chair and stepping swiftly between William and the study door.

She shook her head at him. 'You're not getting out of it that easily. Mavis can answer the door.'

'No, she can't,' he said sharply. 'I sent her on a message when I came in, so there's only us here.'

The person who had rung the bell now kept their finger on the buzzer for a few seconds. Annoyed at the disruption, Olivia strode across the room and peered through the window. A man in RAF uniform was walking away from the front door. She turned to her father. 'Too late, he's gone, although I'm sure he'll call back if it's that important.'

'He?' questioned William.

She shook her head. 'Never mind who was at the front door, you've more important things to worry about.'

William started towards the door of his study, but Olivia had had enough. 'You're a foolish, selfish old man, who's more bothered about an uninvited guest than you are about your dying wife. You should be thoroughly ashamed of yourself, because I know I am.' Turning on her heel, she left the study and headed across the hall to her mother's room. She knocked briefly before entering. 'Honestly, Mum, you've got to keep warm,' she insisted as she slipped her mother's forearm back under the blankets. 'You're as cold as ice …' She broke off as her words caught up with her and realisation dawned.

A week after Olivia confronted her father, she found herself sitting between him and her grandparents at the head of a small congregation at St Michael's church.

Olivia held Nana's hand as the vicar's words swept over her.

'Catherine Campbell, the much-loved wife of William ...'

Olivia fought back the urge to shout 'Lies!' at the top of her voice, for this was neither the time nor the place. Since her mother's passing, she had become more vocal with her opinion of her father, which had caused their relationship to become more explosive than ever. Where she would once have feared him losing his temper and throwing the first thing that came to hand in her direction, she now had the courage to throw it right back, because for the first time in her life she didn't have to worry about upsetting her mother.

Now, hearing Nana and Pops quietly weeping for the loss of their daughter, Olivia shot her father a sidelong glance as they got to their feet. He was keeping his head bowed, but even so Olivia very much doubted he was shedding any tears. It was her belief that her father had kept himself from his wife so that he could deal with her passing when it came. Which infuriated Olivia, because he should have cared more for the feelings of his dying wife than he did for his own, but that was William, he was selfish to the core.

She turned her attention to the vicar, who was leading the congregation out to the graveyard. As they emerged into the brilliant sunshine, Olivia followed the vicar to her mother's burial plot. She watched the pallbearers lower her mother's coffin into the ground. For the first time in her life, Olivia felt truly alone. The vicar's words faded into the background and she found herself gazing at her father. Was that a tear he was wiping from the end of his nose? And if it was, then it was too little too late, as far as Olivia was concerned.

The vicar fell silent and Nana leaned forward, a single rose in her hand. She let it fall on to the top of the coffin and her husband followed suit, followed by Olivia. She looked over to her father as he dropped a lily.

Her emotions getting the better of her, Olivia turned away from the graveside.

'Liv!'

Olivia spun round, half expecting to see her mother, but it was her grandmother who had spoken. Hearing what she had thought to be her mother's voice, Olivia allowed the pent-up tears of anger to flow. 'Why give her flowers now, Nana? He should have done that when she was there to receive them for herself,' she said, her eyes flicking in the direction of her father, who was staring into the grave.

Her grandmother slipped her hand into Olivia's. 'If you don't know by now that your father's not very good at expressing his emotions, you never will.'

Olivia wiped her eyes with the back of her hand and shook her head. 'He's good at showing his anger, and that's an emotion.'

Her grandmother raised an eyebrow. 'Anger is a far easier emotion to deal with than remorse. That's why you're letting your anger get the better of you now.'

'I have every reason to be angry with him,' Olivia argued.

Her grandmother began to walk slowly back to the church. 'Well, you shouldn't be, because it doesn't do you any good. You should allow yourself to grieve.'

'If I start crying, I'll never stop,' Olivia muttered.

Her grandmother shot her a sidelong glance. 'So, it's all right for you, but not for him?'

Olivia's mouth dropped open. 'How can you say that? I've been with Mum all the way! He's the one who's neglected her, not me.'

'It's different for your father. He had a very different upbringing to you, and he's a man – they find it a lot harder to cope with these things than we do.' She gave her granddaughter's hand a reassuring jiggle. 'I know you stayed with your mother, Liv, and no one's trying to take that away from you. I'm just saying, it's different strokes for different folks.'

'But he's always been the same, Nana,' Olivia protested. 'He's always had a bad temper, throwing things like a spoilt brat that can't get their own way, you know he has, and that was before Mum got ill.'

Her grandmother nodded placatingly. 'True, but lots of men suffer from quick tempers – I think it's in their nature. But that doesn't mean to say he doesn't love you and your mother.'

'Pops isn't like that!' said Olivia.

Nana stopped to allow some of the mourners to pass. 'He can be, although I agree he doesn't throw things, 'cos he knows I'd chuck them straight back at him if he did, and I'm a better aim.'

A smile faltered on Olivia's lips but she was determined to prove her point. 'Ted's dad wasn't a violent man.'

'He wasn't an honourable man either, from what I gather,' her grandmother said stiffly.

Olivia fell quiet. She didn't want to get into the well-worn argument about Ted and his father, not with her grandparents, who had been dismayed to hear the news of their granddaughter's condition. She steered the subject back to her father.

60

'Do you really think he loved Mum?'

Her grandmother nodded decidedly. 'Very much so. He was a different man back then, younger, more care-free, and he had a good career ahead of him. If his father hadn't died so unexpectedly I daresay you'd have had a very different upbringing.'

Olivia nodded. 'That's what Mum said.'

'He'd gone from being second in command to fac-tory owner in a heartbeat, and people tried to take advantage of your father's vulnerable position, so he had to learn fast and change the way he handled things – either that or watch the factory go under and see himself out on the streets with a wife and child in tow.'

'How could they have been so callous?' said Olivia. 'You'd think they'd try to help someone who'd just suffered a loss, not kick them whilst they're down.'

Her grandmother shrugged. 'It's just business. Dog eat dog, as they say.'

'But he turned things around, so why is he still so ill-tempered?'

A smile flashed across the older woman's face. 'Because he learned you can't take your foot off the pedal, not even for a moment, because there's always someone in the wings waiting to take advantage. That's why he didn't trust Ted, and rightly so as it turned out.'

'You're making it sound like Dad's been hard done by, yet you and I both know how poorly paid his work-ers are, and as for his tenants,' Olivia went on rashly, 'I saw Ted's house with my own eyes.'

Her grandmother's brow shot towards her hairline. 'I know you did, and that's not all he showed you!' She waved a dismissive hand. 'I know your father doesn't

61

keep his properties in the best condition, but neither does he charge through the nose for his rent like some of them do.'

Olivia threw her grandmother a sidelong glance. 'Still no excuse.'

Nana wagged a reproving finger. 'It's very easy to judge others from the outside, but walk a day in your father's shoes and I daresay you'd feel differently.'

'There's still no reason for him to be mean to me,' said Oliva after some thought, 'throwing things at me, shaking me and making sure I never had any friends. It wasn't my fault his father died.' She thought she had her grandmother there, until she saw the wry look on the old woman's face.

'Remember how I said some folk tried to take advantage of your father's vulnerability after his father passed?'

Olivia nodded mutely.

'Well, some of the factory lads tried to pull the wool over your father's eyes, saying that they'd worked more hours than they had, and that they'd been underpaid. He fell for it at first because he only had their word for it, but after a while he realised he'd been lied to. Of course this shattered his trust in his employees. Not only that, but when he demanded the money back they refused. He sacked them on the spot for their dishonesty, and because he knew they wouldn't be able to pay the rent, he also evicted them.' She dipped her head to one side. 'Word soon got out, and everyone started behaving themselves. Your father learned that if he wanted people to behave he had to toughen up, which he did; the trouble was, he applied that to his family as well as his workers. He couldn't spend as much time with you as he wished, so he ensured you toed the line by setting down strict rules. When your mother started to grow increasingly ill, he figured he could make her better by literally ordering her to do so.' Sighing, she shook her head sadly. 'I feel sorry for him, because he's not the man he was.'

'So if he was no longer the man my mother married, why did she stay with him?'

'Because she loved him, and she knew it wasn't his fault, and I suppose she hoped he'd mellow as time went by, and become the caring, loving man he had once been.'

Olivia looked over her shoulder and saw her father and grandfather making their way up the path. She encouraged her grandmother forward again. 'I dread to think what life is going to be like, now it's just the two of us.'

Her grandmother looked at her in surprise. 'I thought you'd promised your mother that you'd make a new life for yourself should the worst happen. Do you not intend to honour that promise?'

Olivia nodded hesitantly. 'Ye-es, I suppose so, but I haven't really given it much thought. In truth, I wouldn't know where to start.'

'How about doing as she suggested and joining one of the services? Maybe learn a trade and do your bit for the war effort at the same time? If your mother had been well enough, I'm sure she'd have been out there helping the WI serve tea, or fire-watching – probably both, only they don't pay, of course, and you'll need to earn a wage if you're to become independent.'

'Independent?' said Olivia. 'I like the sound of that.'

Nana smiled wistfully. 'You remind me of your mother so much – both cut from the same cloth, as it were.'

Olivia looked at her grandmother from under thick lashes. 'What do you think Dad'll say if I tell him I'm applying for one of the services?'

The older woman glanced back at her son-in-law. 'I shouldn't imagine he'll try to stop you. He's got enough on his plate keeping that factory going, and it's not as if he's ever home much.'

Olivia also glanced at her father. 'I don't like the thought of knocking around in that house on my own all day. I'll only dwell on Mum and what should have been.'

Nana pulled a face. 'Why not come and stay with Pops and me? Goodness only knows we've always wanted to spend more time with you, and this will be the perfect opportunity before you go off – if that's what you decide to do, of course.'

Olivia stopped walking and turned to face her grandmother. 'Do you really think they'd want me?' She glanced down at her ample figure. 'I'm not exactly in peak condition.'

'They'd be grateful to have a smart woman like yourself in the ranks,' her grandmother retorted. 'As for being in peak condition, that's what they're there for, to whip you into shape. No one goes into the forces the same way they come out.'

A glint of hope entered Olivia's eye. 'You really think they'll have me?'

Nana nodded assuredly. 'As sure as eggs are eggs, they'd be mad not to.'

'And can I really stay with you, or do you need to ask Pops first?'

Her grandmother squeezed her hand. 'Your grandfather might wear the trousers in our house, but it's me that runs it! Besides, he dotes on you, you know he does. He'll be made up when he hears we've a house guest.'

Feeling more confident, Olivia turned back to meet her father. 'Can I have a word?'

William nodded curtly.

'I've been talking with Nana and we've both agreed that I'll be very lonely in the house with you out at work all day, so she's very kindly offered to let me stay with her and Pops for a while, until I make up my mind what I want to do with myself.'

Her father gave her grandmother a look of contempt. 'Has she now? Well, don't you mind me, I'm sure I'll be able to cope on my own,' he said stiffly.

Olivia smiled uncertainly. She hadn't been expecting him to object, even if it was in a roundabout way. She thought she might as well lay her cards on the table. 'I'm thinking about applying for the services – that way I'll be out from under your feet and I'll be able to support myself. What do you think?'

He shrugged in a dismissive manner. 'I'm sure it doesn't matter what I think, Olivia. You're a grown woman who can think for herself – apparently,' he added in a sulky undertone.

Olivia walked on in silence whilst she tried to work out her father's mood. When her mother had been alive, he had continually made snide comments aimed at Olivia's reluctance to leave home, so why on earth was he objecting now? She looked at him to see if he was going to add anything else to the conversation, but his mouth was firmly closed. Apparently he had no more to say on the matter. Unable to read his thoughts, she continued, 'Would it be all right if I left today?'

Turning to face her, William gave an impatient sigh. 'You've never asked me for my opinion before, so why start now?' He went on before she had a chance to respond, 'I couldn't get you out of the house when your mother was alive, so I suppose your desire to leave before she's cold in her grave speaks volumes.'

Olivia stared at him, open-mouthed. 'That's not it at all. I only stayed around before so that I could take care of Mum, you know I did.'

Her father shrugged. 'Do as you see fit.' He walked on.

Olivia stared after him. Why couldn't he just say what he wanted? Reluctant as she might feel, she would stay if he really wanted her to – she wouldn't leave anyone on their own if it made them unhappy. She started as her grandmother's hand touched her elbow.

'Everything all right, Liv?'

Olivia shrugged. 'I don't know. He makes out like he doesn't want me to leave, but when I ask him outright for his opinion he won't give it ...' she hesitated, '... apart from implying that he thinks I'm leaving because of him.'

Her grandmother drew a deep breath. 'He's trying to manipulate you, Liv. It's a trait of your father's, is that.'

'I know,' said Olivia. 'He's always been the same, but normally, if you don't do as he wishes, he'll tell you outright, but not today.'

'Because he knows he can't control you any more,' said Nana astutely. 'He realises his only chance is to guilt you into doing what he wants, but you mustn't let him, because he's doing it for selfish reasons, and that's not on. He used to try it with your mother, only she wouldn't stand for it, of course.' She smiled. 'She did him a lot of good, did your mother.'

'So, what should I do?'

Nana slipped her hand through the crook of Olivia's elbow. 'Whatever you want to do, as long as it's what you want and no one else.' She stared pointedly at her son-in-law.

'You don't think my leaving would make him miserable?' Olivia asked uncertainly.

'He's already miserable, Liv,' Nana said decidedly. 'You staying will just make the two of you miserable, and what good will that do?'

Olivia mulled over her grandmother's words. 'If it were anyone else I'd not even contemplate leaving, but I do believe that Dad and I living under the same roof will only lead to unhappiness and bitterness on both sides, him because he knows he's holding me back, and me because I know he's being unfair.' She nodded thoughtfully. 'I need to make a clean break, and I reckon it's better to do it sooner rather than later.'

'Strike whilst the iron's hot,' her grandmother agreed.

When they arrived back at the house Olivia left the mourners in the lounge to seek out her father, whom she wasn't surprised to find leafing through some work papers in his study. She rapped her knuckles against the door to gain his attention. He looked up fleetingly before turning his attention back to the papers on his desk. He spoke abruptly. 'Yes?'

Olivia entered the room and closed the door behind her. 'I've been giving it some more thought, and after everyone's gone, I shall collect my things and move in with Nana and Pops. It'll be nice to spend some time with them before I leave.'

He shuffled the papers into a neat pile, placed them in a folder then gazed intently at her before speaking. 'Leave? I take it that means you're planning to apply?'

Oliva nodded.

'You really think they're after women like you?' His eyes rested on her stomach. 'Only I'd assumed they wanted women who were fit and healthy, and you don't exactly look either of those to me.'

Olivia blushed. Her father had voiced the same reservation that she'd raised with her grandmother. 'Nana says they soon whip you into shape once you've joined, so not only will I be getting out from under your feet, but I'll be getting into shape just like you always said I should.'

Her father looked sceptical. 'They've got their work cut out for them then,' he said spitefully.

Olivia stared at him in disbelief. 'And to think I was worried about how you'd cope without me.' Shaking her head sadly, she laid her hand on the door handle just as her father called out to her from behind.

'You leave this house and you'd better take everything with you, because you shan't be coming back.'

She stood frozen to the spot, her hand still on the handle. She knew that this was another way of manipulating her into staying, because she couldn't possibly take everything with her in one go. She thought of her mother, and how she had stood for none of her husband's nonsense. She addressed him without turning. 'If you want me to stay, you're going to have to say it, no more games.'

There was a moment's hesitation when Olivia thought her father might actually say the words she was certain he was longing to voice.

'Close the door on your way out,' William replied quietly.

Olivia turned the handle and walked out. Closing the door behind her, she leaned against it whilst she came to terms with what had just transpired. She listened intently, waiting to see if she could hear the regretful footfall of her father as he hurried to take back words spoken in haste, but there was nothing. A tear trickled down her cheek as she went up to her bedroom. To change her mind now would be to resign herself to the life of a spinster who'd never been lucky enough to marry. She had no choice but to follow through and leave her past life behind.

She entered her bedroom and took down the suitcase from the top of her wardrobe, then methodically began to pack her most treasured possessions. Once she'd finished, she glanced briefly around the room, making sure that she hadn't forgotten anything. Heaving the case off her bed, she descended the stairs and headed towards the front door. As she passed her mother's room she decided to take one last look before leaving. She wandered over to the window which looked out over the garden. Her mother had spent many an hour gazing at the tulips and dahlias which filled the flower bed outside. Turning, Olivia's eye fell on her mother's dressing table. She picked up the mother-of-pearl-backed mirror and gazed at her reflection. How many times had she brushed her mother's hair with the matching hairbrush? She recalled the last morning her mother had been alive.

'Having my hair brushed always makes me feel better,' Catherine had said, as Olivia gently patted her mother's hair into place, 'like I'm still part of things.'

She had smiled as Olivia held up the mirror so that she could see the result of her efforts. 'You should be a hairdresser, Liv. It's not easy making me look presentable these days, yet you still manage it.'

Now, as silent tears escaped, she flipped open the catches of her suitcase and placed the mirror and hairbrush on top of her clothes and was about to turn away when she saw the small keepsake box which she had given her mother for her last birthday. Picking it up, she placed it beside the mirror and hairbrush. She closed the case and headed back towards the front door. Glancing in the direction of her father's study, she wondered briefly whether she should tell him she was about to leave, then thought better of it. That would be playing the same game as him. She had said she was leaving, and he hadn't tried to stop her.

Olivia opened the front door, breathed in the evening air, and closed it firmly behind her. If her father was silly enough to turn his back on her, then there was nothing that could be done about it. She would step forward into a new life, with exciting opportunities, just as her mother had wanted her to do.

A fortnight after burying her mother, Olivia headed for the town hall, which they were using to recruit volunteers. Once she got there, she joined the end of the queue which stretched along the length of the pavement. She glanced curiously around at the other women to get the measure of those who had chosen to sign up. She couldn't help noticing that they were all considerably slimmer than she was. A small group of men further up the queue had evidently noticed the same thing, sniggering and making rude gestures in her direction. Turning her back, Olivia did her best to ignore them, but if anything it made matters worse as they now had to speak louder in order to make sure she heard their opinions.

A woman who was a few years younger than Olivia turned to see what was causing so much hilarity. She glanced at Olivia before shooting the men a look of disgust. 'They may look old enough to join up, but they're certainly not acting it,' she muttered.

A faint blush tinged Olivia's cheeks. 'Don't worry, I'm used to it.'

The girl shook her head. 'Well, you shouldn't be. My mam always taught me, if you can't say anything nice then you should keep your mouth shut.' Turning to face Olivia, she held out a hand so that the men might see. 'I'm Maude Harris.'

Olivia gratefully shook the other girl's hand. 'Hello, Maude, I'm Olivia, Liv for short.'

Maude smiled pleasantly. 'Hello, Liv.' She glanced along the length of the queue. 'What made you decide to join up?'

'I've been caring for my mother until she passed away a few weeks ago, and then I decided to make myself useful and get paid whilst I'm about it. You?'

'Sorry to hear about your mam,' Maude said sincerely. She glanced down at her ring finger. 'I was engaged until I caught the bugger cheating on me with my best pal, Sally.'

'Flamin' Nora!' said Olivia, causing Maude to giggle. 'Did you wallop him?'

Maude grinned. 'I didn't have to. I went round to his mam's to give him his ring back, only he wasn't there. Of course she wanted to know why I was returning the ring, so I told her. Just as I was about to hand the ring over, he walked in ...' she sighed wistfully, '... and she picked up her frying pan and chased him out of the house and down the street.' A beam split her face in two. 'I bet she gave him a good walloping when she caught up with him.'

Olivia nodded approvingly. 'Good for her!'

'I decided I needed a fresh start, so I handed my notice in at Woolies, and here I am.' Maude checked on the queue ahead of them. 'What are you hoping for?'

Olivia shrugged. 'Not bothered.' She glanced down at her rotund figure. 'Beggars can't be choosers. I'll have whatever they give me.'

Maude frowned at her disapprovingly. 'Stop putting yourself down.' She indicated the group of men who had turned their attentions to a spotty youth with milk-bottle glasses. 'You've got people lining up to do that for you.'

Olivia turned to look at the men, whose taunting had caused the young boy to turn crimson. 'Why can't they leave people alone?' she said angrily.

'Because picking on other people makes them feel better about themselves,' Maude said.

'I don't feel good about myself, but I wouldn't want to make someone else miserable, just to make myself feel better.'

Maude smiled. 'That's because you're a nice person.' Seeing people in front of her shuffle forward in the queue, she followed suit. 'I'm hoping to join the WAAF,' she confided.

'Oh? Why the WAAF in particular?' Olivia asked, with a hint of curiosity.

Maude shrugged. 'I like the uniform.'

Olivia giggled then looked down at her feet. 'I don't think it matters what uniform they give me – if they've got any to fit me, that is.'

Maude tutted her disapproval. 'The way you carry on, anyone'd think you were the size of an elephant!'

A deep blush swept Olivia's neckline. 'I've got eyes in my head, Maude, and whilst those boys may only be making fun of me to make themselves feel better, that's not why my father said it.'

Maude's eyes widened with horror. 'Your own father?'

Olivia nodded. 'He doesn't believe in sugar-coating things; it's his way of trying to gee me up into looking after myself.'

Maude shook her head. 'Blimey, with pep talks like that no wonder you've a low opinion of yourself. Take it from me, you're fine as you are.'

The girls had reached the top of the line and Olivia bade Maude good luck as her new friend handed the corporal her papers.

It seemed to her that he had barely glanced at them before beckoning Olivia to step forward. He went through her details then told her to go home and wait.

'Well?' said Maude, who was waiting to one side.

'He said to go home and wait,' said Olivia. 'You?'

'Same,' she grinned. 'Wouldn't it be smashing if we ended up doing our training together? It's much easier starting something new with a friend, don't you think?'

'I do,' said Olivia, 'because I'm not very confident around new people.'

Maude jerked her head in the direction of the door. 'I reckon you'll soon come out of your shell once you've been in the services for a few days!' She opened her handbag and rooted through the contents, eventually pulling out a piece of paper and a pencil. 'How about we swap addresses? If I get my papers first, I'll come and tell you, and vice versa?'

Olivia beamed. 'Good idea! Or, if you fancy it, you could come to mine now for a cuppa – if you're free, that is?'

'Even better!' said Maude.

Together the two girls made their way to Olivia's grandparents' house, chattering with anticipatory excitement about their new venture.

*

Olivia heard the letterbox snap shut. She looked across the table to her grandmother who gave her an encouraging nod. 'Go on, then! What are you waiting for?'

She pushed her chair back from the table and trotted through to the hallway, only to return a few moments later with an official-looking letter which she propped up against the jar of Robertson's jam.

'Aren't you going to open it?' asked Pops, his eyes fixed on the letter.

'What if it says thanks but no thanks?' said Olivia, nervously nibbling the nail edge of her thumb.

Nana rolled her eyes. 'It won't! So for goodness' sake open it and let us know what it says!'

Taking a deep breath, Olivia took the butter knife, slit the envelope open and read the contents. She looked up, her eyes shining with surprised excitement. 'I'm in the WAAF and going to Innsworth in Gloucester.'

'Told you!' said her grandfather smugly. 'They need girls like you in the WAAF.'

They all turned as someone knocked on the back door. 'It's me, Maude!' called a familiar voice.

'Come in, luv,' said Nana. 'Do you fancy a cuppa?'

Maude nodded. 'That'd be lovely, ta.' She flourished an envelope at Olivia as she sat down on the chair next to hers. 'I've ... ooo!' Spying Olivia's letter, she stopped short. 'Is that what I think it is?'

Olivia beamed with pride. 'Training in Innswo—' She got no further before being engulfed by Maude who was jabbering 'Me too, me too!' excitedly.

'What wonderful news!' said Nana. 'Liv was hoping you'd be stationed together.'

Eyeing his granddaughter, Pops removed the wooden pipe from between his teeth and peered into the bowl. 'Are you going to tell your father?'

Olivia shrugged. 'I would if I thought he was interested, but he told me not to bother going back.'

Nana looked dismayed. 'He didn't mean it, Liv. You said yourself it was his way of making you stay without saying he wanted you to.'

'I'm thirty-one years old,' said Olivia stiffly, 'which is too old to be playing silly beggars – not that that stops him, mind you. Perhaps this will teach him a lesson that he needs to think before he speaks.'

Maude looked at Olivia with surprise. 'You don't really expect him to change, do you?'

'No, I don't,' said Olivia, 'which is why I'm not going to waste my time going round there.'

Nana tutted in a disappointed fashion. 'I think it's a shame when a family falls apart.'

'Don't tell me, tell him!' said Olivia irritably. 'He's the one acting like a child.'

'Two wrongs don't make a right.' Nana poured the water from the kettle into a large earthenware teapot. 'Besides, your father has always acted like a child in these matters; it's up to you to be the adult.'

'Fine!' said Olivia. 'Only I'll tell him in a letter, because I'm not giving him the satisfaction of slamming the door in my face, or hanging up on me.'

Her grandmother smiled appreciatively. 'Good girl, Liv. You know it makes sense, and it would make your mother happy to know that you'd taken the moral high ground.'

'I know she would be,' said Olivia, giving her grandmother a fond smile. 'You remind me of her at times.'

'It's all part of becoming an adult, Liv.' She set the teapot down on the table. 'Now who's up for one of my fruitless scones?'

Chapter Three

July 1940

Olivia and Maude stood in line as they waited to be kitted out. 'I can't wait to get my uniform,' Maude said excitedly. 'A brand-new start away from Sally and that cheating pig.'

Olivia smiled. Maude was gradually easing off on the insults towards her ex-best friend and ex-fiancé, which Olivia took to be a sign that her friend was moving on.

'I don't much care what uniform they put me in,' Olivia sighed. 'I'll still end up looking like one of the balloons.'

Maude wagged a reproving finger. 'Don't be daft, you'll look lovely.'

A chuckle escaped Olivia's lips as her friend was handed a uniform, on top of which lay the biggest pair of knickers either of the girls had ever seen. 'What are these for?' said Maude, holding up the knickers with a look of distaste.

The corporal grinned. 'Them's what they call the passion killers. Ain't you ever seen a pair of bloomers before?'

'Cheeky devil!' tutted Maude. 'I don't wear bloomers.'

The man chuckled and waggled his eyebrows suggestively. 'Oh aye, what do you wear, then?'

Maude glanced haughtily at him. 'Never you mind!'

He gave her a playful wink. 'Have you had your jabs yet?'

'I beg your pardon!' said Maude.

He grinned. 'You know, jabs, needles, injections.'

Maude turned anxiously to Olivia. 'Please tell me he's joking?'

Olivia grimaced. 'I'm afraid he's telling the truth.'

With Olivia the next in line, the corporal cast a scrutinising eye over her figure before collecting the various garments from the shelving behind him and handing them over. Olivia waited for the obligatory flippant remark regarding her size, and was pleasantly surprised when he asked her to move on.

Leaving the hut behind them, Maude turned to Olivia. 'Do you think we can lie and say we've already had them?'

Olivia shook her head. 'They're not stupid. Besides, I'd rather have an injection than come down with something nasty.'

Maude reluctantly agreed. 'I suppose one little injection can't hurt.'

A few days later, both Olivia and Maude were laid up in bed after receiving several injections, one of which had disagreed with most of the girls in their billet.

'Famous last words,' moaned Maude, pulling her knees up to her chest.

'I don't want to eat anything ever again,' groaned Olivia.

'I hope Sally and the snake have to suffer injections like this,' said Maude.

Olivia smiled briefly, before grimacing. 'I hope we don't have to have any more.'

The girl in the bunk opposite Olivia's turned a sweaty face towards them. 'I asked and they said we'd had our lot, thank God.' She sank back down.

'At least they're not making us march round that soddin' yard,' muttered Maude, and a general murmur of agreement came from the rest of the girls.

They soon recovered from their ordeal, and after several weeks of what seemed like relentless drill and square-bashing, both girls passed their initial training.

Having gone down a dress size, Olivia admired her reflection in the mirror of the ablutions.

'You look marvellous,' said Maude as she emerged from the cubicle. 'Carry on as you are and you'll have a tummy flatter than mine.'

Olivia roared with laughter. 'Trust me, that's never going to happen.'

Maude washed her hands in the sink next to Olivia's. 'Don't be so negative! You've already lost a few inches from your waist. Keep going and you'll be fit as a fiddle.'

Olivia smiled shyly at Maude. Childbirth didn't leave anyone with a flat stomach, not that she was about to say that to Maude. 'I wonder what we'll be doing now that we've passed training.'

Maude dried her hands and adjusted her cap. 'I hope it's nothing too strenuous. I find my kitbag hard enough to lift!'

Olivia opened the door to the ablutions and together they headed to the ops room. 'I don't think they give the heavy jobs to the Waafs – they save them for the fellers.'

The corporal who was responsible for handing out the girls' postings approached them. 'Looks like you two are off to RAF Chigwell.'

Olivia glanced down at her envelope. 'What will we be doing when we get there?'

'Fabric workers,' said the corporal. Seeing the blank look on their faces, he added, 'You're going to be making and repairing the barrage balloons.'

When Ted had first arrived in RAF Speke, he'd had high hopes of rekindling his friendship with Toff. His only dilemma was, he didn't know where she currently lived. He had looked through the Kelly's directory, but the only Campbells mentioned had a different initial to hers. He had of course realised that she would probably be married by now, but that didn't help matters, so he had decided to bite the bullet and visit the house on Aigburth Drive. To most people this would seem a risky manoeuvre, but Ted knew otherwise. Mr Campbell never answered his own front door – that was the job of the housemaid, Mavis, and whilst Ted knew who Mavis was, he had never met her, so he had no fear of her recognising him. When she answered the door he would simply ask where he could find Olivia, explaining that he was an old friend who had moved away a long time ago – what could be the harm in that? With it all worked out, he had arrived at the Campbells', but despite his best efforts it seemed that no one was coming to answer the door. At one point, he felt sure that he had heard raised voices, so he had kept his finger on the bell for a few seconds, hoping to gain their attention, but he still got no response. With no alternative he had decided to call back another day.

Several months had gone by and even though he had fully intended to try the house again, there always seemed to be something more important to do. It wasn't until a chance meeting with one of the boys who used to work alongside him in the Campbells' factory that things changed.

'Blimey! Is that Ted Hewitt?'

Leaning back in his seat, Ted caught sight of the familiar face. 'Andy Evans, as I live and breathe!'

Grinning, Andy walked over to join him. 'Well I'll be, I never thought we'd see you round this neck of the woods again!'

Ted laughed. 'I bet Campbell thought the same. Looks like you're not the only one in for a shock.'

Andy's eyes grew wide. 'You're not seriously thinking of going back there, are you?'

'Already have, not that I saw anyone. Besides, it's a free world,' said Ted, adding, 'Well, Britain is at any rate.'

Andy eyed him with bemused admiration. 'You've got bigger balls than me!'

Ted looked annoyed. Out of everyone, he didn't think Andy would have considered him to be a thief. 'Don't tell me you believed that pile of old claptrap?'

Andy held his hands up in a placating fashion. 'You've got to admit, it did look a bit suspicious the way you and your old feller took off without bothering to say ta-ra first, and then old Campbell and his daughter doing a moonlight flit only to reappear a few month's later,' he shrugged, 'tongues were bound to wag.'

Ted looked at him, confused. 'Sorry, Andy, but you've lost me. What's Olivia and Campbell's disappearance got to do with his stupid fish?'

Andy mirrored Ted's confusion. 'Fish?'

Ted excused himself to his fellow diners. He was not about to explain Campbell's accusation in front of his pals, because whilst he knew there was no truth in it, some folk might believe there was no smoke without fire. He gestured for Andy to join him at an empty table away from everyone else. As they sat down, Ted told Andy about Campbell's accusation and ultimatum.

Andy stared back agog. 'That's not what we heard at all! Far from it.'

Ted eyed him, intrigued. 'Why, what did you hear?'

Andy looked awkward. 'You know what the factory's like for rumours – probably best to ignore it really. So, how are you?'

Ted shook his head. 'Oh no, you don't. What did you hear?'

Andy drew a deep breath. 'There's probably nothing in it, but one of the girls who worked in the office said she had to go round to see Campbell in his house a few months after you left. She said she caught a glimpse of Olivia and she reckoned Olivia looked ...' he eyed Ted nervously, '... big.'

Ted rolled his eyes. 'So, she put a bit of weight on, hardly the crime of the century!'

Andy shook his head before leaning forward and lowering his voice to just above a whisper. 'She said Olivia looked like she was going to pop.' Realising he still wasn't being clear, he cut to the chase. 'Pregnant.'

Ted's eyes were out on stalks. 'Was she sure Olivia wasn't just overweight? She was always a bigger girl – she could've passed for sixteen when she was thirteen ...' Seeing the look on Andy's face, his voice trailed off.

'Not long after she seen them, Campbell went away on business, and he told everyone he'd sent Olivia to finishing school around the same time.' His cheeks bloomed in guilty embarrassment. 'Sorry, mate, but you and Olivia became hot gossip, and you know what some folk are like, they won't let it lie. Some of them even made it their business to find out what was going on.'

The colour drained from Ted's face. 'And?' he said, his voice just audible.

Andy pulled a brief grimace. 'Olivia came back but there was no baby, and she'd lost an awful lot of weight ...' He hesitated for a moment. 'I don't mean to pry, but we all kind of assumed you were the father, and that's why you'd disappeared without trace, although if she never told you ...' Seeing the look on Ted's face, he nodded slowly. 'I see.'

'I didn't have a clue,' said Ted quietly. 'Although it does explain why Campbell invented that cock and bull story about me nickin' fish.'

Andy fiddled with the end of his tie. 'He wanted rid before you got wind of the truth.' He gave Ted a grim smile. 'Don't get me wrong, mate, but I can't see you and Campbell playing happy families, can you?'

Ted gave a mirthless laugh. 'Nope.' He pushed his hands through his hair. 'Does anyone know what happened to Olivia?'

Andy shook his head. 'Not a clue, although I do know her mam's health took a turn for the worse after she come back from her ...' he gave a shallow cough, '... finishing school.'

Ted wrung his cap in his hands. 'I swear I didn't know.'

Andy nodded. 'I believe you, mate, although you might get a few funny looks if you bump into any of the lads you used to work with, because as rumours go, someone spread it round that Campbell had paid you to scarper and never show your face around these parts again – not that I believed it,' he added hastily.

Ted looked at the clock above the door to the NAAFI. 'Thanks for filling me in.'

Andy nodded. 'No problem.' He was about to get up when a thought occurred to him. 'What are you going to do?'

Ted's chair scraped across the floor as he got to his feet. 'I'm going to find Toff, after I've told her old feller what I think of him.' He rammed his hat on to his head and left the NAAFI without a backward glance.

Olivia's tongue slipped between her lips as she tried to twist the rope she was holding into a reef knot. As her hands looped round each other she pulled them apart, hoping to see something which resembled what the officer had shown them earlier, only to find that once again, her rope remained unknotted. She looked over to Maude, who was frowning at her own attempt at a knot.

'For crying out loud,' Olivia hissed from the corner of her mouth, 'whoever thought tying a knot would prove so difficult?'

'It reminds me of the magician me mam and dad took me to see when I was little, only he tied knots, then they untied themselves.' Maude considered this for a moment before adding, 'A bit like what I'm doing, I suppose, because it doesn't matter how much I twist this stupid rope round, it still comes out looking nothing like what Officer Haughton did.'

'We've got to master this,' said Olivia, her tone full of determination, 'else we'll be sent for canteen staff, and I had enough of peeling spuds when we did our initial training. I'll be hanged if I let a length of rope send me back to the kitchen.'

Maude nodded emphatically. 'I spoke to one of the girls when I nipped to the lavvy earlier, and she said she was just like us at first, but they go over and over it until you can tie them in your sleep. She said they make sure you get it right because it could turn out to be the difference between life and death.'

Olivia grimaced at the piece of rope in her hands. 'Blimey!'

Maude continued, 'She also said she's seen some of the balloons come back in shreds. She reckoned they were in better shape than the fellers who'd been operating them ...' She fell silent as Officer Haughton, who had overheard them whispering, looked in her direction.

'Aircraftwoman Harris! You've obviously mastered the reef knot to the point you can stand idly chatting – perhaps you would like to demonstrate your expertise to the rest of the class?'

Flushing red to the tips of her ears, Maude reluctantly walked to the front of the class where she tried in vain to knot the dreaded rope whilst the other girls looked on.

Pressing his lips into a grim line, the officer took the rope from her unresisting hands and tied it with ease, retaining eye contact with Maude. He handed the rope back to her complete with knot. 'I don't want to hear another peep out of you until you can tie that knot with your eyes closed.'

Nodding mutely, Maude returned to her seat.

Olivia cast her a sympathetic smile as Officer Haughton slowly demonstrated the knot to the class, adding that none of them would be allowed to leave the room until they also could tie the knot with their eyes shut.

By the time Maude had managed this, the rest of the class had gone, apart from Olivia, who gave her friend a small, quiet round of applause. Officer Haughton smothered a yawn behind his hand before dismissing them.

As they left the room, Maude turned to Olivia. 'When Haughton asked me to stand up in front of everyone, I wanted the earth to swallow me up, because I knew I hadn't a cat in hell's chance of getting it right, but perhaps it was for the best, because I'm a dab hand now.'

'I think you did us all a favour. None of us were getting it right, and I'm sure some of the girls were peeping through their lashes.'

Maude's eyes rounded. 'I don't think I'd have dared do that in case Haughton caught me!' She glanced towards the NAAFI. 'How about we go to the dance later?' Seeing the doubtful look on Olivia's face, she quickly added, 'Oh, please say yes! I don't like going without you, and I know you say you're a bit rusty, but you'll soon get into the swing of things …' She eyed her friend eagerly. 'Please?'

Olivia had been standing with her arms folded across her chest, but seeing the hopeful look on Maude's face, she relented. 'As long as I don't have to dance with any men!'

Maude gave a whoop of joy. She knew why Olivia didn't want to dance with any of the men, but she felt that the men on their base were very different from the ones in the queue outside the town hall that day. Not that Olivia agreed.

'They're all pigs and that's all there is to it' had been her reply when Maude had broached the subject.

Later that evening, Maude threaded her arm through Olivia's as they approached the doors to the NAAFI. 'Let's go and show them how it's done, shall we?'

Olivia beamed. 'I must say, I'm rather looking forward to this. I used to dance a lot with my mother, before she became too ill that is.' She pushed open the door to the NAAFI. 'If a tune came on the wireless, Mum would call out for me to come and join her, and as soon as I arrived she would take me in her arms and dance me around the living room, saying that it was good practice for the day I met my Prince Charming, but that was ever such a long time ago. I hope I can remember the steps.'

'You'll soon get the hang of it,' said Maude as she led the way to the counter.

Olivia glanced around the sea of male faces. She had told Maude that she didn't wish to dance with any of the men because she feared they would make fun of her weight, which was partly true, but the main reason was because of what had happened the last time she had said 'yes' to a member of the opposite sex.

The two women spent the entire evening dancing together, and Olivia could hardly believe her eyes when she looked at the clock above the door. 'The time's flown by.'

Maude jerked her head towards the table which they were using for respite whenever they needed a break. 'Shall we call it a night?'

Olivia nodded. 'Rather! My feet are killing me, although I've had a wonderful time. Thanks for persuading me to come, Maude, I've really enjoyed myself.'

Maude performed a mock curtsey. 'You're welcome. I told you you'd soon get back into the swing of things.'

'And you were right!' said Olivia as she sipped the last of her lemonade. 'Dancing's thirsty work.'

Nodding, Maude slipped her foot out of her shoe and rubbed her toes. 'Painful, too!'

Olivia grimaced. 'Sorry about that ...' She was about to continue when she found herself being interrupted by a man in a corporal's uniform. She looked up at him. 'Can I help you?'

He held out a hand. 'Would you like to dance?'

Olivia looked at Maude, who was pulling encouraging faces. Whether it was the euphoria of the dance which had caused her better judgement to temporarily lapse, Olivia could not say, but to her surprise she found herself taking the man's hand.

Smiling, the airman led her on to the dance floor. Placing his arm around her waist, he turned to face a group of young airmen, all of whom were grinning at him as though he had just made a hilarious joke. He turned his attention back to Olivia, a grin matching those of his friends etched on his face. In that moment, Olivia knew exactly why they were behaving in such a manner. Not prepared to be the butt of their joke, she tried to push him away, but he held on to her firmly and turned back to his friends. 'There's certainly plenty to hold on to!' he said, much to their delight.

One of them called back, 'Oi, Tony, what are you and Celeste going to call your first kid? Babar?'

Laughing fit to burst, the airman tightened his grip as Olivia squirmed in his arms. 'Come on, love, give us a kiss.' Burning with humiliation, Olivia brought her hand back and slapped him hard across the face, instantly quelling his mirth. Holding a hand to his cheek, he returned to his pals, who were now reeling with laughter at the sight of their friend.

Hot tears of humiliation flowing down her cheeks, Olivia left the NAAFI without waiting for Maude.

She was halfway to the ablutions when Maude arrived at her side. 'Ignore them, Liv. They're vile, spiteful bullies who should be reported ...'

'No!' said Olivia abruptly. 'It'll just make things worse.'

'You can't let them get away with that,' Maude protested.

But Olivia was adamant. 'They, or rather he, didn't get away with anything. I should imagine he'll be wearing my handprint on his face for the rest of the evening, which should raise a few questions, not that he'll tell the truth.'

'Serves him right,' muttered Maude, who was feeling guilty for encouraging Olivia to accept the man's invitation.

'I hope he doesn't report me,' Olivia said bitterly.

Maude's brow shot towards her hairline. '*Him* report *you*?'

Olivia nodded. 'Didn't you see his stripes? He's a corporal, Maude. I shouldn't have slapped him.'

'But he was being horrible ...' Maude began, only to fall silent as Olivia continued to shake her head.

'Sticks and stones,' said Olivia, adding, 'and he's a man, they stick up for each other, so there's no point in reporting him. It'll be his word against mine, and no one will believe me. Sorry, Maude, but I've already gone through enough humiliation for one evening.'

Maude placed an arm around Olivia's shoulders. 'I'm sorry he was so horrible. Had I known what his intentions were, I never would have encouraged you to say yes.'

Olivia shrugged. 'It's my own fault.' She gave a mirthless laugh. 'I should have known better. They're all the same – one look at me and they think I'm easy.'

A wrinkle creased Maude's brow. 'I'm sure that's not true.'

Olivia shook her head. 'It is, trust me.'

Confused as to why her friend would think such a thing, Maude pressed her for more information. 'Why would they think you're easy? It doesn't make sense.'

'They assume I must be desperate.' Olivia shook her head. 'Just ignore me.'

But Maude was a true friend, and if something was bothering her pal, she was determined to get to the bottom of it. 'I will not ignore you, Liv. There's obviously a reason why you'd think such a thing. Has someone said something to make you think like that – an old boyfriend, perhaps?'

Olivia stared mutely at her feet.

After a little more thought, Maude had another guess. 'Your father?'

Olivia's gaze flicked up to meet Maude's.

'Well, I wouldn't listen to him. Was it over a boy?'

Olivia nodded slowly.

Maude shook her head. 'Your father's an old fuddy-duddy if he thinks a kiss and cuddle makes you easy. It's not as if he got you in the family way ...'

Olivia's silence spoke volumes.

Maude clasped a hand to her mouth before lowering it and taking Olivia in a tight embrace. 'Oh Liv, I'm so sorry, I had no idea.'

Olivia wiped a tear from her cheek and made an attempt at a light-hearted giggle. 'So you see, he's right.'

Maude shook her head. 'I may not know all the facts, but I'd wager it was your one and only?'

Olivia nodded. 'It's better if I tell you the full story ...'

Maude listened in silence as Olivia told her of Ted, their relationship, and how he had left Liverpool.

Maude blew her cheeks out slowly. 'And I thought I had it rough being cheated on, but after listening to you, I think I got off lightly.' She threaded her arm through Olivia's. 'And to think, there I was banging on about my trivial problems, whilst you were suffering in silence.'

'Your problems weren't trivial, and you're better off talking it through rather than letting it fester for years on end like I did,' said Olivia earnestly. 'I know I could have talked things through with Mum, but I didn't want to upset her, not when she was so poorly.'

Maude squeezed Olivia's arm. 'Do you know what happened to your baby?'

'Stillborn,' said Olivia, the word barely above a whisper.

Maude's bottom lip trembled. 'Was it a boy or a girl?'

Olivia blushed. 'My father said the less I knew, the easier it would be to say goodbye.' Blinking back the tears, she fought to control her emotions before adding, 'I never even got the chance to do that.'

Maude chewed her bottom lip, nervous that her next comment might cause her friend to become more upset, but she felt it only right to bring the matter up. 'Every time you've spoken about your father, you've never had anything good to say about him. Are you sure his advice was given with your best interest in mind?'

Olivia gave a sarcastic laugh. 'Not with hindsight, but at the time I thought it was, although I admit I was so scared and confused, I think I'd have followed the devil through the gates of hell had someone told me to do so.'

Maude nodded slowly. 'Are you sure Ted knew the truth?'

Olivia nodded. 'I read the letter.'

Maude looked horrified. 'He wrote you a letter?'

Olivia corrected herself. 'Not exactly. His father wrote a letter to say they were leaving Liverpool because of the rumours.'

'I thought you said only you, your father and your mother knew?' said Maude innocently.

'That's right.' Olivia gave Maude a sidelong glance. 'You think my father was lying, don't you?'

'Don't you?'

Olivia began to tremble as the guilt of her previous thoughts caught up with her. 'I didn't, but as time's gone by I'm not so sure, and that makes things worse because I've blamed Ted for everything, which isn't fair.' She held a hand to her forehead. 'Oh my God, Maude, what have I done?'

Maude looked at her in astonishment. 'What do you mean, what have you done? You've not done anything. Your father, on the other hand ...'

'I listened to him, Maude, and I should have known better. I even blamed Ted for our baby being still-born because my father said the stress had probably caused it.'

'I'm sorry, Liv, but your father's a wicked man, with a lot to answer for. He knew you were too young to think for yourself.' Maude quickly did the maths in her head before hissing, 'You were fourteen! I don't know what I'd have done had I got myself into that situation at your age.'

Olivia looked ashamed. 'You wouldn't have got yourself into that situation, though.'

'How do you know that?' said Maude firmly. 'I've never been put in that position so I don't know how I would have reacted. Girls do all sorts of silly things when boys are involved – you were just unlucky.'

Olivia smiled through her tears. 'You're a good pal, Maude Harris.'

Maude blushed. 'I don't like seeing women being taken advantage of, or being lied to.'

'Poor Ted,' Olivia said softly. 'I've thought so badly of him all these years, and he might not have done anything wrong.'

'Are you going to try and find him?'

Olivia looked doubtful. 'I wouldn't know where to start. Besides, what would be the point?'

Threading her arm through Olivia's, Maude pulled her close. 'I suppose you're right, and I hope you know you can come and talk to me whenever you feel the need.'

Olivia nodded. She felt better than she had in years. Telling Maude her secret was like releasing a floodgate of pent-up emotions and guilt. She turned her thoughts to her father. She had written to him twice since joining the WAAF, letting him know on each occasion where she could be reached should he need to do so, but so far he hadn't written back. Should she write again? She pictured her mother, and knew at once the answer to be yes. She smiled as she imagined what her mother would say if she were here now.

'*Your father's a silly man, Liv, who doesn't know how to express himself properly. That's why he bullies people into doing what he thinks is right for them. His heart's in the right place, if perhaps a little misguided.*'

Olivia heaved a sigh. Her father was most probably the reason why Ted had left Liverpool, but supposing he hadn't and their baby had survived? Could she and Ted really have brought up a child on their own? Even if they had, what would society have had to say on the matter? She knew the answer as soon as the question entered her mind. Society would have been unforgiving and judgemental. She and Ted would have been ridiculed and persecuted to the point where they would wish they had never met – and not just them but their baby too, and it would have been unfair to put a child through that. No, she might not like her father for what she believed he had done and the way he had treated her, but he had been doing what he thought best at the time, when all was said and done; he had had to think on his feet. She supposed many a father would have reacted the same way under the circumstances.

Ted thumped his fist against the Campbells' front door. He had been standing outside for the past five minutes, shouting, yelling and peering through the downstairs windows, but there was no sign of life. He pushed his hair back with one hand before fitting the blue-grey cap back on to his head. He may have been happy enough to leave the first time he got no reply from the house, but things were different now, and he was prepared to stand here all day if that's what it took. He went to hammer his fist against the door when he heard the sound of approaching footsteps from the other side. The door opened a crack and a woman peered through; seeing the RAF uniform encouraged her to open it a little further. 'Hello?'

Ted pulled his mouth into what he hoped was a warm, welcoming and above all trustworthy smile. 'Hello. Is Mr Campbell or his daughter available?'

His heart dropped as the maid shook her head. 'I'm afraid not.'

'Do you know where I might find either of them?'

She nodded. 'May I ask who's asking?'

'An old friend of the family.' He looked down at his uniform. 'I've been away for a while so I thought I'd drop by to catch up.'

The maid eyed him with suspicion, and with her next question Ted realised why. 'You're a friend of Mr Campbell's?'

Ted gave himself a mental telling-off. Of course she was looking suspicious – Mr Campbell didn't have any friends – but it was too late; to retract the statement would make him a liar. Taking a deep breath, he spoke clearly. 'When I say family friend, I really mean a friend of Olivia's. I don't think her father liked me very much.'

Grinning, she glanced over her shoulder then slipped out of the house, pulling the door to behind her. 'Miss Olivia's not lived here since the day of her mam's funeral.' Seeing the surprise on Ted's face, she continued, 'Sorry, I didn't realise you weren't aware ... did you know her mam?'

Ted shook his head. 'I knew she was ill, but that was a long time ago.'

The girl nodded. 'She was like an angel, heaven sent, not like her husband.' She checked over her shoulder before continuing. 'Miss Olivia went to stay with her grandparents straight after the funeral – not that none of us blamed her, of course ...' She got no further. The door behind her was wrenched open and Mr Campbell stood in the doorway, glowering down at her.

'Get inside!' he roared before turning his attention to Ted. 'Who the hell are you and what do you want with my daughter?'

Ted watched the poor maid dash back inside before replying. 'Don't you recognise me?' His eyes bored into William's.

William studied Ted's face with a look of total incomprehension. 'Should I?'

Ted shrugged. 'I think I'd remember evicting a father and son under false pretences, accusing them of stealing when I knew all along that they'd done nothing wrong ...'

William raised his cane in a threatening manner. He had evicted plenty of people over the years – what made this man think he was any different? 'Get off my property!' he bellowed.

Realising that William hadn't clicked, Ted spoke frankly. 'Is that any way to treat the father of your grandchild?' He was pleased to see the colour drain from the older man's face.

His eyes darting wildly around, William hastily descended the steps and didn't stop walking until he was a good distance from the house. He turned to face

Ted, who had followed him. 'I don't know what you've heard, but it's all lies. You're no more a father than I am a grandfather, so if it's a cushy spot around the family table and a place in the company you're after, you can forget it.'

Ted looked at him in shocked disbelief. 'So it's true! You told a pack of lies because you feared what might happen if I stayed!'

William Campbell looked blank. 'Why else would you be here?'

'To see Olivia!' Ted snapped. 'And to find out what happened to our child.'

'Well, she's not here,' said William. 'You can come in and see for yourself.' He held an arm out towards the house.

'I already know she's not here,' said Ted. 'What I want to know is where I can find her.'

'Why? What's in it for you? There is no child, so what do you want with Olivia?' William glanced at Ted's wedding finger. 'A married man chasing after an old flame! Didn't your wife come with a dowry?'

Ted clenched his fists and battled to regain his composure. He stared at William through dull eyes. 'It's all black and white to you, isn't it? People are only ever after one thing …' He shook his head sadly. 'What on earth did your wife ever see in you, I wonder?'

William looked at Ted as though he had punched him in the stomach. 'Don't you dare bring my wife into this. She was a good, honest woman …'

'And what did she make of your lies?' said Ted. William quickly averted his eyes, and Ted stuffed his hands into his pockets. 'You didn't tell her, did you?'

William strode past Ted without making eye contact. 'I don't have to explain myself to the likes of you.'

Ted nodded. 'You're right, you don't. There's plenty of people around who'll know where Olivia is.'

William stopped abruptly. Without turning, he spoke quietly. 'Has it never occurred to you that she didn't want to bring a child up with you, a boy?' He hesitated, waiting for a response, and when none came he continued, 'She was fourteen years old, for crying out loud, and she knew you'd try and make her keep the child, so she asked me to help sort things out.' Turning round to face Ted, even William was surprised at the words which left his lips next: 'I had no choice, Edward. Do you really think I wanted my daughter to abort my grandchild?' He took a step towards Ted. 'Obviously somebody's been blabbing, but if they told you the truth you'll know that Olivia never came back with a child in her arms.'

Ted searched William's face as he recalled Andy's words. According to rumour, Olivia had disappeared only to return a few month's later with no sign of a child in tow. He glared at the older man. 'I'll bet you forced her into it.'

William eyed Ted stoically. 'I can see why you'd think that, Edward, but I couldn't force her into doing anything she didn't want to, including keeping her away from you. It was Olivia's decision, and I think it was the right one under the circumstances. No husband, fourteen years old, and with a mother who was already ill.' He leaned on the top of his cane. 'Babies are hard work and they don't come cheap. Olivia didn't always make the right choices, you being one of them.' He held up a hand to quell Ted's attempt to protest. 'I'm not saying you wouldn't have tried your best, only that your best wouldn't have been good enough. Think it through – just how would you have cared for a mother and child when you couldn't even look after yourself properly?' He turned away. 'Good-bye, Edward.'

Ted mulled over William's last comment as he watched the old man enter the house and close the door behind him. He had come here full of defiance but was leaving with his tail tucked well and truly between his legs. He didn't blame Toff for aborting their baby, and even though he disliked her father intensely, he could see that, for once, the old man had been talking sense when he said that they had both been incapable of bringing up a child. Even though he would have liked to see Toff again, how could he face her knowing that she had gone through hell on her own, because of their mutual indiscretion? He could hardly wipe away the tears which had fallen some sixteen years earlier. His words of apology would be meaningless. Wishing he could have been there to hold her hand and tell her everything was going to be all right wouldn't help her now. Toff had moved on – he glanced at his wedding ring – and so had he. This thought gave him cause to pause. Her father hadn't mentioned her being married, which Ted was certain he would have done if that had been the case, because it would have been another reason to discourage Ted from pursuing her. He cursed softly beneath his breath. 'You're a married man, daydreaming about a woman you haven't seen in over sixteen years!'

He'd gone to the Campbells' looking for answers and, like it or not, he'd got them. Pondering on this, he left the gravelled driveway and turned on to Aigburth Drive. He was sorry for all she had endured, but he should leave her in peace to get on with her future and concentrate on his own marriage instead of chasing rainbows.

Chapter Four

Olivia eyed Maude thoughtfully. 'What do you think?'

'About becoming a balloon operator?' Maude shrugged. 'I s'pose we could give it a whirl and see how we get on, and Officer ...' she hesitated, 'What was his name again?'

'Bailey,' Olivia said promptly.

'That's right,' Maude continued. 'Officer Bailey seemed to think we'd do well, and it would make a pleasant change from sewing.' She hesitated, thinking she might have sounded as if she was unhappy with her work. 'Don't get me wrong, I know that sewing's an important role, but we don't get to see much action, and we did say we wanted adventure and excitement ...'

Olivia agreed heartily. 'The only thing we have to fear is pricking our fingers on a needle, and I know we should be grateful that we're tucked away relatively safe and sound, but I'd rather be out there in the thick of it, helping to thwart Jerry.'

Maude smiled. 'That's exactly how I feel, so I say we give it a go and see how we get on.' Her eyes glistened. 'We'll be the first female balloon operators, Liv.'

'Pioneers,' Olivia agreed.

With their minds made up, the girls wasted no time in seeking out Officer Bailey and informing him of their decision.

He beamed down at them. 'Well done, girls! You're the sort of women we're after, the kind who aren't afraid to roll up their sleeves and get their hands dirty. I admire your courage, because I daresay you've seen these balloons when something goes wrong – it's not a pretty sight!'

Maude nodded uncertainly. Now she came to think of it, they had seen balloons which had practically been ripped to shreds, and whilst it was hard work piecing them back together, it was probably a far cry from being there when disaster struck. Once out of Officer Bailey's earshot, she wasted no time in voicing her concerns to Olivia.

'Every time we get a balloon in for repair, it's always been up in the air when things have gone wrong, so the only way you can get hurt is when it comes back down. I should imagine you'd have plenty of time to get out of the way – what do you think?'

Olivia wasn't so sure. 'Those balloons are tethered by thick wires; I should imagine they could cause a lot of damage when they break free.'

Maude looked down at her petite frame. 'On the other hand, it can't be that hard if he thinks I could do it.'

Olivia glanced at her own ample figure. 'Perhaps he thought I was enough to keep us both grounded?'

One of the girls who had been on their shift when the officer had asked for volunteers piped up as she passed by. 'From what I hear, you have to pass a medical before they accept you, and one of the tests is to see how much weight you can lift. After that you'll be sent on a training course and they'll make sure you're capable of doing the task in hand, so I doubt you'll be in that much danger.'

Maude smiled confidently at Olivia. 'That doesn't sound too bad. If it's not for us then we're no worse off than when we started.'

Olivia agreed. A few days later, having both passed the medical, the friends were told to gather their belongings and get into the back of a lorry bound for Pucklechurch in Gloucestershire. The journey was an arduous one, not helped by the stale corned beef sandwiches which had been supplied by the cookhouse.

Olivia peeled back the crust to look at the dry tinned meat. 'It's going to be hard enough getting this down without bringing it back up five minutes later ...' She closed her eyes as the lorry sailed over a series of lumps and potholes, then opened them again as the road levelled out, and placed the sandwich back in its wrappings. 'I'll save that for when we break down.'

'Don't you mean *if*?' enquired Maude.

With the lorry lurching across another set of potholes, Olivia shook her head. 'Nope.'

Despite Olivia's doubts, the lorry drew to a halt outside the entrance to their new RAF base. 'Thank goodness for that,' said Olivia as she half jumped, half slid over the lorry's tailgate.

Maude landed neatly beside her. 'I say we sign in then go and get summat to eat.'

'Sounds good to me,' agreed Olivia. 'I don't care what it is, as long as it's edible.'

A stern-faced Waaf was walking towards them, clipboard in hand. She introduced herself as Corporal Walker then proceeded to call out their names. With everyone accounted for, she led them over to the hut where they would be staying, opened the door and waved a vague hand in the direction of the beds. 'You need to make your beds, put your stuff away and tidy round. After that you can grab a bite to eat in the cookhouse. Any questions?'

Olivia was crossing her fingers that no one would ask anything when one of the Waafs further down the room mumbled something inaudible.

Corporal Walker looked around expectantly. 'Did someone say something?'

A rather embarrassed Waaf stepped forward, smiling apologetically. 'Sorry, Corporal Walker, but I'm starving.' She glanced around at the other girls. 'We all are.'

Corporal Walker looked around the sea of faces all nodding their agreement. 'Didn't they provide a packed lunch?'

In answer Olivia took out her sandwiches and handed them to the corporal, who wrinkled her nose as she looked at the pathetic offering. 'Honestly!' she tutted angrily. 'How do they expect an army to march on this rubbish? Right. Choose a bed, then get yourselves down to the cookhouse. You can make your beds when you come back. I'll take this,' she held up the offending sandwich, 'with me, by way of explanation should anyone ask why you've not sorted your billet out before getting something to eat.'

There was an enthusiastic murmur of thanks from the girls, then they all hastily chose their beds before heading en masse for the cookhouse.

'I like Corporal Walker,' Maude said as they joined the end of the queue a the counter.

'Me too,' Olivia agreed. 'I'm glad she's in charge. If that was Haughton he'd have told us to eat up and shut up. Let's hope all the corps are as nice as Walker.' Olivia was blissfully unaware that a corporal was sitting at the table beside the queue listening to every word she spoke.

'Aha! The new recruits! Whilst I can't speak for the others, I'd like to think I'm as nice as Corporal Walker, although not as pretty.'

Turning, Olivia saw a man around the same age as herself, with bright blue eyes, made all the more vibrant by his dark brown hair and thick black brows. He was grinning up at her.

After her last experience with a man presenting a friendly exterior, Olivia had reminded herself that even tigers smile. She stared icily back.

He swivelled in his chair to face her properly. 'I take it you are here for balloon training?'

Olivia nodded stiffly. 'We've come from RAF Chigwell, where we've been sewing balloons,' she said, then added defensively, 'so we're not completely clueless.'

He raised his brow. 'I'm sure you're not, and for what it's worth I'm a firm believer in getting to know your trade from the bottom up, as it were.'

Keen to call a halt to the conversation, Olivia turned to the woman serving behind the counter. 'Any cheese and pickle?' The woman nodded and handed over a sandwich. Olivia waited for Maude to choose hers before they found themselves a table. To her horror, the corporal used his foot to push the chair opposite his away from the table, gesturing for her to sit down.

Determined not to take him up on his offer, Olivia shook her head. 'Thanks very much, but ...'

The corporal leaned across the table, his hand outstretched. 'I'm Corporal Ralph Stebbins. I'll be instructing you for part of the course.'

Olivia cursed inwardly. She could hardly walk away now. Taking the proffered seat, she shook his hand. 'ACW Campbell and this is my pal ACW Harris.' Wishing wholeheartedly that she hadn't bothered going to the NAAFI for something to eat, she glanced around, half expecting to see a few sniggering airmen, but it appeared Corporal Stebbins was the only man in the room.

Ralph indicated the empty plate in front of him. 'The grub's not bad here.' He twinkled at her from across the table. 'What made you volunteer?'

'We wanted to get out from behind the scenes,' said Olivia. 'See a bit of action.'

He nodded slowly. 'Then you've come to the right place. We're the first form of defence in an air raid, so you'll definitely see a lot more than you would stuck behind a sewing machine. But I have to warn you, it's not easy – as you'll soon find out.' He gave her a wink so fleeting that Olivia wasn't sure whether she'd imagined it.

She had no idea whether the corporal was being genuine or not, but as long as she didn't fall for the bait, it didn't really matter. 'We're up for a challenge, aren't we, Maude?'

'Wouldn't be here otherwise,' Maude agreed. She glanced around the cookhouse. 'What's the social life like?'

A shadow of a smile appeared on Ralph's lips as he glanced at Olivia. 'The NAAFI hold a dance once a week, but it's not been much cop, although I'm hoping it's going to get a whole lot better.' He twinkled again at Olivia. 'Do you go dancing much?'

'No,' Olivia said bluntly. 'But when we do, we go off base.' She was praying that the handsome corporal wasn't going to suggest that she and Maude attend a NAAFI dance, because she didn't wish to offend him if his motives were innocent.

He eyed her inquisitively. 'Oh? Is the NAAFI not good enough for you?'

Olivia shot him an icy glance. 'I never said there was anything wrong with the NAAFI. I prefer to keep work and pleasure separate.'

He smiled warmly at her, melting her icy façade. 'That's a shame, because I think it's important that new recruits attend the dances on base. It's a good way to get to know everyone, which is imperative when you're working as a team.' He glanced at the clock above the door and stood up. 'Well, much as I'd like to, I can't sit around chatting. I'll see you both in the morning.' He touched his cap and Olivia and Maude wished him good night.

Maude waited until the corporal had left the building before nudging Olivia. 'Someone's got their eye on you! He wasn't even put off when you were shooting him daggers.' She giggled. 'Teacher's pet!'

'I don't know about that,' Olivia said uncertainly. 'He's probably working out how to have fun at my expense, just like the last feller who pretended to show an interest in me.'

Maude frowned. 'Come on, Liv, you can't compare him to that ratbag.'

Olivia was unconvinced. 'I've got eyes in my head, and Corporal Stebbins is drop-dead gorgeous. If he's interested in me it's only to see whether I can hold a barrage balloon down on my own.'

'Well, I'd be very surprised if he turned out to be a rotter,' said Maude defensively. 'He seemed very open and honest to me. Besides, he can't be mean when he's teaching you – I'm sure that's against the rules.'

Olivia laughed. 'I hope you're right,' and she meant every word of it. Ever since Ted, she had built a barrier to stop anyone from hurting her again, but this man had walked straight through it without so much as a by your leave; he'd not even been put off by her frosty attitude. She couldn't explain why he was the first man in such a long time to reach out and touch her, but she was glad he had, because there was something fascinating about him. She supposed it was the way he looked at her, as though he knew her inside out. She thought of his bright blue eyes and how they had twinkled at her, and a faint smile tweaked her lips.

Maude grinned at Olivia. 'Doesn't take much to guess who is causing that smile.'

Olivia pulled a face. 'You'd have to be blind not to see how incredibly good-looking he is, which makes me question why he was being so nice to me.'

Maude rolled her eyes. 'Is it really so impossible for you to believe he might actually find you attractive?'

Olivia looked down at her waistline and nodded. 'Yes. Not just because I'm a big girl, but ... In the words of my father, I'm second-hand goods, which no one in their right mind would want.'

Maude glowered. 'I don't know your father personally, nor would I want to, but I know how spiteful he can be from the things you've told me, and I wouldn't listen to a word that left his lips, never mind believe any of it, so why would you?'

Olivia shrugged. 'Because it's true.' She lowered her voice, 'I've already had a baby out of wedlock, and even though I don't broadcast it, I reckon I must have some sort of invisible writing on my forehead which tells all the fellers what I'm like.'

'Well, if that's the case then they should be queuing up, because you're a wonderful woman with a kind heart who would go out of her way to help a complete stranger like me.'

Olivia frowned. 'I don't recall helping you.'

'I've not told you this, but when I found my ex Billy and Sally together, for a moment I thought they were being unfaithful because of something I'd done,' Maude held up a hand as Olivia opened her mouth to protest, 'and that maybe I wasn't a very nice person, which is why they'd turned to each other, but when I told you, you didn't even hesitate before asking if I'd walloped him.'

Olivia giggled. 'Only because he deserved it!'

'Exactly! You never doubted who was at fault for a second, and it made me realise that if a complete stranger didn't doubt me, then why should I?'

Olivia mulled this over for a few moments. 'If I'm so nice, then why aren't I fighting the fellers off?'

Maude eyed her reprovingly. 'Because you've got barriers up. Even I can see them.'

Olivia looked surprised. 'Is it really that obvious?' She recalled Maude's earlier words. 'Was I really shooting him daggers?'

'I'm afraid so.'

'Oh dear. I didn't mean to be rude. I just didn't want him to have his fun at my expense ...' Olivia chewed thoughtfully on her sandwich for a moment. 'So they're not trying it on because they think I'm desperate?'

'Not at all!' Maude scoffed. 'They can't see past that huge front you put up, because you won't let them.'

Olivia frowned. 'So how did Ralph – I mean Corporal Stebbins – manage to get through?'

Maude smiled. 'Who knows? Maybe you let him, or maybe he didn't see the barriers.'

'But why him and not everyone else?'

'Because he's special?' Maude suggested. 'I don't know the reason, Liv, but does there have to be one? Can't you just wait and see what happens?'

'Looks like I'll have to.' Despite her calm words, Olivia knew she would probably be awake most of the night trying to work out what set Ralph aside from every other man, although in her mind she thought she might already know the answer. When he had looked at her with his eyes of deepest blue, he hadn't

112

just looked into her eyes but into her soul, and judging by the way his eyes twinkled he liked what he saw.

Ralph Stebbins made his way back to his billet. So *that* was ACW Campbell. He'd done his research prior to the new recruits' arrival, because it was always good to know who you were dealing with and their different attributes. He had no doubt in his mind that with an attitude like hers, she would make a damn fine balloon operator, and if her paperwork was anything to go by, she'd also make a damn fine wife!

Reveille sounded and for a moment Olivia had forgotten where she was, but as she stared bleary-eyed around the Nissen hut she remembered that today was going to be her first day of training with Corporal Ralph Stebbins. She swung her legs out of bed and gently shook Maude's shoulder.

'Rise and shine!' Maude tried to pull the blankets over her ears but Olivia whisked them away. 'Come on, we've got to get kitted out with our new clothing, and I'd rather be first in the queue so that we don't run the risk of being given leftovers.'

Reluctantly, Maude gathered up her washbag and followed her friend to the ablutions. 'I don't see why we need new uniforms. We've not had these that long.'

Olivia shrugged. 'It's all going to be outside, so I daresay they'll be kitting us out with thick pullovers, gloves, scarves, wellies – you know the kind of thing.'

Later that morning they lined up eagerly, waiting to receive their warm outdoor clothing, but Maude's face fell when she saw her battledress. 'Trousers?' she said incredulously, her voice full of distaste. The man handed her a pair of gum boots and she handed them straight back. 'I'm not wearing these! They're men's!'

He beamed and pushed them back to her. 'They might be a bit big, I'll grant you, but with a few extra pairs of socks and a bit of newspaper you'll soon get a good fit, and think how warm you'll be!'

'I don't want to be warm!' Maude protested.

He placed his knuckles on the counter. 'What were you expecting?'

'Big coats, hats, scarves and gloves, *not* trousers and – and gum boots!' she finished in withering tones.

He roared with laughter. 'Someone's in for one hell of a wake-up call.'

Maude turned to Olivia. 'What does he mean by that?'

'He's probably just teasing, you know what these fellers can be like,' Olivia said reassuringly, though she had seen the wry look on the man's face when Maude had told him what she was expecting to wear – clearly he thought the girls had bitten off more than they could chew.

As they left the hut with their new fatigues, Olivia spoke candidly. 'We'll just have to see what the day brings. We've already agreed that this might not be our cup of tea, and if it's not then we'll return to sewing.' She held up her armful of clothes. 'Be grateful you're not a big girl. I reckon I'll be a dead ringer for Oliver Hardy in this get-up!'

Picturing the image in her mind, Maude giggled. 'All my stuff's too big, so I guess that'll make me Stan!'

Olivia stifled a chuckle. 'What a pair we'll make! I bet Corporal Stebbins'll think twice when he sees me in this little lot.'

'Neither of us need worry about any men coming near us, not when we're wearing the same clothes as them,' Maude said ruefully. 'I felt like the cock of the walk in my WAAF uniform. I even wished that Billy and Sally could see me looking so smart, but I think I'd die of embarrassment if they saw me in my battledress!'

Back in their hut they changed into their new uniforms. 'Just as I thought,' Olivia stated as she regarded her reflection in the mirror. 'If Corporal Stebbins was interested then this get-up will soon change his mind.'

William Campbell stood outside the door to his wife's bedroom, his hand on the handle, fighting the pointless urge to twist it open. His father had taught him from an early age that if you want to be successful in life, you can't give in to your emotions. William had taken this with a pinch of salt, believing his father to be a stick-in-the-mud who was trapped in the past, and Catherine had proved him right, until the day his father passed away, of course. That was when he realised that emotions made you weak and an easy target for just about everyone around you.

He had been delighted when Catherine had agreed to be his wife, because he believed himself unworthy of the love of such a beautiful, kind-hearted woman, but love him she had, and William had grown to accept that love, allowing himself to love her back as much as she loved him. Even after his father's death,

William's love for Catherine had still burned bright, but when she began to fall ill, it felt as though his world was crumbling around him. Having lost his father was bad enough, but the thought of losing her was far worse. He'd never felt pain like that in his whole life. He had spoken at length to the doctors, but they were of equal mind when it came to the outcome. Catherine would suffer a long-drawn-out deterioration, taking her from the woman he loved to a shadow of her former self. William knew then that he couldn't stand to watch someone so angelic and true suffer such a horrible demise. He had decided to throw himself into his work, only coming home when he had to, and keeping as far away from Catherine as he could so that when she finally passed away, his pain would not be so great.

He banged his fist against the door. So why hadn't it worked? Why did he still feel such pain?

Mavis must have heard him thump the door, because she shot out of one of the upstairs rooms and leaned over the banister. 'Is everything all right?'

William stood back from the door. 'Fine. Get on with your work.'

He watched as she retreated back to the room next to Olivia's. Why had he been so stubborn when Olivia asked if he wanted her to stay? Of course he had, but why not say so? *Because you don't deserve her love either*, came a voice from the depths of his mind. *You know what you did, and you know that if she knew the truth, she'd not want to be anywhere near you, and what's more you don't blame her!* He pictured Edward, standing in the middle of his driveway, looking smart and grown-up in his RAF uniform. *A decent man after all*, the voice said chidingly, *but then again, that's not why you did it, is it, William? You did it because you worried what would become of your precious family, so precious that you couldn't bear to be near them!* His inner voice laughed at him scornfully. *What a fool you've been, keeping everyone you love at arm's length for fear of getting hurt, and it didn't make one iota of difference, other than ensuring you'd die a lonely old man.* But I did it for their own good, William thought miserably. And he had, but it didn't make any difference. The sacrifice he had made in order to protect them also harmed them, or it would if they ever found out. He shook his head. He was being an emotional, sentimental old fool. *Emotions are for the weak and feeble*, he reminded himself. *Olivia is better off without you, and Catherine is finally at peace.*

He walked across the hall and entered his study. He would take his mind off things by doing some work. As he strode across to his desk, his eyes fell on two letters folded in two and tucked down beside his inkwell. He picked the first up and read the contents.

Dear Dad,

Well, here I am in Innsworth. If you need me for anything you can ring me at the NAAFI or write to me here. I shall let you know whenever I move on.

He picked up the next and glanced at the words, which read much the same as the first, except that she was now in Pucklechurch. Why couldn't his daughter let him punish himself for what he'd done? Why did she insist on taunting him with what could have been?

If he told her the truth, that would sure as hell guarantee she never contacted him again. The mere thought caused him to turn pale. He couldn't tell her, not ever; the words would catch in his throat. He had never told a soul of his actions, because even the most hard-hearted individual would be taken aback if they heard the truth. He was not a God-fearing man, despite his strict Catholic upbringing, but if there was a God, William felt sure he would be sent to hell for his actions. He would just have to hope that Olivia gave up on him.

April 1941

Olivia beamed proudly as she marched along with her fellow Waafs. After ten weeks of training she was finally passing out. Her chest swelled with pride as she and Maude whipped off a smart salute.

Maude was also beaming with pride, and quite rightly so. Being a great deal smaller than the rest of the girls, she had to try a lot harder than everyone else, but her efforts had paid off and she was passing out, top of their class, with the new rank of Leading Aircraftwoman.

'And I thought you said *I* was meant to be the teacher's pet,' Olivia had teased earlier that morning as she watched Maude begin to stitch her new insignia.

Maude viewed her work with a critical eye before turning it to Olivia. 'What do you think?'

Olivia nodded. 'Very smart.'

'And to think I thought I'd not pass muster!' said Maude with a disbelieving chuckle. 'I can't wait to go to the dance tonight!' She sighed happily. 'First female balloon operators!'

'Sounds good, doesn't it?' Olivia gazed out of the window on to the parade ground where they would be passing out. 'I reckon we'll go down in history for this, Maude, and that's something to be proud of.'

Maude finished the stitching and bit the thread. 'I bet you're looking forward to the dance.'

Olivia rolled her eyes. 'And why would you think that?'

'Because Stebbins is going to be there, and with this being our last night, who knows what the evening may bring?' Maude waggled her eyebrows suggestively.

Olivia gave a wry smile. She had got to know the corporal well over the past ten weeks, and in that time he had proved himself to be every bit the professional when it came to his job. So much so, she had begun to think that he had only shown an interest in her because he believed she would do well in her new position, which would reflect favourably on himself. After all, this was a new venture, and if Ralph proved that women could do as well as men when it came to operating the balloons, he might find himself being promoted. It was for this reason that she had said yes when he had first asked her to dance, and she was glad she had, because dancing with him was preferable to dancing with Maude, and his professional attitude had proved she could trust him.

'He likes to get the most out of his girls, which is why he's so nice,' she reasoned.

Maude didn't look convinced. 'If that's the case, then why does he spend more time training you than the rest of us?'

'Maybe he thinks I need a little more help than the rest of you,' Olivia suggested.

Maude shook her head. 'No chance. You're stronger than most of us, so you don't struggle as much. If you think about it, there's a lot of girls who need more help than you.'

Olivia had thought about it, and Maude was right. Whilst Ralph would give instructions to the ones who were struggling, when it came to Olivia he used a more tactile approach. When demonstrating how to splice a line or work the winch, his hands would linger over the top of hers. Then there was the time she had had difficulty with one of the ropes. Instead of getting her to stand to one side whilst he showed her, he had placed his arms around her shoulders and held the ropes with her, brushing his cheek against hers as he calmly relayed his instructions. When he had let go, he had grinned at her, praising her for her efforts, and his eyelid had briefly fluttered just as it had when she first met him in the cookhouse. Was this his way of winking without being seen by others?

Maude's voice cut across her thoughts. 'I've seen the way he looks at you when the two of you dance, and believe you me, he doesn't look at the other girls that way. I'm not the only one who's noticed either.'

'Who else?' said Olivia, her stomach lurching unpleasantly at the thought of people gossiping behind her back.

'Only a couple of the Waafs in our billet, but don't worry. They think it's rather sweet, not to mention how lucky you are to have Sexy Stebbins after you!'

Olivia gave a shriek of laughter. 'Sexy Stebbins! Who made that one up?'

Maude grinned. 'No idea. You know what it's like in the WAAF – I heard it through the grapevine.'

'If Sexy Stebbins really was interested in me, he wouldn't dance with other women,' said Olivia.

'Could you imagine if you were the only woman he danced with?' Maude scoffed. 'He'd be for the high jump for showing favouritism – you know he would. If you ask me, he's keeping his hand close to his chest for your own good as well as his, because you know what some women can be like. Only he can't help himself, which is why he brushes against you and pays you that extra bit of attention.'

Now, as Olivia finished the salute, she swung her hand down by her side. If Maude was right, then tonight could be very interesting indeed!

As the sergeant barked the order for them to 'dismiss', a huge cheer erupted from the girls on the yard. Looking around the sea of happy faces, Olivia caught the eye of Corporal Stebbins who was smiling at her as though she were the only woman on the yard. Smiling shyly back, Olivia's cheeks turned pink. She was being silly. Ralph was proud of his accomplishment. That's why he was smiling. On the other hand, his eyes hadn't left hers. Looking down at her feet she felt the blush deepen, and when she looked back up, he was still looking in her direction.

Maude placed a hand around Olivia's shoulders and waved to Corporal Stebbins, who waved back. 'I swear if I ever lose you in a crowd, I'll know where to find you if he's about,' Maude chuckled. 'How can you think his warmth towards you is merely platonic?'

Olivia shrugged. 'Because he's not done anything to convince me otherwise.' She hesitated. 'Seeing as how tonight's our last night, would you mind helping me with my make-up?'

'Course I will,' said Maude. 'Not that you need much.'

'Thanks, Maude.' Since being in Pucklechurch, Olivia's confidence had grown, but she hadn't managed to shed any more weight despite the hard, labour-intensive work, and she said as much to Maude.

'You're growing bigger muscles,' Maude assured her friend, flexing her own bicep, 'we all are, so try not to be too disappointed.' She looked hopefully at Olivia. 'Does this mean you're going to let me pluck your eyebrows?'

'Are they that bad?' Olivia asked.

Maude pulled a hesitant face. 'I wouldn't say bad exactly, but a shaped eyebrow can really accentuate your eyes, and whilst I've only ever done my own, I should imagine doing someone else's should be much easier.'

Inside the hut, Maude fetched her tweezers from her handbag and ordered Olivia to sit still and not move, if she valued her eyeballs.

Olivia instantly leaned away. 'Hold your horses! What do mean, if I value my eyeballs?'

'If you're going to wriggle around, I might catch you by accident, so it's easier if you sit still,' Maude explained.

Maude was three quarters through the first eyebrow when Olivia called for a break. 'My eyes keep watering. Have you got a tissue?'

'Honestly, Liv, the dance'll be over at this rate.'

Olivia eyed her left eyebrow. 'You've taken loads out, and my skin's all pink. No wonder my eyes are watering – it's in sympathy for my eyebrows!'

Giggling, Maude handed her friend a tissue. 'It always hurts more the first time. After you've been doing it for a while, it's not so bad.'

Olivia finished dabbing her eyes and sat up straight. 'I daresay the skin toughens up. Come on, then, let's get it over with!'

When Maude had finished, they turned their attention to Olivia's hair, putting it into a number of styles before settling on having it curled under at the back and rolled back on top.

'There!' said Maude as she pinned the last roll into place. 'Perfection.' She handed the mirror to Olivia who gasped at her reflection.

'I look like my mum,' she breathed.

Maude beamed. 'Are you pleased?'

Olivia nodded. 'Thanks, Maude, I owe you one.'

Maude waved a vague hand. 'Don't be daft, that's what pals are for! Besides, I rather enjoy doing this sort of thing.'

With both girls looking their best, they entered the NAAFI, and Olivia found herself looking around the room, hoping to spot Ralph. It seemed, however, that the handsome corporal was not about. Maude must also have been looking for him because she gave Olivia a disappointed smile.

'Perhaps he's had to do some extra work, what with it being our last evening in Pucklechurch,' she suggested.

'Perhaps.' Olivia set her handbag down on an empty table. 'Or perhaps he's getting an early night, ready for the next batch of recruits.'

Maude nudged her in the ribs. 'I *knew* he wouldn't let us down.'

Olivia followed her gaze to Ralph who had just walked through the doors. His eyes scanned the room before settling on Olivia. He smiled.

'He's coming over!' hissed Maude from the corner of her mouth.

'Shhh!' Olivia hissed back.

Ralph smiled down at the girls. 'Might I have the pleasure of buying the first ever female balloon operators a drink?'

'Stout, please,' said Maude.

'And I'll have a lemonade, thank you,' Olivia said primly. The last thing she wanted was to get drunk and make a fool of herself in front of Ralph.

They waited until he was out of earshot before speaking. 'He's never offered to buy us drinks before,' said Maude approvingly.

'On the other hand, today is a day for celebration, and not just for us. Corporal Stebbins can be just as pleased with his efforts as we can with ours. After all, with this proving to be a success, it opens up more opportunities for more Waafs to train as balloon operators, freeing up more men, and I daresay he'll get a giant pat on the back for that.'

They fell silent as Ralph returned with the drinks which he placed on the table. He held out a hand to Olivia. 'May I?'

Olivia nodded happily. When all was said and done, Ralph Stebbins was a smashing chap who had helped them make history. If he hadn't been so handsome, she very much doubted she and Maude would be discussing romantic notions. Taking his hand, she gazed into his eyes which twinkled delightfully. *He sees me as a sister figure*, Olivia told herself, *no more, no less, and there's nothing wrong with that.*

He slid his arm around her waist, took her other hand in his and stepped into the dance. Olivia felt her tummy flutter as he led her around the floor. Was it her imagination or was he holding her tighter than he had in the past?

'You've no idea how glad I am that you've passed out today, and not just because I'm pleased for you,' said Ralph, gazing into her eyes, 'but because I'm no longer your corporal, which means I'm free to …' He hesitated.

'To what?' said Olivia, her heart in her mouth. This did not sound like the sort of conversation any brother and sister would be having.

He half smiled. 'To dance the night away with you and not care two hoots what anyone else thinks – something I've wanted to do since the first day we met.'

Olivia felt a wave of disappointment sweep over her. She had thought he was going to say he was free to kiss her. She chastised herself for thinking so foolishly and resolved to keep the conversation going before he realised anything was amiss. 'You were worried before?'

He pulled a face. 'They like to discourage that sort of thing, but now that you're no longer under my wing …'

'You're free to do what you want?'

'Precisely! You don't mind, do you?'

Olivia restrained herself from giving a heartfelt sigh. Corporal Stebbins was a cut above every girl in their platoon, and he wanted to dance with the safe bet, the girl who wouldn't have any expectations. That was why he wanted to dance with her, because he believed she wouldn't hold on to any foolish notions. She shrugged. 'I can't see any reason to object.'

He grinned down at her, and this time there was no mistaking the wink. 'Good, because I wouldn't want to dance with anyone else.'

Olivia felt her impatience beginning to grow. He was sending her mixed messages, whether he intended to or not, and it was unfair for him to continue. She voiced the thought uppermost in her mind. 'Why me, though? There are a lot of girls in here who would jump at the chance to spend their last evening with you – or is that why?'

He furrowed his brow. 'I'm not sure I follow ...'

Olivia felt a blush begin to make its way up her neck-line. 'Are you only dancing with me so that you don't have to dance with the other girls?'

He looked genuinely shocked. 'That's not the case at all! I want to dance with you because I like you – a lot, have done since the day you arrived.'

Olivia stared at him. 'How can you have liked me? If I remember rightly, I was rather distant.'

He grinned. 'You don't always need to speak to someone to know whether you like them or not. I've always thought you can tell what a person's like just by looking into their eyes.'

She smiled apologetically. 'I'm sorry, ignore me.' She decided to change the subject. 'It's a shame we won't get to see each other again.'

'What makes you say that?' he asked.

'Because you're going to be staying in Pucklechurch and I'm going to Shirehampton,' Olivia said matter-of-factly.

He grinned. 'Ah, well that's where you're wrong, because I'm coming with you, if only for a couple of nights – not as your corporal, but as an observer, to see how successful this trial run is. You may have passed muster but you're not out of the woods quite yet – we've still got to see how this works out in the real world.'

Olivia looked at him in astonishment. 'Really?'

He nodded. 'Just to make sure everything runs smoothly.'

'It'll be nice to have you close by,' she said, 'like a sort of safety net.'

He gave her a quizzical look. 'Is that the only reason?'

'Of course not! You've been a good friend as well as an excellent teacher.'

Ralph continued smiling down at her. 'How come nobody's snapped you up?'

Olivia's smile faded in an instant. Was he hinting that he wanted to snap her up for himself, or was he just being kind? She chastised herself inwardly. He'd soon change his opinion of her if he knew the truth behind her past. Used goods, that's how her own father had described her. Not that she would ever let Ralph find out the truth. She thought about this. Here she was wishing for him to make his feelings clear, but what if he did? The truth would have to come out sooner or later, and that would never do. She glanced to where Maude had been sitting, but her seat was empty. Casting an eye around the room, she spied her friend dancing with another of the Waafs in their billet. Aware that she hadn't answered the question, she glanced back at Ralph. 'My mother was desperately ill, so I stayed at home to look after her.' As the words left her lips she felt a warm glow invade her cheeks. *It's not so much that I'm lying to Ralph*, she told herself, *just being careful with the truth.*

'And you wondered what I saw in you?' said Ralph softly. 'I knew you were special, and this just proves it. Not many would be as selfless as you.'

Olivia felt the blush deepen. If Ralph really saw her in such a light, perhaps he could forgive a misguided mistake from her youth. She turned her attention back to the people dancing around them. If Ralph was the sort of man who valued personality over looks, then maybe, just maybe she was in with a chance.

July 1941

With the May Blitz far behind them, life at RAF Speke had begun to return to normal, or as normal as things could get considering most of the city lay in ruins.

Whenever any of the airmen had a moment to spare, they would go into the city and help with the clear-up. It was on one of these trips that Ted bumped into Mavis, the maid who had answered the door of the Campbells' residence. He and a few of the others were clearing some debris from around one of the shops when he caught her reflection in the shattered glass.

He hadn't recognised her straight away, but as she came closer, the penny dropped.

He turned to face her. 'Hello! Mind where you step, it's still not safe.'

She looked at the half-collapsed building. 'Thank God the Luftwaffe stopped when they did.'

He nodded. 'Unlucky for Russia, but lucky for us!' He eyed her awkwardly. 'I hope I didn't get you into too much trouble when I called round to see old Campbell.'

She waved a carefree hand. 'Don't worry, his bark's worse than his bite. I've got used to it over the years.'

'Did he say anything after I'd left?' Ted asked.

She nodded. 'He said I should've slammed the door in your face. He doesn't like most folk, but it was obvious you'd rattled his cage. What did you say to annoy him so?'

Ted stepped to one side and gestured for her to come closer. 'Remember how I said I used to be friends with his daughter?'

Mavis gave him a startled look. 'Are you the …'

Ted nodded grimly. 'I was her boyfriend, which is why he wasn't pleased to see me.'

She looked down at her feet. 'Did you know she was – *you know*?'

'Not at the time,' said Ted truthfully. 'I moved away, you see, and when I came back I bumped into an old pal who told me of the rumours, and that's why I called, to see if those rumours were true. Olivia's father tried to deny it at first, but when I made him aware that I knew about the baby, that's when he told me what she'd done.' He shrugged. 'I don't blame her – it must have been very difficult.'

The girl held out a hand. 'I'm Mavis, although I suspect you already knew that.'

He gave her an apologetic grin. 'I'm afraid so, and for the record, I'm Ted.'

She smiled shyly. 'I know who you are, because I overheard Miss Olivia and her mother talking about you.' She blushed. 'I wasn't eavesdropping – they were in the same room as me. I think they sometimes forget that staff have ears.'

He shrugged dismissively. 'Don't worry about it. You can't help it if people talk in front of you ...' He hesitated. 'I don't suppose you ever heard why Olivia made such a momentous decision without seeking me out first? I blamed her father, but of course he denied it was his idea.'

The maid gave him a wry glance. 'You're bang on the money. There was no way Campbell was going to give you and Miss Olivia a chance to meet up, not when he'd got everything so neatly worked out.'

'I thought as much,' said Ted. 'I couldn't see her doing something like that off her own bat.'

Mavis agreed. 'He arranged everything, from the birth to the adoption, or at least that was the plan until, well, you know.'

Ted stared at her with a blank expression. 'Sorry, did you say adoption?'

She nodded sadly. 'That was the idea, but it's the only part of his plan that didn't come to fruition.'

'Are you certain?' Ted asked urgently. 'Because that's not what he told me – far from it, in fact.'

She nodded. 'As true as I'm stood here. Why? What did he tell you?'

'He told me she had the baby aborted,' Ted said.

Mavis's eyes widened with horror. 'Oh no, that's not what happened at all. It couldn't anyway, because she was too far gone. You must have misunderstood.'

Ted shook his head. 'I know what he said, he made it very clear.'

'Why on earth would he tell you that?'

'I don't know.' Ted looked up sharply. 'But if she didn't have an abortion and there was no adoption, then what happened to the baby?'

Her lips formed a grim line. 'Stillborn. They buried the baby not far from the hospital where she gave birth.'

'Where was that?'

'I don't know, although I gather it was far away because that was the whole idea, to take Miss Olivia away from prying eyes and wagging tongues so that she could give birth in peace. That way she could return to Liverpool and lead a normal life as though nothing had happened.'

Ted frowned, deep in thought. 'If she was going ahead with the birth, then why on earth didn't she tell me ...' He fell silent, clapping a hand to his forehead. 'Stupid, stupid, stupid!' He stared at Mavis. 'Because he got rid of me before she had the chance.'

Mavis eyed him awkwardly. 'I was in the room next to her mother's when he came back from seeing you. He told Miss Olivia that you and your father had found out about the pregnancy and legged it.'

Ted's jaw practically hit the floor. 'The filthy rotten ...' He stopped himself before a stream of obscenities could leave his lips. 'And she believed him?'

Mavis shrugged. 'He made it sound plausible. He had a letter off your dad explaining that you'd heard the rumours ...'

'Rumours that I'd nicked his stupid fish!' said Ted. 'Not ...' he lowered his voice, '... not got his daughter in the family way.' He stopped abruptly. 'Only you couldn't have believed him, because if you had I daresay you'd have torn a strip off me when you found out who I was.'

She smiled. 'You'd hardly come calling if you'd done a runner.'

He smiled back. 'That's true.'

Mavis appeared to be thinking. 'He never told anyone else he'd had fish nicked, so he must have made that bit up just to get rid of you.'

'And it worked,' Ted said bitterly.

'He's always been good at getting people to do what he wants,' Mavis admitted. 'Miss Olivia was no match for him.'

'What did her mother think?' Ted asked curiously.

'She agreed with her husband because she thought you'd run off.'

Ted rested his chin against his forefinger and thumb. 'Only why not tell me the truth? Why make up an abortion?'

She looked at him darkly. 'Because he didn't want you coming round or getting in touch with Miss Olivia, because that way you'd find out the truth, and more to the point, so would she.'

'True,' Ted agreed. 'Golly, how I'd like to see Olivia again, just to let her know that I didn't leave her in the lurch. I don't suppose …' He eyed her hopefully.

Mavis shook her head. 'Sorry, the last I heard she was thinking about joining up, but that was over a year ago. She could be anywhere by now.'

'Her father probably knows,' said Ted, 'but he's not going to tell me, so … her grandparents?'

Mavis nodded eagerly. 'Of course! She went to stay with her grandparents after the funeral whilst she worked out what she wanted to do.'

Ted grinned. 'Then it's her grandparents whom I shall see. I believe they lived on Ullet Road?'

She nodded. 'Still do as far as I know.'

Ted thanked her profusely for her honesty. 'I won't tell a soul where I got my information from,' he assured her.

A look of relief swept her face. 'Thanks. I don't think Campbell would be too pleased if he knew I'd been gossiping about his family.'

'I should think not,' Ted agreed, 'especially when he's worked hard to cover up the truth.' A thought suddenly dawned on him. 'If it wasn't for you, I'd never have even tried to find Olivia – what would have been the point?'

'Like I said before, he's good at manipulating people, that's why he's so rich.'

Thanking Mavis for her help Ted wandered back to the men who were doing their best to steady a pillar of bricks as they tried to safely bring the wall they were working on down to the ground. An image of William Campbell formed in his mind's eye. Now he thought about it, the older man hadn't appeared remotely upset by the fact his daughter had had an abortion. He wondered what Olivia would say if she ever found out the truth. He knew the answer. She would be furious as well as heartbroken at the lies her father had told in order to keep the two of them apart. Well, it would serve William right to be found out, Ted concluded. He tried to remember a phrase his father used to quote when he caught Ted fibbing as a child. He nodded. 'Oh what a tangled web we weave, when first we practise to deceive,' he said beneath his breath. William had dug himself a very deep hole from which he could not escape, and it was all his own doing.

Olivia stared open-mouthed as they jumped out of the lorry. 'It's a farm,' she said to the WAAF MT driver who had driven them to their first site. 'You must've taken a wrong turn.'

The driver shook her head. 'Sorry, ducks, but this is your new home.' She jerked her head in the direction of a couple of wooden huts. 'And they're your new billets.'

'Oh, bugger,' said Maude as she cast an eye around the open fields, large hangars and wooden huts.

Another truck had pulled up behind theirs and more Waafs descended, all looking just as unimpressed with their new surroundings.

Corporal Stebbins laid a hand on Olivia's shoulder. 'Welcome to RAF Shirehampton.'

'Well, I needn't worry about meeting a feller out here,' Maude said conversationally. 'The most I'm going to run into is a sheep or a cow.'

'Where's the NAAFI, the cookhouse ...' Olivia pulled an anxious face, '... the ablutions?'

Ralph grinned. 'You'll be doing your own cooking, and the ablutions are behind your billet. The truck comes round once a week to empty them.'

Olivia heaved a sigh of relief. 'Thank goodness for that.'

Ralph led the girls around the site, which didn't take long, before stepping inside their billet. 'This will be your new home.'

The girls scanned the interior of the hut, which wasn't actually too bad. The beds were of sturdy construction, the floor had been swept clean and there was no sign of damp.

He smiled at them. 'The rations lorry will be calling by later on this afternoon. When the men were here, they took it in turns to do the cooking.'

'Excuse me, Corporal, but what do we do for fun?' asked one of the girls from the other lorry.

Ralph turned to address her. 'You get one twenty-four-hour and two evening passes a week.'

'You'll have to take us out and show us the sights,' giggled the Waaf.

Olivia peered round to see who had spoken and her eyes rested on a busty blonde with a tiny waist. Olivia felt her cheeks redden.

Ralph glanced around the rest of the Waafs. 'Any more questions?'

The bolshie blonde held up a hand. 'Are you single?'

The comment was met by a ripple of giggles.

Ralph wagged a reproving finger. 'Has anyone got any questions regarding their new site?' With no further response, he left them to settle in.

'Bagsie the hot corporal,' said the blonde as she placed her kitbag on one of the beds.

Maude looked at Olivia who was running a finger over the top of her locker. 'Someone's a bit brassy.'

Olivia shrugged. 'She's only having a bit of fun. Besides, she's more his type than I am.'

Maude looked at her in surprise. 'How do you know? Anyway, I doubt it, you're the sort of girl that Ralph goes for.'

A Waaf from the same bus as the blonde placed her things on the bed next to Maude's. 'If you're on about Beth Moreton, then you've hit the nail on the head. She goes through men like water.' She held out a hand. 'I'm Josie Cotter.'

Maude and Olivia took it in turns to introduce themselves. 'You know her, then?' said Olivia, jerking her head in the direction of the girl called Beth.

Josie nodded. 'We did our training together, and she was brassy from the word go, although I agree that Corporal Stebbins is a bit of all right.'

Maude smiled. 'They called him Sexy Stebbins in Pucklechurch,' she glanced at Olivia, 'and he's got his eye on our Liv here.'

'Lucky bugger,' sighed Josie. She looked at Maude. 'Have you got a feller?'

Maude shook her head. 'No chance – been there, done that, watched the sod run off with me best pal.'

Josie rolled her eyes. 'Bit like Beth, was she, your pal?'

Maude shrugged. 'She wasn't as forthright as Beth. We'd known each other since I can remember, which is why it came as such a shock.'

'At least Beth doesn't hide her true feelings,' said Josie, then turned her attention to Olivia. 'So, are you and Corporal Stebbins official?'

Beth, who had been earwigging from the comfort of her newly claimed bed, called over to them. 'What's that about Corporal Stebbins?'

Josie shook her head. 'Nothing.'

Getting up from her bed, Beth headed over to them, her eyes fixed on Olivia. 'Did I hear right? Are you courting Corporal Stebbins?'

Olivia shook her head. 'No ...' she began before being cut off by Beth, who was nodding in a knowing fashion.

'I see, so it's a case of wishful thinking.' Beth returned to her bed.

'He's interested in Olivia, though, he's made that quite clear,' said Maude defensively.

Beth raised her beautifully arched eyebrows. 'There's a big difference between feeling sorry for someone and being interested in them romantically. I think it's obvious to anyone that it's the former.'

Josie frowned at Beth. 'What's that supposed to mean?'

Beth shrugged. 'Corporal Stebbins can get any woman he wants.'

'And?' said Maude.

Moving towards Maude, Beth lowered her voice. 'Don't ask me to spell it out.'

'You don't have to,' said Olivia, who had heard Beth's words. 'I know exactly what you're driving at because it's written all over your face.'

Beth looked at Maude and Josie, who were staring at her in an unfriendly fashion. 'What?'

'You really don't know?' said Maude incredulously.

Beth looked at them, her face a picture of feigned concern. 'I didn't want to see the poor girl getting her hopes up just to be humiliated. I was *trying* to be nice.'

'Bloody hell,' breathed Josie, 'I'd hate to see you being nasty to someone.'

As Beth walked away Olivia turned to Josie and Maude. 'She's only saying what everyone else is thinking.'

'No, she's not,' said a girl in the bed across from Olivia's. 'Or at least she's not speaking for me.'

Olivia smiled. 'Thanks, but I can't help thinking she might be right. Perhaps Ralph's just being kind.'

'Poppycock!' exclaimed Maude. 'He was drawn to you like a moth to the flame.'

Olivia was unpacking her belongings into the locker beside her bed. 'Pretty big flame,' she said, adding, 'although they do say there's a lid for every pot.'

Maude looked smug. 'There you are!'

Josie looked over to where Beth stood, admiring her reflection in a hand-held mirror. 'She thinks a lot of herself, does Beth.'

'I can see why,' said Olivia honestly. 'She's beautiful with a body to match ...' she tilted her head from one side to the other whilst looking at the other girl, '... although that hair's straight from a bottle if I'm any judge.'

'I reckon you're right,' sniffed Maude. 'I won't tell you what my mam says about bottle blondes.'

Josie leaned forward in a conspiratorial fashion. 'Fur coat, no knickers?'

Giggling, Maude nodded. 'Spot on.' She smiled at Josie. 'Where are you from? Me and Liv here are from Liverpool.'

'Maidstone in Kent,' said Josie promptly.

'We were balloon fabric workers before retraining. What about you?' said Olivia.

'I was packing parachutes, but I volunteered for this because I'm not keen on working in a factory, or rather, in factory-type conditions,' Josie explained.

'We volunteered because we wanted to see a bit of action,' Maude admitted. 'I can't wait to get stuck in tomorrow.'

Olivia nodded. 'Getting out there and doing it for real!' She had visions of them rushing to the rescue, winching the balloons out and saving the country from the sort of nightmare the Blitz had released on Liverpool as well as many other parts of the country. She thought back to the phone call she had received from Nana and Pops.

'I'm so glad you aren't here, Liv, 'cos the buggers nigh on flattened the city, not that we're going to let it get us down. The Luftwaffe might have crushed our homes but they'll never destroy our spirit,' Nana had said defiantly. 'It'd take a lot more than a few bombs to do that.'

Olivia had smiled. It was typical of the Liverpudlian spirit to describe the Blitz as 'a few bombs'.

The following morning, the girls were up betimes, and after a hearty breakfast of toast and porridge they headed out to see what the day had in store for them.

Olivia was pleased to see Ralph, who smiled as his eyes met hers. The Waafs shuffled into two lines, and a sergeant whom none of them had seen before strutted towards them. Staring dreamily at Ralph, Olivia listened as the sergeant welcomed them to their new site and ran through his instructions for the day. He then produced a piece of paper and read out everyone's duties, and Olivia was relieved to hear that she and Maude were on the winch, whilst their new friend Josie was in charge of the cooking. When the order came for them to fall out, each Waaf set about her business, and a short while later they all beamed proudly at the balloons which floated high above.

Ralph came over to join Olivia and Maude on their winch truck. 'Well?'

'Loved every minute,' said Olivia. 'Miles better than sewing them together.'

'Better paid too,' agreed Maude.

'Glad to hear it,' said Ralph, then turned to Olivia. 'I'm going out to the local for a meal tonight and I was wondering if you'd like to join me? I'm sure I can organise for you to have one of your evening passes at short notice.'

'Love to,' said Olivia, wishing that Beth had been around to hear him ask her.

He beamed. 'It's a nice evening, and the walk's pleasant enough. How about I meet you by the gate around five?'

'Look forward to it,' said Olivia, and she meant every word. He hadn't gone more than ten paces before she gave a small squeal of excitement. 'I'm going to have dinner with Ralph!'

Maude giggled as Olivia led the way to their billet. 'Do you think it's a date?'

'I hope so, because I'd love to see the look on that Beth's face when she finds out!' Olivia's grin broadened as a young airman walked past. 'Oh look, it's that airman, the one who couldn't keep his eyes off you earlier!'

Maude smiled as the airman waved to her. 'Corporal Stanley Williams,' she informed Olivia. 'He was so busy watching me, he tripped over one of the wires and got a right rollicking.'

'He looks nice,' said Olivia. 'I wonder if he'd consider double dating?'

Maude gave a snort of contempt. 'Don't care if he does. I've sworn off men, you know I have.'

Olivia began walking towards their billet. 'We'll see.'

'There's nothing *to* see,' Maude assured her as they entered the billet.

Beth looked up from getting something from her kit-bag. 'Someone's in good spirits. My hands are in ruins after holding them stupid wires.' She held up a hand which was covered in blisters.

Olivia beamed happily at the other girl. 'We had a wonderful first day, didn't we, Maude?'

Maude agreed heartily. 'And one of us is going to be topping it off with a wonderful evening out with the handsome Corporal Stebbins.'

Olivia's smile broadened at the sight of Beth face, which had dropped at Maude's words. 'I don't believe you!'

Olivia nodded. ''Fraid so! We're going out for dinner. Enjoy your fried Spam!'

Maude wrinkled her nostrils. 'Don't rub it in.'

Olivia beamed with satisfaction as Beth stormed out of the billet, a look of disbelieving fury etched across her face.

'Well, you got to see the look on her face. Was it everything you imagined?' Maude asked as the door to their billet slammed shut in Beth's wake.

Olivia nodded happily. 'I feel like the cat who got the cream! And even if it isn't a date, I never said it was, just that we were going for dinner, which is true!'

'Clever girl! I wonder if she'll tell the others?'

Olivia shrugged. 'Don't care if she does.' She had often wondered what Ralph's feelings towards her were, but Beth had made it plain how she felt about the handsome corporal, and if she had been his type, surely Ralph would have asked her out to dinner and not Olivia?

At five o'clock, she headed towards the picket fence, where Ralph stood waiting for her, holding his arm out as she approached. She slipped her arm through his and together they struck out in the direction of the pub.

Turning his head, he gave her one of his secretive winks. 'I see you ditched your battledress.'

'Golly, yes. It's great for working in, but that's where it ends.' She watched him from the corner of her eye as they walked along – the square jaw, chiselled features and deep blue eyes – oh, how lucky was she to be spending the evening with him.

'How long have you been in the RAF?' she asked.

'Since war broke out. I used to work in a bank, doing the same job day in, day out, hardly exciting, so when

142

Chamberlain made his announcement I jumped at the chance, and here I am.'

'Glad you did it?'

He nodded. 'Enough to know I want to stay on when it's all over. How about you?'

Olivia smiled. 'I've got nothing to go back to. My mum died just before I joined, and my father ...' Her smile faded. 'My father has his own life.'

He cocked an eyebrow. 'Not close, then?'

She shook her head. 'Couldn't be emotionally further apart if he were on the moon.'

Ralph looked surprised. 'That's a shame. Personally I get on well with both my parents.'

Olivia watched the butterflies as they flittered around the wild flowers which skirted the hedgerows. 'Do you have any siblings?'

Ralph shook his head. 'I'm like you, an only child.'

Olivia paused mid-step. 'How did you know I'm an only child?'

Ralph hesitated before answering. 'I seem to recall you saying you'd stayed at home to look after your mother, so I assumed you must be the only child.'

Olivia was impressed that he had remembered her very words. 'Fancy you remembering that.'

Again, he gave her one of his private winks, whilst tapping his forefinger against his temple. 'Up here for thinking, down there for dancing.'

Olivia laughed. 'That's why you're the teacher and I'm the pupil.' She glanced at the road ahead. 'Have you been to this pub before?'

He nodded. 'They do a cracking meat and potato pie, if you like pies, that is.'

Olivia grinned. 'Love them, only steak and kidney's my favourite.'

Ralph sighed wistfully. 'Now you're talking. I love a good steak and kidney pie,' he grimaced, 'although I can't stand those vile canned kidneys they try and get us to choke down. You won't have had them yet, and take it from me, you'll pass when they drop them off with your rations.'

She laughed. 'So you're not keen on them, then?'

He held up a finger. 'Kidneys should never be served in a tin – a bit like egg should never be powdered.'

Olivia wrinkled her nose in solidarity. 'It's one of the many things I won't miss when this dreadful business comes to an end.'

Ralph held up a hand indicating a large stone public house to the side of the road ahead of them. 'Here we are, the Rose and Crown.'

Stepping across the threshold, Olivia followed Ralph to the bar, where a dumpy woman with a cheery face greeted them. 'Hello, my dears, what can I get you?'

'I'll have a pint of your best bitter, and ...' Ralph looked at Olivia who ordered a half of mild.

The woman got two glasses and held the first under the pump handle as she explained the menu choices. 'We don't bother with written menus any more 'cos we don't know what we'll be having from one day to the next, so today's choice is either meat and potato pie with all the trimmings, or fish and chips.'

'I'll have the meat and potato pie, please,' Ralph said promptly. 'Liv?' Before she could answer he quickly added, 'Do you mind if I call you Liv?'

144

'Not at all,' said Olivia, enjoying his familiarity. 'And make that two meat and potato pies, please.'

The woman finished pouring their drinks and handed them over. 'If you'd like to take a pew, I'll bring your meals out when they're ready.'

Ralph handed the money over before joining Olivia at the window seat she had chosen. 'It's a lovely little spot, this, isn't it?' she said, staring out at the meadows across the way.

'I wonder what they're having back at the station?' said Ralph as the aroma of pie being cooked wafted towards them.

Olivia grinned. 'Fried Spam with bubble and squeak, much to Beth's disgust, although I don't think that's the reason why she got so upset.'

He cocked an eyebrow. 'Oh? Sounds interesting.'

Olivia told him how she had explained to Beth about her planned evening.

Ralph drummed his fingers on the table top as he tried to place Beth, although he soon remembered after a quick, rather unflattering description by Olivia.

'The busty, brassy blonde, eh?' he chuckled. 'I remember her now, the shy wallflower.'

Olivia, who had just taken a sip of her drink, began to cough. 'Are you sure we're talking about the same girl?'

He grinned and then winked, and this time, there was no doubting his action. 'The RAF's full of Beths. They work their way through the base, moving from one poor sucker to the next. The war's created a play-ground for women like her.'

Olivia hesitated. She didn't like the other girl much, and according to what Josie had said, Beth certainly had had a lot of male companions, but to suggest she worked her way through the entire base seemed a trifle unfair. At the same time, she was pleased to hear that Ralph didn't approve of women like her, and just to make sure she asked the question uppermost in her thoughts. 'So not your type, then?'

He pulled a disapproving face. 'God, no. She's the sort of girl my father warned me about – fast and easy.'

Olivia stared at him, the thought of her indiscretion flying through her mind, and the smile vanished from her lips as she imagined what he would say if he knew the truth about her past. Ralph looked at her with concern. 'Sorry, did I say something amiss?'

Olivia shook her head hastily. 'Not at all,' she lied.

Ralph took her hand in his. 'Are you sure I didn't say anything to upset you? Only you look a bit preoccupied.'

Olivia smiled briefly. 'I was just thinking about Beth. Do you think we might be judging her unfairly?'

He stared into his drink before looking up. 'You only have to hear the way she talks to know she's hardly the Virgin Mary when it comes to the opposite sex.'

The barmaid brought over the cutlery and condiments and placed them in the middle of the table. Hearing his words, there wasn't a doubt in Olivia's mind that he would tar her with the same brush if he knew her history, which was unfair. She had been so young at the time, and she had regretted her actions ever since, so much so that she hadn't so much as kissed a man since, but she highly doubted that would matter to Ralph or his father. She had been so happy when he had asked her to join him, but whether he intended to take it further or not didn't matter any

146

more, because she knew she would have to reject any advances he made.

The woman bustled towards them carrying two plates, with a tea towel to protect her hands from the heat. She placed them on the table. 'Mind out – those plates are hot,' she warned.

Olivia looked at the delicious fare before her. 'Do you know, this is the first pub meal I've had since leaving Liverpool?'

'We'll have to do something about that,' said Ralph as he lightly shook the salt cellar over his food.

Olivia smiled, but inside she was kicking herself. *One mistake,* she thought, *and I'm going to pay for it for the rest of my life. I could have had it made with Ralph, but there's not a cat in hell's chance I'm risking him finding out the truth, and seeing as I can't lie to him forever, it looks as though it's over before it even started.*

Once they'd finished their meals, Ralph ordered them another round of drinks – 'For the road,' he told Olivia.

Olivia had steered the conversation to the war and its progression, something which Ralph was happy to give his opinion on. As the evening wore on, the topic of conversation turned to life before the war. Ralph spoke of his home life, and his failed relationship with his long-term girlfriend, who had cheated on him with another man. From Ralph's description, the woman had sounded a dead ringer for Beth. This revelation made it clear to Olivia that Ralph's dislike of women like Beth stemmed from his last relationship. This brought another thought to her attention. Ralph didn't like cheats and that's what he believed Beth to be, but

Olivia wasn't a cheat. Would he feel so badly if he knew the truth? Gazing into his sparkling blue eyes that shone with warmth, she thought it most likely that Ralph would forgive her past, especially when he knew she'd not been with a man since.

Ralph then turned the conversation towards Olivia's home life. 'I know you say you and your father are poles apart, but surely wartime might bring on a reconciliation?'

Olivia shrugged. 'You'd think so, but I can't see him relenting any time soon.'

'Maybe if you paid him a visit?' Ralph suggested. 'It's a shame to see father and daughter at odds.'

'Tell him, not me,' said Olivia.

Ralph nodded thoughtfully. 'If you ever wanted to go and see him, I wouldn't mind coming with you if you thought it might make things easier.'

Olivia smiled. 'I might just take you up on that. You're the sort of feller my father would approve of.'

'Oh?' said Ralph. 'He likes devilishly handsome chaps, does he?'

Olivia took a playful swipe at his arm. 'He likes anyone with ambition,' she said plainly, 'and with you being a bank clerk, then working your way up the ladder in the RAF, my father would definitely approve.'

The evening had come to an end and as they stood outside the door to her billet it occurred to Olivia that even if he did try to kiss her – and she very much doubted he would – she had no idea how she would feel after all this time. Just as the thought was running through her mind, Ralph leaned forward and placed his hand around the back of Olivia's neck, but she instinctively pulled back with a light-hearted giggle. 'Corporal Stebbins, you should know better than to kiss a lady on the first date, if indeed that's what this is.'

Smiling, Ralph leaned back. 'Quite right too.' He gave her another of his winks. 'Goodnight, Liv.'

She bade him goodnight before hurrying into the billet where Maude and Josie were eagerly awaiting her return.

'How'd it go?' Maude asked before Olivia had time to say 'hello'.

'Good,' said Olivia.

The girls stared at her. 'Is that it?' said Maude, disappointed.

Olivia shrugged. 'The food was lovely ...'

'Oh, come on, Liv!' Maude said in hushed tones. 'Did he try and kiss you?'

'Oh, that,' said Olivia in a preoccupied fashion, 'yes, he did.'

'And?' asked Josie, getting impatient.

'And I turned him down,' Olivia said simply.

Maude stared agog at Olivia. 'Why on earth would you do that?'

Olivia had been asking herself the same question as she entered the billet. She shrugged. 'It was instinctive.'

Maude eyed her friend thoughtfully. 'I know you, Liv, and there's more to this than meets the eye. What are you not telling us?'

'I just don't think we're a good match,' Olivia said truthfully.

Josie, who had been perched on the edge of her bed, eager to hear the gossip, now sat back. 'I don't get it. Why do you think you're not a good match?'

Olivia looked in the direction of Beth's slumbering figure before turning to Maude. 'You were right about him not liking fast women.'

Maude nodded. 'That's because he's a gentleman!'

'Indeed,' said Olivia. She stifled a yawn with the back of her hand. 'I'm ready for bed. Early start and all that.'

Maude stared intently at Olivia. 'I'm off to the lavvy. Do you need to go before bed?'

Olivia shook her head. 'I'm fine, thanks ...'

Standing up, Maude whisked Olivia's washbag out of her locker and pointed towards the ablutions. 'You've not brushed your teeth, nor removed your make-up.'

Sighing heavily, Olivia bade Josie good night before following Maude to the ablutions. Once they were inside, Maude checked to make sure the cubicles were empty before speaking her thoughts. 'What happened, Liv? You were keen on Ralph before, crowing about an evening out with him, and he even tried to kiss you, yet you turned him down? What's it all about?'

Olivia relayed Ralph's opinion on women like Beth word for word. 'He thinks she's a tart – what's worse is I did too – yet we're peas in a pod, only Beth didn't get pregnant when she was fourteen, so if anything I'm more of a tart than her!' She let out a gasp as Maude slapped the back of her hand.

'Don't you dare call yourself that!' said Maude angrily.

Olivia grimaced. 'That's what Ralph would think if he knew the truth.'

Maude frowned. 'Surely not? You were only kids, and like you say, you've only ever been with one man.'

Olivia wetted her flannel under the sink tap. 'I hope you're right, Maude, because I really like him.'

'Then why in God's name did you shun his attempt to kiss you?' asked Maude incredulously.

'Because I don't like lying to people, and Ralph's a good man who's been badly hurt in the past.' Olivia spoke thickly through her flannel as she ran it over her lips.

'You're not lying exactly,' Maude said, 'just omitting to tell the truth. You'd only be lying if he asked you outright and you denied it.'

Olivia regarded her friend uncertainly. 'I think that might be stretching things a tad, Maude, but it doesn't matter. He probably won't want to see me after tonight.'

'If he really likes you, then he will,' Maude reassured her. 'And if you want my opinion, you're not doing anything wrong by not telling him about Ted. I bet lots of couples have skeletons in their closets which they don't want their partner to find out about.'

Olivia briskly brushed her teeth. 'Ralph's going back to Pucklechurch tomorrow, where he'll most likely meet another woman, so I'm probably fussing over nothing.'

'Wait and see,' said Maude.

With nothing more to say on the matter, the girls went back to their billet and changed for bed. Settling down to go to sleep, Olivia thought of Ralph. He was handsome, polite and charming, everything a woman could want. She looked over to where Beth lay. She didn't much like the other girl, but she hadn't liked the way Ralph had been so vocal in his opinion of her without knowing the facts. She drew a deep breath before letting it out. He had assumed Beth was easy because she had passed comment about him being single, but that was all he had to go on. Olivia had initially felt the other woman to be a threat, and when Josie had told them of Beth courting a lot of men, Olivia had jumped at the opportunity to label the other woman as being loose, but in reality, nobody but Beth knew whether she'd slept with any of those men. Sitting up, she pummelled her pillow and sighed. She herself was always being judged for her appearance, yet here she was doing the same to Beth, just because the other girl was strikingly beautiful – and why? Because Olivia was frightened that Ralph might find Beth more attractive than her. With that thought in mind, she fell into a sleep riddled with nightmares where Beth found out the truth about her past and broadcast it to the entire base, and Olivia's father turned up, wagging a reproving finger and saying, 'I told you so.'

Chapter Five

September 1941

Ted stood on the platform of Lime Street Station, holding a bouquet of chrysanthemums and dahlias. He looked at the wilted petals which lay on the floor by his feet. He felt certain that his nerves were transferring to the flowers, which had looked just fine when he had bought them on his way to the station. He mulled this thought over. He couldn't help feeling that most men would be filled with excited anticipation at the thought of meeting their wife after such a long break, so why was it that Ted was filled with nervous apprehension? Yet he definitely was. Beads of sweat were forming on his brow, his mouth had gone dry, and thinking about it now, it was his trembling fingers which had caused the petals to fall. His stomach lurched unpleasantly as a train appeared in the distance. He ran a finger around his shirt collar, then mopped his brow with his handkerchief. He scanned the line of carriages pulling into the station. As the second to last carriage rolled past, his eyes locked with Isobel's, scanning the platform for his presence. He saw a small, fleeting smile twitch her lips, so he did the same back. Telling himself that he had nothing to be nervous about, he walked towards her carriage.

When he had left Mavis, his plan had been to seek out Olivia's grandparents, but then he had thought of his wife. It was not fair to Isobel for him to be chasing the past when he had problems within his own marriage. So he had dismissed the idea. There was no point in crying over spilt milk, and whilst he would have liked to clear his name, dragging up the past would inevitably open up old wounds for Olivia, which wasn't fair.

Now, as he drew level with the station clock, he glanced at the time. Isobel hadn't set foot off the carriage, yet he was already counting down the hours until she left. Ted tutted impatiently. What was wrong with him? Despite her reluctance for Ted to join the forces, she had been the one to make the suggestion that she could come and visit him in Speke, so she was making an effort; he should be pleased. A suspicious frown creased his forehead as he wondered what had driven his wife to come all this way. It was most unlike Isobel to put herself out – if anything, he thought she would have waited for him to get leave so that he could go and visit her. He stood outside her carriage and waited for the guard to open the door. Stepping forward, Ted held up his hand to receive her suitcase.

'Hello, darling, I trust you had a pleasant journey?' he said, his lips brushing her cheek as she turned her head.

Taking a tissue from her handbag, she wiped Ted's kiss from her face, then glanced briefly at him before looking around the station with disdain. 'Arduous,' she replied sullenly.

Ted offered her the crook of his elbow and was pleased when she took it. Picking up her suitcase in his other hand, he led the way out of the station. 'I thought you might like to see where I used to live before we check you into the B&B, as it's on the way,' he said conversationally

She rolled her eyes. 'Do we have to? I'm exhausted after the journey and that tiresome little oik who shared my carriage didn't stop jabbering the whole time. I'd far rather go to the B&B and get a few hours' rest. I think I can feel one of my migraines coming on.'

It was all Ted could do to stop himself heaving an exasperated sigh. He'd far rather she'd stayed at home if all she was going to do was moan and criticise everything, not that he could say so. 'Of course, dear, I should've been more considerate. I'll get us a taxi.' He hailed a taxi and gave the driver the address of the B&B as he settled into his seat. As the cab wound its way through the streets, Ted asked after their friends in Plymouth – how they were, where they were and for any news. Never averting her eyes from the passing scenery, she replied to all his questions with one-word answers, as though she found his conversation tiresome in the extreme. When they arrived at their destination, Ted paid the cabbie and led her up the steps to the boarding house. He knocked lightly on the door, which was swiftly answered by a middle-aged woman with a warm smile.

'Ah! Mr Hewitt, you've arrived!' She glanced at Isobel. 'Hello, Mrs Hewitt. I trust you are well?'

Isobel gave her the briefest of smiles before turning to Ted. 'Can I go up now?'

Ted gave the older woman an apologetic glance. 'Hello, Mrs Armitage, we're both well, thank you, but my wife's rather tired from the journey and would like a few hours' rest, so if our room's ready?'

Mrs Armitage nodded in an understanding fashion. 'I'll take you up.' As they reached the upper floor, she opened the door to a pleasant room and handed Ted the key. 'Holler if you need anything.'

'How about an elevator,' said Isobel sourly.

Ted cringed inwardly as he saw Mrs Armitage's friendly smile freeze then falter. Bidding them a pleasant afternoon, she hastily descended the stairs. Watching her disappear from view, Ted half wished he could have gone with her.

Closing the door, Ted placed Isobel's suitcase on top of the chest of drawers, then turned to face her, but she had already kicked off her shoes and was lying on the double bed with her back to him. Sighing, he lay down on the bed next to her and reached over to touch her shoulder, but she shrugged him off irritably. 'Do leave me alone, Ted. Can't you find something to entertain yourself that doesn't involve me?'

Pulling his hand away, Ted stood up from the bed. 'Shall I come back in a few hours?'

She nodded silently.

He descended the stairs and made his way to the front door of the property where he nearly collided with Mrs Armitage, who raised her eyebrows in surprise. 'You leaving already?'

'My wife needs her sleep so I said I'd call back later.'

She smiled kindly. 'I expect she'll feel more like herself after a nap – it's a long way from Plymouth to Liverpool.'

He nodded. He wished he could have assured her that she was right, but Isobel was always snappy and irritable, or at least she was around Ted. He wondered what had happened to the girl he had courted all those years ago. She never used to be so miserable; he'd never have asked her to marry him if she had been. He had hoped that absence might have made her heart grow fonder, but so far this didn't seem to be the case.

Ted returned to the boarding house later that day, hoping to find his wife in a sunnier disposition, but instead of finding her vitalised and refreshed, she was annoyed that he had left her on her own for so long.

'Where have you been? I've been sitting here bored out of my brains!' she snapped as he walked into the bedroom.

Ted found himself apologising, something which was common when he was with Isobel. 'Sorry, Issy ...'

'Isobel!' she said stiffly. 'I'm not two years old!'

He drew a deep breath. 'Sorry, Isobel, I didn't realise you'd be awake.'

She eyed him critically before glancing in the direction of the window. 'Are you going to take me out?'

He nodded. 'As I said, I thought we could go and see where I used to live.'

She pulled a face. 'I didn't come all this way to see some grotty slum. Surely you can take me somewhere better than that?'

Ted failed to hide his disappointment. 'I thought you'd want to see where I grew up.'

She shrugged her disinterest. 'If you insist.' She shot him a sidelong glance. 'Why did you get a room with a double bed? You know I need my space – sharing a bed makes me irritable, which is why we have separate bedrooms back home. You'll have to find somewhere else to stay.' She tutted beneath her breath, 'Really, Edward, do you never think of anyone else?'

Ted fought the impulse to say, *Don't you?* Biting his tongue, he replied through stiff lips, 'Sorry, I forgot. I'll stay at Speke.' He wondered what his colleagues would say when he returned to base later on. They would probably think that Isobel hadn't arrived. He rolled his eyes. He wasn't looking forward to telling them that his wife didn't want her own husband anywhere near her.

Ted's plan had been to walk to Fisher Street, but he didn't fancy having to listen to Isobel whine on about how she didn't like Liverpool, so instead he hailed a taxi and a short while later they arrived at his former home, where Ted pointed out the house he used to share with his father.

Isobel was regarding the area with a wrinkled nose. 'You must be glad you got out of this hovel.'

Ted looked at the taxi driver who had shot her an angry glance in the rear-view mirror. Ted opened the door and got out, then went round to the cabby's window. 'Sorry about this, mate, but do you mind waiting here whilst I have a word with the missus?'

The taxi driver glanced to the far side of his cab where Isobel was waiting for Ted to open her door so that she might get out. He glanced back at Ted. 'Rather you than me, pal.'

Thanking the driver, Ted opened Isobel's door.

She pouted up at him from where she sat in the car. 'Oh no, really, Edward? Why do we have to get out?'

Without replying, Ted took her by the hand and led her away from the taxi where he might speak without being overheard. 'It may be a hovel to you but it was home to me, and a good one too, and I won't have you insulting my city in front of fellow Scousers.'

She rolled her eyes. 'That's always been your problem, Edward. You've never been keen to get out of the gutter, but content just to lie on your back watching the stars roll by.'

He glared at her. How dare she be so rude? Had she really come all this way just to insult him? But the biggest question that sprang to mind was, did he really want to spend the next two days being criticised? He decided the answer was no. 'Why did you come here, Issy?'

Her nostrils flared angrily. 'I told you already, don't call me that!'

He shrugged. 'You call me Edward despite my objections.'

'Because you're not a child, and Ted is a child's name,' she retorted, then added, 'and if you must know, I came to ask you about your intentions for our future.'

Ted blinked. 'How on earth do I know what the future holds? The war could go on for years yet.'

'I meant when it's over,' she said icily.

Ted frowned. 'What are you driving at?'

'I want to know when you're going to be a man and demand your share in the garage,' said Isobel. 'I didn't marry you with the intention of living hand to mouth,

159

and that's what it'll be like if you don't grab the bull by the horns and demand they make you an equal partner.'

Ted stared at her in humorous disbelief. 'You mean to tell me you came all this way to ask me to demand a partnership in a business I have no desire to be involved with?'

She sighed breathily. 'No flaming ambition …' She hesitated. 'Or do you intend to climb the ranks in the RAF?'

He shook his head. 'I'm happy as I am, thank you very much.' Adding in the privacy of his head, *Although I'll be a lot happier when you're on the train back to Plymouth.*

She raised her arms before flapping them down by her sides. 'So that's it? You expect me to live in a poky flat with no prospects?'

He shrugged. 'I'm not stopping you from joining up.'

She shot him a withering glance. 'I'm not like you, Edward. I know where my place is, and it's not running around taking orders from others.'

He shrugged. 'That's your prerogative, but I think you should know that since coming back to Liverpool I find myself reluctant to return to Plymouth. It was never my intention to leave Liverpool the first time around, and now that I'm back I've decided that this is where I'd like to raise my family.'

She spluttered in disbelief. 'Me? Have children, in this hellhole? I don't think so.'

He pulled his lips into a grimace. 'Well, I'm not going back to Plymouth, so we'll have to live here, besides, Plymouth is full of Navy, and when the war ends I intend to remain in the RAF.'

She stared around her, aghast. 'If you think I'd move up here, then you've lost your mind!' She shook her head. 'You either come back to Plymouth and join your father's business or ...'

Ted raised an eyebrow. 'Or what?'

She ignored his question. 'I should never have agreed to marry you, only I thought you'd change, and that I could make you see your worth, but fat chance of that! I was foolish to think I could change you.'

Ted wrinkled his brow. 'What are you saying?'

She drew a deep breath. 'I'm saying that if you don't change and start putting me first, then I shall have no choice but to file for a divorce.'

He eyed her incredulously. Surely she couldn't be serious? She must be calling his bluff, hoping to bully him into doing what she wanted him to do – well, it wouldn't work, not this time. 'I can't change, and you shouldn't want me to, so I guess the ball's in your court.'

Isobel's eyes widened with shock before narrowing in anger. 'Fine! Don't say I didn't warn you.'

Ted stuffed his hands into his pockets in an unyielding manner. 'You have to do what you think best.'

Her jaw dropped. 'You're seriously choosing this ... this ... cesspit over me?'

He shrugged. 'You're the one handing out ultimatums, not me.'

She shook her head. 'My mother always did say you can't polish a turd.'

Ted roared with laughter, which infuriated Isobel. 'Stop it! Stop laughing at me!' she demanded, her voice turning shrill.

But Ted couldn't stop. The tears were rolling down his cheeks as he tried to compose himself, but it was useless. He held his arm up in front of his face, as Isobel threw her handbag at him. 'You're a pig, a mean, rude, thoughtless pig!'

'Pot, kettle, black,' he said unsteadily.

She marched back to the taxi and opened the door of the taxi. 'I want to go back to the B&B.'

Ted nodded. 'I think that's a good idea. You're obviously still tired ...'

She spun round, her eyes spitting fire. 'Don't you dare patronise me, Edward Hewitt.'

He held his hands up in a placating manner. 'I didn't mean to. Let me take you to the bed and breakfast ...'

She cut him off without apology. 'I'm not going anywhere with you. You can sod off and go to hell as far as I'm concerned,' she looked around her with a disapproving eye, 'although I rather feel you're already there ...'

Ted ran his tongue around the inside of his cheek. For two pins he would have agreed that being in Isobel's company was probably very like being in hell, but he had no wish to throw fuel on to an already burning fire. 'As you wish. I shall call round in the morning.'

She shot him a withering look before getting into the car and rolling the window down. 'Don't bother.'

Ted shook his head. 'Don't be silly, Issy ...' but Isobel had already ordered the taxi to leave, so Ted found himself addressing thin air.

Seeing the taxi disappear into the distance, he made his way to the nearest tram stop. He knew now that Isobel had only agreed to marry him because she thought he would become a partner in the business. Whistling softly, he turned his thoughts to Toff, and how she had accepted him despite the fact that he was so much poorer than she was. It was that rotten father of hers that had been the problem. William Campbell was just like Isobel, despising anyone that wasn't just like him. Ted tried to envisage how his life would have turned out had he and Toff still been together. He heaved a heartfelt sigh. There was no point in dwelling on the past.

He held up a hand and jumped on to the back of a tram as it slowed. He would speak to Isobel in the morning and see if they couldn't come to some kind of agreement.

The next morning Ted was up betimes. The previous evening had not been a pleasant one for him, with a whole host of questions being fired at him as to why he wasn't staying with his wife. Rather than explain that he was married to a sourpuss, he had said that there had been a mistake with the booking and she was in a single bed.

He arrived at the boarding house shortly after breakfast and knocked on the door. Mrs Armitage appeared, with her usual warm smile, until she saw whom she was addressing.

'Oh, Mr Hewitt.'

He nodded. 'My wife and I decided it might be better if I stayed at my base last night. May I come in?'

She looked past him awkwardly, nodded and stood to one side. He was about to ascend the stairs when she called him through to a private room in the back.

Believing that Isobel had probably said numerous things to upset the landlady, he was about to apologise when she cut him off.

'I'm ever so sorry, Mr Hewitt, but your wife left before breakfast.'

Ted stared at her in disbelief. 'Are you sure?'

She nodded. 'She said you'd settle the bill, and that she wouldn't be returning.'

Ted stared at her for a second or two before pulling out his wallet and handing her some money. 'Keep the change.'

'Are you sure? She didn't have any breakfast,' said Mrs Armitage, counting the coins.

He nodded. 'Positive, and thank you. I daresay she wasn't the easiest of guests.'

The older woman drew a deep breath. 'Liverpool's not for everyone. I'm sure she'll be a lot happier when she gets back to Plymouth.'

'Let's hope so.'

With that said, he left the house and headed back into town. He knew Isobel had been furious with him, but it wasn't as if this was the first episode; she seemed to spend most of her time being furious with him over one thing or another. No doubt she was doing this to scare him, as a form of punishment. He shook his head sadly. Oh, to have his time over again!

October 1941

Despite their initial worries over the lack of facilities on site compared to Pucklechurch, Olivia and Maude soon got used to things, and were thoroughly enjoying the thrill of being the first to arms when it came to defending their country.

'Much more satisfying when you're doing it for real,' Olivia said as she secured the winch. 'Knowing that we're making the Luftwaffe's job a lot harder makes my heart sing.'

'I worried we might make a mess of things as soon as Ralph left,' Maude admitted, 'but he did a grand job training us. We run like clockwork, and that's thanks to him. What time's he arriving, do you know?'

Olivia jumped down from the winch. 'He said it'll be some time later on this afternoon.'

'Well, I can't wait to tell him how well we've done without him here to supervise us,' said Maude, 'although I daresay you'll have plenty of time to fill him in on all the goss if he takes you out to dinner.'

Olivia shrugged. 'He didn't mention anything about going for dinner in his letter, so I haven't booked an evening pass.' She hesitated. 'Do you think I should have, just in case?'

Maude pursed her lips. 'Not if your heart's not in it, and I hope you don't mind me saying so, but you're hardly jumping for joy at the thought of seeing him.'

Olivia looked around her to make sure that Beth wasn't in earshot. 'I'm not, although I don't want Beth to know that.'

Maude eyed her curiously. 'I thought we'd been through all this, and agreed that it would be best to see how things pan out?'

Olivia scratched the top of her head. 'I did, but ... Oh, I don't know.' She sighed.

'What's up?'

'Even if he does accept my past, I'm not sure I like the way he thinks about women,' Olivia confessed. 'I know I don't like Beth, but with good reason – she was really mean about my size, and I'd not said a word to provoke her.' She hesitated again, because whilst she'd not said a word against Beth, Josie and Maude had, and Olivia had agreed with them. If Beth had overheard that part of the conversation, then maybe that was provocation enough? Only she couldn't prove what Beth had or hadn't heard, so she continued, 'But Ralph's done the exact same thing to Beth – cast judgement without getting to know her. Surely two wrongs don't make a right?'

Maude pulled a face. 'Beth sets herself up for a fall by the way she acts. You didn't do anything to cause her to be nasty to you. It sounds to me like Ralph can be a bit outspoken and over-opinionated, but he's good reason, if he's been cheated on.' She waggled her ring finger at Olivia. 'I was bitter about men for a long time after Billy, so I know where Ralph's coming from. He probably doesn't mean the things he says about Beth – it's probably more a case of once bitten twice shy. He makes assumptions from his past.' Tilting her head to one side, she eyed Olivia shrewdly. 'You had a bad experience with that horrible little corporal in Chigwell, and it took you a long time to get over it. I seem to remember that you were convinced that Ralph's motive for pursuing you was that he thought you'd offer yourself up, but you couldn't have been more wrong.'

Olivia grimaced. 'Are you saying I'm as bad as Ralph and Beth?'

Maude thought about this for a minute before shaking her head. 'No, I'm saying it's human nature. No one likes to have their feelings hurt, so they learn from past mistakes by not replicating them.'

'I suppose you're right,' Olivia said. 'It's not that he's being mean, he's just trying to make sure he doesn't fall for a woman like his ex again. Do you think that's why he likes me? Because he thinks no one else will have me, so he needn't worry I'll run off with any of his pals?'

Maude shook her head briskly. 'No, I do not! I think he likes you because you're a smashing lass, with a heart of gold, and that's why he knows you'd never do the dirty on him.'

Olivia smiled shyly. 'Thanks, Maude, I hope you're right.'

Maude grinned. 'Course I am. I reckon you and Ralph are a match made in heaven, because you're both helping each other to get over unpleasant experiences.'

Olivia pulled the face of someone who has just had an epiphany. 'Like you and Stanley!'

Maude's eyes glazed over in a dreamy fashion. 'That's right! I was just the same as you were with Ralph, thinking the worst without giving him a chance.'

'I know,' Olivia said, 'but I bet you're glad you did now.'

'I am,' Maude confessed, 'but I'll not forget how nerve-racking it was to take the plunge, especially after last time. I didn't fancy giving him my heart, just to have him crush it, like Billy did.'

Olivia smiled at her affectionately. 'I'm so glad you gave him a chance.'

'Only because you made me see how unreasonable I was being, and I'm glad you did, because Stanley's nothing like Billy.' Shading her eyes from the sun with one hand, Maude pointed to an army imp which had come through the gated picket fence. 'Isn't that Ralph? I thought you said he was arriving later on this afternoon?'

Olivia squinted as she tried to get a better look at the driver behind the wheel. 'Blimey! He must've got away earlier than he expected.'

Ralph pulled the car up beside them and wound down the window. 'Hello, girls, how's tricks?'

Maude beamed proudly. 'Things are going really well! I reckon we could do it in our sleep.'

'Excellent! That means I've done a good job!' He turned his attention to Olivia. 'Fancy coming for a spin? I thought we could go back to the Rose and Crown, seeing as you liked it so much last time. My treat, of course.'

Olivia shook her head. 'You never mentioned any-thing about going out, so I didn't arrange to have an evening's pass ...'

'Only it's not evening, is it?' said Ralph. 'It's lunch-time, which means you've a few hours to spare.'

'A pass is a pass,' reasoned Olivia, 'and I've not got one.'

Ralph winked at her. 'Don't worry about that. Come on, hop in.'

Olivia reluctantly slid into the passenger seat. 'You'd better not get me into trouble, Ralph Stebbins!'

Ralph beamed at her before waving a hand to Maude. 'Tell her not to be such a worrywart, Maude.'

Chuckling, Maude waved them goodbye. 'Enjoy your meal!'

As they approached the gate, Ralph flashed a grin at the guard, who pulled the gate open for them to pass through.

Olivia glanced over her shoulder to the guard who was shutting the gate behind them. 'Why didn't he want to see our passes?'

Ralph tapped the side of his nose with his forefinger. 'Sometimes it's not what you know, but who you know, and Percy owes me a favour.'

Olivia looked curious. 'Blimey, that must be some favour.'

Ralph nodded. 'I'm sworn to secrecy, of course, but let's just say I've got him out of shtook a couple of times recently.'

Olivia nodded. 'You scratch my back?'

He grinned. 'That's the ticket.' Taking one hand off the steering wheel, he adjusted his tie and cleared his throat. 'I've been giving some thought to our relationship.'

'Oh? Sounds ominous.'

'I think we should decide where our relationship's going. I'm not keen on casual dating, but on the other hand I don't want to push you into something you're not ready for.'

She averted her attention to the countryside rolling past her window. 'I'm not sure I want to be victim to a wartime romance. I don't fancy having my heart broken again.'

He looked surprised. 'Again?'

She chided herself for speaking without thinking first, but it was too late, the words were out, and he deserved some kind of explanation, even if it didn't contain the full nitty gritty. 'I was in love once, and I thought he felt the same about me – turns out I was wrong.'

Ralph's expression turned wooden. 'Let me guess, he cheated on you?'

Olivia shook her head. 'Not that I know of. Let's just say he wasn't the man I thought he was.'

Ralph shrugged. 'But I'm not him, and whatever he did, you can be assured I won't follow in his footsteps, because I won't, you know.'

'And I'm not saying you will,' said Olivia reasonably, 'but we're living in uncertain times. None of us know what the next five minutes hold, never mind the next five days!'

He gave her a long, calculating stare. 'So, you're saying you don't want a serious relationship in case one of us buys it?'

She gave him an appealing look. 'You see it all the time, Ralph – men and women rushing into things, only to have this damned war tear them apart ...' She shrugged helplessly. 'That's not for me.'

He smiled, but Olivia could see he was disappointed. 'At least you're honest.'

Olivia grimaced inwardly because she wasn't being entirely truthful. The war wasn't the only reason why she didn't want to commit to Ralph. She wanted to be honest with him, but she didn't have the guts to tell him the truth about her past, and that was no way to start a relationship, especially with someone you really liked.

When Ralph dropped her off a few hours later, he held her hands in his as they stood outside her billet.

'I really enjoyed being with you this afternoon, Liv, and if waiting for the war to come to an end is what it takes, then I'm more than happy to wait.'

The moonlight twinkled in his eyes as he gazed down at her, and Olivia found herself wishing that he would forget her earlier words and kiss her, because at this moment her heart was in charge of her head, and her heart was looking at him with desire, pure, passionate desire. Whether he could read her thoughts or not, Olivia couldn't be certain, but when he leaned forward and kissed her softly on the lips, she made no effort to pull away.

Drawing back, Ralph smiled. 'Couldn't resist, but don't worry, I promise to be a gentleman and a man of my word, although I can't promise not to fall in love with you.'

Nor I you, Olivia thought privately. She looked at him from under her lashes. 'I don't want you to get the wrong impression ...'

He held up his fingers, imitating a scout. 'I promise not to kiss and tell.'

Olivia smiled. 'Good, because there's nothing to tell. We're just two good friends ...'

Ralph gestured towards the billet, where Maude and Josie were beating a hasty retreat from the window. 'I wonder if that's what they think?'

Olivia rolled her eyes. 'Oh bugger, they're going to put two and two together and come up with five!'

'Then you'd best get in there before they get the tom-toms out!' Ralph said.

Olivia bade him goodbye and entered the billet, where she saw Maude and Josie mugging furiously at her. 'Before you start, it's not what you think!' she insisted.

'Pfft!' said Maude dismissively. 'We've got eyes in our heads! He kissed you, what more is there to know?'

'What were you doing looking out of the window in the first place?' Olivia demanded.

Josie grinned. 'We thought we heard voices ... And we thought right!'

Maude held up a hand. 'Hold your horses! Stop trying to sidetrack, and tell us what we don't know!'

Olivia shot her a wry glance. 'You always were a sharp one, Maude Harris.' She sat on the edge of her bed. 'I think that kiss was what you'd call getting caught up in the moment.' She held up a hand to silence Maude, who had opened her mouth to speak. 'We've already agreed to keep things on a friendship-only basis, so don't go reading something into it.'

'It's a start, though, isn't it?' Maude said shrewdly.

Olivia fixed her friend with a coy smile. 'Maybe.'

Ralph pulled the car up by the gate and leaned out of the window to thank Percy for the favour.

Percy jerked his head in the direction of the women's billet. 'When you said you wanted to take one of the girls out, I assumed you meant Beth or someone like her. You could've knocked me down with a feather when I seen that Olivia in the passenger seat!'

A smirk flashed across Ralph's face. 'That's the difference between me and you, Percy.'

Percy rubbed his chin between his finger and thumb. 'I daresay she's a lovely lass, but why Olivia? I'd have thought a handsome chap like you would have his pick of the crop and that Beth's a real sort. If I were in your position, I'd have chosen her.'

Ralph wagged a reproving finger. 'That's because you don't think ahead, Percy, and there's more to Olivia than meets the eye – a lot more – and I'm not talking about her girth either!'

Percy stifled a snigger as Ralph pulled through the gate. 'I guess it takes all sorts.'

Ralph waved and headed down the road. Percy was right, it did take all sorts, which was why, if you were clever, and thought with your brains rather than your loins, you got the real cream of the crop.

Women like Beth were ten a penny, but Olivia? Women like her were a rarity. She hadn't joined the forces because she was in need of money or to improve her circumstances. If anything, going into the forces could be viewed as a step back for the only child of a rich widower. Olivia was a woman of means, and to the right man she was worth her weight in gold – and Ralph was determined that man would be him.

He'd always known he wasn't cut out to be a nobody like the private on the gate, which was why he was doing his best to climb up the ladder, but he also knew that unless you were lucky enough to be born into a privileged, wealthy family, then there was only so far you could go. If he was to reach the top, he needed someone like Olivia and her family behind him. Once he got there? Well, that was a different matter. As far as he was aware, they couldn't strip you of your ranking for getting a divorce.

November 1941

Ted looked with anticipation at the young airman who was handing out the mail. Despite having written to Isobel numerous times he hadn't received a single letter in return.

The airman looked around, spied Ted and walked over to him. 'There you go,' he said, handing over an envelope.

Ted thanked him then looked at the writing on the envelope and sighed. It was from his father. He slit it open with his knife and read the contents.

Dear Ted,

After reading your last letter I went round to your flat to pay Isobel a visit. I'm not having her upset you when you're so far away, and in my opinion she's a spoiled little madam who needs bringing down a peg or two! As expected, I got a real frosty welcome. In order to break the ice I asked how she had found Liverpool. As you've already said, she was far from complimentary! She said she hated the city and everything about it. She also said you'd taken leave of your senses because you were intending to live in Liverpool once the war was over. I said that that was your choice, and that a good wife should stand by her husband's decisions. I could tell she was shocked that I had stood up for you by the look on her face. I thought that might be an end to the matter, but she then went on to say that you were only staying in Liverpool because there was nothing left for you in Plymouth, and she suggested that if I made you partner in the firm, you might have a change of heart. I asked her why it was so important for her to stay in Plymouth and that's when she dropped a bombshell. She said she had no intention of bringing her baby up so far away from her parents – she even asked how I'd feel having my only grandchild halfway across the country.

Obviously I was surprised, so I asked her outright if she was pregnant, and she said that she was, although it hadn't been confirmed by a doctor yet because it was still early days, what with her falling pregnant on her trip to Liverpool …

Ted stared at the words in disbelief. He hadn't gone near Issy in Liverpool, so if she was pregnant, he couldn't possibly be the father. What was she playing at? He tutted silently to himself. He knew full well what she was playing at. She hadn't been able to manipulate him, so she thought she'd manipulate his father instead. Well, he'd soon put a stop to that! He made his way to the phone, waited for it to become free and then phoned the garage.

Craig's voice came down the line. 'Good morning, Hewitt's and Lyle, how may I help you?'

'Hi Dad, it's Ted.'

He could hear his father chuckling. 'I take it you got my letter?'

'Yes, I did,' said Ted firmly. 'I can't believe she's trying to manipulate you by suggesting she might be pregnant – the nerve of that woman! She wouldn't let me near her when she came to Liverpool, so if she is pregnant, it won't be by me.'

'Now why am I not surprised to hear that?' his father said wryly. 'She asked me to keep the pregnancy quiet as it was still early days and I agreed, but there was no way I was keeping that to myself!' Craig sighed. 'You know me and Rob are happy to make you a partner, but not if you don't want to be.'

'I don't, Dad, you know I don't, and the only reason she wants me to be a partner is for the money, even though I've told her it doesn't work that way.' He ran his fingers down the length of the telephone cord. 'I'd like to know what's going on inside that head of hers. She was the one handing out the threats, then leaving Liverpool at the crack of dawn. I've not heard a peep from her since she got back to Plymouth. What could she possibly hope to achieve by getting you to make me a partner when she won't even speak to me?'

There was a long pause before Craig spoke slowly down the receiver. 'There is one thing I can think of ...' He tailed off.

'Are you still there, Dad?' Ted asked.

'Ye-es,' said Craig, and Ted could hear the uncertainty in his father's voice when he asked his next question. 'Do you love her, Ted?'

Ted had to think about this before answering. 'I suppose so, or at least I did in the beginning, but ...' He sighed. 'I don't know, Dad.'

'How would you react if she were to ask for a divorce?' said Craig tentatively.

Ted ran his hand across his face. 'To be honest, Dad, she already has.'

'*What?*' Craig said incredulously. 'Why didn't you say something before?'

'Because I didn't want to worry you. Besides, I thought it was an empty threat, and her insistence on being pregnant proves I'm right, because why would you want to be pregnant by a man you intended to divorce?'

There was another long pause before Craig next spoke. 'What did you say when she said that to you?'

Ted sighed heavily. 'I'm sorry to say, I wasn't particularly bothered. All she ever does is pick fault and criticise, and you don't do that to someone if you love them.'

'So, you'd welcome it then?' Craig said impatiently.

'I would, but I doubt it will happen now, as she's obviously no intention of going through with her threats.'

'I've had an idea,' said Craig. 'Leave it with me.'

'What are you going to do?'

The operator's voice came down the receiver informing them that their time was at an end.

'Take care of yourself, son. I'll be in touch.'

Ted heard the receiver on his father's end click down. He frowned as he tried to work out what his father had meant, then shrugged. No doubt he would find out in due course.

March 1942

Olivia swore as Beth wrenched the brake on the winch, snapping the wire. 'What the hell are you doing?' she shouted over the roar of the wind. She raced round the other side of the truck and ran after the trailing wire as it whipped around. 'Didn't you hear the order to stop winch?'

'It's too windy!' yelled Beth, as she too tried to grab the end of the wire. 'I can hardly hear myself think.'

Olivia yelled out in pain as she grabbed the wire and felt it pull painfully through her fingers. Leaping in front of Olivia, Beth held on to the wire further up. She looked wildly around her for help, which came in the form of Josie and Maude and several other girls, all of whom were racing towards them, along with the sergeant who had given the order to 'stop winch'.

Together they managed to bring the balloon back under control, and when they eventually got it grounded, several other Waafs ran to deflate the balloon before it could take to the skies once more.

Back in the hut the sergeant glared angrily at Beth.

'You can't afford to daydream, ACW Moreton, you're damned lucky no one was killed.'

'I'm sorry, Sarge,' sniffed Beth, 'I didn't hear ...'

Ralph, who had been recalled to Shirehampton to cover for a Waaf who had previously been injured by a winch wire, tutted under his breath. 'Probably dreaming about some feller or other.'

Olivia stared at him. She may not particularly like Beth, but it was unfair for Ralph to automatically assume she was daydreaming about men, especially when during the briefing, they had been told that with the wind being so loud, it would be a miracle if they could hear each other, so to shout as loud as they could. The unfairness of his accusation caused her to speak out on Beth's behalf.

'You couldn't hear a thing out there, Sarge,' she reasoned. 'I certainly never heard the order to stop winch.' She glanced briefly at Beth, who looked at her in stunned silence.

The flight sergeant looked hard at both girls before coming to a conclusion. 'I suppose if neither of you heard the order ...'

Olivia nodded, so he continued, 'In that case I shall write in my report that the conditions were such that instructions could not be heard.'

Beth breathed a sigh of relief. Not carrying out an order was a serious offence which could lead to her being court-martialled.

As they were dismissed from their debriefing, Ralph caught hold of Olivia's elbow and pulled her over to one side. 'Why are you sticking up for her?'

Olivia was careful not to make eye contact when she replied. 'Because I didn't hear him either.'

Ralph looked to where Beth was waiting for Olivia. 'I hope you're telling the truth, because people like Beth aren't worth getting court-martialled for.'

She jerked her head in Beth's direction. 'We've had our differences, and we'll never be best pals, but it's only fair I tell the truth.'

Ralph nodded. 'Shall I see you for lunch tomorrow?'

Olivia shook her head. 'I'm on guard duty two till four, then again from eight till ten.'

The flight sergeant excused himself as he walked between them, and Olivia took this as an opportunity to leave. Swiftly bidding Ralph goodbye, she made her way over to Beth, who smiled gratefully at her.

'Thanks for what you did back there,' she said humbly.

Olivia smiled. 'I'm sure you'd have pulled the brake had you heard the instruction.'

Beth looked back at Ralph who was jogging to catch up with the flight sergeant. 'Why has he got it in for me?'

'I don't think he's got it in for you,' Olivia replied untruthfully.

Beth looked surprised. 'Don't you? Only he's always giving me disapproving looks, and what he said back there was so unfair. He obviously thinks I'm some kind of maneater who can't stop thinking about her next course.'

Olivia roared with laughter, causing several people to turn their heads. Hastily smothering her mirth behind her hand, she looked at Beth sympathetically. 'I'm sure he doesn't think that.'

'You're close to him. Has he said anything to you?' Beth asked cautiously.

Olivia was surprised to find she was feeling sorry for Beth. Did the girl not realise that dating a lot of men got you a reputation? She decided to play devil's advocate. 'Have you ever thought that going out with lots of men might give people the wrong idea?'

Beth stared at her. 'He's said something, hasn't he?'

Olivia pulled a face. 'You can be very forthright with your opinions – you certainly were when it came to my weight.'

Beth looked rueful. 'Sorry about that. I didn't mean to upset you, only I've got eyes in my head and I saw the way you looked at me when I asked if he was single. Talk about daggers – you could tell you'd already made up your mind.'

Olivia blushed. Had she really given Beth a filthy look? She cast her mind back to their first meeting. She had certainly been annoyed that Beth had asked him such a blunt question, because she was jealous of Beth's appearance. 'Sorry, I didn't realise I had, but thinking back, I was a little put out when you were so direct.' She shrugged. 'I was worried he might like you more than me.'

Beth nodded. 'That's pretty much what I thought.' She held out a hand of friendship. 'Can we call it pax?'

Olivia giggled. 'I've not heard that expression since I was a kid, but yes, I don't see why not.'

Beth smiled happily. 'Just for the record, I know what Josie told you, because I have ears as well as eyes, and yes, I've had a lot of boyfriends, but I've never gone the whole way, no matter what anyone might think. I'm waiting till I get a ring on my finger. Until then I'm going to keep on dating until I find the right one – it's just my luck that I seem to attract idiots.'

'When you put it like that, it doesn't seem so bad.' As they were being so honest, Olivia decided to ask the question uppermost in her thoughts. 'Is Ralph the sort of feller you normally go for?'

Beth shook her head. 'I don't have a type as such. I'm waiting for Mr Right to come along and I thought that feller might be Ralph. I was pinning my hopes on him being the sort of feller who liked blonde women with big boobs.'

Olivia broke into giggles once more. 'Oh gosh, Beth, is that all you see yourself as?'

Beth nodded sincerely. 'Or at least I know that's what most men see me as, including officers and sergeants.' She shrugged in a matter-of-fact fashion. 'I'm used to it. I can't win – men find me attractive but women see me as a threat.'

Olivia smiled. She had always found the reverse of Beth's experience. 'Most women like me because they don't regard me as competition, and men just want to be my friend.' She looked over to where Josie and Maude were eyeing them curiously.

Beth followed Olivia's line of sight. 'Bet they'd love to know what we're talking about.'

Olivia grinned. 'I think we should go and tell them.'

Beth looked uncertain. 'Do you think they'd regard me any differently if we did? I know that Josie's already made up her mind.'

Olivia nodded firmly. 'That's because she doesn't know you properly.'

Beth shrugged. 'I can but try, although when I've tried to make friends in the past, some of them have accused me of having ulterior motives.'

'Ulterior motives? Like what?'

Beth looked peeved. 'Getting close to them so that I could steal their boyfriend, which is something I would never do. Who wants a man who would cheat on his girlfriend?'

Olivia wondered what Ralph would say when she told him the truth about Beth, then chided herself inwardly. Ralph had been judge, jury and executioner when it came to women like Beth. He would say that Olivia was naive for believing her and that Beth was lying. It was men like Ralph who labelled Beth without trying to get to know her first, just as he had assumed Olivia was a 'good girl' because everyone knew that big women couldn't be fast and easy, not when men didn't want them. She liked Ralph, she really did, but she found his opinions a little trying at times.

Maude eyed Beth warily as they approached. 'Everything all right?'

Beth nodded. 'I was just thanking Olivia for speaking up.'

'And we were just saying how appearances can be deceptive,' Olivia added conversationally.

'Appearances?' said Josie, as she regarded Beth coolly.

'How some people think I'm easy just because of the way I look,' said Beth.

'And others assume I'm not because I'm overweight,' Olivia added.

'Are you talking about anybody in particular?' said Maude diplomatically.

'Men,' Beth and Olivia said in unison.

Beth giggled as Josie gave an audible sigh of relief. 'And some women, she added.'

'Be fair!' said Josie. 'You must have dated most of the men in training.'

Beth gave a half-shrug. 'I went out to dances, meals and the cinema, I'm not sure you'd call it dating. I never committed to any of them ... or slept with any of them.'

'Oh,' said Josie quietly. 'I thought ...'

'You didn't think,' corrected Beth, 'you *assumed*!'

'But what about what you said to Sexy Stebbins when you first laid eyes on him?'

'What's wrong with asking someone if they're single?' Beth replied reasonably.

Maude pointed at Olivia. 'What about what you said to our Liv?'

Beth lowered her gaze. 'I was being mean, for which I've apologised.'

'And I accepted Beth's apology,' Olivia said quickly, 'because I kind of cast the first stone without knowing it.' Seeing the doubtful look on Maude's face, she ran over the conversation she and Beth had just had.

Maude, who hadn't taken her eyes off Beth, nodded slowly. 'I see. Well, I suppose we're all a bit guilty of making assumptions without getting to know the facts first.'

Josie gave Beth an embarrassed smile. 'And I'm sorry for assuming the worst. I'll know better next time.'

Beth smiled. 'Perhaps I should have been more open, only I've learned through bitter experience that people will think what they want, regardless of the truth.'

Josie nodded. 'Just goes to show, you can't judge a book by its cover.'

'Exactly,' said Olivia, adding in the privacy of her own mind, *because you think I'm holier than thou, and never been kissed, which just goes to show how deceptive looks can be!*

Since the telephone conversation with his father, Ted had expected Isobel to break her silence in one form or another, but weeks had gone by and there was still no communication between them. He had fought the temptation to ring his father back and ask if there had been any developments from his side, because he knew his father would tell him to have patience. So it came as a huge relief when a large envelope arrived for him, bearing the Plymouth postmark.

Expecting it to be something to do with his father's business, he was surprised to find inside a set of papers with a covering letter from a solicitor's firm in Plymouth. Fearing he was in trouble for something he had no clue about, he quickly scanned the page before him. To his surprise it was a petition for divorce from Isobel.

Ted got off his bed and made his way to the NAAFI. He wondered why it had taken Isobel so long to decide she wanted a divorce, especially when she hadn't answered any of his letters. He frowned. It didn't make sense – despite what she had said in Liverpool, she had tried to persuade his father to take him on as a partner, so what had changed her mind? Ted tutted to himself. His father must have told her he had no intention of taking Ted on and that he knew she had been lying about her trip to Liverpool and the alleged pregnancy.

Picking up the phone, he gave the operator the details of his father's garage and waited for someone to answer.

'Dad?'

'Ted!' said Craig, sounding delighted. 'How's my boy doing?'

'Do you know anything about Isobel petitioning for divorce?'

'Oho! When did you get that?' said Craig.

'This morning. So you did know something about it, then?'

The smile in Craig's voice was evident to hear. 'I didn't know whether she would or not, but I suspected she would go for it.' Realising he wasn't making any sense, he added, 'Me and Rob drew up some false documents making you a partner and gave them to Isobel, to see what she would do.'

'And?' said Ted, slow on the uptake.

'And she asked you for a divorce,' sighed Craig.

There was a short silence before Ted spoke next. 'So, she asked you to make me a partner so that she could benefit from the divorce?'

'I'm afraid that's the gist of it, yes.'

'Only I'm not really a partner?'

Again, Ted could hear the smile in his father's voice. 'Nope.'

Ted grinned. 'You wily old sod!'

Craig laughed down the phone. 'Sign those papers and send them back as soon as you can. By the time Isobel realises it's a hoax it'll be too late, the divorce will be final and there won't be a damned thing she can do about it.'

'Cor, I wish I could see the look on her face when that day comes.' Ted chuckled. 'Talk about spitting feathers!'

'I should imagine she'll not be best pleased,' Craig agreed.

'Thanks, Dad.'

'For what?'

'For bringing things to a head, and making her show her true colours.'

'Ah, don't be daft, you already knew her for what she was,' said Craig. 'I just gave things a bit of a nudge.'

'Well, I'm glad you did,' said Ted. 'I'll sign and send them back without delay.'

'Good on you, Ted. Let me know how you go.'

Ted took a pen and signed on the dotted line. He was relieved that his sham of a marriage was over, but he did feel a smidgen of regret, as he had once loved Isobel and thought she felt the same way about him, and even when things had started to get rocky, he had always hoped that things would work out. After all, no one wants to think they'll get divorced when they're making their wedding vows. He sighed. He'd married the wrong girl.

An image of Toff formed in his mind. Young, sweet, with a heart of gold. He wished he could go back to the day his father had whisked him off to Plymouth. If he could, he would have ignored William's allegations and gone to the house. They may have been too young to have a baby, but at least he could have been with her when she gave birth, and who knows? His presence alone could have been enough to save their child. He tried to imagine what Olivia must have thought of him when her father returned to say that he had left without saying goodbye. He shook his head miserably. She would have been heartbroken because the one man she thought she could truly rely on had dropped her like a hot cake and hightailed it to the other end of the country. He couldn't bear for her to think badly of him. In that moment Ted made up his mind. He would wait until the divorce was settled, then seek out her grandparents and try to make contact. He hesitated – why couldn't he go before the divorce came through? No. If Isobel found out that he had gone to see his first love, she would probably name Olivia in the divorce and she didn't deserve that. He would have to be patient.

William Campbell stared out across the factory floor whilst his employees went about their work. It seemed odd to him that you could be the loneliest person in the world when you were surrounded by so many people. Yet he was. True, he had plenty of people to talk to, but they all worked for him in one way or another, so were, therefore, beneath him. He knew from his father that it was unthinkable to befriend someone who worked for you, as it would give them ideas above their station, and likely as not they would try to take advantage of their position. He had friends of a sort, but he was not about to discuss his innermost thoughts with any of them.

His thoughts turned to Olivia. He knew from her letters that she was in Shirehampton and that she was enjoying her new life in the WAAF. He drew a deep breath. In some respects he supposed it must be wonderful to be happy when you had nothing but your comrades. Which led him to another thought: Olivia had walked away from the factory, the house, the wealthy lifestyle in favour of ... nothing. Was it because she knew she could come back if it didn't work out? He shook his head. He had told her she wasn't to come back, something which he had said in haste, but she had heeded his words.

He sighed heavily. The people below him belonged to him during the day, but they would go home to loving families once the whistle blew, and that's where their true lives were. He thought about his own work life, and it occurred to him that the whistle never blew as far as he was concerned. He was working whether he was at home or in the factory. In fact, his business was the last thing on his mind when he went to bed and the first thing he thought of when he woke. He never switched off, he wouldn't know how to. Every decision he made was based on the business. His stomach lurched unpleasantly. It was the whole reason why he had objected to Olivia and Edward's relationship. He knew Edward would use Olivia to wiggle his way into William's life, and once he got his feet under the table, William would never be able to get rid of him. As a result, William had been forced to make some major sacrifices. He'd had no choice, and that was all Edward's fault. Everything he had done had been with his family's best interest in mind. You couldn't afford to think with your heart in situations like that, because it would only land you in deep water. Far better to shut it out and think logically. So why was his head now allowing his heart to be heard?

Olivia stared at the letter in her hands.

Maude looked up curiously. 'What's up?'

'It's from my dad ...' Olivia said, turning the envelope over in her hands.

'Do you think it's bad news?' said Josie tentatively.

Olivia shrugged. 'I've not heard a word since the day I left, so I suppose it must be.'

Beth came up behind them. 'For goodness' sake, just open it!' She took a bite out of her toast and sat down next to Olivia.

Olivia slit the envelope open and scanned the contents.

Olivia,

I trust you are well. Liverpool looks very different from when you saw it last, but we're a resilient lot. If you ever come back to take a look perhaps you could call by? It would be nice to see you after all this time.

Olivia frowned as she finished the letter. She looked up into the expectant faces of Maude, Josie and Beth. 'He didn't say much apart from suggesting I might call in if I were passing.'

'Perhaps he's missing you?' Maude volunteered.

Olivia chuckled. 'No, not my dad.'

Maude shrugged. 'He's been on his own for a long time now – he's had a while to think about things.'

Olivia looked doubtful. 'He's not like other people, trust me. I lived with him long enough.'

'He's opened the door, which is a start,' Beth said.

Olivia nodded. She hadn't had any intention of going back to Liverpool, but should she consider it? She knew her grandparents would be in favour of her doing so, especially if they got to see her whilst she was there. She thought of Ralph's proposal that he might accompany her and imagined her father's face if she turned up with Ralph on her arm. He would undoubtedly approve, but on the other hand, she didn't want him to think that she was trying to impress him, nor did she want to give Ralph the wrong impression. She stared at the letter. *What do you want, William Campbell?*

June 1942

As Ted had anticipated, the last few months had been volatile, but not because of the war. Isobel's solicitor had informed her of Ted's father's ruse regarding his partnership in the business, and she had not been happy, demanding that her solicitor make the paperwork she had been handed legal. When he had told her that this wasn't possible, she had rung the NAAFI in RAF Speke and demanded to speak to Ted.

'Your father's an idiot!' she had fumed down the receiver, heedless of the listening operator. 'Didn't he realise he needed a legal document drawn up, and that he couldn't make you a partner in a handwritten letter? You'll have to tell him to do it properly!'

'And why would I do that?' said Ted, his tone level.

'Because your stupid father has duped you, Ted! Blimey, talk about the apple not falling far from the tree!'

'It's not me who's been duped,' Ted replied quietly. There was a long pause, so he continued, 'I told you I didn't want to be a partner and I meant it, but you went behind my back to get my father to sign me up without my knowledge, and you did that because you wanted a divorce but only when I had a legal stake in the business.' He chuckled softly. 'Sorry to disappoint you, *Issy*, but I haven't got two pennies to rub together, never mind a third of a successful business.'

He held the receiver away from his ear as Isobel shrieked angrily down the line before slamming the phone down.

Now, Ted folded the decree absolute and pushed it into his pocket. He started walking, then stopped, removed his wedding ring and placed it in the same pocket as his divorce papers. Smiling, he set off once more. He had made a promise to himself that as soon as his divorce came through he would go and see Olivia's grandparents. Having looked them up in the Kelly's directory earlier that morning, he confidently made his way to their home in Ullet Road.

When he arrived he hesitated before rapping the knocker. He had expected a maid to answer and was surprised when a small, white-haired woman opened the door a crack. 'Hello?'

'Mrs Barnham?'

Nodding, she eyed him quizzically, but seeing the uniform she opened the door a little further. 'Can I help you?'

Ted nodded. 'I'm looking for your granddaughter, Olivia Campbell.'

She looked surprised. 'Oh, I'm afraid she doesn't live here, dear, she's in …' She stopped short as an elderly man appeared and hushed her into silence.

'Good God, woman, don't you know there's a war on?' He pulled her gently to one side and stared accusingly at Ted. 'Who are you?'

Ted took a deep breath. He had no idea how her grandparents would feel when they knew who he was, especially if Olivia had told them that he had left her in the lurch when he found out she was pregnant, which was what her father had told her. He decided to approach the matter side on. 'I'm an old friend of Olivia's. I know she's not living with her father any more …' he noticed with some satisfaction how Olivia's grandfather rolled his eyes at the mention of William, '… because I called round when I first got back. I asked him where she lived but he wasn't exactly forthcoming.'

'Doesn't surprise me,' tutted Mrs Barnham.

Ted opened his mouth to continue, then shut it again. He had meant to skirt the issue of his relationship with Olivia, but he didn't feel comfortable deceiving the Barnhams in such a manner. He held an outstretched hand towards Mr Barnham. 'I'm Edward Hewitt, Olivia knows me as Ted.'

'Ivor!' squealed Mrs Barnham as her husband's fist connected with Ted's jaw.

Ted held up his hands in a placating manner as Ivor came forward, his fists held up ready for another swing. 'Scoundrel,' roared Ivor, 'blackguard!'

'I can understand why you're angry, Mr Barnham,' said Ted hastily, 'but you haven't heard my side of things.'

'Nor do I wish to!' bellowed Mr Barnham, waving his wife back as she pleaded with him to calm down.

'Ivor! Please think of your blood pressure! You know what Doctor Baker said!'

Speaking quickly, Ted tried to explain himself. 'I didn't know Olivia was pregnant, her father evicted us so we wouldn't find out ...'

He ducked as Ivor extended his arm, his finger pointing towards the street. 'Leave!'

Mrs Barnham placed a retaining arm across her husband's chest. 'Let him speak, Ivor.'

Ted smiled gratefully at the older woman who wagged a reproving finger. 'Whether you knew or not, you still got our granddaughter pregnant.'

'I know, and I'm sorry,' said Ted. 'Believe me, if I could turn back the hands of time I would, and had I known the truth I would never have left Olivia.' He rubbed his jaw. 'She was my first love.'

Mrs Barnham nodded. 'And you hers, but why are you here?'

'Because I want to set the record straight. I don't want Olivia to think badly of me, even though I can't do any-thing to change what happened. I need her to know that I wasn't the man her father painted me to be.'

Mrs Barnham rested her hand over his. 'You weren't a man at all, but a boy, and that's where the problem lay.' She turned to face her husband who was still look-ing furious. 'It's not up to us whether Olivia speaks to Ted – only she can make that decision.'

'He shouldn't be allowed anywhere near her, Matilda,' growled Ivor. 'I don't see what good can come of it.'

She raised a questioning brow. 'Do you not? Because I do. Our Liv's confidence took a real nosedive after this one left. She thought herself incapable of judging someone and started to believe everything her father told her, and look where that got her.' She sighed. 'If Ted tells her the truth, she'll know she didn't get him wrong. It's rotten when you can't trust your own mind.'

'Well, I'm not giving him her address,' said Ivor, folding his arms across his chest.

'You could give her mine?' suggested Ted.

Mrs Barnham smiled. 'What a good idea. If you don't hear from her you'll know she's not interested.'

'That's good enough for me,' Ted said. 'I promise to let bygones be bygones if that's her decision.' As he spoke he took a piece of paper from his pocket and began scribbling his details down. He handed it to Mrs Barnham. 'I promise I won't bother you again.'

She took the paper from him, before casting her husband a sideways glance. 'Liv wasn't the only one who suffered in all this. Ted's father had to leave his home town because of their naivety.' She looked at Ted. 'I daresay your father wasn't best pleased with you.'

Ted shrugged. 'As I said, we didn't know about the pregnancy. According to Campbell, we were being evicted because I'd stolen his precious koi, only I didn't and my father knows I'm not a thief.'

Ivor looked up. 'He never mentioned any of his koi going missing, and he would if he really thought someone had stolen them.'

'There you are!' said Mrs Barnham reasonably. 'He blamed Ted in order to get rid of him.'

'I know he didn't mention it to anyone else either,' Ted volunteered. He looked Ivor square in the eye. 'I really didn't know, although I understand that's not much of an excuse.'

Ivor heaved a sigh. 'What's done is done.' He nursed the knuckles on the hand he had used to hit Ted with. 'Sorry about punching you.'

Smiling, Ted rubbed his jaw. 'Fair do's. You've got a mean right hook on you there, Mr Barnham, and I guess it's the least I deserve.'

Ivor's eyes flicked towards the paper in his wife's hands. 'We'll pass it on.'

Thanking the Barnhams for their help, Ted made his way back to the tram stop. All he had to do now was hope Olivia wrote to him.

*

Maude entered the billet with a clutch of letters in her hands and handed them out to their recipients.

'One from Ralph and one from Nana and Pops,' said Olivia. Slitting Ralph's open first, she read the contents.

Dearest Liv,

I knew it would happen sooner or later, but I suppose I was hoping I'd be lucky and spend the war close to you, but unfortunately the RAF have other ideas and as a consequence I'm being posted to the land of jellied eels, so I fear it might be some time before I see you next.

I'm glad we managed to sort out the 'Beth business', even if it was by accident.

Olivia grinned. Ralph was referring to his last day in Shirehampton. She had been on guard duty with Beth when Ralph had come by. He had acknowledged both women before turning his attention to Olivia and asking whether she would like to go dancing with him in the village hall the following evening.

'I'm sorry, Ralph, I've already arranged to go with Beth and the girls to see *Dumbo* at the Metropole.'

Ralph had tutted as he shot Beth a withering glance. Fearing Beth might have seen or heard him, Olivia looked at her friend, and was glad to see she had her back turned to them.

Ralph looked imploringly at Olivia. 'Why her?' he said sulkily. 'I can understand you wanting to spend your time with Maude and Josie because they're nice girls, but why Beth?'

'Because she's a nice girl too,' Olivia said quietly. 'You'd know that if you gave her a chance.'

Ralph regarded Beth doubtfully. 'She hides it well.'

Olivia smiled. 'She does, because she knows what people think when they see her, so she's very defensive, but if you took the time to get to know her, like I did, you'd see a different side.'

'I don't think there's enough time in the world for that,' Ralph said cynically. 'I know you mean well, but mind you don't get yourself a reputation for hanging around with her – you know how judgemental people can be.'

Olivia's brow had shot towards her hairline. Talk about the pot calling the kettle black! Why couldn't Ralph see that he was being a hypocrite? Not to mention grossly unfair – he'd never spent more than a few seconds in Beth's company. Well, he could jolly well do so now. 'I've got to nip to the lavvy, do you mind stepping in for a minute or two?'

Ralph looked at Beth, who had turned to approach them, then looked at Olivia. 'Go on then, but be quick.'

Grinning, Olivia hurried off to the ablutions, keeping her fingers crossed that Ralph would be eating his words by the time she returned, and was pleased to see that not only were Ralph and Beth deep in conversation, but they weren't arguing.

Beth beckoned her over. 'Trust you to miss all the fun!'

'What happened?' said Olivia, looking eagerly around her.

'We had a WAAF officer trying to pass through with no ID, so I told her she couldn't come in,' Beth said in excited tones. 'She got really stroppy, tried to push past and called me an imbecile, but I stood my ground and told her to turn around.'

Ralph nodded approvingly. 'Credit where credit's due, Beth wouldn't take no for an answer and sent her packing, which is admirable, because most people would've buckled under the pressure when faced with an angry officer.'

Beth nodded primly. 'Rules are there to be obeyed, I don't care how many stripes you have on your arm!'

Olivia had tried to swallow her smile; she didn't want Ralph to see how pleased she was that the two of them were talking.

Now, as she continued to read the letter, she felt her heart drop. Despite her words, she feared she was beginning to fall for him, because the thought of him leaving for London – or at least she presumed it to be London after his jellied eels comment – was causing her heart to ache.

'Everything all right?' said Maude.

'Ralph's been posted London way,' Olivia said miserably, 'and we all know what it's like down there.'

Maude grimaced. 'Do you know when?'

'Couple of weeks, and he doesn't think he'll have time to see me before he goes.'

'Oh Liv, I am sorry.' Maude sat beside Olivia and placed an arm around her shoulders. 'I swear the RAF do it on purpose.' She glanced at the other letter. 'Why don't you see what your nan's got to say? You never know, it might cheer you up.'

Olivia opened the envelope from her grandparents.

Darling Liv,

I don't know quite how to say this, but we had a surprise visit the other week from Edward Hewitt.

With her heart beating as though it was trying to come out of her chest, Olivia let the paper drop through her fingers.

Maude rushed over and picked the letter up. 'Oh no, what now?'

Olivia shook her head. 'It's not bad …' she hesitated, '… or at least I don't think it is.' She took the letter back from Maude. 'Ted's been to see Nana and Pops.'

'Who's Ted?' asked Beth inquisitively.

Maude's eyes widened as she waved Beth into silence. '*The* Ted?'

Olivia nodded. 'I can't imagine why he's turned up after all these years, let alone why he'd go and visit my grandparents. He's got some nerve, I'll give him that.'

Josie looked from Maude to Olivia. 'Is anyone going to tell me and Beth who Ted is?'

Maude eyed the paper clutched between Olivia's fingers. 'Only one way to find out.'

Nodding, Olivia turned her attention to the letter. 'You'd best tell Beth and Josie about Ted whilst I read.'

Maude looked uncertain. 'What, everything?'

Olivia nodded. 'They won't blab and I know they won't judge me either.'

As you can imagine, your Pops wasn't best pleased and I'm afraid to say he gave Edward a piece of his mind, as well as a right hook! Needless to say, neither of us wanted to talk to him, but you have to give people a chance, so we let him say his piece and I've agreed to pass his details on so that you might get in contact should you wish to. Now I'm not one to interfere, but I think it might be in your interest to at least give him a chance to give his side of the story. Anyway, with that being said I've written his address at the bottom of this letter.

Pops's gout is playing up again, but he doesn't do himself any favours ...

Olivia turned the paper over and glanced at the address on the bottom. She looked up at Maude and Beth, who was looking slightly stunned. 'He's in RAF Speke!'

'You're a bit of a dark horse,' said Beth quietly. 'Did your grandparents say anything else?'

Olivia shrugged. 'Only that Pops gave him what for, as well as a right hook.' She waited for Josie to stop giggling before continuing, 'Nana did say that she thought it a good idea to hear his side of things.'

Maude nodded. 'I agree. You've said yourself you've had doubts as to what your father told you regarding Ted's sudden disappearance, and I've already given my opinion – you know I wouldn't trust your father as far as I could throw him.'

'I know, but it all happened such a long time ago. What's the sense in dragging it all up again? I can't see why he'd want to! It's not as if any good could come of it. At best he'll deny any knowledge, but that still won't change the outcome.'

'Only it would mean that you'd know the truth,' Josie said levelly, 'and that alone could help you understand what really went on. I wonder if that's why your father wrote to you?'

Olivia's mouth hung open. 'Of course! I'd forgotten about that, but it makes sense now. I bet Ted went to see Dad first and that's why Dad wrote to me, because he wants to speak to me before Ted has a chance to.' She shook her head. 'My God, are there no lengths that man won't go to to cover his tracks?'

'So you *do* think he was lying?' said Maude.

'It certainly looks that way,' Olivia confirmed. 'All this time and not a word, but as soon as Ted turns up, bingo!'

'So, are you going to write to Ted?' Maude asked hopefully. 'Only if you want my opinion, I reckon your nan's right. And on top of that, Ted has a right to clear his name, and you have a right to know the truth.'

Olivia nodded. 'I'll write to him after I come off duty.' She turned anxiously to her friends. 'Please don't tell anyone else that I'm writing to an old flame, because they might not understand.'

Beth nodded definitely. 'Mum's the word.'

Maude agreed heartily. 'That goes for me too.'

'And me,' said Josie.

Olivia continued to read the rest of her grandmother's letter in a half-hearted fashion, because she couldn't keep her thoughts from Ted and why he had turned up after all these years. She wondered if he was married and whether he had any children. He obviously knew about her being pregnant, but how? She tried to imagine what Ted must look like now, some eighteen years or so since she last saw him. Her mind turned guiltily to Ralph, who had written to tell her he was going to be operating in one of the most dangerous parts of the country, and here she was daydreaming about her first love. Should she get back in touch with Ted, or would it be seen as disloyal to Ralph? She mulled this over for a moment or so before asking Maude's opinion.

'As long as you're only contacting Ted to hear what he has to say, I don't see what harm it could do,' Maude said. 'It's not as though you're considering rekindling your relationship, and besides, you and Ralph aren't even courting, not officially at any rate.'

Feeling better about the matter, Olivia nodded. 'You're right. I'll write back to him, and he can tell me his side of the story. After that we can go our separate ways.'

Ralph frowned. 'I don't quite understand why I'm getting into trouble for this. I was merely standing in for one of the Waafs whilst she nipped to the lavvy. If you want to have a go at someone, you should be talking to the officer who tried to gain access to an RAF base without any identification.'

'The reason why we wanted to talk to you on the matter is because you weren't down for duty that day, and we wanted to confirm what you were doing there,' said the flight officer, exasperated. 'We need to know that your reasons are legitimate.'

Ralph shook his head. 'Why wouldn't they be?'

The flight officer drew a deep breath. 'The officer in question suggested that you were with your girlfriend, and that you shouldn't have been there, and you weren't behaving in a professional manner. She says you were unreliable and that you should be court-martialled along with the Waaf concerned.'

Ralph stared open-mouthed at the flight officer. 'She's wasn't my girlfriend.'

The flight officer shrugged. 'I'm sorry, but I have to take her allegations seriously because they've been raised. The Waaf who was with you will also be called for an interview, so you're not the only one taking the blame.'

'It's obvious to anyone that the officer is trying to deflect attention away from herself,' Ralph said furiously. 'Why is anyone even listening to her?'

'She's a right to her opinion, and as it's raised a few eyebrows it's considered to have merit.'

Ralph wanted to shout at the unfairness of it all, but he knew to do so would only make matters worse. He wondered how Beth must be feeling having received the same summons.

Ted's heart skipped a beat as he held the envelope addressed with unfamiliar writing in his hands. Having ruled out everyone else, he thought it had to be from Olivia or her grandparents, but either way he hoped it would give him an answer. He slit the envelope open and skipped to Olivia's signature at the end. He smiled.

Hello Ted,

I've heard from my grandparents that you went to pay them a visit, but that's about all. I don't know what you have to say, but I am prepared to hear your side, even though it can't change the past. Perhaps it'll help draw a line under things.

I am currently serving in RAF Shirehampton, so you can either ring or write to me here, whichever suits.
Hoping this letter finds you well.
Olivia

He drew a deep breath. He'd hardly been expecting instant forgiveness, but it was a start, and that's all he could ask for.

Chapter Six

Ralph entered the room and gave a small nod of recognition to Beth who was sitting on the far side of the table. The past few weeks had been anything but fun. He should have been in London by now with the rest of his platoon, but he had been held back whilst an investigation had been carried out – something which had spread around his fellow men like wildfire. Olivia had apologised profusely for getting him into trouble, and even though he had assured her it was not her fault, there was a tiny part of him that did blame her. After all, had she been the one on duty as she should have been, the WAAF officer would not have been able to make such wild accusations, and neither he nor Beth would be going through this ordeal. Seeing Beth now, her big blue eyes surrounded by a thatch of dark lashes, her blonde hair peeking out beneath her cap, and her … He turned his attention away from her breasts, which accentuated her tiny waist. Not an officer alive would think Ralph had not been flirting with her whilst on duty – they would probably believe he had sent Olivia off so that he could be alone with the other woman. He sat down opposite his flight officer and waited for the accusations to fly, and fly they did. Denying any wrongdoing on her part, the WAAF officer turned the focus on to Beth and Ralph, claiming they'd been incompetent.

It was hours later by the time he and Beth emerged from the meeting. Having been proven innocent of any wrongdoing, they were in the clear – not that you would have known that from Beth's face, which was still wet with tears.

'Beth!' Ralph jogged after her. 'Hold up.'

Beth turned to face him. 'I'm sorry, Ralph, and I know it's not your fault, but I'd rather you didn't speak to me.'

He fished around in his pocket then handed her a fresh handkerchief. 'Here, use this.'

Taking the hanky, Beth dabbed her eyes. 'Thanks.'

He chucked her under the chin with his forefinger. 'Cheer up! We won, we should be celebrating, not crying.'

She gave a short giggle. 'I know, I think it was all the pressure. I felt sure they were going to take her side.'

He nodded. 'But they didn't, so dry your eyes and I'll arrange for someone to take you back to Shirehampton.'

Beth looked up sharply. 'Couldn't you take me? I don't fancy making small talk with someone I don't know, especially when they'll most likely be fishing for information.'

Ralph smiled, revealing a dazzling set of perfect white teeth. 'They all love a bit of gossip when it's not about them.' He looked in the direction of the ops room. 'If you hang on here I'll go and ask Flight if it's all right for me to drive you.'

Beth stood outside the ops room as she waited for Ralph. The sun was blazing down and she wished she could take off her hat and jacket, even if just for a minute or so to cool down. The room in which they had held the investigation had been hot and stuffy, with no means of ventilation, and with the accusations weighing heavily on her mind, she had got hotter and hotter, made worse by the fear that her sweaty face made her appear guilty.

Ralph reappeared, jiggling a set of keys, and smiled broadly at her. 'Done.' He walked towards one of the cars and opened the passenger door for Beth. 'M'lady!'

'Thanks, Jeeves,' Beth chuckled as she slid into the passenger seat. She blanched as her tights connected with the hot leather. 'It's worse in here than it is out there!' she moaned.

Ralph rolled down the window and placed his arm across the back of Beth's seat as he looked over his shoulder to reverse.

As they left the base, Beth tried to roll her window down but it was stuck fast. 'Damn and blast. It's like a sodding oven in here.' She looked at Ralph, her hand on her cap. 'Do you mind?'

He shook his head. 'Not a bit. You'll melt with that on.'

Beth thankfully removed her cap. 'I wouldn't mind taking my jacket off as well.'

Ralph shrugged. 'Go for your life, I won't tell if you don't.'

Beth leaned forward, her arms behind her back, and wriggled around until she managed to get her arms out of the sleeves. She cast her jacket on to the back seat with a sigh of relief, although the effort of all the wriggling had left her hotter than ever.

Ralph glanced at her. 'Funny how things turn out.'

She mopped her brow with the hanky he had given her. 'How'd you mean?'

'If someone had told me a couple of months ago that the two of us would be on the same side, I'd have laughed at them.'

Beth nodded. 'I'd agree with you there ...' She hesitated. 'Why did you dislike me so much? I've never done anything to you.'

He pulled a face. 'You reminded me of my ex. I assumed you were cut from the same cloth, as it were.'

'What did she do exactly?' Beth asked.

His jaw flinched. 'Cheated on me. I did everything for that woman – fancy clothes, meals out, the works – but apparently, it wasn't enough for her.'

Beth turned her attention from the road to Ralph. 'She was a fool to treat you the way she did, but her loss is Olivia's gain.'

Ralph eyed her curiously. 'Try telling that to Liv. You do know the two of us aren't official, don't you?'

Beth nodded. 'Although I think it's only a matter of time.'

Ralph smiled. 'Perhaps you could put in a good word for me.'

Beth began to fan her face with her hand. 'Can't we see if we can do something about my window? I'll melt if I have to sit here much longer.' As she spoke, she loosened her tie and undid the first two buttons of her blouse.

To her alarm, Ralph swerved the car off the road and into a lay-by hidden behind a row of trees. 'What's wrong, is it the engine?'

Ralph turned the engine off. 'The car's fine, but I can't fix your window whilst we're on the move.'

Beth heaved a sigh of relief. 'Thanks, Ralph, you're ever so thoughtful. Most men would leave me to boil, probably hoping I'd remove more clothing!'

'Oh well,' chuckled Ralph, 'in that case ...'

Beth giggled as he pretended to grab the crank handle. 'Olivia's one lucky woman to have a man like you, Ralph. I shall tell her she's a fool to leave you dangling, I know I wouldn't.'

'What can I say?' said Ralph. He was leaning across Beth to reach the window winder, which he clasped firmly in one hand. 'I'm a real catch!' he half chuckled, half grunted as he pushed hard, forcing the winder free.

Feeling the cool air hit her face, Beth put her neck back to allow the flow to cool as much of her as possible. 'You sure are ...' she breathed. Holding her tie in one hand, she began to pull it loose and closed her eyes, feeling the air caress the heat of her skin. When she opened her eyes, she saw Ralph's face, inches away from her own, his eyes fixed on hers, his lips millimetres away from her mouth. Beth let out a squeal of alarm.

'W-what are you doing?' she stammered.

Ralph's forehead wrinkled. 'What am *I* doing?' he said, his tone incredulous. '*You're* the one who started stripping off, telling me how much you liked me! Good God, woman, you practically threw yourself at me!'

Beth gaped at him. 'I was hot! You could see I was.'

Ralph gripped the crank arm, got out of the car and spun the engine into life. Climbing back into his seat, he cast Beth a withering glance. 'I know you were hot all right, you made that perfectly obvious. Don't worry, Beth, I'm not angry at you,' he shook his head, 'I'm angry at myself, for falling for your act!'

'*Act?*' she cried. 'What act?'

Taking his cap from his head, he pretended to throw it on to the back seat before pulling at his tie and fluttering his eyelashes. 'Oh Ralph, I'm so hot! I do wish you could do something to cool me down, just pull over whilst I take my clothes off!'

Beth shook her head fiercely. 'That's not what I said, nothing like it! Why are you twisting things?'

Ralph snorted in disbelief. 'I'm not twisting anything, or are my eyes playing up? Did you not remove your cap, jacket and tie, and undo the buttons on your blouse?'

'I was hot!' Beth insisted indignantly.

Ralph's jaw stiffened. 'I doubt that's the way Olivia will see it.' He turned on to the main road, causing the man coming from behind to swerve wildly, honking his horn. As Ralph speeded along the road they caught up with a group of squaddies sitting in the back of a lorry with the canvas flaps rolled back. Seeing Beth's flushed cheeks and unkempt appearance, they began making cat calls and wolf whistles as they nudged each other and pointed at Beth.

Looking down, Beth realised that she still hadn't done her buttons up. God only knows what they must have thought she and Ralph had been up to. She hastily buttoned her blouse and pulled her tie back into place

'You don't have to be a genius to know what they're all thinking,' said Ralph as he pulled past the lorry of jeering squaddies.

Beth shook her head. 'I didn't mean to give you the wrong impression, honest to God I didn't, Ralph,' she spluttered. 'Please don't say anything to Olivia. She's been lovely to me, I'd never do anything to hurt her.'

Ralph pulled a cynical face. 'Could've fooled me.'

Tears brimmed in Beth's eyes. 'Please, Ralph, I can't lose Liv and the girls.'

Ralph shot her a reproving glance. 'Give me one good reason why I shouldn't!'

'Because I didn't mean to give you the wrong impression, and ...' she faltered, '... and because whether I gave you the wrong impression or not, you shouldn't have acted on it, so you're as guilty as me!'

Ralph slammed his foot on the brake, causing Beth to lunge forward in her seat, before hitting the accelerator, making her fly backwards. 'You poisonous little bitch!'

'It's true ...' Beth mumbled quietly.

'I've just been through one hell of an ordeal defending your honour, to get you out of shtook, and why? Because your best pal wanted me to spend time with you so that I would realise what a nice girl you are!' He slammed his palm down on to the steering wheel. 'What an idiot! I knew you were a wrong 'un from the very beginning, yet here I am nearly getting court-martialled for you! You!' he repeated scathingly.

'I didn't ask Olivia to go to the lavvy,' Beth said defensively.

'Maybe not, but the end result's still the same. If only she knew what a mistake she'd made.'

Beth hid her face behind her hands. 'Please don't say anything!'

Ralph's face remained wooden as he rounded the next curve in the road. After a minute or so, his expression softened slightly. He shot her a sidelong glance. 'I'd never do anything to hurt Liv, and if you say you didn't mean to egg me on, then I shall have to believe you. But if you ever do anything like this again . . .'

'I won't!' said Beth hastily.

'Then I think it best if we keep this little . . . misunderstanding between the two of us. Agreed?'

Beth nodded fervently. 'Agreed.'

It felt as if the remainder of the journey took a lifetime, and by the time they reached Shirehampton Beth couldn't wait to get out of the car. Slamming the passenger door shut, she made her way to the ablutions so that she might wash the tears which had stained her cheeks.

She had hoped that Ralph would leave without stopping to say hello, but to her dismay she heard him ask the guard for Olivia's whereabouts. She opened the door to the ablutions, walked over to the nearest sink and splashed her face with cold water. She wondered what Ralph was going to say to her friend. Would he keep his word? She gazed at her reflection. Had she given him the wrong impression? It was plain for any-one to see that she was melting in her seat. She winced as the memory of his lips so close to hers came to the forefront of her mind. He'd tried to kiss her, then, when she refused his advances, he'd turned the blame on her. She stared at her face in the mirror. Ralph was the one at fault, not her, but he'd almost made her believe that she was the instigator. If she believed it, then there was no doubt that Olivia, Maude and Josie would also believe it. She tried to fight back tears of frustration as they welled in her eyes. Ralph Stebbins was a dirty rot-ten hypocrite, and there wasn't a damned thing she could do about it. If she told Olivia, Ralph would tell his side, which would sound far worse, and Olivia would believe him, and Beth would lose her friends as a result.

She washed the fresh tears away. What was he say-ing to Olivia? The thought was driving her barmy. She left the ablutions, her face tingling as the sun's rays hit her wet cheeks. From the corner of her eye she could see Ralph standing outside the cookhouse next to Olivia. Beth was determined not to catch their eyes, so she lowered her head as she hurried towards their bil-let. She had her hand on the door handle when Olivia called over to her.

'Beth! Don't rush off, come and tell your side of events.'

Beth froze. What did Olivia mean by 'her side of events'? Looking up, she saw that Olivia was smiling as she beckoned Beth to join them. Realising that Ralph couldn't have said anything amiss, Beth reluctantly went over.

Eyeing her with sympathy, Olivia placed a hand on Beth's shoulder. 'Ralph told me you were upset, but I didn't think you'd still be crying. What did they say to you? Ralph's told me his version, but it looks like he's underestimated how upsetting you found the whole process.'

Beth shot Ralph a glance from under her lashes. 'If you don't mind, I'd rather not talk about it,' she said quietly. Glancing up, she gave Olivia a small smile. 'It's been a long day and I've not had anything to eat.'

Olivia jerked her head in the direction of the cook-house. 'The girls have done quite a good stew ...' She fell silent as Beth shook her head.

'Thanks all the same, but I think I'll give it a miss. Ta-ra, Liv.' Turning on her heel, she started back to their billet.

Olivia called after her. 'Beth?'

Beth half turned.

'You really are tired – you forgot to thank Ralph for the lift!'

Beth's heart sank into the pit of her stomach as she turned her head and saw Ralph, a smug smile etched on his lips. The last thing she wanted to do was thank him, but without appearing rude, she had no choice. 'Thanks.' The word caught in her throat, and as she walked away, she could hear Ralph telling Olivia that it had been a testing day and it didn't matter. Knowing that her friend was wondering why Beth had been so short was one thing, but hearing Ralph blame it on the stress of the day rather than the truth was a different matter entirely. He was despicable, detestable, a liar and a fraud. Determined not to let his words upset her, she fought back the tears which threatened to fall once more. She would have to work something out, because she couldn't stand to see Ralph acting holier than thou, when nothing could be further from the truth. No matter what he may say, it was he who tried to kiss Beth, not the other way round, and even though he and Olivia weren't official, everyone knew it was only a matter of time.

Ralph sat on the train which would take him to London. Ever since leaving Shirehampton he had asked himself the same question. *Why had he been so stupid?* And each time he had come up with the same answer. Because he had been thinking with his loins rather than his head. He gazed glumly out of the rain-speckled window as they passed through a tunnel. If Beth were to tell Olivia of his actions, there wasn't a doubt in his mind that Olivia wouldn't want to see him again. He had worked hard to get her to trust him and he was certain that he was getting ever closer to her agreeing to be his belle.

So why risk everything for a quick fumble? Especially with Beth? He pictured her as she had sat next to him in the car, her face glistening with sweat, her lips swollen from the heat, and her chest ... He screwed up his eyes, dismissing the image. He would have to keep his fingers crossed that Beth kept her promise to remain quiet, at least until he had a chance to slip a wedding ring on Olivia's finger. After that it wouldn't matter who she told, because it would be too late.

August 1942

Ted waited with nervous anticipation as the Waaf who had answered the telephone went to fetch Olivia. He had rehearsed what he wanted to say over and over until he had got it down pat, because a three-minute call wasn't long, and he had a lot to get across. He had one chance to plead his case. If he didn't use the right words, she might slam the phone down and refuse to speak to him ever again.

'Hello?' Olivia's voice came down the receiver, full of anticipation.

'Toff?'

As soon as Olivia heard him call her by her old pet name, she felt the years melt away. 'Hello, Ted.'

'He smiled; her voice was as he remembered. 'I've a million and one things to tell you, but first things first, how are you?'

'I'm doing well, although a bit surprised to hear your voice after all these years.'

'I can imagine,' said Ted. 'Is there any chance we could meet up for a chat?'

Olivia hesitated. She had loved Ted once, very much so, and he had broken her heart as well as her faith in men. 'Can you not just tell me over the phone?'

'I've a lot to say and I'd rather talk in private, which is nigh on impossible when I'm using the phone in the NAAFI,' Ted said reasonably, 'or any phone for that matter. There's always the chance of crossed wires, and I don't wish to air my dirty laundry in public. I think you'll understand when you hear what I have to say.'

Olivia hesitated. She hadn't anticipated that he would ask to meet her in person. She had assumed he

216

would say his piece and that would be an end to the matter.

'Can you really not tell me over the phone?' she asked hopefully.

'Sorry, Toff, but no. I went to your house hoping to see you, but obviously you weren't there. Your father was, though, and he said some pretty damning things. I'm pretty sure you don't know about them, but I can guarantee you wouldn't want just any Tom, Dick or Harry hearing his accusations.'

Oliva rolled her eyes. What on earth had her father said now? She pursed her lips in thought. Surely there could be no harm in her paying her grandparents a visit, especially as she hadn't seen them since joining the WAAF. If she arranged to meet Ted for ten minutes in a public place, then where could be the harm in that?

'I'll see if I can get a bit of leave. I'm due some, so I can't see it being a problem. I'll write to let you know when I'm coming home.'

Ted wanted to whoop with joy. 'Brilliant! Just let me know and I'll come and meet you at the station.'

Startled by his response, Olivia spoke quickly. 'I'm coming back to see my grandparents, Ted. I don't mind meeting you for ten minutes, but that's all. A lot of water has passed under the bridge since I saw you last, and I don't fancy taking a trip back up river.'

'I see,' Ted said dejectedly. 'Only I think it best if I tell you the full story. That way you can choose whether to tell your folks or not.'

Olivia swallowed hard. Whatever her father had said, it sounded bad. 'Fair enough. I'll get back to you as soon as I know the dates.' She hesitated. 'It's a long haul from Shirehampton to Liverpool. I hope you're not messing me around, Ted.'

When he spoke next, she could hear the sincerity in his voice. 'The last thing I want to do is hurt you, and the only reason I'm getting back in touch is to set the record straight. If you don't want to see me again after that, then I'll respect your decision.'

'Thanks, Ted.'

He could hear the relief in her voice. 'Ta-ra, Toff.' He waited until he heard her receiver click down before hanging up. He'd made contact and she had agreed to come and see him in Liverpool. This was going to be his one shot at winning her back. He mustn't mess it up, not this time.

Olivia walked back to the billet where Maude and Josie were eagerly waiting her arrival.

She had hardly stepped foot through the door before an impatient Maude spoke up. 'Spill the beans!'

Josie nodded encouragingly. 'Don't keep us in suspenders!'

'I'm going to go home on leave,' said Olivia. She glanced around the billet, then lowered her voice. 'He wants to meet me at the station so that he can explain the situation before I have a chance to talk to my grand-parents. He said it's to do with something Dad said.'

Maude rolled her eyes. 'No surprises there! We guessed he'd put his oar in somewhere along the line.'

'If he only wants to make pitiful excuses for why he ran off, I'll swing for him, I swear I will. I'm not carting myself halfway across the country just so that he can make himself feel better.'

'Do you really think that's what this is about?' asked Maude doubtfully. 'Only I'd have thought he'd rather leave sleeping dogs lie than rake up the past, and don't you think it's a bit odd, him going to see your old feller? He's either stupid or arrogant, because most men would expect to be greeted down the barrel of a shotgun for leaving a girl in the lurch.'

Olivia nibbled the corner of her lip as she considered this. 'So you think there's more to this than meets the eye?'

'I should say so,' said Maude. 'Unless you think him stupid or arrogant, of course?'

Olivia shook her head decidedly. 'No, he might have got frightened off when he heard I was pregnant, but he's neither stupid nor arrogant.'

'Not like Ralph then,' said Josie, much to Olivia's surprise.

'Sorry?'

'He's a bit arrogant, don't you think? The way he used to talk about Beth, like he was better than her?'

'I know my Stanley's not exactly keen on him either,' Maude put in. 'He reckons Ralph struts his stuff like he's the cock of the walk.'

Olivia frowned. 'Why are you picking on Ralph?'

'We're not picking on him,' Josie said hastily, 'and you yourself said you weren't keen on the way he used to speak about Beth,' she added a touch reproachfully.

Olivia looked at Maude. 'You never told me that Stanley didn't like him.'

Maude shrugged. 'It's different with fellers. Stanley just wants to get his head down and do his duty, and he's not a stickler for the rules like Ralph – he'll accept the odd bit of baccy even if he's not too sure where it came from, whereas Ralph wouldn't dream of doing something like that. I s'pose Stanley's a little wary of Ralph, a lot of the fellers are.' She reached over and placed a comforting hand over Olivia's. 'I'm not saying that there's anything wrong with following the rules. Stanley and Ralph are just cut from a different cloth, that's all.'

Olivia was sure her friends weren't trying to be mean about Ralph, and Josie was right in saying that Olivia had often questioned Ralph's behaviour towards women. In fact, she had noticed the way that Ralph eyed men of lower rank, like they were lazy, or not trying hard enough. One thing her friends' observations had done was bring up her own doubts as to what she should tell Ralph, and she said as much to Josie and Maude, whilst keeping an eye on the occupants of the billet to make sure no one was earwigging. 'We may not be an item, but I wouldn't like him to think I was gadding off meeting other men, especially not old flames, and you know what the RAF's like for gossip.'

'I know what you're saying, but you know we won't say owt,' Maude reassured her, 'and everyone knows you've family in Liverpool, so it won't look suspicious you going there on leave. If someone does see you with Ted, you can say you bumped into him at the station – it's up to them to prove otherwise.'

Olivia nodded. 'You're right. I'm not doing anything wrong, so why do I feel like I am?'

''Cos you're honest to the bone, and you don't want to hurt Ralph's feelings,' said Josie promptly. She hesitated. 'Are you going to tell Beth?'

Olivia shook her head. 'I'll tell her I'm going home on leave but nothing else. It's not that I don't trust her, but she's been very distant since that business with the officer. I know she says she doesn't blame me, but she's a lot quieter than she used to be.'

Maude nodded. 'No matter what she says, something happened, and I reckon it was to do with you, because you're the only one she seems to be avoiding.'

Josie looked at Olivia inquisitively. 'Have you mentioned it to Ralph? I know you were thinking about it.'

Olivia pulled a face. 'Yes, but he insists that everything was fine when he dropped her off, which is odd, because I saw her and she definitely wasn't acting like everything was all right.'

Maude gave a small shrug. 'Then again, men aren't known for noticing this kind of thing.'

Olivia removed her skirt and slipped it on to a hanger. 'She was really worried about what would happen in the meeting. All I can think is that the experience took its toll – I just wish she'd talk it through.'

'Time's a good healer, she'll come round in the end,' Maude said firmly. 'She probably thinks it's best to keep herself to herself for now.'

Olivia nodded, but she wasn't so sure. There was no doubt in her mind that Beth was deliberately avoiding her, and only her.

Ted jogged up the steps to Lime Street Station. Olivia's train was due any minute, and he was determined to be there when she arrived. He walked the length of the platform, nervously fingering the flowers, only stopping after he saw a few petals fall to the ground. This was exactly what had happened the last time he had been here, although the nerves he felt this time were different from the last, and he very much hoped the outcome would prove different too.

His heart rose in his chest as he heard the sound of a train approaching the station. He was about to see Olivia for the first time in eighteen years – provided she hadn't got a case of cold feet, of course, he thought glumly. He stared along the carriages which chugged slowly past. His heart fell. There was no sign of Olivia. He thought back to the last time he had seen her. Would he even recognise her again? He knew he'd changed a lot over the years, so he presumed she must have too. He conjured up an image of her in his mind. Locks of ebony, green eyes, and the prettiest smile he had ever seen. As the train drew to a halt, the passengers began to alight. He knew she'd be in uniform, so he concentrated on the Waafs, but unless she'd changed a lot, she wasn't here. He scanned the crowd heading for the exit. Was it possible he'd missed her? He felt sure she would be keeping an eager eye out for him. With the train now empty, he dropped his arm which was carrying the bouquet and walked back along the platform. He was nearing the other end when a plump Waaf, standing with her back to him, her hair curled under, caught his eye. She was looking expectantly around her, as if she was waiting for someone. Ted coughed politely. 'Toff?'

Olivia turned to face him. 'Ted!'

He nodded, before hastily lifting the flowers up and thrusting them towards her. 'Long time no see, I trust you had a good journey.' He fired the words out in a barrage of nerves.

She took the flowers and sniffed the delicate scent. 'Thanks, Ted.' She glanced shyly at him. 'You look well.'

His eyes locked with hers. 'As do you.'

She blushed. 'I've put on a few pounds since I saw you last, but ...' She had been about to say that pregnancy did that sort of thing to a woman's figure, then changed her mind. She had to give him a chance.

He continued to gaze into her eyes, which sparkled at him, just as they had all those years ago. 'I can't say I've noticed ...' Realising that it was rude to stare, he glanced around the building. 'Looks a bit different to the last time you were here.'

Olivia glanced at the domed ceiling which had clearly suffered bomb damage. 'It certainly does ...' She sighed impatiently. 'I really don't wish to be rude, but can you speak your piece? I can't pretend I find this easy.'

Ted shook his head. 'Not here. I thought we could go to the Crown Hotel.'

She looked at him dubiously. 'A hotel? Why would you want to take me to a hotel?'

Ted could see that she was suspicious of his suggestion, so he quickly explained his reason. 'No funny business. I booked a room so that we can talk in private, but if you'd rather not, I completely understand.'

Olivia stared at him defensively. He looked genuine enough, but if he was planning some kind of seedy rendezvous then he could jolly well think again! She spoke in a cool manner. 'In whose name?'

Seeing the fire in her eyes, Ted swallowed before continuing. 'Mr and Mrs Hewitt, but please believe me, I only did it so that we could talk without being overheard. I think you'll understand when you hear what I have to say, but honest to God, Toff, no hanky panky, I'll swear on anything you want.'

She pursed her lips. 'I've a very dear friend called Ralph, and I don't want it getting back to him that I've shared a hotel room with my ...' she broke off for a moment, before carrying on, '... a man.'

Ted's heart sank. He didn't know who this Ralph was, but Olivia clearly thought a lot of him. 'I'm sorry, I wasn't thinking.' He looked at her from under his brows. 'What do you suggest?'

Olivia drew a deep breath. When it came down to it, she couldn't think of anywhere sufficiently private for them to discuss the pregnancy and whatever else Ted had on his mind, and the last thing she needed was for someone to overhear their conversation. She heaved a sigh. 'Seeing as you've already booked the room, we may as well go there.'

'Are you sure?'

She nodded. 'It may not be my ideal, but I can't think of anywhere else.'

They spent the short walk to the hotel in silence. When they arrived at the Crown, Olivia waited whilst Ted booked in at reception. The whole time she stood beside him, her nerves were telling her to forget the whole thing and go to her grandparents', but a spark of curiosity was getting the better of her. Not only that, but to walk out now would be unfair. Ted deserved a chance. He got the key and together they ascended the stairs to their room.

Once inside, Ted placed her suitcase on the bed and wandered over to the window. He turned to face her. 'You get a good view from here, although it's not one you'd remember.'

Olivia walked cautiously towards the window and looked over the city before her. 'Oh, Ted.' She put a hand to her mouth. 'I knew it was bad, of course I did, but I didn't realise it was *this* bad.' She turned to face him. 'Were you here, during the Blitz?'

He nodded. 'It was like hell on earth. I honestly thought we'd had it. I've never seen so many planes, it's a wonder anything's left.'

She leaned against the chest of drawers, her back to the window. 'So I see, only we didn't come here to discuss the war.'

Ted drew a deep breath. 'I don't know exactly what your father told you, but whatever it was, it wasn't true. He turned up at our house, accused me of stealing and said that if we didn't leave Liverpool on the next train he'd report me and Dad to the scuffers.' He rubbed the back of his neck with the palm of his hand. 'Your father's a powerful man, with friends in high places. We couldn't take the risk, so we left.'

Olivia wanted to believe him with every bone in her body, but she was reluctant to do so until she'd heard more. 'Stealing what exactly?' she asked quietly.

'His koi carp,' Ted said bluntly. He shoved his hands into his pockets. 'It would be his word against mine, and you don't have to be Einstein to know who they'd believe. I swear I didn't know about the pregnancy until I came back to Liverpool.' He told her about the chance encounter with his old workmate.

Olivia listened in stunned silence. 'So, he really was lying?'

Ted gazed into her eyes. 'It pains me to think you believed I'd run off, because nothing could be further from the truth. Wild horses couldn't have pulled me away had I known you were carrying our baby. I'd have done anything to look after you.'

Olivia nodded. 'Why couldn't you have told me that over the telephone?'

He gazed at the floor before looking up. His eyes, when they met hers, spoke volumes. 'There's more.'

She felt her heart plummet. What had her father said that was making him look at her in such a dark and foreboding manner?

'As I said on the telephone,' he went on, 'I went to Aigburth Drive hoping to find you, but the only person I saw was your father,' being a man of his word, Ted was determined to keep Mavis's involvement quiet. 'I told him I knew the truth and that I wanted to speak to you, but he refused to tell me where you were, so I said I'd find you for myself.' He blew his cheeks out. 'I thought he was going to cave my head in with that new cane of his, he was mad as fire, but he's not stupid, he knew I'd be quicker than him, so he took a different tack.' He drew a deep breath before letting it out slowly. 'He told me you'd had an abortion ...'

'*What?*' squeaked Olivia. She clutched one of the bedknobs for support. 'It's not true, Ted, I'd never ...'

He held up a hand. 'I know you didn't. I can't say who because I swore I wouldn't tell, but someone in the know told me that your father was lying and that our baby was stillborn. I can't understand what he had to gain from telling such a whopper, other than to keep me away from you, of course.'

'Well, I'd have found out he'd been lying to me for the past eighteen years for a start,' Olivia said bitterly.

'I'll never forgive your father for the lies he's told, but there's no sense in dwelling on the past,' Ted said. 'I'd like to take some flowers to the grave wherever that may be. I know you went to Scotland, but no more than that. I don't even know if our baby was a boy or a girl.'

Olivia looked at him shamefaced. 'Neither do I. They never told me, and when I asked Dad he said it was best all round for me to pretend it never happened, so the less I knew the better.'

Ted looked at her aghast. 'He seriously said that? As if you could walk away and forget all about it?'

Olivia sighed heavily. 'My father's not exactly in touch with his emotions, he probably thinks that's possible.' Her eyes flicked up to meet his. 'It's not, of course.'

Ted stood up from leaning against the bedstead. 'What about the funeral? What did they put on the headstone? Was there a headstone?'

Olivia held her head in her hands. 'I don't know, Ted. I'd just given birth, and it was quite an ordeal. I was ashamed of my condition, ashamed of my age and the fact that I was with my father and not my husband. I didn't want to draw any more attention to myself than necessary, and when Dad said he'd take care of everything I was more than happy for him to do so. I just wanted to get home and pretend none of it had ever happened.' As she looked up he could see her cheeks were wet with tears. 'You should have seen the way they were looking at me, Ted; it was like I was the worst person in the world. I just wanted to get as far away from them as I could, not dwell on my disgrace.'

Ted started towards her, his arms held out. His eyes locked with hers, imploring her to allow him to comfort her. Olivia did nothing to rebuke his attempt and he engulfed her in a tight embrace, speaking soothingly into her ear. 'I'm so sorry you had to go through that on your own. Things would have been different had I known.'

Olivia felt a bubble of desire begin to slowly rise in her body as he continued to hold her. Fearing what might happen if she didn't break off his embrace, she pushed him away and dried her eyes. 'Don't, Ted. I know you mean well, but we've been here once before many years ago, and I've no wish to go there again.'

Ted hung his head in shame. 'Sorry, I just wanted to make you feel better.'

She nodded. 'Like last time ...'

He sank down on to the bed. 'I know.' He looked at her through anxious eyes. 'I know I haven't the right to ask, but I really would like to go and pay my respects, only I wouldn't know where to start. Do you think your father would tell you if you asked him outright?'

Olivia shrugged. 'When I told him I was joining up he told me to get out and never return. In fact, he's only recently got in contact with me, and I reckon that's because he wants to see if I've heard from you.' She

228

gave him a grim smile. 'He suggested I might pop round if I'm in Liverpool, so I can ask, but I don't know whether I'll get an answer.'

Ted gave her a fleeting smile. 'Thanks. Have you arranged to see him whilst you're home?'

Olivia nodded. 'Can't say I'm looking forward to it, especially as I'm going to be asking him about the past. He wasn't keen on talking about it then, and I should imagine he's even less keen to talk about it now.'

'Sorry if I'm opening old wounds,' Ted said, 'but it's important to me. It may sound silly, but I don't want our child to think I didn't even bother to say goodbye.'

Olivia bowed her head in shame. 'It doesn't sound silly at all, Ted. Truth be told, I feel terrible for not asking more questions. It wasn't because I didn't care, but I didn't want to revisit the past.' She looked up at him. 'I've always wanted to let him or her know that I was sorry, but I've spent so long burying it, I'm terrified of acknowledging the truth. I'd certainly not be brave enough to do it on my own, so if he tells me where our baby's buried, could I come with you?'

Ted gazed at her mournfully. 'Of course you can. In fact, I rather hoped you would.'

Her bottom lip wobbled as she smiled. 'Thanks, Ted.'

He tucked a loose lock of hair behind her ear before placing a tentative arm around her shoulders and was pleased to see she didn't shy away. 'Are you sure you want to do this? Because once you see that grave, there's no going back, no pretending it didn't happen.'

She blinked at him. 'I need to do it. Pretending nothing happened never worked, I realise that now. I just hid it in the depths of my mind hoping it would go away, but it's still there, and that's where it'll stay, slowly eating away at me, until I face the truth.' She gazed out of the window. 'Pretending something didn't happen doesn't make it disappear.' She turned her gaze to Ted, and she could see the empathy in his eyes. 'I shall do the best I can to find out where our baby's buried. If Dad won't tell me, I'll ring the registrar's office in Glasgow, they're bound to have it on record.'

'Good idea,' said Ted. 'Let me know if I can do anything. I don't mind making a few phone calls, although I don't know whether they're allowed to give out that kind of information.'

'I'll cross that bridge when or rather if I come to it,' said Olivia. She smiled at Ted. 'I won't deny I was worried about seeing you again after all these years, but I'm glad I did.' Her eyes rested on his ring finger. 'Not married?'

He also looked down at his finger. 'I was, only I wasn't rich or ambitious enough for her.'

Olivia raised her eyebrows. 'You mean you were too good for her!'

She couldn't imagine why any woman wouldn't find Ted to be enough, and whilst she was sad to hear that his marriage had not worked out, she also felt a sense of relief, which brought another thought to the forefront of her mind. Olivia had told herself as well as her friends that she had held back with Ralph because she didn't think he'd approve if he found out about her past, but now that she was here in front of Ted, she had to wonder whether that was just an excuse and the real reason was because she had never stopped loving Ted.

Ted opened the door to their room. 'I won't walk you out in case someone sees us.'

She smiled. 'Ever the gent.'

'I try.' He grinned before kissing her lightly on the cheek. 'Ta-ra, Toff.'

Olivia began to descend the stairs then turned to look at him from over her shoulder. 'Goodbye, Ted. I'll be in touch.'

Ted watched as she disappeared from view, then went back into the room, closed the door and walked over to the window, where he continued to watch as she exited the hotel and walked down the street. He crossed his fingers. Toff had said she had a close friend called Ralph, but just how close were they? If he was to stand any chance of winning her back, he'd know within the next few ... He grinned. Olivia had turned to look up at the room he was in. He waved at her from the window and she waved back. Turning away from the window, he had to refrain from keeping the strut out of his stride. It was early days, too early for him to act as if he'd won his belle, because that's how he still saw her, even after all these years. His feelings had never faded. A pang of guilt stabbed him. Could Toff be the reason why his marriage had failed? Because he had been secretly yearning for his past love? Had he been distant with Isobel? He shook his head. His heart might never have belonged to Isobel, but he had done all he could to make the marriage work, and who knows? If Isobel had treated him half as well as he had treated her, perhaps he wouldn't be yearning for Toff ... A small smile curved his lips. He knew that wasn't true. He hadn't broken things off with Toff because he'd lost his love for her – they'd been forced apart, which was totally different. It might seem presumptuous of him to want to carry on where they'd left off, but he couldn't help the way he felt. To him nothing had changed – in fact, if anything, absence had only made his heart grow fonder.

Outside, Olivia scolded herself for turning round to look up at the window. Although if she hadn't, she would never have known that he was watching her, and she needed to know.

Walking away from her first love, it felt as though no time had passed since their last encounter. The desire for love and companionship had returned with lightning speed, and when he had held her in the hotel room, her body had ached for him to go further, to share the lovemaking that had made her feel so loved and wanted, but she was older and wiser now. She knew that sex wasn't always shared between lovers; sometimes it was a reaction to an emotion which should not be confused with love. A glimmer of guilt flickered in her mind as she thought of Ralph, and how patient he had been. She had never felt a passion towards Ralph as she did towards Ted, which was odd, because Ralph was what you'd call typically handsome. She swapped her suitcase from one hand to the other. If she felt more passion towards Ted, then it was because he was Ted. It had nothing to do with looks, it was his soul which she desired. She chastised herself. Ralph was a lovely man, a little judgemental, but otherwise kind, courteous and God only knows he was patient. A small voice from the back of her mind spoke its thoughts. *But he doesn't love you, Liv, not the same way*

Ted does. Ted's love is plain to see, there's a passion, a desire, a connection – Ralph has none of that. She faltered mid-step. She had never considered that Ralph didn't have strong feelings for her before. He certainly spoke as though he did, yet this thought had entered her mind with such clarity, she wondered whether it was true. Or was she just trying to make excuses to get back to a time in her life when she was truly happy, before it all went wrong?

Olivia hadn't planned to see her father until the day she was due to leave for Shirehampton, but Ted had lit a fire in her belly and she was determined to strike whilst the iron was hot. She waited for the tram which would take her on the first leg of her journey to Aigburth Drive. She wasn't looking forward to seeing her father, but he had brought this on himself; she wasn't the one in the wrong. She would have to be firm, and make sure he knew she wouldn't take silence for an answer.

With her mind made up, Beth knocked on the door of her flight officer and waited until she heard a gruff voice from the other side ordering 'Enter'.

She walked in and saluted smartly.

'Stand at ease.' The officer eyed her expectantly. 'What brings you to my office?'

'I'd like to be considered for a different posting, sir.'

'Really, and why would that be?' he said, pulling a sheet of paper towards him and reaching for his pen. 'I was under the impression that you were happy here.'

'I am, but . . .' said Beth, only to be chopped off before she could get the rest of her sentence out.

'Then I don't see any reason to post you elsewhere. Was there anything else?'

Beth shook her head. She knew it had been a long shot.

'Jolly good, dismiss.'

Beth saluted before leaving. Ever since her encounter with Ralph, she had felt uneasy in Olivia's presence. Wanting desperately to tell her friend the truth but fearing the consequences of doing so, the guilt was driving her to distraction. Especially when she overheard one of the Waafs telling Olivia how lucky she was to have a man like Ralph courting her affection.

'Gettin' my feller to write more than a few lines is like tryin' to get blood out of a stone! But Ralph must write to you a couple of times a week, and such lengthy letters too. He's obviously smitten!'

Beth had wanted to stand up and tell the whole billet exactly what Ralph was like, but of course she couldn't. She was finding it harder and harder to hold her tongue, so when Olivia announced she was going home on leave, Beth thought this would be the ideal time to request a transfer. If she was granted her wish, she would be gone before Olivia returned.

Now, as she crossed the yard, she heard Josie call out her name.

Beth waited for Josie to catch up.

'What's up? You look like you've found a penny and lost a pound!'

Beth shrugged. She hadn't planned on telling the girls she was asking for a new posting until she had one foot out of the door, but she was so upset with the flight officer's decision she didn't bother to hide the

234

fact that she wanted to leave Shirehampton. 'Had my request for a move denied.'

Josie looked stunned. 'I didn't know you wanted to move. Has something happened?'

Beth shook her head. 'They say a change is as good as a rest. I thought it might be nice to see somewhere new, maybe a bit closer to a town.'

Josie nodded. 'It can be a bit boring out here. I've often longed for Innsworth, and I never thought I'd say that.'

Beth smiled wistfully. 'I wish I was back there.'

'This doesn't have anything to do with that spiteful officer, does it, the one who dobbed you and Ralph in?'

Beth gave a shrug. 'I suppose that was the straw that broke the camel's back.'

'Oh,' said Josie, 'I thought everything was all right before that? Have you really been unhappy for that long?'

'I've not, it's …' Beth heaved a sigh, 'it's complicated.'

Josie placed her hand on top of Beth's shoulder and gave it a comforting squeeze. 'You know you can talk to me about anything, don't you?'

Beth nodded. 'Of course.' Her eyes flickered towards the cookhouse. 'Sorry, Josie, but I'm already running a tad late.'

Josie nodded. 'Promise me you'll come for a chat should you need to?'

Beth nodded and waved goodbye as she headed in the opposite direction.

Josie promptly made for their billet. Until that business with the officer, Beth had been quite vocal about her happiness at Shirehampton, saying how it was the first base she'd ever had proper girlfriends, and that she enjoyed being part of a group. Hearing her say now that the officer's complaint was the straw that broke the camel's back suggested she had been unhappy prior to the incident, and Josie found this hard to believe.

She entered the hut and saw Maude. Making her way over, Josie told Maude of Beth's denied request for a transfer, and her reasons for it.

Maude shook her head. 'Beth was fine before the investigation. Olivia's right when she says Beth changed the day she came back – only that was ages ago. I don't think it's any coincidence that Beth waited until Olivia went on leave before asking for a new posting. The only thing I don't understand is why. I can't imagine Beth seriously holds Olivia responsible, not after all this time.'

'And she got proven innocent,' said Josie, 'so there's no need for her to give it a second thought, but it's almost like she's brooding over it.'

'Do you think we should say something?' said Maude.

Josie shrugged. 'I've already tried asking her, but she said it was complicated.'

'Hmmm,' said Maude thoughtfully, 'that sounds to me like an excuse not to tell the truth.'

Josie ran her tongue over her bottom lip. 'Do you think it has anything to do with Ralph?'

Maude frowned. 'I don't see how.'

Josie eyed Maude wretchedly. 'I know we say we got Beth wrong, but I'm not so sure. What if she tried it on with Ralph whilst she was away, and he turned her down, and now she feels guilty?'

Maude's eyes widened with the enormity of her friend's suggestion. 'Blimey, Josie, you don't pull your punches, do you?'

Josie shrugged. 'I just can't think why she's so distant, and Olivia's right when she says Beth's only odd around her, because she's fine with the rest of us.'

'Which is why I don't think she's done anything, because if she had she'd feel just as guilty around us because we're close friends with Liv. Besides, we know how Ralph feels about women like that. He didn't want to know Beth and was vocal in his judgement that she was promiscuous, so he'd be the first to blow the whistle if she'd done anything improper.'

Josie blew her cheeks out. 'Well, that's me fresh out of ideas.'

Maude looked thoughtful. 'It's been pretty dull round here lately. How about an evening out? Perhaps that would cheer her up – I know it would cheer me up.'

Josie nodded. 'She did say she missed being close to a town, so perhaps this is a case of cabin fever?'

'Could be,' said Maude. 'Beth's probably missing some male companionship. Let's face it, we've not got a lot of men on base, and the ones we have got are either old as the hills or ugly as sin.'

Josie burst out laughing. 'When you put it that way, it's easy to see why she's fed up.'

Beth entered the hut and headed for her friends. 'What's tickled your fancy?'

'Maude's description of the men on base,' giggled Josie. She straightened her face. 'We've been saying how it would be nice to get off base for a bit, what do you reckon?'

Beth nodded gladly. 'I could do with letting my hair down. When do you have in mind?'

Maude shrugged. 'As soon as we can arrange for passes.'

Beth and Josie began to discuss different options for their evening out, whilst Maude sat, her chin on her knuckles, deep in thought. They had readily jumped to the conclusion of cabin fever, but there had to be more to it than that. She would wait until Olivia returned and see whether Beth was still giving their friend a wide berth.

Olivia knocked on the front door, noting how odd it felt to knock on the door which was once her home. As she waited, she half hoped that her father would not be there so that she wouldn't have to confront her demons, but after a moment or so she heard light footsteps approaching the door and assumed it had to be Mavis.

The door opened a crack and an elderly lady peered through the gap. 'Can I help you?'

Olivia nodded. 'Is my father at home?'

The door opened further. 'Sorry?'

'My father?' She held out a hand, 'I'm Olivia Campbell.'

The door now fully opened and the old lady ushered her in. 'Goodness me! I am sorry, Miss Campbell, I thought we were expecting you on Wednesday?'

Olivia nodded. 'Change of plans. Is he here?'

The elderly maid gave a grim smile, one that was familiar to anyone who dealt with William Campbell. 'He's in his study, I'll let him know you're here.'

'Thank you,' said Olivia. 'Is Mavis not around?'

'Oh goodness me, no, she left to join the ATS. I'm Annie, her replacement.'

Olivia watched as the old woman made her way to the study. She wondered what else had changed in her absence. As she gazed around her, her eyes automatically focused on the door to her mother's bedroom. Aigburth House was a considerable size; she was surprised her father hadn't decided to move somewhere a little smaller, perhaps a nice flat or bungalow. Her heart skipped a beat as her father emerged from his study. He was walking a lot more slowly than she remembered, although he was still using the horrible cane which he had brought back from Scotland. She eyed the silver handle, thanking the powers that be that he hadn't had it to hand the day she had run to Ted, because she might not be here today if he had.

Her father gave her a grunt of recognition, before indicating she go ahead of him into the living room.

She waited for him to sit down before taking the seat opposite. She smiled fleetingly at him. 'How are you?'

He shrugged in a petulant manner. 'As well as can be expected when living on my own.' His eyes met hers. 'You?'

She nodded. 'I'm doing well,' quickly adding, before she could chicken out, 'I saw Ted earlier.'

Her father bristled. 'Did you now? By God, has that man no shame? Anyone else would've left well alone

– just goes to show how desperate he is to get his foot through the door.'

Olivia waited patiently for her father to finish. Her face impassive, she asked him outright, 'Why did you tell him I'd had an abortion?' She watched his face carefully. He didn't look shocked, and his eyes weren't darting around his head as he tried to seek an excuse. For once, it looked as if she was going to get the truth.

'You're better off without him,' he said simply.

'And is that why you accused him of stealing your koi? Because you needed to get rid of him before he found out I was pregnant?'

William gave his daughter a calculating stare before answering. 'I did what I thought was best at the time.'

She nodded. 'So you kept telling me. I remember you saying it was better for me not to know anything about my baby, not even the sex, and maybe you were right at the time, but a lot of water has gone under the bridge since then, and I'm no longer the naive chit of a girl I once was, which is why I've come to see you. In short, I want to know more.'

Her father shot her a glance. 'Funny how you're only asking now *he's* turned up on the scene.'

Olivia eyed him levelly. 'I always wanted to know, I just didn't have the courage to ask, and yes, that's down to Ted, but it was always there. Olivia knew her father was trying to deflect the conversation, something she wouldn't allow. Where did you bury our baby, *your* grandchild?'

William stared at her. Out of all the questions he expected her to ask, this obviously had not been one of them, and for the first time in her life, Olivia found her father was almost lost for words. 'I – I can't remember,' he said lamely.

Olivia felt her temper beginning to rise. If Ted hadn't turned up on the scene she very much suspected her father would not have had an issue with answering her question; he was only pretending not to remember to spite Ted. 'What do you mean, you can't remember? How many babies have you buried, Dad?'

He shot her a reproving glance. 'Don't be ridiculous, Liv. It was a long time ago, I can't remember everything that happened around that time. You weren't the only one who was distraught.'

She almost choked at his outlandish statement. 'Distraught? You? You've never been distraught in your life, not even when your own wife was dying!'

Despite his initial appearance, William had more gusto than Olivia bargained for. He stood up so sharply his chair toppled over behind him. His face purple with rage, he bellowed, 'How *dare* you!' He thrust his arm out in the direction of the living room door. 'Get out!'

Olivia shook her head. 'If you want me out, you'll have to tell me where my baby's buried. Tell me that and I'll leave, and I promise you'll never see me again.'

To her surprise, William picked up his chair and sank back into his seat. 'But that's not what I want.'

'Then stop pushing me away and tell me where my baby's buried,' she said coolly.

His jaw flinched. 'I know you'll say I'm wrong, but you were happy enough leaving things be. Why stir things up now, Olivia? It's been over eighteen years!'

Olivia leaned forward. 'Only I wasn't happy leaving things be, I just didn't have the courage to address the issue, and no matter what you think of him, Ted has given me that courage, and not so that he can get his feet under the table, but because he wants to pay his respects, acknowledge the birth and death of his own child, something which you denied him. And I want to do the same. You think I put it all behind me, but I didn't – perhaps this will allow me to do so.' She waved a vague hand. 'I don't even know what name you put on the headstone, or didn't you put a name? Maybe just our surname?' She hesitated. 'Did you put in loving memory?' Seeing his blank expression, her next words were spoken in hollow tones. 'Please tell me there was a headstone ...'

He folded his hands over the top of the cane's handle and rested his chin on them. 'You have to believe me when I say I did what I thought best at the time.'

A tear trickled down her cheek. 'Only it's not about you or me, it's acknowledging the existence of a child, and showing your respect.'

'I did what I thought best,' William repeated quietly.

'So you keep saying,' snapped Olivia. She looked at the deep lines which creased her father's face. She might not agree with his decisions, or even like him all that much, but he was an old man, set in his ways and of a different generation. She relented slightly. 'Just tell me the name of the church – the vicar will have a record of the burial.'

William lowered his head. 'Too long ago.'

Olivia flapped her arms down by her side in exasperation. 'Fine! I'll contact every church in Glasgow myself!'

But William wasn't listening. 'Don't do this, Olivia, it'll only cause more pain.'

Olivia stared at him, deeply confused. 'I don't understand why you won't tell me!'

William sighed heavily. 'Because there was no burial. I thought it best to have a cremation.'

Olivia's hand flew to her mouth and she began to gabble her incomprehension. 'Why on earth would you do something like that? You don't even believe in cremation, so why do it to your own flesh and blood?'

'Because I thought it for the best,' snapped William irritably. 'That baby brought nothing but trouble from the moment it was conceived – better if it was erased from history.'

Olivia jumped up, tears streaming down her face, and ran to the door. 'It? *It?* I know you can be a mean, cantankerous pig of a man, but to refer to your own grandchild as "*it*"? How can you sit there and cast the blame on an innocent child?' She didn't wait for him to answer. 'I hate you!' She left the room and ran across the hall.

Her father stumbled as he tried to get to his feet. 'Olivia, wait!'

'You're a heartless vile, old man,' she yelled. 'I never want to see you again as long as I live!' She raced down the drive, so upset that she didn't stop running until she had reached Aigburth Road. Seeing a bus just about to pull away from the stand, she waved at the clippie who was looking out for potential passengers. 'Wait!'

She jumped on to the back of the bus and quickly took a seat before the clippie rang the bell. Turning to face the window so that she might hide her tears from the other passengers, she hastily wiped her face dry with the palms of her hands. The clippie approached her tentatively and asked her for the fare, which Olivia handed over, careful to keep her eyes lowered.

The clippie smiled shyly as she gave Olivia her ticket. 'Are you all right, luvvy?'

Olivia nodded. 'Not been home for a while,' she mumbled by way of explanation for her tears.

The clippie nodded slowly. 'Probably come as quite a shock seeing the city looking the way it does.' With the presumption that this was what Olivia had been referring to, she carried on up the aisle taking fares.

Relieved that the young girl hadn't continued, Olivia replayed the conversation with her father in her mind. How could he have her baby cremated when it went against his religion? Did he really hate the baby that much? What sort of man hated a baby?

By the time she reached her grandparents', Olivia decided it best all round if she kept the unplanned meeting with her father to herself. There was no sense in upsetting Nana and Pops, who would be devastated at her revelation. She would tell them of her meeting with Ted and leave it at that. When it came to her planned visit to her father, she would make an excuse and hope they didn't push the matter.

When she arrived at their house on Ullet Road, all thoughts of her father dissipated as she hugged her grandparents for the first time in a long while. It was lovely to see them both looking so well. Naturally they were inquisitive about her time with Ted, but Olivia kept most of the conversation to herself, simply telling them what Ted had already told them, adding that the two of them had made their peace and gone their separate ways. She felt awful lying to them, but knew if she spoke the truth her grandparents would insist she go to her father immediately and ask where her baby was buried.

However, the next morning as they sat down for breakfast, her grandmother raised the subject of Wednesday's visit, and was dismayed when Olivia told her she had changed her mind.

'Your mother would be ever so upset to think you and your father were no longer on speaking terms, and you did say you'd go and see him whilst you were home,' said Nana reasonably.

'Only because she didn't know the truth,' said Olivia firmly. 'No one knows what that man's really like. If they did, they wouldn't ask me to go and see him.'

'No one, meaning me?' Nana enquired. 'Because if that's what you think, you couldn't be more wrong. Me and your grandfather knew your father before he met our Catherine. We've seen how callous he can be, but he was different with our Catherine – you too, for that matter.'

Olivia stared at her grandmother in disbelief. 'Even if that was the case, it was only until his father died – that's when he showed his true colours.'

Nana wagged a reproving finger. 'I know he did wrong by you and Ted, but he thought he was doing the right thing, and whilst I know you believe him to be heartless, his heart was in the right place, even if misguided.'

Olivia heaved a sigh. 'Believe me, Nana, he might have put on a good show for the outside world, you and Pops included, but I know what it was like living with him. I know the real William Campbell, and if you thought him cruel and callous before, you haven't a clue how vile that man can be.'

Her grandmother's eyebrows shot towards her hairline. 'Liv! What on earth would make you say such a thing? I thought you two had started to mend bridges. What's happened to make you change your mind, and why are you so angry?'

Olivia stared at the jar of Robertson's jam. How could she tell her grandmother why she hated him so much without revealing the truth? She cast the older woman a fleeting glance. 'Maybe I'll visit him next time I'm home.'

Her grandmother shook her head in a chiding fashion. 'He's not getting any younger, and with this war, none of us can be sure of a tomorrow.'

'Fingers crossed,' muttered Olivia beneath her breath, although, as it turned out, not quietly enough as far as her grandmother was concerned.

'That's enough! I don't care what he's done, you shouldn't say things like that.'

Something inside Olivia snapped. 'Really? So it wouldn't bother you to know that he'd had my baby, your great-grandchild, cremated?'

Olivia's grandmother reeled backwards, clutching one of the dining chairs and sinking into it, a hand to her forehead. She stared at Olivia. 'I don't know what poisonous little wretch told you that, but ...'

Olivia cut her grandmother off without apology. 'He did. I went to see him today. I didn't tell you because I didn't want you knowing what he'd said, but I'm sorry,

Nana, I couldn't sit by and hear you trying to make excuses for his behaviour when I knew what he'd done.'

Nana shook her head in disbelief. 'But he's Catholic, he doesn't believe in cremation, or rather he does, but not in a positive sense.'

'I know,' said Olivia. Her fingers trembling, she fished her handkerchief out of her pocket and blew her nose loudly before continuing. 'Why condemn your own flesh and blood in such a fashion?'

Nana placed a comforting hand over Olivia's. 'I've no idea, Liv, I can't imagine what was going through his mind at the time. Did he say anything else?'

Olivia shook her head. 'I told him what I thought of him before I ran out. I didn't want to stay in that house a second longer than necessary.'

'I don't blame you,' said her grandfather gruffly. Until now he had stayed out of the conversation. 'The man's twisted. I think you're wise to cut your losses and chop him out of your life.'

His wife looked doubtful. 'I know what he did was wrong, and I can't fathom why he would do such a thing, but I'm not sure it's in Liv's best interests to cut her father out of her life. Like it or not, he is her father.'

'Biologically,' said Olivia simply, 'but it takes more than that to be father. I agree with Pops.'

Nana frowned at her husband. 'Well, you shouldn't listen to everything your grandfather tells you …' She rapidly tapped her forefinger against her lips. 'There's something about all of this which is troubling me.'

'Troubling all of us,' said Pops.

Nana eyed her husband. 'Where did you put my old diaries?'

'In the attic. Why?'

She pursed her lips. 'I seem to remember him coming back from Glasgow with a different tale to the one he's told our Liv, and I'm hoping I wrote it down in my diary.'

'Doesn't matter what he told you,' said Olivia. 'The man's full of lies. I very much doubt he'd know the truth if it slapped him in the face.'

Placing both hands on the arms of his chair, Pops got to his feet. 'Well, I for one don't intend to waste another second trying to work out what's going on in that man's mind, not when our Liv's going to be catching a train in a couple of days.'

Nana nodded apologetically. 'You're right.' She smiled at Olivia. 'What would you like to do with the rest of your time with us?'

Olivia sighed, grateful that the conversation concerning her father was at an end. 'How about lunch at Lyons …' she paused, '… please tell me Lyons is still there?'

Her grandmother nodded. 'It was one of the lucky ones.'

Olivia gathered the empty plates. 'Do they still do those lovely fruit tartlets?'

Pops grinned. 'They certainly do, and they're just as good as they ever were.'

'Then Lyons it is!'

Olivia's time with her grandparents had been memorable. They had done all the things they used to do when she was a child, going for strolls through Sefton Park, feeding the ducks, and taking the tram to Princes Park for a picnic. They had even taken her for a wander around the city, showing her where Blacklers and Lewis's new stores could be found, and in the evenings they had played cribbage and rummy, and Nana's favourite, draughts, whilst they reminisced on the things they used to do with her mother before she had become unwell. The day trips to New Brighton fair, and the open-air swimming pool, or further afield to Southport where they ate cockles as they walked barefoot along the beach which stretched as far as the eye could see. Olivia enjoyed reliving these good times because none of them included her father, who had always insisted that he was too busy with work to go with them.

A few days later it was with a heavy heart that Olivia boarded the train which would take her on the first leg of her journey. She leaned out of the window as her grandmother clutched her husband's hand.

'Don't forget to write!' called Nana. 'And make sure you keep your eye on the stops – you don't want to get off in the wrong place!'

'She's old enough to look after herself, Matilda,' said Pops, and turned his attention back to Olivia as the train wheels gained traction. 'Ta-ra, queen!'

Giving them a wobbly smile, Olivia waved back. 'I will! Love you!'

Nana was just calling back that she loved Olivia too, when the train driver blew the whistle, causing her to start.

They waved until their granddaughter had disappeared from view.

Tucking her hand into the crook of her husband's elbow, Matilda told Ivor, 'We need to find my old diaries in the attic.'

He pulled a disgruntled face. 'Why? Just so you can see what William told you back in the day? I don't see as it matters what he says, the man doesn't know how to tell the truth. It wouldn't surprise me if he believes his own lies.'

Her eyes flashed up at him. 'So you think he's lying?'

Her husband gave a half-shrug. 'I can't see why, although if he were, it would be a real humdinger!'

She tutted irritably. 'I reckon you're too lazy to go into the attic to check.'

'It's nothing to do with me being lazy, although I'll admit I don't relish the idea of going up there, because I can't see what good can come from it.'

Nana sucked her lips in before letting them out with a smacking noise. 'Because there's something really fishy about all of this, and I think we should have questioned him a long time ago, instead of turning a blind eye and taking his word on everything. Let's face it, Ivor, we were both surprised at how well he handled the situation.'

Her husband's patience was beginning to wear thin. 'What could he possibly be hiding that was so awful? No matter which way you look at it, our great-grandchild didn't make it. In my book, that's as bad as it gets.'

Matilda agreed with her husband, but deep down she had an uneasy feeling that William was hiding something much bigger than the death of their great-grandchild. The question was, what?

*

Back in Shirehampton Maude and Josie were eager to hear their friend's news regarding her trip home to Liverpool.

'What's the city like?' asked Maude, as Olivia joined them at their table. 'Mam and Dad say it's not too bad, and not to worry, but I've heard the news reports same as the rest of you, and I think they're playing it down so as not to upset me.'

Olivia set her lips into a grim line. 'It's bad, Maude, but the people are in good spirits, which is what's important.'

Maude nodded. 'I thought as much.' She gently blew over the surface of her tea. 'So how did it go with Ted?'

Olivia briefly considered her answer. 'Good. As you'd imagine, it was a bit awkward at first, but once we got talking it was as if no time had passed.'

Gazing steadily at Olivia, Josie rested the side of her face against the palm of her hand. 'What news did he have on your father?'

Olivia took a deep breath before telling them everything, from the moment she stepped off the train in Lime Street Station to the moment she got back on.

'Bloody hell!' breathed Josie. 'I reckon your grandfather's right, Liv, you want to cut that man out of your life like you would a cancer.'

Maude agreed. 'I don't understand. My father's nothing like yours, and if that's what money does to a person, then I think you're better off without it.'

'Me too,' said Olivia. 'I can't think why Nana wants me to have anything to do with him, but she does.' She glanced around the empty hut. 'Where's Beth?'

Maude and Josie exchanged glances.

Olivia gave them a questioning look. 'What?'

'As soon as you'd gone she applied to be transferred,' said Josie.

'Only she got turned down,' Maude added hastily.

Olivia looked at them, surprised. 'She asked to be moved? But why?'

'That's what we've been wondering,' said Maude. She leaned forward conspiratorially. 'She says she wants to go somewhere with a bit more life, so we've taken her on a couple of trips out to make her feel better, but she's still insisting she wants to leave Shirehampton. Josie asked whether it was to do with that officer, and she said the officer was the straw that broke the camel's back.'

A frown creased Olivia's brow. 'But that happened ages ago and she was acquitted, so why would she still want to leave?'

Josie looked at Maude who nodded approvingly.

'We reckon it's summat to do with Ralph,' said Josie, 'because whenever we mention his name, she rolls her eyes or gets up and leaves the room ...'

'And her face dropped when she heard you were back,' Maude added.

'Me?' said Olivia, her voice full of astonishment. 'What've I done?'

'Nothing!' said Josie. 'As I said, we think it's something to do with Ralph. Everyone knows how he keen he is on you, which is why I think she's treating you the same as she does him.'

Olivia's shoulders sagged as a thought occurred to her. 'You don't think he's been mean to her again, do you? Only I remember the day they came back, and

Beth was quieter than I thought she'd be, but Ralph was his usual self, quite upbeat, and I know how horrible he can be when he talks about women being free and easy. He might not have meant to have upset her, but you know what fellers can be like – speak first, think later!'

Josie looked at Maude who shot her a warning glance, but Josie continued anyway. 'I know we all said we believed Beth when she said she wasn't a maneater, but I'm not so sure.' She went on quickly as she saw a doubtful look cross Olivia's face, 'We know she had her sights set on Ralph from the moment she clapped eyes on him, and that you two only became friends because you ...' she sought the right words, '... embellished the truth, which got her off the hook. I reckon she spun you a yarn to make herself look better and we all fell for it.'

'What are you saying?' said Olivia, although she had a nasty feeling in the pit of her stomach that she knew exactly what her friend was driving at.

'I'm saying, I think she tried to kiss Ralph or to win his favour after the inquest, and we all know how Ralph feels about women like that, so we know he'd have turned her down flat, which must be why she gets annoyed when we mention his name, and she doesn't like being around you because she feels guilty.'

'Perhaps you should ask Ralph if anything happened,' said Maude. 'Because you deserve to know if you're lying with wolves.'

Olivia looked doubtful. 'Ralph would have been crowing it from the rooftops if that had happened. He was always determined that I was trusting the wrong person, and I don't think he'd miss an opportunity to let me know he'd been right all along.'

Josie shrugged. 'Maybe so, but I can't see the harm in asking.'

'I can!' said Olivia. 'If Beth hasn't done anything then how will that make me look?'

'Like a concerned friend, who wants to know why her pal wants to leave Shirehampton,' said Maude matter-of-factly.

'Or are you worried we might have hit the nail on the head?' asked Josie guardedly.

Olivia got to her feet. 'Shan't be a mo.' She headed for the telephone. She felt rather uncomfortable at the thought of asking Ralph whether her friend had made any advances towards him, because if the answer was no, and she hoped that would be the case, then she would have to explain why she had ever suspected Beth of turning into a Judas, when she had been the one trying to convince Ralph of her friend's good character.

She gave a small smile as she heard Ralph's voice. 'Hello, Liv! How'd Liverpool go?'

She felt a stab of conscience as she pictured Ted smiling down at her from the hotel window. 'Good, but I'm not ringing about Liverpool, I'm phoning to ask if you know what's up with Beth.'

There was a pause before he spoke. 'Why, what's she said?'

There was something in his voice which concerned Olivia. 'Nothing, only she put in for a transfer, and nobody knows why.'

'Did you try asking?'

'No, because I was in Liverpool when all this happened, but the girls did, and they said she wasn't very forthcoming whenever they raised the subject.'

'It's not a crime to want to leave Shirehampton,' Ralph said plainly.

'I know, but she must be unhappy, don't you think?'

'Maybe she's run out of men ...'

His comment cut through Olivia like a knife. Why was he being so mean? Last time she spoke to him about Beth he had been singing her praises, so what had changed? She decided to take the matter in hand. 'Did something happen between the two of you when you were in Pucklechurch?'

'Like what?' said Ralph, only Olivia could tell by the tone in his voice that he knew full well what she was getting at.

'Did she make any advances towards you?' The words left her lips in a rush. Hearing his silence, she twisted her finger around the telephone cord as she waited anxiously for his response.

There was a distinct pause as though he was thinking carefully. 'I wouldn't worry about it – I didn't.'

'What's that supposed to mean?' said Olivia, almost dreading his answer.

'I think she got carried away in the heat of the moment – kind of understandable. I expect she regrets it now, though.'

'What did she do?' snapped Olivia.

'I'd rather not go into it and I expect she feels silly, and when all's said and done, she can't change the past. What's the point of worrying when she's already gone?'

'Only she hasn't gone anywhere,' sighed Olivia, 'because she got refused.'

'Why didn't you tell me that before?' said Ralph, clearly annoyed. 'I'd never have opened my mouth had I known she was still in Shirehampton.'

Olivia frowned. 'What does it matter if she's still here?'

Ralph appeared to falter before answering. 'Because you've got to live with her knowing the truth, which isn't going to be easy, and I daresay you won't be able to leave sleeping dogs lie.' He tutted loudly. 'Honestly, Liv, talk about giving someone half a story!'

'Like what you've given me, you mean?' said Olivia sulkily. 'I don't even know what she did.'

'Just as well, given the circumstances,' said Ralph petulantly.

Olivia was confused. Why was Ralph annoyed with her? Surely she should be annoyed with him for not warning her about Beth's indiscretion, whatever that might be. She said as much.

'I didn't tell you because I didn't think it worth mentioning,' said Ralph. 'Are you saying you tell me everything?'

An image of Ted flashed into Olivia's conscience. Guilt swamped her and she spoke as truthfully as she could. 'If one of your friends had acted inappropriately with me, I'd tell you straight away.'

'There's no point in arguing the whys and wherefores,' said Ralph testily. 'What's done is done – we can't all be as perfect as Saint Liv.'

'There's no need to be rude,' said Olivia. 'I really can't see what I've done that's so wrong.'

'Evidently,' snapped Ralph. He paused, and when he spoke next he sounded tired. 'You're making a lot of fuss, for someone who refuses to become my girl. Perhaps this might be the push you need to make up your mind about what you want.' He sighed heavily. 'It's been a long day and there's a queue a mile long waiting to use the phone, so if you don't mind I'll be getting off.'

Unable to think of a response that wouldn't cause conflict, Olivia said goodbye. She walked back to Maude and Josie.

'Well?' said Josie as Olivia sat down on a chair. She relayed the gist of the telephone conversation.

'I reckon he knows he should've said summat and he feels guilty, so he's trying to lay the blame on you,' said Josie.

'I don't know,' said Olivia quietly. 'There's something he's not telling me. He was reasonable until he found out that Beth had been denied her request for a transfer, but after he knew that he got really upset, saying that I should have told him that first, because he wouldn't have said anything if I'd done so.'

Maude sat forward. 'That is odd. What's Beth's whereabouts got to do with the price of fish?'

'Did he think she'd already left base?' asked Josie thoughtfully.

Olivia nodded. 'Definitely. Why?'

'Well, you can ask Beth her side of things now, can't you?' said Josie. 'But if she'd gone you'd probably have left sleeping dogs lie ...' She looked at Olivia, whose mouth had dropped open. 'What?'

'That's exactly what Ralph said, that I'd not be able to leave sleeping dogs lie with Beth still on base.'

Maude raised her eyebrow. 'Then isn't the real question, why is Ralph worried about you hearing Beth's version of events?'

Chapter Seven

Matilda Barnham sat by the fire leafing through one of her old diaries. Despite her husband's insistence that it was a waste of his time going into the attic, she had appealed to his better nature with a bowl of scouse, and had shortly been rewarded with two diaries from 1923 and 1924.

She settled on the pages covering the week commencing the twenty-third of December and ran her finger down the daily jottings until she got to the day Olivia and her father had returned from Glasgow. Her eyes scanned the writing looking for any mention of William. She found one entry which referred to a conversation that had taken place between her daughter and her son-in-law.

Our poor Catherine's broken hearted, after hearing their first grandchild wasn't strong enough to make it. She asked William if there was any chance of burying the baby at St Michael's, so that the family might visit the grave, but he said it was too late as he'd already buried the child in Glasgow ...

'I knew it,' she muttered between pursed lips, 'I blooming well knew it!'

Ivor looked up from his bowl of scouse. 'Knew what?'

She turned the diary to show him, but he shrugged. 'I can't read that without my glasses.'

She read the entry, then looked at him expectantly. 'Told you he was lying!' she said with an air of triumph.

Her husband took another spoonful of scouse. 'Tell me something I don't know.'

'But why tell our Liv he'd had the baby cremated when he clearly didn't?'

Ivor swallowed his mouthful. 'Why tell Ted she'd had the baby aborted? Who knows why that man lies, what's more, who cares?'

'I do!' snapped Matilda. 'Someone needs to have a word with William and let him know we can see through his lies.'

Ivor dipped his spoon in the bowl of half-eaten stew. He knew he shouldn't have let himself be swayed by the promise of his favourite dish. 'What are you planning, woman?'

She drew herself up to her full height, all four foot ten inches of it. 'Nobody else dares to stand up to that man, but he's broken our Liv's heart in more ways than one and it's about time he was stopped.'

Ivor stirred his spoon round as he looked for the best bits. 'It'll end in tears, and they'll likely be yours.'

'That's as maybe, but it's about time this nonsense stopped.' Getting up from her seat, she collected her coat, hat and scarf from the cloakroom.

'How are you going to get there?' said Ivor, hastily wiping his lips with his napkin.

'Walk – it'll only take me ten minutes or so – besides, it'll give me a chance to gather my thoughts.' Stepping back into the room, she picked up the diary and pushed it into her handbag. 'Shan't be long.'

'Hold on, woman, I'll come with you.' Ivor pushed back his chair and was about to get to his feet when his wife's hand landed on his shoulder.

'No, you won't. Ivor this is something I need to do on my own.'

'He's not going to like being questioned, and we all know he's a temper on him,' Ivor said, his features etched with concern.

Matilda's eyes flashed. 'As have I, the difference being, I'm fighting for something, so if you want to worry about anyone, worry about him.'

'Well, if you're not back in an hour I'm coming round,' he said firmly.

'Why?'

He grinned. 'To help you dispose of the body.'

William Campbell was sitting in his study going over his company's finances when someone rang the front doorbell. 'Annie!' he bellowed. He cocked his ears waiting for a response, then, sighing heavily, he pushed his chair back and peered through the side window. A frown lined his brow as his eyes settled on Matilda Barnham. What the hell did she want? Just as he was debating whether to pretend there was no one at home, he heard Annie crossing the hallway. Trust the old bat to finally put in an appearance when he didn't wish her to. He heard the old maid run through her salutations before coming to the study. His thoughts were to tell Annie to lie, but as she entered the room, so did Matilda.

Annie gabbled an apology for Matilda's unannounced arrival before being brusquely dismissed by her employer.

Matilda's expression was wooden. 'William.'

He nodded. 'Matilda. What brings you here?'

She opened her handbag and showed him her diary.

William frowned. 'Whose is that?'

She gave him a brittle smile. 'Mine.'

He nodded slowly. Had she finally lost her marbles? He looked past her. 'Are you here on your own?' Before she could answer, he added, 'Does Ivor know you're out?'

She pursed her lips. 'Why did you tell Liv that you'd had her baby cremated?'

He stared at her. 'What on earth are you on about?'

'You heard,' she said simply. 'Now answer the question.'

William was about to say that he had said it because it was true, when the penny dropped. She had brought her diary round because she had memorialised what her daughter had told her when William and Liv returned from Glasgow. Thinking on his feet, he replied, 'Because she deserves to know the truth. I lied to Catherine because I knew it would upset her if I told her of the cremation.'

Matilda eyed him warily. He looked like he was telling the truth, but there again, he often did. 'Why all the smoke and mirrors? Olivia would have been none the wiser if you'd carried on with the lie, so why now?'

'Because she wanted to pay her respects. I could hardly send her to grieve in a churchyard, knowing full well that her baby wasn't there – even I wouldn't go that far.'

'All these lies, William … If you'd just told the truth from the start …'

He rallied. 'If I'd told the truth from the start, goodness only knows what would have happened to Liv. Her reputation would have been shot to pieces, her credibility in the toilet, and for what? The baby didn't make it, so she wouldn't have been any better off than she is now, but she would have been dragging round the reputation for being fast and loose. You know as well as I do how harmful getting a name like that can be. She would have been ridiculed and judged by everyone – she'd never have recovered from such a scandal.'

Matilda stared back at him. 'You're the one who would've lost out the most, though, aren't you, William? All your contacts and employees knowing that your underage daughter had had a child with one of your workers? You'd never have lived it down. You pretend you did all this for Liv, but you didn't, you did it for yourself.' She shook her head angrily. 'God forgive me, but thank goodness that baby didn't survive because I dread to think what you would have done if it had.'

William looked at her as though she had hit him in the face with a spade. 'What the hell are you accusing me of?'

'I'm saying I think you'd go to any lengths to protect your precious factory.' She eyed him levelly. 'Tell me I'm wrong!'

'I'll admit, it was better for everyone that the baby didn't survive, but if you think for a moment it died by my hand, then you'd better find yourself a good lawyer, because I will drag you and your husband through every court in the land, until you've not a penny to your name.' He paused, then added spitefully, 'Not that it was your money in the first place.'

'I never said you'd murder your own grandchild, I simply said ...'

'Well don't,' roared William. He eyed her with disdain. 'Good God, woman, that might be the heathen kind of behaviour you're used to, but let's not forget, it was me who got you out of that gutter and if you don't want to find yourself sharing a roof with ten others, I suggest you keep your libellous trap shut!'

'Are you threatening me?' said Matilda, scarcely able to believe the turn the conversation had taken.

'Too bloody right I am. You open that big mouth of yours to anyone else and all this will have been for naught.'

'I've not said a word to anyone,' Matilda spluttered.

'So, your husband doesn't know your thoughts?'

'Well, obviously I've said something to Ivor,' she replied meekly.

'And what was his response?' William asked. 'I don't see him anywhere.'

She looked down guiltily. 'He said I should leave well alone.'

He nodded. 'At least one of you has some sense.'

'I just want the lies to stop. It's not fair on Liv,' Matilda said quietly.

'Nor is making up wild accusations,' William said.

She looked up at him. 'No more lies?'

He eyed her carefully. 'No more accusations?'

She nodded.

'Then let that be an end to the matter.' He gestured to the study door.

Matilda took the hint and stepped into the hallway.

On the walk back to Ullet Road, she thanked her stars that she had refused her husband's offer to come with her to confront their son-in-law. He would have been furious that she had unwittingly suggested William might have murdered his own grandchild – at least this way he need never be any the wiser. She mulled this over. It was hardly fair of her to shout that William should refrain from lying to his daughter if she was considering lying to her husband. She drew a deep breath. Ivor would be angry at first but he would soon calm down.

William sank into the chair behind his desk and poured himself a large brandy. The damned woman had got him so flustered he had nearly blurted out a part truth. He took a large swig from the glass. His threats to throw the Barnhams out of their home had worked and he was certain he had seen the last of them. He even doubted that they would tell Olivia of their accusations for fear of reprisals. He took another swig. His father had taught him long ago that liars have to have good memories, and he had been right. William had told so many untruths he could no longer remember what he had said, and to whom he had said it. The only thing he could be certain of was the truth, and he would take that to the grave.

*

Blissfully unaware of the confrontation between her grandmother and father, Olivia smoothed out Ted's latest epistle. He had written to her every day since their encounter in Liverpool, and Olivia loved receiving his letters. When she had walked away from the Crown Hotel, she had very much wanted to turn back and sink into his arms as she had done all those years ago, but her head had forbidden her. Even though she was sure in her heart that Ted wouldn't hurt her for the world, there was still a small part of Olivia that was terrified of having her heart broken beyond repair yet again. Even if Ted didn't do it directly, they were at war with Germany, bombings were frequent, and you could buy it at any moment. The thought of gaining the love of her life back just to have him torn from her by the Luftwaffe was more than she could bear.

In his letters he wrote of his life in Plymouth, the garage, his father, their small cottage by the sea. It seemed an idyllic existence, and Olivia wished she had been able to share it with him. She began to read the latest letter.

Dearest Toff,

I'm very much looking forward to seeing you again and hearing your news. I understand that things were a little sensitive in our last meeting, but I would hope that things will be different this time. I've loved receiving your letters, and hearing about your friends and life in Shirehampton – I feel as though I've met Maude and Josie. I'm glad things worked out for you once you left Liverpool . . .

Olivia placed the letter down on her lap. In her letters to Ted she had been evasive about her life after he'd left, but she'd told him heaps about her time in the WAAF. She supposed the anguish of her father's revelation was still too raw, and even though she didn't blame Ted, it could come across as though she did.

She picked up the letter and read on, a smile blooming on her cheeks. Ted was coming to see her! She folded the letter and placed it with the others in her mother's small keepsake box, which she kept in her locker.

As she headed out to tell the girls about Ted's imminent arrival, her thoughts turned to Beth, and Ralph's revelations. If she confronted her, she was certain Beth would deny everything, and with Ralph clamming up on the subject Olivia couldn't even say exactly what it was that she was accusing Beth of.

'I'd look ridiculous making half-cocked accusations,' she said to Josie and Maude as they patrolled the picket fence. 'I can hardly say what he told me, because it doesn't even make sense – it's more an implication than an accusation.'

Maude nodded. 'He's left you without a leg to stand on.' She hesitated. 'I know this probably isn't the time, but have you heard from Ted?' She chuckled. 'Silly question, considering the amount of mail you get!'

Olivia gave her a shy smile. 'I just got a letter from him. He's written to say he'll be coming to see me in a week or so – he's going to book a B&B.'

'Good thinking,' said Josie approvingly, 'although it's a long way for him to come for little to no information, don't you think?'

'I suppose so, but I feel partly responsible because it's my father who's caused all this.'

'That's hardly your fault!' Maude said indignantly.

Olivia gave her a resigned smile. 'That may be so, but it doesn't stop me from blaming myself.'

'And is that the only reason you're meeting up?' Maude asked with a wry smile.

Olivia looked around to check that no one was close by before answering. 'Last time we saw each other it was a little fractious because I didn't know what Ted was going to say, but after we'd gone through every-thing, I found myself wishing I had more time to talk to him. We've got so much unfinished business, and I don't mean with our baby, but our relationship, because it didn't end properly. It's kind of like we're still in limbo, even all these years later. Ted meant an awful lot to me at one time ...' she paused, '... in fact Ted meant everything to me. He was my whole world, my escape from Dad, my shoulder to cry on and my confi-dant, and even though we've corresponded a lot, it's not the same as seeing him face-to-face.'

Josie's eyebrows neared her hairline. 'Blimey, sounds more like love than friends.'

'It was,' said Olivia simply. 'You don't think we'd have got that intimate otherwise?'

Maude shrugged. 'Caught up in a moment of passion?'

Olivia shook her head. 'After finding me kissing Ted, my father told me I was never to see him again. I refused and that's when things got nasty. I ran to Ted because he was my safe haven. When he opened his front door I started to cry, so he held me close and comforted me.' She shrugged. 'One thing led to another, it seemed so natural at the time.'

'So had your father not been such a pig, you probably would never have fallen pregnant?' said Josie thoughtfully.

Olivia nodded. 'I turned to Ted because I had no one else to turn to, and I could hardly talk to Mum because she would have agreed with Dad that I was too young to be kissing boys.'

'Do you reckon he realises that he's partly to blame for everything that ensued as a result of his behaviour?' said Josie tentatively.

Olivia laughed. 'God no, he thinks I'm a hussy.'

Maude shook her head. 'There's none so blind as those that will not see.'

'That's my dad all over. There's no reasoning with him, he won't even try to listen.' Olivia eyed her two friends curiously. 'Do you think it's wrong of me to meet Ted?'

Josie and Maude exchanged glances. 'No-o,' said Josie slowly, 'because you've a legitimate reason.'

'Are you going to tell Ralph you're meeting him?' Maude asked.

Olivia pulled a face. 'That's the thing, I'm not going to tell Ralph, but only because I don't want him to get the wrong idea.' She eyed her friends anxiously. 'I'm going to spend the week in town with Ted – that way people won't wonder where I'm going every morning. I'm owed leave, so I can't see it being a problem.'

'I think it's a good idea,' said Maude. 'A week's not long, and you need to spend as much time as you can in each other's company, in order to work out where your true feelings lie.'

Josie felt she had no choice but to play devil's advocate. 'Won't it look a bit suspicious if you don't tell Ralph and he finds out on the grapevine? A bit like you, when Ralph told you about Beth.'

Olivia pursed her lips. 'This is totally different. Beth made a move on him and he kept it to himself. I'm meeting Ted for a very different reason.'

Josie blushed awkwardly. 'Yes, you're meeting him so that you can discuss what happened to the baby you shared when you were fourteen.'

Olivia's mouth dropped open. 'Whose side are you on?'

Maude quickly intervened. 'She's on your side, Liv, we both are, but you have to admit, it is a bit like pot and kettle. You know it would look far less suspicious if you told Ralph beforehand. You don't have to mention your relationship with Ted, just say he's an old friend – where's the harm in that?'

Olivia backed down. 'You're right, I should tell Ralph, but I can't, because I'd be lying if I said I was only meeting Ted as an old friend, or to discuss my father. The truth is I'm meeting Ted for much more than that. He meant – *means* – an awful lot to me, and the feelings I had for him are resurfacing, and I already know he's keen on me, he's as good as said so.'

'Golly,' breathed Maude. 'What are you going to do about Ralph?'

Olivia rubbed her forehead. 'I don't know. It's not like we're official or anything, but I like Ralph a lot. In fact, if Ted hadn't shown up, I think we could have made a go of it, which is why I'm reluctant to say anything just yet, in case my feelings for Ted are misguided.'

Josie nodded slowly. 'Reliving your youth type of thing?'

'That's it in a nutshell. When I see Ted the years melt away and I feel like a kid again, when everything was all right, my mum was still alive, and I had a wonderful friend, who I loved very much. Who wouldn't want that back?'

'So, you want to make sure that the feelings you have now aren't based on bygone times?' said Maude, who was beginning to understand why her friend was in such emotional turmoil.

'I don't want to give Ralph up to chase a pipe dream.' Olivia hesitated. 'Does that make me a bad person?'

'No!' said Maude quickly. 'For once in your life you're looking out for yourself, and it's about time too if you ask me. Hang it all, Liv, you and Ralph are only friends – good ones, I'll grant you, but that's where it ends.'

'Thanks, girls,' said Olivia. 'I suppose all this uncertainty is the real reason why I don't want to rock the boat with Beth. She knows about Ted and I don't want to give her an excuse to go blabbing to Ralph.'

'Would she, though?' said Josie.

'Don't see why not,' said Maude. 'They say hell hath no fury like a woman scorned, and if Ralph rejected her advances, I think she'd take pleasure in rubbing his nose in things.'

'Then why didn't she do it when she had the opportunity?' Josie asked. 'You'd have thought it was the ideal time to tell him about Liv and Ted, but she didn't.'

'True,' Olivia admitted.

'Unless she really was caught up in the moment and regretted it straight away,' said Josie, 'because that's the only reason I can think of for her not spilling the beans.'

'Acting on impulse?' said Olivia thoughtfully. 'I suppose it's possible. They were very fraught circumstances – not that that's an excuse, mind you.'

'When you put it like that, even though she was wrong, perhaps she really regrets her actions and can't bear to see you every day,' Josie said.

'Now that makes much more sense,' said Olivia. 'It was probably something and nothing, but she feels guilty after I stood up for her when the balloon broke loose that time.'

'There you have it,' Josie agreed. 'So, what are you going to do about it?'

Olivia shrugged. 'Can't see as there's much I can do, because I still don't have any detailed information, and after our chat about Ted I'm not in a position to badger Ralph to tell me the truth.'

'Shame, though,' said Maude. 'One silly mistake and she's been punishing herself for months.'

'I'd like to tell her to forget all about it,' said Olivia, 'but I can hardly do that when I don't know what I'm telling her to forget.' She glanced at the Waafs who were coming towards them to take over patrolling the fence. 'That's us done for the night. Anyone fancy a cuppa before bed?'

Maude yawned widely, setting off a chain reaction in her friends. 'Not for me, ta, I'm whacked.'

'Me too,' yawned Josie, 'all this thinking's done me in.'

Olivia stifled a yawn with the back of her hand. 'Crikey, we'd best get to bed whilst we've the energy.'

The girls had a quick chat with the next shift before making their way back to their billet.

'Thanks for helping me work a few things out,' said Olivia. 'It's a lot easier with friends to talk to.'

Maude placed her arm through Olivia's. 'That's what friends are for.'

Ted's train pulled into the station at Shirehampton and he immediately began to scan the platform for Olivia, and was delighted when he saw her waving at him. He pulled his kitbag out from under the seat and made his way to the door of the carriage, pushing the window down. As the train drew to a halt, he leaned out and twisted the handle of the door, grinning at Olivia who was smiling shyly at him.

'Hello, queen!'

She beamed at him. 'Hello, Ted. Good journey?'

He nodded in a carefree manner. 'Not too bad, but you know how it is, changing trains every other station – as long as you know which station's which, of course.' He chuckled softly. 'I got off at the wrong stop twice. I think it's silly painting out the signs, when all you have to do is ask the guard where you are.'

'Ahh,' said Olivia knowingly, 'but if you had a German accent he wouldn't give you the answer!'

'No pulling the wool over their eyes, eh?' laughed Ted, and instinctively went to take Olivia's hand in his before checking himself. He quickly apologised. 'Old habits die hard, eh?'

Olivia smiled. This was precisely what she had been talking about with Maude and Josie – being with Ted was like sliding on a pair of comfortable slippers. 'Do you think that's what we are? An old habit?'

He ran a hand over the back of his neck. 'I don't know, Toff. I suppose only time will tell.' He shot her a sidelong glance. 'Does Ralph know I'm here?'

Olivia swallowed. 'I thought it best not to worry him, and I didn't fancy explaining my past in case he didn't understand.'

Ted looked at her curiously. 'You mean he doesn't know you've had a baby?'

She shook her head, her eyes growing wide at the very idea. 'Gosh, no, he's very opinionated on those kinds of matters. He doesn't even like it if a woman's a bit vocal, he thinks it brassy.'

Ted pulled a face. 'He sounds a bit like your father.'

Olivia opened her mouth to rebut the idea, but when she thought about it, she supposed Ted was right – Ralph was very judgemental, just like her father. A slight line creased her brow. How on earth had she got so close to someone like her father without realising it?

As they left the station Olivia told Ted what had happened to their child. She watched his face as she relayed the information. She could see the hurt her news was causing him.

'What the hell's wrong with him?' spluttered Ted. 'I've never known anyone tell so many lies.'

'Unfortunately, this time he's telling the truth,' Olivia said miserably. 'I'm so sorry, Ted. You must wish I'd stayed in my garden and allowed you to pass by all those years ago.'

'Don't be daft. I looked forward to our meetings; it was a little ray of sunshine in an otherwise dull and cloudy life.'

'But the trouble and heartache I've caused,' Olivia insisted. 'You and your dad had to leave your home, your jobs, your friends and family – how can that have been worth it?'

Ted turned to face her. 'Because I met you, you goose, and that meant more to me than the rest of it put together. The only regret I have is letting you go home that day, because had you stayed with me, things would have been very different.'

'But my father would never have stood for it. He'd have thrown you out and …'

'And you'd have come to Plymouth with me,' said Ted determinedly.

Olivia smiled up at him. 'My mum, Ted, you're forgetting about her. I could never have left her – never mind the fact I was underage. My father would have sent for the police, and had you and your father accused of kidnap.'

'I suppose you're right. It seems so easy, but in reality it would never have worked.' He looked at her wedding finger. 'How come you never married, or did you?'

She shook her head. 'I practically lived like an old maid, looking after Mum because Dad was always working. By the time she passed on, war had broken out and I could finally escape my father.'

'Gosh,' said Ted, 'a double-edged sword, then?'

275

She nodded. 'Dreadful because I lost my mum, but elating because I could finally leave home.'

'And this Ralph?' Ted asked cautiously. 'You said in Liverpool that he's an important friend, but how important?'

'Very, or he was,' said Olivia, 'but now I'm not so sure – no prizes for guessing why.'

A slow smile spread across Ted's cheeks. 'Because of me?'

'Seeing you has reminded me of what we had, how we felt for each other …'

'Me too,' said Ted. 'If I'm honest, the thought of seeing you again gave me the courage to end an unhappy marriage.' He smiled. 'I knew you'd never have treated me the way Isobel did, you were never bothered about money.'

'If there's one thing my father taught me, it's that money means nothing if you don't have love. I hope he learns that one day.'

They were both quiet for a moment, then Ted spoke up. 'I'm just thinking about our baby. When someone's cremated I believe their ashes are scattered in a certain area, a bit like a plot. Couldn't we go to the crematorium to pay our respects?'

Olivia turned to look at him, her eyes sparkling with hope. 'Of course we could. I was so angry with my dad I hadn't even thought of that.'

'All we have to do is find out the name of the crematorium …' said Ted.

She shook her head. 'If you're asking me to ask my father, then I'm afraid the answer's no. I told him I never wanted to see him again and I meant it.

However, I should imagine there's only one crematorium in Glasgow, and even if there's more than one, they'll have records, they have to by law.'

'Then are we agreed?'

Olivia nodded. 'I shall make some enquiries.' She rolled her eyes. 'It was hard enough travelling from Shirehampton to Liverpool – I dread to think what it will be like going to Glasgow!'

'At least we'll have each other for company,' said Ted.

Gazing into Ted's twinkling blue eyes, Olivia realised she was going to have to have a serious chat with Ralph, and the sooner the better.

Beth was not having a good day. It had been Josie's turn to cook lunch and she had decided to make them a concoction of leftovers, mainly consisting of spam and cabbage, which was fine for most of them, but the plentiful cabbage had had a rather unfortunate effect on Maude, who had to keep dashing to the ablutions. In fact her trips had become so frequent she had been excused guard duty for the day, leaving Beth to man the fence by herself. To make matters worse, whilst she was patrolling, a military car approached the gate and she saw a familiar but unwelcome face behind the wheel. It was Ralph, and he did not look pleased to see her. She shot him a withering glance. 'What?'

'I haven't come to see you, if that's what you're thinking,' Ralph said.

'Glad to hear it.'

He parked the car and walked towards her. 'I'm here to surprise Liv. Do you know where she is?'

Beth stared unblinkingly at him. 'How can you pretend nothing happened? How can you look her in the eye and tell her how much you care for her when just a few weeks ago you tried to kiss me?'

'I'd never have tried to kiss you, had you not thrown yourself at me. Call it a gut reaction, one I very much regret. You might be a pretty face, but that's where it ends. Olivia's got breeding.'

Beth laughed scornfully. 'Which is more than you've got.'

He shook his head. 'Maybe, but I've got a brain, which is why I chose Liv over the likes of you.'

Beth stared at him. When she first found out that Ralph had asked Olivia on a date, she had assumed it was because he was attracted to a woman with a fuller figure, but that couldn't be right, because he had practically pounced on Beth in the car. Only if he didn't find Olivia attractive, why had he asked her out? And what did he mean when he said he'd chosen Olivia over Beth? He'd made it sound as though he'd picked her out of a line-up, but he couldn't have, because he didn't have a clue who Olivia was before she arrived for training. She mulled this over for a second or two. When they applied for training, they'd had to write down all manner of personal information so that the officers could choose the best recruits for the job.

Her head snapped up. 'You knew who she was before you'd even clapped eyes on her, and that's what you found so attractive – her father's wealth.' Seeing the look on Ralph's face, Beth knew she'd hit the nail on the head. 'Of all the poisonous, malicious, calculating ...'

He shrugged his indifference. 'You can't prove anything.'

Beth stared at him and reached a decision. 'I've been so frightened of telling Liv because I knew you'd twist things, and I might lose her as a friend, but the truth is I've already lost her, and the way I see it, I may as well get hung for a sheep as a lamb. After all, what have I got to lose?'

Stepping forward, Ralph grabbed her wrist in his hand and twisted it viciously. 'One word and I'll make you out to be the biggest slut who ever walked the earth. I'll say Olivia was lying to save your bacon that day you let the balloon go, and I know the sergeant will believe me, because he was eager to have you court-martialled then.'

Beth spoke through gritted teeth. 'I don't care any more, Ralph, can't you see?' She pulled her wrist but he tightened his grip.

'Oh, you will,' said Ralph, 'I'll make sure of it.'

'Liv!' cried Beth as she looked over his shoulder.

Ralph immediately released his grip on her wrist and spun round to explain himself, only to find himself addressing thin air. He turned back. 'You little ...' But Beth had gone, running across the camp and hurtling into the women's ablutions. Chasing after her, he cautiously entered the block. 'Beth?'

He was about to walk in when her voice came from the cubicle nearest him. 'Go away, Ralph.'

'Not until you give me your word,' he said firmly. He banged the door with his fist. 'I'm not playing around, Beth.'

'Neither am I!' said Beth, her voice thick with tears.

Ralph spoke through gritted teeth. 'If you tell her that I tried to kiss you, I'll deny every word. She believed you to be a tart before and I'll make sure she believes it again.'

'Fine!' said Beth. 'And I'll tell her you only asked her out because you knew her father had money.'

'Like I told you outside,' said Ralph, 'tell her what you want, you can't prove anything. I'll tell her you made the whole thing up because I'd turned you down.'

'You turn me down!' Beth said scathingly. 'That's rich when you're the one who tried to kiss me.'

'Prove it!' said Ralph. He turned to leave when another thought occurred to him. 'Liv said you'd put in for a transfer but been refused?' He waited, but there was no reply. 'Good news! As you've left the fence unguarded I'm going to get you out of here so fast your feet won't touch the ground!'

As she heard him leave the ablutions, Beth broke down in tears. Through no fault of her own, her time in Shirehampton had come to an end, maybe even her time in the WAAF, and why? Because she had turned down a hideous beast of a man. She dried her eyes and opened the door to the cubicle, then let out a stifled scream. She was not alone as she had thought. Maude was standing in front of her, tears streaming down her face. She held out her arms and took Beth in a tight embrace. 'I heard every word.'

Beth sobbed thankfully into Maude's shoulder. 'I've been living in a nightmare.'

Maude smoothed Beth's hair back from her face. 'Come with me.'

They exited the ablutions and Maude was about to walk Beth over to the officers' office when she had an idea. She turned to Beth. 'Can you do me a favour?'

Beth nodded.

'Go to the billet and stay there until I come and get you.'

Beth went to nod, then stopped, a frown wrinkling her brow. 'You're not going to try and tackle Ralph on your own, are you, because he can be pretty vicious if he thinks he's cornered.'

Maude shook her head. 'I'm not that daft. Go inside and I'll get you when I'm ready.'

Olivia and Ted were savouring their last day together with a walk through the town. They had spent the past few days enjoying each other's company, but strictly as friends. When they had gone to see a film, there was no canoodling in the back row, dancing was done at arm's length, and their leisurely walks along the head-land had been side by side, rather than arm in arm. They were specifically doing things they'd never done together before, so that they could see whether their feelings for each other were those of adults chasing their youth, or of two people who truly loved each other. And the answer couldn't have been clearer. Whenever Olivia looked into his eyes, it was as if she was looking into his soul, and she had found a part of herself in there.

Now, as they stopped to study a shop window, Ted spoke frankly. 'I know it's a pretty rotten thing for me to say, because I feel badly for Ralph, but I can't wait for you to telephone him and let him know you'll never

281

be more than friends so that I can hold your hand and show the world you're mine!'

A small smile curved her lips. 'I must admit I'm not looking forward to breaking the news, because he's been so patient, but it will come as a huge relief when I do.' She gave a heartfelt sigh. 'I wish he'd been there when I telephoned this morning.'

'You can always try again later,' said Ted.

Olivia didn't particularly want to break the news by telephone, but who knew when she would see Ralph again? And she was desperate to be in a committed relationship with Ted where they could express their feelings. 'I'll try as soon as I get back to base.'

He had gone to smooth the hair down on the back of her head then stopped himself. 'As soon as you've told Ralph, I'm going to pick you up in my arms and kiss you like you've never been kissed before.'

Olivia looked down at herself. 'Good luck on that one. I'd be surprised if you could get my feet off the ground.' She giggled as Ted cracked his knuckles.

'I always did like a challenge!' he chuckled, before adding, 'Mind you, I think all this weight business is in your head – you look perfect to me.'

Olivia smiled at him. 'You really don't see any change in me, do you?'

His eyes travelled the length of her body. 'Nope.'

She tilted her head to one side. 'How would you like to come with me to the balloon site and meet my friends? They know all about you, and seeing as we've not so much as had a peck on the cheek, I can't see the harm.'

'Are you sure it's a good idea?' asked Ted. 'You don't want word to get back to Ralph before you've had a chance to speak to him yourself.'

Olivia shrugged. 'We're still just friends, Ted, we've not done anything wrong. So, yes, I am sure, although I'll understand if you'd rather not.'

Ted beamed. 'You daft goose, of course I'd love to meet your friends!'

Olivia hurried over to the bus stand to flag down the cream and green single decker which was approaching. 'Come on, Ted!'

They got on the bus and Ted paid the clippie.

Taking the seat nearest the window, Olivia felt as though her cheeks were going to burst from smiling so much. 'I can't wait for you to meet them ...' Her thoughts turned to Beth – would the other girl use Ted's visit as ammunition? She'd already told Ted about the situation with Beth, and now she shared her concerns with him.

He rubbed the back of his neck. 'She doesn't sound much of a pal if that's what she does behind your back,' he said thoughtfully. 'On the other hand, as she already knows about me, I agree with you, if she was going to stir the pot she'd have done it by now.'

Olivia nodded. 'I can't understand why she didn't. It's such a shame, because I really liked her.'

Ted appeared to be mulling something over. After a moment or so he voiced his thoughts. 'You don't suppose Ralph's lying, do you?'

Olivia pulled a face. 'It had crossed my mind, but she would have said, if it had been vice versa, and after all his outspoken opinions, I doubt he'd have had the gall to show his face if that were the case.'

They arrived outside the base and alighted from the bus. Olivia waved at Maude who was swiftly approaching them. 'Maude, meet Ted, Ted, this is Maude.'

'Hello, Ted,' Maude said hurriedly, then she turned to Olivia. 'Can I have a quick word?'

A concerned frown creased Olivia's brow. 'What's up?'

'It's Ralph ...' said Maude, only to be cut off by a voice hailing them from behind her.

Olivia's eyes grew wide as she stared at Maude. 'I think I know what you wanted to see me for. Thanks for the heads up, but looks like we're too late.' She looked past Maude to Ralph. 'Hello, Ralph, I tried telephoning you earlier.'

'You've been looking for me?' Ralph was talking to Olivia but staring at Ted.

Olivia looked at him awkwardly. 'This is Ted, an old friend of mine from Liverpool.'

Ralph acknowledged Ted with a nod before turning his attention to Olivia. 'As you've probably guessed, I decided to surprise you with a spot of leave.' He glanced at Ted again. 'Looks like I'm the one in for a surprise.'

Ted stepped forward. 'Perhaps I should leave you two to it.' He glanced at Maude. 'Has someone put the kettle on?'

Reluctantly, Maude nodded and was about to walk away when Olivia spoke up. 'Hang on a mo, Maude, aren't you meant to be on fence duty?'

Maude was staring at Ralph. 'I am, but I had a bit of a dicky tummy, so it was just Beth for a while.'

Olivia looked from Ralph to Maude – both of them looked as though they were hiding something. She glanced around. 'Where's Beth now?'

Ralph quickly cut in. 'Probably chasing after some feller.'

Maude shot him an icy glance. 'I think she's in the billet.' She prayed for Olivia to stop asking questions because she really wanted to get her friend away from Ralph so that she might have a word with her in private.

Tired of the awkward silence when there was clearly something amiss, Olivia spoke out. 'Somebody needs to tell me what's going on.'

Ralph shrugged. 'Damned if I know, but whatever it is has nothing to do with me.'

Maude hissed inwardly.

Olivia arched an eyebrow. 'Maude?'

Maude stared icily at Ralph. 'You know how we thought Beth had made a pass at Ralph and that's why she was being off with you?'

Olivia was careful not to look in Ted's direction as she nodded. 'What of it?'

'We were wrong,' said Maude simply, then turned her attention to Ralph. 'In fact, we couldn't have been more wrong if we tried. It wasn't Beth who made a pass at Ralph, but the other way round.'

Ralph laughed incredulously. 'Who told you that crock of rubbish?' He rolled his eyes sarcastically. 'Let me guess, it was Beth. Now I wonder why she would make up a thing like that ...'

To his surprise, Maude cut him off without apology. 'Wrong, Beth didn't say a word.'

Ralph looked at her, utterly perplexed. 'Then who did? 'Cos whoever it was has stitched me up good and proper – you, too, if you're really stupid enough to swallow any bit of gossip that comes your way.'

Maude waited for him to finish. 'It was you, Ralph, you were the one who told me.'

He gawped at her, his chin dropping, then began to huff and puff as he tried to find the right words. 'Barmy!' he snapped, pointing at Maude. 'Stark, raving bonkers. I've only just seen you, so tell me how I've managed to make such outlandish comments without anyone else hearing me? Not just that, but why would I say something so ludicrous to Liv's best pal?'

'Didn't you listen when I told you why I wasn't on duty?' said Maude, her words falling like ice. 'Or did you not twig?'

He shrugged. 'You had a dicky tummy? What's that got to do with anything?'

'Everything,' said Maude. 'I've been in and out of the lavvy all afternoon, although I'm better now, thanks for asking.' She gave him a meaningful look as she saw realisation dawn on his face. 'Penny finally dropped?'

He swallowed. 'It was a joke, we were playing a game. Surely you didn't believe ...'

Maude walked towards Ralph until she was inches away from his face. She pointed to the billet, her finger shaking with anger. 'Beth's in there crying her bloody eyes out, does that sound like a joke to you?' She was about to walk away when her anger got the better of her. She brought her hand round in an arc and slapped Ralph across the face. 'That's for Beth.' She turned to Olivia. 'He made Beth promise not to tell you that he was the one who'd tried it on with her, because if she did, he'd say it was her that tried it on with him, and that you'd believe him 'cos you thought she was a tart before.' She looked at Olivia, her eyes filled with sorrow. 'That's not all. It seems he only asked you out because your father has money.'

Ted, who had been quietly waiting for Maude to take him for a cup of tea, looked up at this. 'He said *what*?'

Ralph looked wildly around him for someone to back him up, but it was clear he was on his own. He decided his only form of defence was to turn the tables on Olivia. 'You're no better, turning up with him! Is that why you were trying to find out where I was, so that you could bring him back here?'

'No,' said Olivia, still reeling from hearing Maude's revelations. 'I wanted to talk to you ...'

'What utter rot!' said Ralph. 'You wanted to make sure the coast was clear for you and lover boy here.'

'Don't judge me by your actions,' Olivia said quietly.

Ralph stared at her in disgust. 'I don't know why I'd expect any different. After all, if you lie down with dogs you get fleas. You've been around Beth so long you've started acting like a tart ...' He got no further. Ted's fist had connected with his jaw, lifting him clean off the ground.

'Say that again!' roared Ted.

Maude refrained from giving Ted a small round of applause.

Ted stood over Ralph. 'I don't know much about you or what you've done to try and make Beth shut up, but I will tell you this. If you don't leave this base right now and never come back, I'll make sure you wish you had.'

Ralph stood up. Rubbing his chin with his hand, he turned on his heel, but not before muttering a parting shot at Olivia. 'You've got a mirror, you must've wondered why I asked you out.'

Olivia placed a restraining hand on Ted's arm. 'Don't bother, Ted, he's not worth it.'

Maude jerked her head back towards the billet. 'I told Beth to stay in there until I'd told Ralph exactly what I thought of him in front of our flight officer.' She smiled. 'Giving him a slap across the chops was far more satisfying.'

'You've got gumption,' said Ted, 'I'll give you that.'

Olivia was looking less celebratory. 'I think I'd better go and see Beth. I've got some apologising to do.'

'I can't believe we fell for his lies,' Maude said ruefully. 'I feel such an idiot.'

'What I don't understand is why Beth never told us,' Olivia said.

'I do,' Maude said. 'Let's face it, Liv, whether we admit it or not, we all thought badly of Beth from the word go, and even when we thought we were wrong, there's always a tiny part of you that remains suspicious. Beth must have realised that out of the two of them we'd believe Mr Holier Than Thou over her. If she'd told us the truth, she'd have been hanging herself – we'd have thought she was trying to blacken his name before he had a chance to speak.'

Olivia set off for the billet. 'Come on, Ted, you can't come in but I can bring Beth out.'

Beth, however, had already appeared in the doorway to the billet and was looking cautiously around her. She looked at Olivia, then Maude, who nodded encouragingly.

'Has anyone seen Ralph?' Beth asked.

'Seen him, slapped him,' said Maude, and nodded at Ted, 'punched him in the face and sent him packing.'

Beth's hand flew to her mouth. 'You don't know what he's like! He'll go straight to the top and spin a yarn of lies, he'll have you court-martialled, he'll …'

Olivia placed her arm around Beth's shoulders. 'He won't be doing any of that, because he got caught out good and proper. He might be able to bully one person into keeping quiet when it's his word against theirs, but there were too many witnesses, all of whom will shoot his reputation down in flames should he be stupid enough to say anything.' She noticed Beth massaging her wrist. 'What have you done to your arm?' She pulled Beth's hand up to have a closer examination. 'Did he do this to you?'

Beth nodded. 'He's worse than I thought, Liv. He was mad as fire when I told him I was going to tell you everything. He tried to frighten me into holding my tongue, but I got free and legged it into the ablutions.' She smiled at Maude. 'I ran into the first cubicle and locked the door in case he was desperate enough to come in.'

Maude took up the rest of the story. 'I was in the furthest lavvy away from the door,' she grimaced, 'wishing I'd not eaten so much of Josie's cabbage, when I heard someone come in. I stayed quiet because I could hear they were really upset, then two seconds later I heard a man's voice. Well, that surprised me for a start. I didn't recognise him at first, but then I recognised Beth's voice, and as Ralph started doling out threats. I realised what was going on, but I kept quiet so that I could hear the whole story.'

Olivia shook her head. 'Ralph's an intelligent man, why on earth didn't he check the cubicles were empty before spouting off?'

'I thought that,' said Beth.

Maude voiced her theory. 'When I ran to the lavvy I wanted to check that no one else was in there, so I pushed all the doors open until I got to the last one. Ralph must have seen the majority of doors open and assumed no one was in there, bar Beth who was in the first cubicle. After all, most people go to the nearest one when they get the urge!' She grinned apologetically at Ted. 'Sorry about all this, Ted, it's not how I envisaged our first conversation going.'

Ted chuckled. 'Don't worry, it's hardly your fault, although I think you've probably put me off cabbage for life.'

Maude's cheeks flushed pink as she began to giggle, then Olivia and Beth joined in, and pretty soon they were all laughing fit to burst – which intrigued Josie, who had just left the kitchen. 'What's so amusing?'

'Too long a story,' said Olivia, stifling her chuckles, then added, 'Ted, meet Josie.'

The two shook hands. 'Nice to meet you finally,' said Josie. 'Have you come for a quick gander before heading back to Liverpool?'

Ted nodded. 'In fact, I'd better get a move on. I'd completely lost track of the time what with all the excitement.'

'What excitement?' Josie pouted. 'I always miss the fun!'

Olivia's eyebrows shot towards her hairline. 'In this case you should count yourself lucky, but I'll let the girls explain whilst I see Ted off.'

They said their goodbyes to Ted, wishing him a safe journey, and hoping it wouldn't be too long before they met again, and that they would have more time together on his next visit.

Olivia walked him to the gate. 'I feel so embarrassed, Ted.'

He looked at her in surprise. 'Why?'

'Because I've been such a fool, falling for Ralph's tales, believing that he was a gentleman who had high standards, yet you saw through him before you'd even met.'

'You had your suspicions, though,' Ted said reasonably. 'For a start, you didn't like the way he spoke about Beth, which is why you mentioned it to me.'

She cast her eyes skyward. 'That's why I tried to get them talking, so that Ralph would see what Beth was really like ...' She thought back. 'Blimey, Ted, had I not nipped off to the lavvy that day, I might never have seen his true colours.'

'Would it have mattered?' Ted asked. 'You were planning on telling him there was no future for the two of you.'

'But everything is all down to chance, don't you think? If you'd not gone to see my grandparents I might well have settled for Ralph, completely unaware of his real intentions. I might even have married him!' She gave a mirthless laugh. 'I bet Ralph would've laid it on pretty thick with my father.'

Ted nodded. 'Your father would've let Ralph charm his way into his life, because Ralph knows the right things to say, yet he'd rather die than have me around.'

She tilted her head to one side. 'Actually, that makes me feel a bit better, knowing that someone as ruthless and seemingly intelligent as my father would have been just as blinkered as me.'

Ted slid his arm around her waist and pulled her close.

'Ted!' giggled Olivia, looking to see if anyone was watching. 'Not here!' she whispered.

Ted glanced around and gave one of the Waafs crossing the yard a little wave, then turned his attention back to Olivia. 'Why not?' He smiled at Olivia's half-hearted attempts to push him away. 'Now that Ralph's out of the picture, you're a free woman. Or rather, you aren't, because you're my woman now.'

Olivia gave up the pretence of pushing him away. 'You're right, and to think I actually felt guilty that I might break Ralph's heart!' She opened her mouth to continue speaking, but Ted had waited long enough. In one swift movement his lips met hers and he was kissing her with such tenderness Olivia felt as though she were light as air in his strong, all-encompassing embrace. She didn't even notice when the bus pulled up beside them.

'I want to say don't go, but I know you have to,' she said miserably. 'I can't believe you've been here for a week, because it feels like you've hardly been here any time at all.'

He nodded. 'I know. I wish I could stay.' He kissed her briefly on the tip of her nose. 'I'll phone as soon as I'm back in Liverpool, and I'll write every day.'

'Me too!' said Olivia ardently. 'I miss you already.'

She gazed longingly at Ted as he took a window seat on the bus. Breathing on the window, he drew a heart shape with his finger.

Olivia beamed at him, but her face soon fell as the bus pulled away. She watched until it was out of sight before turning back.

Seeing Maude and Beth back on guard duty, she gave them a small wave. As she drew nearer, she glanced at Beth's wrist. 'Are we going to report Ralph for that?'

Beth shook her head. 'I think he's suffered enough, and if I'm honest I'd rather forget the whole affair.' She brightened. 'I take it you and Ted have decided to give things a go?'

Olivia nodded. 'That's why I'd been ringing Ralph's barracks, so that I could tell him we hadn't got a future.' She sighed guiltily. 'Golly, how I wish I'd rung him sooner – that way none of this would ever have happened.'

'Well, I don't,' Beth said, 'because if he hadn't shown up shouting the odds, you lot would still have thought badly of me, and I'd have lost my dearest friends.'

Olivia grimaced. 'You shouldn't have had to go through any of that. You should have been able to talk to us, knowing that we would believe and support you. I'm so sorry we let you down.'

Beth gave her a grim smile. 'That's what happens when you've got a reputation, no matter how false it may be.'

Olivia remembered her father's words when it came to a girl's reputation. 'I'm so angry at my father and the trouble he's caused, but when I think of your situation and the unfairness of it all, I realise that my life would have been very different if word had got around I was pregnant at fourteen.'

'Hung, drawn and quartered before you'd left school,' Beth agreed.

'He was still wrong for telling all those lies.' Olivia tutted under her breath. 'You'd think that after my father, I'd be able to recognise a liar a mile off!'

'Not necessarily. Ralph was plausible. How were you to know he had his sights set on you before you'd even met ...'

'Sorry?'

Beth explained how Ralph had learned of Olivia's father's estate through the application process.

'Blimey!' breathed Olivia. 'If you put it like that, then no, I didn't stand a chance, because I wasn't aware I was stepping into a game of poker where the only other player already knew my hand.' She gave a short, mirthless laugh. 'He and my father are like peas in a pod.'

'You've certainly had a lucky escape,' Beth agreed.

Olivia smiled happily. 'And I'm with my first love, who wouldn't dream of doing anything to hurt me, and who respects me no matter how big I am.'

Maude tapped Beth on the arm. 'You should've seen Ted when he hit Ralph, defending Liv's honour. Not

294

only was it the most romantic, heroic act I've ever seen, he took Ralph clean off his feet!'

Beth stamped her foot on the ground. 'Oh, damn and blast, I wish I'd known! I'd have liked to have seen that with my own eyes.'

'Well, I've had quite enough excitement for one day,' said Olivia with verve, 'and I've got a lot more to come, because Ted and I are going to go to Glasgow to visit the crematorium so that we might pay our respects, and after today I've decided I want us to visit my father first.'

Maude's eyes nearly popped out of her head. 'Why on earth would you want to do that? I thought you liked Ted?'

Olivia giggled. 'I do, but I want to show my father that he didn't win, and how, despite his best efforts, me and Ted still got together.' She smiled wistfully. 'True love always finds a way.'

'How romantic!' sighed Maude.

'Wouldn't I love to be a fly on the wall when you walk in with Ted.' Beth chuckled. 'Does he know what you've got planned?'

Olivia nibbled her bottom lip. 'No, but I'm hoping he'll agree.'

Maude rolled her eyes. 'That man would jump through hoops of fire for you. Besides, I should imagine he'll quite relish the opportunity to show your father that he finally got his girl.'

Olivia beamed. 'He did, didn't he?'

It was much later on that same evening when Ted rang to say he was safely back at RAF Speke.

'It's going to be a while until I can arrange any more leave,' he told Olivia, 'so I've no idea when we might get to Glasgow.'

'I've been thinking about it,' she said, 'and I'd like us to go and visit my father before we go to the crematorium.'

'O-kay,' said Ted with a hint of hesitation. 'Can I ask why?'

'So that we can show him we're together and he can't split us up, not this time.'

She could hear Ted grinning as he spoke. 'What're you trying to do, kill him?'

'Oh, ha ha,' said Olivia, although Ted could tell by the tone of her voice that she was smiling. 'I just think it will do him good to learn that he can't control everything. He may be a bit long in the tooth, but nothing's going to change the fact that he's my father, and who knows what the future may bring.'

'Are you not worried about his response?'

'Nope, I've not been frightened of my father for some time now. I think that's partly why I want to face him, so that I can show myself as well as him that I'm in control of my own life. Good or bad, I make my own decisions.'

'In that case, I'm right behind you. But I think it would be good to do two birds with one stone, and if we leave it a few months, I should be able to get enough time off to go to Scotland, even if it's just for a few days.'

'I can't wait to see you again,' said Olivia, 'even if our visit proves to be a bit turbulent, what with seeing Dad for the first time since I stormed out.'

Ted's voice was reassuring. 'No matter what happens, he can't stop us being together. I know you believe him to be set in his ways with no hope of change, but he's a lot older now and I daresay he's had enough of the whole matter. He'll probably be pleased you're willing to let bygones be bygones.'

Olivia, however, was far more sceptical. 'I think he'd cut his nose off to spite his face. He's being doing it all his life, so why break the habit of a lifetime?'

'Because he's on his own in that big old house with nothing to do but dwell on his mistakes – what could have been and what should have been,' said Ted. 'So just you see when you can get some leave, I'll do the same, and we'll arrange to meet up.'

Olivia wanted nothing more than for her father to show some emotion, maybe even a flicker of approval that she had done a good job with her life despite his doubts. She mentally crossed her fingers. He might not let her back in after her last outburst, but when he'd shouted for her to wait, there had been a pleading in his tone she had never heard before. She had been too angry to speak to him at the time, for fear she might say something even worse than she already had. She nodded thoughtfully. She'd have to give him one last chance, if for no other reason than she knew her mother would have wanted her to.

Chapter Eight

June 1943

It had only been a few months since Ted and Olivia had become official, but in that time a lot had changed.

It had all begun on a day which had started off so calm. The girls had winched out the balloons and all had seemed well; there was a slight breeze but nothing to cause alarm. When the wind began to pick up, Olivia had been sent to check the weather report and had come back stating that all was well, and there was nothing out of the ordinary to announce.

By the time the storm hit, it was too late. They had tried to bring one of the balloons back down, but the wire which tethered it to the winch snapped free. Josie and Maude had been the nearest to hand, and they had battled in vain to bring the balloon under control, but they simply weren't strong enough and had to give in when Josie, through the effort of pulling, suffered an abdominal strain. With Josie out of action and the balloon lost, Maude had immediately gone to help with one of the other balloons, which exploded as they brought it back to base. Maude had been second closest, and both her hands had been badly burned.

Beth had been lucky in that Corporal Spencer Evans, who hadn't been at Shirehampton for long, had been close by and pulled her out of the way in the nick of time. Something which the other girls had thought more than a coincidence.

'He's been eyeing you up ever since he arrived,' said Maude, as she sat on her bed in their billet, her hands bound in bandages. 'If he hadn't been keeping such a keen eye, he'd not have noticed the wire opposite you was about to snap ...'

Beth had opened her mouth to respond when someone knocked on the door of their billet.

Olivia wrinkled her brow. 'Odd! People don't normally knock ...' She got to her feet and answered the door, and when she put her head back through the doorway she was grinning like a Cheshire cat.

'It seems you have a visitor, Beth.'

Beth's face had fallen. 'Who?'

'Corporal Spencer Evans,' said Olivia, her grin growing wider.

Beth got to her feet and disappeared out of the billet, only to reappear a few minutes later, her cheeks flushed pink with embarrassment.

'Well?' said Maude, eager to hear any gossip.

'He was very sweet,' said Beth, 'asked if I was all right, and whether he could take me out sometime ...'

Both Maude and Olivia squealed with excitement until Beth shook her head.

'I told him no ...' She held up a hand as her friends tried to protest. 'I'm not ready.'

Olivia felt a blush begin to bloom in her cheeks. She knew Beth didn't blame her for Ralph, but she still felt responsible, because had she not been so judgemental of Beth in the first place, perhaps Ralph wouldn't have tried to lie.

Accidents like these were becoming increasingly common for the girls in Balloon Command, and due to their injuries both Maude and Josie had been declared unfit to continue in such demanding duties. At first the girls feared they might be discharged from the WAAF so they were relieved when they were sent for retraining as wireless operators, after which they had been posted to RAF Ramsbury in Wiltshire.

Olivia and Beth had also suffered strains and stresses, but nothing bad enough to keep them from performing their tasks.

Olivia was sitting in their billet when Beth came in with a couple of letters, two of which she handed to Olivia. 'One from Ted and one from Maude.' She looked at the rather poor handwriting on one of the envelopes. 'Poor Maude, I see she's still having difficulty holding a pen.'

'Hardly surprising,' said Olivia. 'It'll take a while for her hands to heal, but at least she'll get better, unlike poor Betty.'

Beth grimaced. Betty had been standing in front of Maude when the balloon exploded, and whilst she was not the first Waaf to die on duty in Shirehampton, she was the first to die from an explosion. The memory of it still haunted their nightmares, especially Maude's.

Olivia opened Ted's letter first.

Darling Toff,

I've finally had the go-ahead for Glasgow. My leave starts at midnight on the 20th July, and ends at midnight on the 24th, so if you want to see your father before we go, how about you get here on the 20th? I could come with you after my shift, then we can catch the late night train ...

She continued to read the rest of his letter and discovered that he had already pencilled in a hotel in Glasgow for three nights, subject to her confirming that she could get the same time off. She placed his letter on the bed beside her.

'Shan't be a mo, just going to see if I can book some leave.'

Beth looked up from Josie's letter. 'At last!'

Olivia hurried off to book her leave and was pleased when it was granted. She hastily returned to the billet and put pen to paper.

'I feel like a kid at Christmas,' she told Beth. 'I've been waiting for this moment for such a long time, I'm not even worried about going to see Dad first.'

'Are you going to tell him you're planning to visit, or are you going to surprise him?'

Olivia stopped writing. 'I don't know what to do for the best. If I tell him I'm coming, I won't be able to back out. On the other hand, he might tell me not to bother, which means I wouldn't be able to speak my piece.'

'Don't tell him then,' said Beth. 'For all you know, he might well have got wind of you and Ted, and realise the reason for your visit, and deny you for that very reason, and I think it would do you a power of good to show him you've moved on with your life and re-united with the man of your dreams.'

Olivia nodded. 'I won't write, but I'll definitely turn up, because you're right, I don't want him to have the chance to turn me away before I get my foot through the door.' She looked at the letter from Josie. 'Has Josie much to say?'

'She's loving her new job, and wants us to visit,' Beth waggled her eyebrows, 'to meet her new beau.'

'Really? What's he like? Where did she meet him?' Olivia fired the questions in quick succession, causing Beth to giggle.

'His name's Clive and he's one of the ground crew on a base not far from Ramsbury. She says he's a real gent and she thinks he might be the one; she also says there's more news to tell, but she doesn't want to take the wind out of Maude's sails so she's going to let Maude spill the beans, although she wishes she could be a fly on the wall when we read what she has to say …' She pulled a face. 'I wonder what that's all about.'

Olivia glanced at Maude's unopened letter. 'No idea, but I daresay we're about to find out …' She slit the envelope open with her finger and gazed speculatively at Beth. 'So that's me, Maude and Josie all with fellers – fancy joining the club? I know Corporal Evans would be like a dog with two tails if only you'd give him the chance.'

'You know I've already told him that I'm not inter-ested in starting a relationship,' Beth protested.

Olivia tutted softly. 'That was a while ago now, and you shouldn't let Rotten Ralph put you off fellers. I didn't.'

'It was different for you, though, you already had your true love waiting in the wings.'

'And you could have yours if only you'd give him a chance, and I think that Spencer is a dear, although maybe I'm not the best judge of character.'

Beth decided to be frank. 'The only fellers that ask me out are the macho type who want to show me off to their pals, hardly the basis for a serious relationship. I know Spencer's not like the rest of them, but there again I thought Ralph was cut from a different cloth.'

'Not all men are bad,' said Olivia, 'but you'll never find out unless you take the plunge, and just for the record I don't think Spencer found it easy to ask you out, even if he had just saved your life.' She shook her head as Beth tried to interrupt. 'He's not cocky like some of them,' she tried to swallow her smile, 'he likes trainspotting, for goodness' sake! I don't think he has a macho bone in his entire body.'

Beth suppressed a giggle. 'That's what I thought, and he does make me laugh, but I don't want to agree to go out with him just to have him start swaggering round like an idiot.'

Olivia pictured Corporal Evans. Ginger-haired, pale-skinned, and an open, honest face. She shook her head. 'If he turns out to be like Ralph, I'll eat my hat – yours, too, if it comes to that.'

Beth looked at the letter which rested on her knees. 'If you're wrong …'

Olivia squealed with delight. 'Good girl! I just know he's going to make you happy!' She gave a contented sigh. She had felt increasingly guilty over Beth's refusal to date, knowing that it was her encounter with Ralph which had formed her decision. As for Ralph himself, no one had seen hide nor hair of him since he'd last set foot in Shirehampton.

She opened Maude's letter.

Dearest Liv,

Guess who I bumped into the other day? He's gorgeous to look at but rotten to the core …

Olivia's head snapped up. 'Maude's seen Ralph.'
Beth's features clouded over. 'What's he done now?'
'Haven't got that far,' Olivia admitted before studying the letter in detail.

I don't think he recognised me at first, and when he did, he couldn't wait to get away, possibly because he's no longer a corporal! Obviously, he wasn't going to tell me what had happened, so I asked around and it turns out he'd been caught with a Waaf when he was meant to be courting the major's daughter. Apparently, it caused a real brouhaha, and he's been demoted because of it!

Olivia gave a short squeal as she read the last bit. She passed the letter over to Beth, who was staring at her, on tenterhooks. She waited until Beth squealed then started laughing. 'Talk about getting your just deserts.'
'And to think he had the nerve to portray himself as holier than thou!'
'I always thought I'd never want to bump into him again, but after hearing that I think I'd quite enjoy the experience,' said Olivia. 'I must include that in my letter to Ted. Thank goodness I haven't sent it yet.'

*

William Campbell rolled his eyes as Annie entered the room. 'For goodness' sake, woman, what now?'

'It's Doctor Palmer come to see you,' Annie said apologetically.

William drew a deep breath before letting it out in a series of barking coughs. Turning puce, he gestured with his hand for her to send him in. Fighting to regain his breath, he scowled at the doctor who stood patiently beside William's bed.

'Well, I needn't ask how you are because I can hear it for myself,' Doctor Palmer said sternly. 'I don't suppose you've been taking the medication I prescribed?' Seeing a tablet bottle on William's bedside table, Doctor Palmer picked it up and peered at the contents. He shook his head disapprovingly. 'How do you ever expect to get better if you don't do as you're told?'

William leaned back against his pillow and wiped his lips, then glanced at the handkerchief which was flecked with a pink froth. He stared wearily at his visitor. 'Can you cure the dying?'

'Who said you're dying?'

'Me,' said William as he locked eyes with the doctor, who didn't try to contradict him. William quietly chuckled. 'My body's had enough, only you're making too much money prescribing your useless potions and pills to admit the truth.'

'Not at all,' said Doctor Palmer indignantly. 'It could be a number of different things, but if you don't let us rule them out we might never get to the crux of the problem.'

William wheezed. 'Wouldn't that suit you fine?' He waved a hand to silence the doctor, who was spluttering a protest. 'I can't say as I blame you. You're in business, same as me, we've all got to earn our living somehow.'

Doctor Palmer furrowed his brow. 'I've a duty of care, I can't stand by and leave you suffering without at least trying to help.'

'And what if I couldn't afford to pay you? What then? Would you still have a duty of care?'

Doctor Palmer's jaw flinched. 'I'm not a charity and medicine doesn't come cheap.'

William nodded, deep in thought. 'My Catherine had polio as a little girl; her parents had to club together with the neighbours to afford the medicine.' He fixed the doctor with an inquisitive gaze. 'Did you meet Catherine?'

Doctor Palmer frowned. 'Of course I met her – I was the one who gave her treatment, you know I did.'

William had been ready to speak, but now he closed his mouth. He appeared to be thinking hard, but after a moment or two he looked up. 'She saw many doctors over the years, for all the good it did her.'

Doctor Palmer gritted his teeth. 'Your wife was suffering with post-polio, which has no cure, all we could do was make her comfortable, but it's different with you, we might be able to do something to help.'

William stared at him, a blank expression on his face. 'Which is why she's dead?'

The doctor stared back at William with an air of confusion. 'Of course it is. What did you think was the cause of her death?'

William shrugged. 'How the hell should I know? I'm not a ruddy doctor!' He heaved a weary sigh. 'Just give me the bill.'

The doctor smiled briefly. 'I can see you're tired so I shall leave you to get some rest.' He put the tablet bottle back on the bedside table. 'Start taking these and you might begin to feel better.'

William picked up the bottle and gave it a shake. 'Daresay they won't make a difference.'

Bidding his patient goodbye, Doctor Palmer went out on to the landing where he found Annie hovering by the top of the stairs. He walked over to her, a look of mild concern on his face. 'Hello, Annie, I was wondering if I might have a quiet word?'

Annie glanced at the door of her employer's bedroom.

Doctor Palmer followed her gaze. 'Don't worry about Mr Campbell, he's catching up on his rest.'

Annie nodded. 'Best make it quick, mind, as I've a pile of ironing to do.'

He eyed her keenly. 'I was wondering if you'd noticed any changes in Mr Campbell, apart from his cough?'

She pulled a face. 'Not really, although his temper hasn't got any better. He's a lot quicker to fly off the handle than he used to be, his memory's gettin' worse and he's allus accusing me of doing summat I shouldn't have.'

He cocked an eyebrow. 'Like what?'

She looked slightly awkward. 'I'm not sure I feel comfortable talking about Mr Campbell behind his back.'

The doctor smiled reassuringly. 'Whatever you say to me will be treated in the strictest confidence.'

Annie appeared to be wrestling with her conscience, before giving in. 'Silly things, like saying I've put too much sugar in his tea or that his food tastes funny and I've put summat in it I shouldn't have. He's even accused me of makin' him ill so that he can't go back to the factory. It's ridiculous, of course, but quite hurtful too, because I wouldn't do that.'

'I'm sure you wouldn't. Mr Campbell's used to controlling everything from his business to his home life; it can't be easy having someone else in charge. My main concern is his refusal to take his medication, because without that, he may never get better, so could you please ensure he takes his tablets, even if you have to crush them up and hide them in his food. It's imperative we get them in his system one way or another.'

She paused for a moment before answering. 'I'll try my best.'

'Thank you, Annie.' He hesitated. 'I think it better that Mr Campbell's condition doesn't become common knowledge, so perhaps keep it under your hat?'

Annie drew the sign of the cross over her left breast with one finger. 'You can trust me, doctor, I won't tell a soul.'

Doctor Palmer headed down the stairs at a brisk pace. If people found out that William Campbell was unwell they'd be quick to take advantage, and William might try to go back to work before he was ready, which could have dire consequences on his health.

Olivia waved to Ted as she got off the train. 'A whole week!' she breathed as he picked her up in his arms, kissed her lightly on the mouth, then put her back down.

Taking a step back, he cast an assessing eye over her. 'Is it me or has something changed? I can't put my finger on it, but you look different.'

Olivia laughed. 'I've lost a stone in weight!'

He placed a loving arm around her shoulders. 'That'll be it.'

She gave him a sidelong glance. 'I think you must be the only person alive who didn't notice how fat I'd got.'

Ted looked down at her and said, 'You've always looked the same to me.'

'I have, haven't I,' mused Olivia, 'which is lovely, but I'm pleased I've lost the weight, and I reckon it's all thanks to you, because ever since you came back into my life, it's just fallen off me!'

'I reckon I lost a few pounds when you suggested going to see your father,' said Ted with feeling. 'I'll do it because you want me to, but I can't say I'm looking forward to it.'

'Me neither,' admitted Olivia, 'but it's only right, Ted. Whether he wants me in his life or not doesn't matter, I'm still his daughter, and I see now that Mum was right, one of us has to be the grown-up.'

'It should be him,' said Ted. 'How old is he anyway?'

'I reckon he must be at least in his mid-sixties,' said Olivia, 'although I couldn't say for sure, because we weren't allowed to mention his age, probably because he was much older than Mum, actually not so far behind Nana and Pops.'

'Is that all?' Ted said. 'He looked around a hundred when I used to work for him!'

A wry smile curved her lips. 'Because he's always frowning, the surly sod.'

'If that's what piles of money does to you, you can keep it.' Ted cocked an eyebrow, and an impish grin appeared on his cheeks. 'It's true what they say.'

Olivia looked up into his eyes which were twinkling down at her. 'What's that?'

He grinned. 'That only the good die young.'

She slapped his arm playfully. 'We're going to see him to keep the peace, not start a war.'

He placed three fingers in the air. 'Scouts honour I'll be a good boy.'

She gave a disbelieving laugh. 'Don't try and tell me you were in the scouts, Edward Hewitt, because I shan't believe you!'

Ted jutted his bottom lip out in feigned hurt. 'Don't you think they'd have had me?'

'No, I do not!' giggled Olivia. 'Always up to no good, that was you!'

He kissed her on the cheek. 'You wouldn't have me any other way.'

She sighed wistfully. 'For my sins.'

Ted held out a hand to hail a tram as it trundled towards them. 'Gosh, it's good to have you home.'

Olivia walked towards the middle of the tram before taking a seat. 'It's good to be back. I do miss Liverpool. The country's all right, but I'm a city girl through and through.'

'Have you any idea what you're going to say to your old feller?'

Olivia nodded. 'I'm going to tell him that we're courting, and that he'll have to get used to it.' She pursed her lips. 'If he tries to suggest you're only with me because of my inheritance, I shall tell him that if that's what he wants to believe then that's fine by me because I know it's not true, then I'll tell him to go boil his head.'

Ted burst out laughing. 'You were doing so well up until that point.'

She grinned mischievously. 'I won't really tell him the last part, because he never does anything I tell him to anyway.'

Ted gave her a grim smile. 'He's a daft old sod. He had it all, beautiful wife, daughter, lovely home and plenty of money – why couldn't he be happy?'

Olivia shook her head. 'I haven't the foggiest, Ted. Mum and Nana used to blame the factory, but if that were the case then he should have sold it and been done with it – it's not like he'd have been short of money.'

The tram journey passed far more quickly than Olivia would have wished, and it seemed she had hardly been in Liverpool for more than ten minutes before she found herself standing outside the door to her father's house. She rang the bell and then, holding Ted's hand, stood back.

There was a flurry of footsteps before the door was opened wide and Annie stood in the entrance, slightly out of breath. She stared at them both for a few seconds before the penny dropped. 'Goodness me, if it isn't Miss Olivia!' Stepping back, she ushered them in before closing the door. 'I do apologise, miss, only I thought you were the doctor.'

'Doctor?' repeated Olivia. 'How come you're expecting the doctor? Dad's never ill!'

Annie fidgeted awkwardly. 'Not expecting him exactly, but he does call in every few days to see how your father's getting on. You see, your father's been unwell for ever such a long time now. I would have written to tell you, but he forbade me from telling anyone, saying if I did, they'd soon come crawling out of the woodwork.'

Olivia removed her jacket. 'That's him all over. He could be knocking on death's door but he'd still be more worried about his money.' She tutted impatiently. 'Where is he?'

Annie glanced in the direction of the stairs. 'In bed, same as he's been these past few months.'

'*Months!*' repeated Olivia, her tone incredulous. 'Shouldn't he be in hospital if he's that unwell?'

Annie rolled her eyes. 'He won't go because he's worried that if word gets out that he's in hospital, they'll fleece him in the factory.' She tutted. 'Poor old Mr Connolly's doing his best to keep things afloat with the business, but he's not cut out to work in an office. Your father only put him in charge because he's the most senior person on the shop floor, and your father's a hard task-master, barking his orders then reprimanding folk because he reckons they're not pulling their weight. He's the same with me, and he's awfully rude to Doctor Palmer.'

'Same old Dad,' muttered Olivia, 'pushing people away when they're trying to help him.' She handed her jacket to Annie. 'I'll just nip up and see him ...'

Annie shot out a detaining arm. 'Make sure you're on your toes – it's not uncommon for him to throw things when he loses his temper.'

Olivia raised her brows. 'Nothing new there, then.'

Annie continued. 'Your father refused to take his medication, claiming it was doing him more harm than good; he's even accused me of making him ill, so Doctor Palmer suggested crushing his tablets and hiding them in his food, which worked just fine until he realised what was going on – that's when he started accusing me of trying to kill him.' She shook her head sadly. 'He won't listen to reason. I tried explaining that I was doing it for his own good, but he's convinced otherwise.'

'So what exactly is the matter with him?'

'He keeps getting infections, whether it be chest, water or the trots.' She grimaced. 'Doctor Palmer says your father keeps getting ill because he's run down and stressed out; not only that but he doesn't take his medication.' She raised her hands and shrugged. 'It's like a vicious circle, not helped by the fact he hardly eats anything because he doesn't trust anyone.'

Olivia patted Annie's hand. 'Don't worry, I'll have a word with him, make him see sense.'

'I hope so,' said Annie.

Looking at Ted, Olivia jerked her head in the direction of the door to her father's room. 'Ready?'

Ted looked doubtful. 'Are you sure it's a good idea, me coming with you? Only he doesn't trust me, never has, and I don't think it's a good idea to exacerbate the situation.'

'He's being cantankerous and bossy because he can, but I won't let him treat us that way, so yes, I do think it's a good idea that you come too. He just needs a stiff talking to.'

Ted took a deep breath and held his hand towards the door. 'After you.'

As she opened the door to her father's room she peered cautiously around the edge. Her father was sitting up in bed, a plate of untouched toast on his lap. Seeing the door open, he grabbed a vase from beside his bed and threw it at the door where it smashed against the frame. 'Sod off,' he bellowed, 'I'm not eating your poisonous crap!'

Olivia pursed her lips and strode into the room. 'I'll have none of that!'

Her father squinted at her, before reaching for his glasses and putting them on. 'Oh,' he said dismissively, 'it's you.'

'It's nice to see you too, Dad,' said Olivia.

He peered at her as she walked towards him. 'I thought you said you were never coming back. Never's not as long as I remember it to be.'

'Well, it's a good job I did,' said Olivia stoutly. 'By all accounts, you've run yourself into the ground, and taken a few others along the way.' She glanced over her shoulder to where Ted stood, half in, half out of the doorway. 'I've brought Ted with me.'

William's jaw flinched as he eyed Ted with disapproval. 'So I see,' he said in withering tones. His eyes flicked towards Olivia. 'What the hell did you bring him for?'

Olivia placed her hand in Ted's as he arrived by her side. 'We've decided to give things a go, and we've been courting for well over ...' Breaking off, she swiftly removed the plate of toast from her father's lap before he sent it hurtling in Ted's direction. 'That's enough,

314

Dad!' she snapped. 'I'm not Annie. You can't boss me around and have a hissy fit just to get your own way.'

'Boss her around?' scoffed William. 'Is that what she's been telling you? Because if it is, she's a liar! She's trying to bump me off, and I can prove it.'

'Oh, don't be ridiculous, she's not trying to do anything of the sort.'

'Really?' he demanded. 'Then how come I found her hiding drugs in my food? Bet she never told you about that, did she?' he finished with an air of triumph.

Olivia sighed heavily. 'She told us you've been refusing to take your medication, so she tried to hide it in your food, yes, but that was for your own good.'

'Poppycock!' snapped William. 'There was nothing wrong with me until they started giving me those damned pills.' He glared at Ted. 'It's the likes of him that have put her up to it, feeble-minded woman that she is.'

'For goodness' sake, Dad, you carry on making statements like that and people are going to think you've gone barmy.'

Her father smiled gleefully. 'And that's part of their plan. If the poison doesn't work they'll have me sectioned, but I'm not falling for that one.'

'You're an idiot,' Olivia mumbled under her breath.

'What?' said William sharply.

'Nothing wrong with your hearing,' Olivia commented.

William folded his arms across his chest. 'If you've just come here to wave *that*,' he nodded his head at Ted, 'under my nose, then you can leave, mission accomplished!'

Olivia also folded her arms across her chest. 'Not until you've had something decent to eat, and taken your tablets,' she said firmly.

He stared at her without blinking for a few seconds before turning to face the window and relaxing his arms. 'Fine, but none of that crap that Annie prepares for me. I want you to make it, agreed?'

'Agreed,' said Olivia. She turned to Ted. 'Fancy scouse for your tea?'

Ted grinned. 'If I must.'

As they left her father, Olivia turned to Ted. 'Did you see him, Ted? He's as skinny as a rake!'

Ted nodded. 'You can see he's not had a decent meal in a long while.' He hesitated before voicing the thought uppermost in his mind. 'I know Annie wouldn't try and hurt your father, but let's face it, he's never going to win any popularity contests. Are you certain someone isn't trying to bump him off, because he seems pretty sure?'

Olivia gave him a long-suffering look. 'Don't you start.'

He shrugged. 'I bet there's a few who'd be grateful to see the back of him, and he probably knows it too, that's why he's so paranoid.'

'If I found crushed up tablets in my food, I think I'd be paranoid as well, especially if I'd done wrong to so many people,' Olivia said reasonably, 'but we don't need to worry about that.'

They entered the kitchen where they found Annie washing the dishes. 'Any joy?' she asked Olivia.

Olivia nodded. 'He's agreed to eat a meal if I make it, but you're right about the medication – he's still convinced you're trying to bump him off, or rather not so much you, as old employees, persuading you to do it for them.'

Annie's lips formed a thin line. 'In the beginning your father was convinced he was dying, and Doctor Palmer warned him at the time that such thoughts could become self-fulfilling prophecies, if you didn't shake them.' She smiled grimly. 'From what I've seen I think the doc's right.'

Olivia looked up at Ted. 'I know we're meant to travel to Glasgow tonight, but would you mind if we stayed here overnight and leave for Glasgow first thing in the morning?'

'Of course I don't mind, take as long as you need. There will be plenty of other opportunities.'

She smiled at him gratefully. 'Thanks, Ted. I know it can't be easy for you to be nice to my father, not after all he's done, but that's why I love you, because you're the better man.'

Ted grinned. 'It's not easy being perfect.'

She aimed a playful swipe at his chest. 'Come on, Mr Perfect, you can help me make the scouse.'

He pulled a face. 'I can peel and chop stuff but that's where it ends.'

'That'll do!' said Olivia. She pointed to a drawer. 'Knives are in there. I'll fetch the veggies.'

Annie looked round expectantly. 'What would you like me to do, dear?'

Olivia chuckled. 'Nothing, thanks, Annie. He's only agreed to eat it if I make it. I certainly won't be telling him Ted had a hand in the preparation, because he'd definitely not touch a mouthful if I did.'

317

'Then I shall leave you to it. If you need me, I shall be in the washroom, darning socks.'

When Annie had left the room Olivia ran a few ideas past Ted. 'If I can get Dad to take his tablets tonight, and another lot before we leave in the morning, then I'd be happy enough to go to Glasgow, stay overnight, visit the crematorium, then head back soon after. That'll give me a few extra days with Dad to get him on the right track. What do you think?'

Ted took the carrots, turnip and swede which Olivia handed him from the pantry and placed them on the table. 'You can only do your best, but if you stay in regular contact and make sure he's doing as he's told, who knows, it might turn things around.'

She brought out the potatoes and headed back to see what, if any, meat they had. 'If he doesn't listen to me, he'll end up in hospital whether he likes it or not,' she said. 'As you say, I can only do my best.'

Ted looked up from the carrot he was peeling. 'I never thought I'd see your father looking so frail.'

She emerged from the pantry with a small portion of rabbit meat. 'Me neither – he's always been rotund.'

Ted put the peeler down. 'Do you think your father's right? Do you think this might be the end of the road?'

Olivia placed the meat on a chopping board and began to dice it. 'He always seems to bounce back from whatever life throws at him, but if he continues not to eat, then I very much fear he might be unsuccessful on this occasion.' She fetched a pan from the hook above the range, added a small amount of lard and lit the stove. 'I came here ready for battle and I've ended up making his tea!' She put the kettle on to boil whilst she browned the meat in the pan.

'That's because you've a heart of gold,' said Ted. He began to dice the rest of the vegetables.

Olivia stirred the meat in the pan. 'Or a glutton for punishment.' She took the pan off the heat and began to add the vegetables. 'I know a lot of people would say he deserved everything he gets, but he's still my dad, I don't like to see him looking so poorly.'

Ted helped her place the remainder of the vegetables in the pan. 'You're a saint, Olivia Campbell.'

She stared at him. 'You never call me by my real name.'

'That's cos to me you're still a shy, fun-loving thirteen-year-old, not the grown-up woman you've become.'

Olivia gave a wry laugh. 'So the expanding waistline and lined forehead weren't a clue?'

He gazed down at her. 'Only I don't see either of those things. I still see you as you were.' He tilted her head so that he could look into her eyes. 'Your eyes haven't changed, still sparkling with life and mischief, still full of love and compassion.'

Feeling embarrassed by such praise, she looked away.

'Don't ever hide your face because you're embarrassed to be seen for who you are. There's nothing wrong with having a big heart and caring for those around you – it's an admirable quality which too few people possess. You should be proud of yourself.'

'I don't think my father would agree with you,' she said quietly.

'Your father never appreciated what was right in front of him, and I pity him for that. He might be rich in fortune, but what good is that if you're poor of heart?'

Olivia poured the boiling water out of the kettle into the pan and put it on to simmer. 'I wish my father could see things the way you do.'

Ted placed his arms around her shoulders and pulled her in for a cuddle. 'If he can't see how wonderful you are, then he must be blind.'

Relaxing into his embrace, Olivia smiled happily. Ted always made her feel good about herself, which was quite an accomplishment considering she had always believed the things her father used to say about her.

Chapter Nine

It was the morning of their trip to Glasgow. Olivia and Ted had spent the previous evening with her father, trying to persuade him to eat, which had proved more challenging than Olivia had first expected, but after seeing Ted heartily tucking into the scouse, William had eventually relented and eaten the lot, followed by a bowl of rice pudding. Then there came the task of getting him to take his tablets, something which he refused to do point blank, until Olivia reasoned that he would likely end up in hospital if he didn't. This seemed enough to convince her father to take them, if only for a day or two.

Now, as she entered his room, a bowl of porridge in her hands, she was grateful to see that his mood seemed to have improved.

'Is that my breakfast?'

She nodded. 'Porridge with a smidge of honey.' Sensing his improved mood, she added, 'Would you like your tablets before or after your breakfast?'

He shrugged. 'Either or.'

She placed the porridge on the table beside his bed so that he could reach it easily, opened the tablet bottle and handed him his medication along with a glass of water, which he took without complaint.

Olivia could have whooped for joy. 'I'm glad to see that you're feeling better – you had me worried for a minute there.' She waited until he had finished his breakfast before broaching the matter of her trip to Glasgow with Ted, something which did not go down well.

'What the hell are you going there for?' he snapped irritably.

'So that we can visit the crematorium and pay our respects.'

He looked up sharply. 'We?'

'Me and Ted,' said Olivia.

'Who?'

'My boyfriend, the one you had your supper with last night?'

William fell silent for a moment as he searched his thoughts. 'You mean Edward Hewitt!' he said testily.

Olivia nodded.

He stuck out his bottom lip. 'How long will you be away?'

'Only overnight. We'll visit the crematorium first thing in the morning and come back on the midday train.'

'The crematorium?'

Olivia sighed. Trying to talk to her father this morning was like trying to get through to a brick wall. 'Yes! The sooner we find it, the sooner we'll be back.'

'It's easy enough to find. Pass me a pen and paper.'

Olivia nodded cautiously. Was her father really going to help her? She rooted around in her handbag for a pen and paper and handed them over.

William wrote the information down, and handed them back.

Olivia glanced at the paper to make sure she could read his writing, then placed it in her handbag. 'Thanks, Dad, I or rather we appreciate it.'

He shrugged. 'Have you prepared anything for me to eat whilst you're away?'

She nodded. 'There's a cheese and pickle sandwich for your lunch and the rest of last night's scouse for your supper. All Annie has to do is heat it up.'

He pulled a disapproving face. 'Tell her I'll be checking it thoroughly.'

She sighed. 'I will. Now I really must dash, because the taxi's probably already here.'

She arrived downstairs to see Ted waiting anxiously for her in the doorway. 'About time, the driver's starting to get impatient.' He picked up their bags and took them to the taxi. 'How's your father?'

'The same as yesterday. He told me to tell Annie he'd be checking the food I prepared for him, but other than that he was actually quite helpful. He wrote down the name and street of the crem so that we'd find it easily. Mind you, he only did it so that we'd be back quickly, I'm not going to kid myself that he did it for our benefit.'

Ted opened the rear door of the taxi for Olivia, then headed round to the other side.

'Who knows? Maybe he's realised it's time to appreciate you.' He instructed the driver to take them to Lime Street Station.

'But that's enough talk about my father,' said Olivia. 'Let's talk about our trip. How do you feel, now that we're on our way?'

'Apprehensive, nervous and relieved that we're finally going to reach some kind of conclusion. You?'

'Same,' said Olivia.

The driver pulled up beside the steps to the platforms and waited for Ted to pay the fare. In the station, they checked that the train sitting idle on the tracks was theirs, then headed for the nearest carriage, which was empty. Ted indicated the door. 'Ladies first.'

Olivia entered the carriage, took a seat by the window and waited for Ted to join her. A few minutes later, the train blew its whistle signalling its imminent departure. Olivia looked out as the train gathered momentum. If she was truthful, going to Glasgow was a grim reminder of her past, something she'd rather forget. Her hopes were that this trip would draw a line under something which was over a long time ago but had been hanging over her ever since.

The train journey was tedious with many stops, lots of changes, and frustrated passengers who had either missed their connections or boarded the wrong train.

'Well, that was an absolute farce,' said Ted as they eventually pulled into Central Station in Glasgow. 'I'm glad the forces are better organised than the railways.'

Olivia yawned sleepily. 'I feel like a shuttlecock in a game of badminton.'

'I can't believe we've got to go through it all again tomorrow!' Ted complained. 'I'll need a break to get over this one.'

Olivia slid her arm through his. 'Let's get a bite to eat then head to the hotel. We've another long day ahead of us tomorrow.'

They found a café not far from the station where they each wolfed down a portion of egg, chips and beans, followed by a bowl of bread and butter pudding with thick custard.

The hotel was much larger than Olivia had anticipated. 'How much do I owe you?' she said as Ted pointed out the grand building.

'Not a sausage,' he insisted. 'I booked the hotel so I'm paying for it.'

Olivia smiled guiltily. 'It looks ever so expensive.'

He pushed the revolving door which led into the lobby. 'I wasn't going to take you to some dive, and as I don't know anywhere in Glasgow I had to go on recommendations, and this place came out on top.' He approached the woman behind the desk and asked for the keys to their rooms.

Smiling, the receptionist made to ring the bell on her counter, but Ted stopped her. 'It's all right, we'll find our own way up.'

She handed Ted the room keys. 'Your rooms are adjacent to each other, top of the stairs, turn left and keep going; breakfast is served between six and nine.'

Ted led the way to their rooms, then held up the two keys. 'Which room would you like?'

Olivia picked one of the keys. 'See you in the morning.'

Ted nodded, then kissed her softly on the cheek. 'Goodnight, Toff.'

'Goodnight, Ted.'

Olivia entered her room and closed the door. She placed her bag on the chest of drawers and drew out her issue pyjamas, then glanced back at the door. Since rekindling their relationship Ted had been every bit the gentleman, something which she both appreciated and admired, although it felt a little odd as if they were starting their relationship in reverse. They had had a child together, yet here they were in separate rooms. She cast her mind back over the last twenty-four hours. She had arrived in Liverpool expecting her father to show her the door once and for all, but had ended up staying the night. She turned her thoughts to what lay ahead regarding her father's ill health. If he continued not to eat or take his medication, then the inevitable would happen. She wished her mum was still alive so that she might ask her advice, because Catherine was particularly good with these kinds of matters, but then again, so was Ted. He spoke with a level head, exploring all avenues before reaching a conclusion; in fact, he very much reminded Olivia of her mother in that respect.

Having separate rooms was the right and proper thing to do, but she would've liked a cuddle from Ted and for him to tell her that everything was going to be all right. She was so deep in thought that she started as someone knocked gently on her door.

'Toff?' Ted's voice came from the corridor outside.

Her heartbeat quickened. Was he going to make an excuse to come into her room and spend the night in her bed? What would she say if he suggested it? 'Yes?' She paused before opening the door a crack.

'I just wanted to check what time you wanted to go down for breakfast in the morning?'

Olivia almost laughed with relief. 'Eight thirty?'

He smiled. 'Eight thirty it is.'

Closing the door softly, she heard the door to Ted's room shut behind him. How could she have doubted his integrity? Relief washed over her as she got herself ready for bed. She set the alarm clock on the bedside cabinet for eight o'clock then slid between the sheets.

It seemed to Olivia that she had only just shut her eyes when the alarm clock beside her bed rang loudly. She pushed down the knob and stared blearily at the face, half convinced that she must have set the wrong time, then her eyes shot open as she saw that it was eight o'clock. She jumped out of bed and headed for the shared bathroom, quickly brushing her teeth before filling the sink with warm water. She ran her flannel over her face, neck, and underarms, rinsed it out, then tied her hair into a neat bun. She rummaged around the inside of her washbag until she found the small bottle of fragranced talcum powder, put a small amount into the palms of her hands and ran them over her chest and arms. She clapped her hands together to rid them of the excess talc. There was nothing worse than talcum powder to make a uniform look messy. She quickly nipped back to her room, dressed and finished packing her bag just as Ted called her name and knocked on the door.

'Coming!' She opened the door and smiled at him as he held his hand towards her.

'Pass me your bag.'

Olivia picked up her holdall. 'In case you'd forgotten, I handle whopping great barrage balloons every day – I think I can manage to carry my own bag.'

His eyebrows raised, he took the bag from her hands. 'I'm sure you can, but that's not the point. I don't feel comfortable watching you carry this round, it goes against my principles.'

They descended the stairs and headed for the dining room. Olivia stared around the elaborately decorated room. 'I bet they don't do sausage baps here!'

Ted pulled out a chair for her. 'This is Glasgow, how posh can it be?'

A waitress approached them, notepad in hand. 'Can I get you some tea?'

Ted nodded. 'A pot for two, please and ...' He eyed the menu quickly, before looking at Olivia with a raised eyebrow.

'Just porridge for me, please,' said Olivia. 'I'm not awfully hungry.'

He nodded briefly. 'Make that two bowls of porridge.'

The waitress went off to get their order, and Olivia glanced at Ted. 'We'll have our brekker and get going.'

'I hope it's not too far.' Ted looked out of the window at the passers-by. 'Have you thought of what you want to say, when we get to the crem?'

She shrugged. 'I think it's one of those I'll-cross-that-bridge-when-I-come-to-it, moments. What about you?'

He reached into his bag and pulled out a small teddy bear which he handed to Olivia. 'Don't laugh, but this was mine when I was little.'

'And you still carry it around with you?' Olivia asked, smiling.

He gave an awkward grin as a blush rose up his neckline. 'Kind of, it was the last thing my mother gave me.'

The amused smile instantly disappeared from Olivia's lips. 'Oh, Ted, I'm sorry for making fun.'

He shrugged. 'I thought I'd ask if I could leave it wherever they scattered the ashes, so that our child had a toy ...' He broke off. 'Oh, Liv, I'm sorry.'

Tears brimmed in Olivia's eyes, and she fished a handkerchief from her handbag. 'Don't apologise, I think it's a beautiful thing to do.' Her lip wobbled. 'You'd have made a brilliant father.'

He smiled. 'I hope I still might one day.'

She blew her nose, then leaned back as the waitress arrived with their breakfast. Olivia picked up her handbag and began to search through its contents, before tipping them out on to her lap.

'Lost summat?' asked Ted, who was craning over the table to see what Olivia was looking for.

She nodded. 'I don't believe it! All this way, and I've forgotten the damned paper.'

Ted frowned. 'What paper's this?'

Stuffing the contents back into her handbag, she zipped it closed. 'The paper with the address of the

329

crem. I meant to bring it with me, but I must have left it in Liverpool.'

The waitress caught Olivia's eye. 'Sorry to interrupt, but if you're talking about the crem in Glasgow, there's only one.'

A look of relief swept over Olivia's features. 'Thank goodness for that! I don't suppose you know where it is?'

The waitress nodded. 'Tresta Road. You can get there on the number six, it'll take you straight to the entrance. I know, because it's the same bus I catch to go home.' She smiled briefly. 'Will there be anything else?'

Olivia shook her head. 'You've been very helpful, thank you.'

As the waitress walked away, Olivia cast Ted a rueful glance. 'I can't believe I forgot something so important.'

Ted gave her a wan smile. 'Not to worry, no harm done.'

'Just as well,' said Olivia, sinking her spoon into the porridge, 'because the name Tresta doesn't ring a bell. I'd have sworn it was far more sombre-sounding than that.'

Ted reached across the table and placed his hand over Olivia's. 'Stop beating yourself up. You heard what the waitress said – there's only one crem in Glasgow. Now get that porridge down you before it goes cold.'

The waitress had been correct with her information, and half an hour or so after leaving the hotel behind, they stood outside the door to the crematorium office. Ted slipped his hand into hers. 'Come on, queen.'

He rapped his knuckles against the office door and waited to be invited inside. A woman in her late fifties opened the door and smiled warmly at them. 'Can I help you?'

Ted nodded. 'I hope so. We're after some information concerning a cremation that took place here in 1923.'

The woman looked surprised. 'Gosh, that was a long time ago.'

Ted nodded. 'It's a bit of a long story, and we've not got much time as we have to be on the midday train back to Liverpool, so I'm afraid we're in a bit of a hurry – sorry.'

She shook her head. 'Not to worry. We keep good records, so it shouldn't be too much bother finding the information you need.' She smiled fleetingly. 'Name and date of death of the deceased?'

Ted swallowed hard. 'Date of death is the same as the date of birth, and I'm afraid there wasn't a name given.'

The woman looked at them sympathetically. 'I see. Well, at least you've got the date to go by.'

Ted told her what it was and she disappeared into the back after telling them to take a seat.

'I'm scared, Ted,' Olivia whispered.

He placed his arm around her shoulders and pulled her close. 'Of what?'

'You were right in what you said before, that once we know where the ashes are, it'll make everything real, because it will.'

'I reckon that's why your father didn't want you to hold the baby, because he feared it would be too much

331

for you to handle. Perhaps he did the right thing, or perhaps he was only putting off the inevitable. Can you deal with your emotions better now than you could when you were younger?'

'Of course I can. I'm a lot older now, I understand things much better.'

'Then maybe that's the answer,' Ted said logically. 'I know I didn't grasp the enormity of my mother's passing when I was six years old, but now I'm an adult I realise how much I missed out on.'

The woman came out from the back and placed a large black ledger on her desk. She placed her glasses which hung on a cord round her neck back on to the brim of her nose, before scanning the page in front of her and placing her index finger on an entry.

Olivia's heart began to race in her chest. *This is it*, she thought to herself, *this is when you're finally going to find out where your baby is.*

'I've looked from the date of death all the way to the end of January, and there's not a single entry for a baby.' The woman removed her spectacles and looked expectantly at them. 'Is there any chance you've made a mistake? Perhaps the cremation took place in Edinburgh?'

Olivia joined the woman by the desk. 'No, I gave birth in the hospital here in Glasgow. There's no way my father would have gone all the way to Edinburgh. He barely left me the whole time I was in Scotland – at most he left for half an hour, which isn't long enough, surely.'

'Not by a long chalk.' The woman pulled an awkward face. 'You say your father handled the funeral side of things – have you checked with him to make sure he definitely went down the road of cremation, and not a burial?'

Olivia heaved a sigh. 'He's told a few stories over the years, so who knows?'

The woman turned the book around so that Olivia and Ted could see for themselves. Olivia ran a finger down the entries, before turning to Ted. 'What shall we do?'

Ted shrugged. 'Not a lot we can do. We can't possibly visit all the churches in Glasgow before we leave.'

The woman took the book and tucked it under her arm. 'I wish I could be of more help, but even if you went to the registrar's office, it would only confirm the date of birth and death, not the place of burial or cremation.'

Nodding in resignation, Olivia turned to Ted. 'We may as well go home. We've done all we can here.'

They thanked the woman for her help and left.

'All this way for nothing,' said Ted.

Olivia threaded her arm through his. 'I wish I had that piece of paper with me, Ted.'

'What good would that do?'

'It'd prove that he's deliberately sent us on the wrong path by making up a false address for a crematorium that doesn't exist,' she said. 'As soon as I get back I'm going to look for that bit of paper.'

Ted hailed the approaching bus. 'Will you say anything to him?'

'No point,' she replied. 'If he's done this, then as far as I'm concerned it's the last straw. I'll continue to make sure he looks after himself, but other than that, I don't want anything to do with him.'

Ted followed Olivia on to the bus, then addressed the clippie. 'Two for Central Station, please.'

She took the fare and handed him the tickets.

He sat next to Olivia. 'That's probably for the best. Sometimes I think he delights in making other people miserable.' He fell silent for moment before adding, 'We don't need your father, we'll make our own memorial, somewhere we can visit to pay our respects.'

Olivia brightened. 'What a grand idea, Ted. Have you anywhere in mind?'

'Well, it could be in a park. All kids love parks, and we could choose a tree and carve the date in the trunk with our initials.'

Smiling, Olivia leaned over and kissed his cheek. 'Thanks, Ted.'

'What for?'

'For being you.'

It was much later that evening before Ted and Olivia got off the train in Lime Street Station.

'Well, that wasn't as bad as I thought it was going to be,' said Olivia.

'Certainly better than the journey up,' Ted agreed. 'Do you fancy grabbing a bite to eat or do you want to get back to your dad's?'

'I can't say I'm in a hurry to see him, so how about a fish supper?'

Ted grinned. 'Sounds good to me.'

'Have you thought about which park we should make the memorial in?

Ted nodded. 'Sefton Park's always been my favourite. We used to have so much fun boating on the lake or playing hide and seek.' He chuckled softly. 'I remember the time you hid in the Palm House, I searched for hours! Plus it's close by, so we can do it before you go back to Shirehampton.'

'That's a lovely idea, Ted.' She gazed lovingly at him. How could her father have believed Ted was only with her for money? He was nothing like that. *Because he's judged Ted by his own standards*, she thought bitterly. *He's done his fair share of smarming up to people in order to get what he wants, so he thinks everyone's the same as him.*

After their fish supper they went back to the house on Aigburth Drive to find Annie waiting for them. She opened the door, her face grim.

'What's he done now?' said Olivia, immediately assuming her father had said or done something to upset the older woman.

Annie wrung her hands. 'He's in hospital.'

Olivia's jaw fell. '*What?* How?'

'He attacked Doctor Palmer.' She shook her head. 'He came on his routine visit this morning and told your father that he was glad to hear that you'd come home and talked sense into him. He asked where you were, but your father wouldn't say, so I told him you'd gone to Glasgow with Ted. Your father threw a vase at the doctor for no reason whatsoever.'

'Did it hit him?' she asked, though her words were muffled by her hand which was covering her open mouth.

Annie nodded ruefully. 'Knocked him out cold, I thought he'd killed him. I rang for another doctor to come, and when he arrived he said that Doctor Palmer would be fine with time, but your father had to go into the hospital, as he was a danger to himself as well as others.'

'He's in a mental hospital?' gasped Olivia, her eyes growing ever wider.

Annie hastily shook her head. 'No, he's on a ward for the elderly in Sefton General.'

Olivia clasped her forehead in her hand. 'Looks like his temper has finally caught up with him,' she said, 'but why he would get so angry over you telling the doctor where I was, goodness only knows.'

Ted shot her a knowing glance. 'Really? After the wild goose chase he's just sent us on? I should imagine he's not looking forward to seeing you, because even he must realise he's gone a step too far this time.'

Annie glanced at the grandfather clock which stood to one side of the staircase. 'Do you mind awfully if I get off home, only I should have left an hour ago.'

Oliva nodded quickly. 'Of course not, and thanks for waiting, Annie.'

Annie gathered her things and left.

Olivia went up the stairs, closely followed by Ted. She pushed the door to her father's bedroom open with her fingertips and stared at the empty bed. 'Well, it's out of my hands now, that's for sure, although I think under the circumstances that he's in the best place.'

Ted placed his arms around her shoulders and kissed the side of her neck. 'They'll soon get him right.'

Olivia blinked back a tear. 'Do you think he's scared?'

Ted rested his chin on her shoulder. 'Blimey, Liv, don't you ever think of yourself?'

'Sorry?'

'We've travelled up to Scotland and back in just over twenty-four hours to pay our respects, only to find your father lied about where he took our child, and you came back with murder in mind, yet you're still putting him first.'

'Because he's helpless, Ted. He's lost control of the factory, his household – because he believes he can't eat because he can't trust the food – and me, because I'm with you.'

Ted kissed the top of her head. 'You really love him, don't you?'

She nodded. 'He's my dad.'

Ted let his arms fall from around her shoulders and stepped back on to the landing. 'Well, there's not a lot we can do tonight, but tomorrow you need to go and see your grandparents and let them know what's going on. After that we can go to the hospital to see your father.'

'What'll happen to the factory?' Olivia asked. 'I know Mr Connolly is in charge, but with Dad in hospital, word might get out, and goodness only knows what'll happen to the factory then.'

Ted blew his cheeks out. 'Your father must have granted someone power of attorney, and I expect it's you. If that's the case, then you can appoint someone to look after the factory until your father's out of hospital.'

'Pops!' said Olivia promptly. 'He was working in the office before he retired – I bet he'd know what to do, and people would be less likely to take advantage if they knew a family member was running things.'

'There you are then!' said Ted.

'So much to think about and so little time to get everything sorted,' Olivia sighed.

'Best get to bed,' said Ted, stifling a yawn behind his hand. 'We've another early start in the morning.'

Olivia cast an eye around the deserted bedroom. The house seemed empty without her father's presence. She pulled herself together and showed Ted to the spare room, where fortunately the bed was already made up. 'I hope you'll be all right here, Ted. I bet you're beginning to wish you'd never got back in touch – talk about baggage!'

His blue eyes twinkled down at her. 'Not a chance – besides, there's never a dull moment with you around.'

She rolled her eyes. 'Not by choice.'

Lifting her chin with the knuckle of his finger, he kissed her softly on the lips. 'Come on, you need to get to bed yourself. It's been a long day, and we've got an even busier one tomorrow.'

The next day, after sorting things out with her father's solicitor, Olivia and Ted went to visit her grandparents.

'Dad needs someone to run the factory, Pops. Do you think you could cope, just until we know for certain what's going on with him?'

Pops grimaced, but seeing the look of disappointment on his granddaughter's face, he quickly rallied. 'Of course I can. I might be a bit rusty, but I'm sure I'll soon get into the swing of things.'

'And I'll help out in my spare time,' said Ted.

With that decided, Olivia and Ted moved on to the next task at hand, visiting her father at the hospital.

William was lying in his bed, pale as the sheets he lay on. He barely looked at her when she leaned over to speak to him.

'Hello, Dad, it's me, Liv.'

He blinked slowly. 'So I see.'

Olivia glanced at Ted before turning her attention back to her father. 'You needn't worry about the factory. Pops has agreed to take charge until you're well enough to return.'

He shot her a withering glance. '*Wonderful!* I won't have a factory to return to, with that blithering idiot in charge.'

Olivia flinched. She decided to mention the trip and see whether that cooled his mood. 'We've been to Glasgow.'

'Bully for you,' said William. He turned over on to his side so that he was facing away from Olivia, indicating that he wasn't interested in her topic of conversation.

Olivia fought the urge to give him a piece of her mind. If he wanted to act like a petulant child, she would treat him like one. She slipped her hand into Ted's. 'There's no point in me staying here if you're going to be rude. I'll nip in to say goodbye before my train leaves for Shirehampton tomorrow afternoon.'

She waited for an indignant response, but when none came, she turned, ready to leave the ward.

'Olivia!'

She stopped in her tracks and spoke without turning back. 'Yes?'

'I'm sorry.'

Assuming he was referring to his rude behaviour, she shrugged dismissively. 'Don't worry about it, I'm not.'

There was a brief pause before he spoke again. 'I'd like to see you tomorrow.'

Olivia spoke quietly. 'You will.'

Without looking back, Olivia and Ted left the hospital and headed for Sefton Park.

'Well, that was a turn-up for the books,' said Ted.

'What was?'

'Your father apologising. I didn't think he apologised to anyone.'

'It's only because he wants me to call in tomorrow, when he'll have had time to make up an excuse for giving us a red herring.'

Ted looked at her in surprise. 'I'd forgotten about that! Did you find the piece of paper with the address in Glasgow?'

'No,' Olivia said glumly. 'I reckon Annie must've chucked it by accident, not that it matters. I'm positive that it wasn't the name of the crem, or the road.'

When they reached Sefton Park, Ted directed Olivia to a large oak tree and patted the trunk. 'Will this do you?'

She smiled. The tree Ted had chosen was the one he had hidden up one summer's evening when they had been playing hide and seek. He had watched Olivia run round the park, trying to find him, then, just as she was about to give up, he had jumped down in front of her, causing her to scream, so she had chased him all the way to the lake, before they had stopped to catch their breath. 'It's perfect, Ted ...' She stopped short as he let go of her hand and started to climb the tree.

Shading her eyes with her hand, she looked up to where Ted was fiddling with something. 'What are you doing?'

He jumped back down and pointed to where he'd been.

Olivia spotted a small hollow further up the trunk, and saw Ted's teddy bear just visible. 'Oh, Ted.'

He beamed. 'Do you approve?'

'Very much so.' She watched him take his penknife from his pocket and check the coast was clear before quickly carving their initials and the date of their baby's birth into the trunk of the tree.

Olivia ran her fingers over the carving. 'It's beautiful, Ted.'

'It's the next best thing,' he said.

Olivia stifled a yawn behind her hand.

Ted squeezed her shoulders. 'Time for home.'

She nodded wearily. 'I'm whacked.'

They headed for Aigburth House at a leisurely pace, and opened the door to the aroma of Woolton pie and mashed potato. Olivia smiled. 'Annie's made us tea.'

Hearing her name, Annie appeared in the kitchen doorway. 'Just in time! Take a seat and I'll bring it through.'

Olivia thought she had never tasted anything so good. The pie was wonderfully filling, and by the time she had cleared her plate she could barely keep her eyes open. As she attempted to ascend the stairs for bed, she stumbled on the bottom step. Ted scooped her up into his arms. 'C'mon, sleeping beauty.'

When Olivia woke the next day, she was surprised to find herself in bed as she couldn't remember getting there. She looked beneath the sheets and gasped. She was wearing pyjamas, but how had she got into them? She was about to get out of bed when someone knocked politely on her bedroom door.

'Are you awake?'

It was Ted.

'Yes?'

'Can I come in?'

Olivia started to pull the sheets up around her, then realised how ridiculous this was. Her pyjamas were perfectly respectable. She quickly ran her fingers through her hair before telling him to come in.

Ted entered, carrying a tray with tea and toast.

Olivia smiled. 'Breakfast in bed?'

He nodded. 'I think it's the least you deserve – you've had a pretty hectic few days … I see Annie managed to get you changed.'

Olivia sighed with relief, causing Ted to laugh. 'Who did you think got you into your pyjamas?'

Olivia blushed. 'I hadn't thought about it.'

Ted grinned. 'Liar.'

Olivia raised a slice of toast to hide her smile. 'So what's the order for today?'

Ted sat down on the end of her bed and grabbed himself a slice of toast. 'You said you'd stop by the hospital this afternoon to see your father before heading back to Shirehampton, but otherwise that's it.'

She put the piece of toast down. 'I'd forgotten about that.'

'Eat up!' Ted insisted. 'I made that for you.'

She looked at the toast which bore signs of being scraped prior to being buttered, and bit into it. Ted always cheered her up. 'It's delicious.' She said, wiping some crumbs from her chest.

'Are you looking forward to getting back to a bit of normality?'

She took a sip of her tea. 'I'm not sure what normality is at the moment. Because even when I go back to Shirehampton, Dad's still going to weigh heavy on my mind.'

'I don't mind popping in to check on him if it makes you feel better ...' He stopped short as Olivia covered her face with her hands.

'Oh Ted, whatever did I do to deserve you?'

He grinned. 'I guess you're just lucky.'

Olivia broke into a fit of giggles. 'I'm going to miss you.'

Ted's face straightened. 'Not half as much as I'm going to miss you.'

Olivia had called by to see her father before she left for Shirehampton, but the matron stopped her from entering the ward. 'I'm sorry, Miss Campbell, but your father's made it plain that he doesn't wish to see you.'

Olivia stared at her, open-mouthed. 'But yesterday he asked me to drop by before I left.'

The matron gave her an apologetic smile. 'Sorry, dear, but we can't go against his wishes.'

'Did he say why?' Olivia asked.

'No, I'm afraid not.'

'So what exactly did he say? And are you certain it's me he doesn't want to see? I know he's not keen on my boyfriend, but he's waiting outside – maybe you could tell my father that I'm on my own today?'

The matron gave her a rueful glance. 'I'm afraid he was very specific,' she smiled grimly, 'and quite rude with it!'

Olivia grimaced. 'He's obviously feeling better if he's being offensive.'

'Not to worry, I'm used to it,' the matron told her.

Olivia shrugged helplessly. 'Then I suppose I have no choice but to leave. I just wish I knew why he'd changed his mind. Will you let him know I called?'

The matron nodded. 'Of course I will, and try not to worry.'

Olivia thanked the woman for her help and went to join Ted.

'That was quick,' he said, hailing an approaching taxi.

'He didn't want to see me,' Olivia said. 'No explanation as to why – probably to punish me for going to back to Shirehampton.'

Ted shook his head. 'Selfish old goat – doesn't he know there's a war on?'

The cab pulled up beside them and Olivia sank gratefully into the back seat. 'He doesn't care as long as he gets his own way.'

Ted instructed the driver to take them to Lime Street Station, then turned his attention back to Olivia. 'Well, he's a silly old fool!'

She rested her head against Ted's shoulder. 'It's his loss, not mine.' But inside, Olivia was worried. War was a serious business, and she would hate to leave things on a bad note with her father, but if he refused to see her, what more could she do?

*

344

William lay in his bed, staring at the ceiling. The matron had come to tell him that his daughter had been to visit but she had done as he requested and turned her away. A tear trickled down his temple. He hadn't refused to see Olivia because he didn't want to see her, but because his memory was getting worse and he was making mistakes, serious ones. He had given Olivia the right name and address to visit in Glasgow, but not for the crematorium. He rolled his eyes as he thought of the consequences which could have resulted from his momentary lapse in concentration, something which seemed to be happening more often these days. How could he have been so stupid? So complacent? He had been so eager to throw her off the scent that he had inadvertently put her on the right track. What would have happened if she'd gone to the address he'd given her? He shuddered at the very thought. His memory of the present was hazy, but when it came to the past, he was as sharp as a knife. He could remember the day she gave birth down to the last detail, and even though he'd not left his name or address, he was sure they would have been able to give Olivia enough information for her to realise the truth. Another tear fell. He couldn't bear that, not after all this time. She wouldn't understand, and if he tried to explain himself, she wouldn't want to listen.

Olivia always thought life was black and white, but William knew different. Life was complicated, and there were numerous choices to be made, most of which had consequences. You couldn't go back and change things if you got it wrong; you had to live with the repercussions – and he had got a lot of things wrong, including choosing the factory over his family. So when Olivia had fallen pregnant, he'd vowed he would not let her ruin her life, the way he had allowed the factory to ruin his. Only, upon reflection, he wasn't certain he'd made the right choice. He pictured her and Edward together. Had he got it wrong? If he had … William closed his eyes. If he had, then it was crucial that Olivia never learn the truth, because if she did, she would walk away from him forever, hating him until her very last breath.

Another tear disappeared into the pillowcase. If he were to refuse to see her, then he would protect them both from the pain caused by the truth, and even though it meant he would never see her again, that was better than facing up to reality. And as he couldn't trust himself not to say something out of place, the only choice he had was to cut her out of his life. The tears fell more freely now. He'd lost her, although in truth he'd already lost her many years ago, when he'd made a decision that would change their lives forever.

Olivia returned to Shirehampton full of tales of her trip to Scotland and her father's ill health.

Beth proved to be an excellent listener and gave her honest opinion on the matter. 'You've tried your best. I don't think there's any more you can do, and Ted's idea to have a memorial in Liverpool is excellent. Trekking up to Glasgow wouldn't have been feasible – at least this way, you can visit any time you want. And as for your father's condition, who knows what's going on inside that head of his? From the stories you've always told, this sounds very typical behaviour, although the paranoia is new.'

She glanced at the letter in Olivia's hand. 'Are you going to read it?'

Olivia nodded and began to read the letter out loud.

Darling Liv,

I never thought I'd be saying this, because I've always gone with the rule of 'once bitten twice shy', but I now find myself engaged for the second time in my life – or should I say the second and last time in my life? Stanley came over for a visit, and took me out for a meal. I didn't think much of it until the waitress came over with a pudding which we hadn't ordered. I told her to take it away and was quite put out when she refused. Stanley urged me to take a look, and when I did, I could see what looked like a piece of metal poking through the top of the sponge. I was about to complain when he told me to take a closer look. I dug it out with my spoon, and when I realised what it was, well, you could have knocked me down with a feather! Stanley took the ring, got down on one knee in front of everybody, and asked me to marry him. I think I'd said yes before he'd finished asking! With hindsight, I was surprised at how quickly I agreed, I didn't even think about it, but then again, this pro-posal was totally different to the last one. When Billy proposed it was more like a suggestion and he hardly whooped for joy when I accepted, whereas Stanley was like a dog with two tails. I'm so happy, Liv, and I can't wait to see you again. Are you able to come over for a visit? I know from what you've said that you've an awful lot on your plate at the minute, but everyone needs a break.

With love,
Maude

'How romantic!' Beth exclaimed. 'Though I can't say I'm especially surprised – it's clear that Stanley is completely smitten.'

Olivia was delighted for her friend and was longing to say so in person, but she knew she wouldn't be allowed any more leave, so she would have to fit her visit into a forty-eight-hour pass.

A few weeks after receiving the letter, Olivia found herself keeping an eagle eye out for Maude and Josie as her train pulled into the station. As it came to a stop, she was pleased to see a familiar face grinning at her from the crowded platform.

She grabbed her bag from under her seat and leapt down to join her friend, who was holding up her hand for Olivia to see. 'What do you think?'

Olivia admired the thin band which encircled her friend's finger. 'Blimey, Maude, I didn't know your engagement ring was gold! Where'd Stanley get that from?'

'It was his great-grandmother's,' said Maude, beaming proudly. 'I told him it was too much, but he insisted. I felt ever so guilty, especially when I met his mam, but she said if it was what Stanley wanted then that was fine by her.' She threaded her arm through Olivia's. 'I can't wait to show you round Ramsbury – it's like heaven compared to Shirehampton.'

'Did Josie not join you, or is she holding a taxi for us?' said Olivia, glancing expectantly towards the cabs lined up outside the station.

Maude gave an apologetic grimace. 'I'm afraid she couldn't come. She was given a forty-eight at the last minute – rotten timing, I know – and whilst she would have loved to see you …'

Olivia nodded her understanding. 'She'd far rather be with Clive, and I can't say as I blame her. You have to snatch every opportunity you can these days!' She glanced at Maude's hands. 'How are they?'

Maude turned them over so that Olivia could see her palms where most of the burning had occurred.

'They look fantastic!' Olivia said. 'I can't believe how much they've improved.'

'They're certainly a lot less sensitive than they were,' Maude agreed.

'According to our flight sergeant, too many women have been laid off with accidents,' Olivia said. 'So our days as balloon operators are numbered.'

Maude hailed a taxi. 'Do you think you'll be sent for retraining, then?'

Olivia nodded. 'Just a matter of time. Me and Beth have been talking about it, and we've decided we'd like to retrain as drivers.'

'Oooh, me too!' said Maude. 'I like being a wireless operator until something goes wrong – it's really upsetting when you get a darky.'

'A darky?' Olivia asked cautiously.

'It's when you've got to guide a pilot in using only radio control because something's gone wrong with his kite. It's the one call we all dread, because their lives are literally in our hands.'

'I hope they need drivers over wireless operators,' Olivia said.

Maude nodded darkly. 'You can't stop yourself from counting them going out and back in again. I'd far rather be back on the balloons.' They climbed into the taxi and she addressed the driver. 'RAF Ramsbury, please.'

'But that's enough about work,' said Olivia. 'When's the wedding, or have you not set a date yet?'

Maude rolled her eyes. 'Trying to get a date fixed so that everyone can attend is nigh on impossible, so we decided to take the first available date at Brougham Terrace, provided we can both get leave, of course.'

'But Stanley's not from Liverpool,' said Olivia. 'Didn't he want to have the wedding in Enfield?'

'No, he said it'd be nice for his parents to get away from London. I did tell him that it would be a bit like jumping out of the frying pan into the fire as far as bomb-damaged cities go, but he says a change is as good as a rest. How's Beth getting on with Spencer?'

'They're a match made in heaven!' said Olivia proudly. 'I'm so glad I persuaded her to give him a chance; I don't think I've ever seen her so happy. He's put a real spring in her step – she's even taken up train spotting.'

Maude shot her friend a look of amused disbelief. '*Beth?* Trainspotting?'

Olivia chuckled. 'Yes, he's really calmed her down.'

As the taxi drew to a halt Maude took out her purse.

'Halves,' said Olivia, also removing her purse from her handbag.

They sorted through their change and thanked the driver for the ride.

'I'll take you for a quick tour of the base, then we can have some lunch in the NAAFI – or the cookhouse, whichever you prefer.'

Olivia shrugged. 'I know a lot of people prefer the NAAFI, but I don't think there's a great deal of difference, not when it comes to the meals at any rate, and at least the cookhouse is free!'

Maude introduced Olivia to the girls she worked with in the control tower, then showed her the billet she shared with the other Waafs.

'God, how I miss a real base,' Olivia sighed wistfully. 'It must be wonderful being somewhere so big and well organised.'

Maude nodded happily. 'Proper cooks doing the food – it's like a hotel compared to Shirehampton.'

'Oh, Maude …' Olivia was watching three Hurricanes as they came in to land.

Maude smiled. 'Magnificent, aren't they?'

'They certainly are, and the men are so brave.'

Maude opened the door to the cookhouse. 'It gives me shivers every time I hear the siren sound for them to scramble, but you should see them, Liv – they run hell for leather towards their kites, never giving a thought for their own safety. I don't think it crosses their minds for a minute that they might not make it back.'

Taking a tray each, they joined the back of the queue. 'I suppose it's better for them not to dwell on what-ifs.

I'm glad Ted's a mechanic – at least he gets to keep both feet firmly on the ground.'

'How is Ted?'

'You know Ted – nothing seems to faze him. I felt a real heel dragging him all the way up to Scotland for no reason, but he was so sweet. Did I tell you about the tree in Sefton Park?'

Maude nodded. 'He's a heart of gold, has Ted. I don't know how you haven't swung for your father. I know he's not well, but that's no excuse for sending you on a wild goose chase.'

Olivia shrugged. 'I don't think he knows what the truth is, he's spun that many lies.' She held up her plate and her ID card for the cook to inspect.

'But why tell you where to go? I just don't get it.'

'Well, it was a red herring,' Olivia said. 'He was deliberately trying to set us off on the wrong track, which was stupid, because there's only one crem in Glasgow and it's called Glasgow Crematorium.'

'What did you father say it was called?' asked Maude as the cook spooned stew on to her plate.

Olivia mulled this over. 'If I'm honest, I'm not entirely sure, but it was something depressing, like you'd expect the name of a crem or cemetery to be.' She hesitated, 'Like graveyard, or gravestones ...' She snapped her fingers. 'Got it! He said it was called Greystones.'

The cook paused halfway through slopping some mashed potato on to Maude's plate. 'Sorry, but I couldn't help overhearing. Did I hear you mention something about Greystones – are you still talking about Glasgow?'

Olivia nodded. 'Have you heard of it?'

The cook nodded. 'I should say so, I lived there most of my life.'

Maude grimaced. 'You lived in a crematorium?'

The cook's eyebrows rose swiftly towards her hair-line. 'Crematorium? Who on earth told you that Greystones was a crematorium?'

'My father,' said Olivia. 'Although of course we now know he was wrong, but if it isn't a crem, what is it?'

The cook pushed her serving spoon into the vege-tables. 'It's an orphanage.'

Chapter Ten

Olivia stared open-mouthed at the cook. 'An *orphanage*?' She turned to Maude. 'I wonder if there's a church nearby.'

Maude stared at Olivia. 'It's a bit of a coincidence, don't you think?'

'What is?'

'Out of all the names your father could have given, he chose one that actually exists.' Maude looked at the cook. 'We know Greystones is in Glasgow, but what street is it on?'

'The corner of Edinburgh and Barrachnie roads.'

'Is there a church near there?' Olivia asked.

The girl nodded. 'We used to walk there every Sunday. Why?'

Olivia smiled. 'Just wondering.' She motioned for Maude to follow her to the back of the room where they sat down far away from everyone else.

'So, what are you thinking?' asked Maude, placing her tray on the table.

'Isn't it obvious? Dad mistook the name of the church for the orphanage!'

Maude pushed her stew around her plate and spoke quietly. 'Please don't get upset, but how do you know that your baby died?'

Olivia swallowed the mouthful she had just taken. 'Dad told me, and before you say I can't believe anything he tells me, do you not think the hospital staff would have said something if my baby had survived?'

'Did you ask?'

Olivia lowered her gaze. 'No. I was too upset at the time, and I had no reason to question him. I thought he had my best interests at heart.' She took another mouthful of stew and chewed thoughtfully before continuing. 'Why would he lie? We'd already agreed to put the baby up for adoption, so he had nothing to lose.'

Maude pulled a disgruntled face. 'Because he's an oddball. You could ask why he told your grandparents that the baby had been buried, but told Ted different. Not a lot of what your father says or does makes much sense, but I keep harking back to that saying "Oh what a tangled web we weave ..."'

Olivia stared at her friend. 'Do you really think he'd give his own grandchild to an orphanage?'

Maude shrugged. 'From what you've said, it sounds as though your father's capable of anything.'

'But why would he do that?' said Olivia. 'It doesn't make sense when he'd already arranged the adoption.'

'Had he?' Maude regarded her friend in a quizzical fashion. 'Did he tell you who the family were, where they lived, or if they had any other children?'

'No,' Olivia conceded, 'but then again, I didn't ask. I was only fourteen.'

'Even so, surely you must have been curious?'

'Dad told me it was best not to know.'

Maude gave an exasperated sigh. 'Honestly, Liv, when are you going to learn that you can't believe a word your father says? What has to happen for you to see through him?'

Olivia looked offended. 'I know full well what my father's like. I've suffered with his lies all my life, but I know his limits, and he wouldn't do something like what you're suggesting because it wasn't necessary. He's always droning on about time being money, so why would he go to those lengths just to turn round and hand the baby over to an orphanage?'

'On the other hand, why would he waste time finding adoptive parents when he could simply hand the baby over to the nearest orphanage?'

Butterflies were forming in Olivia's stomach. Maude was beginning to make a lot of sense. She pushed her plate of stew away. 'I know he can be a selfish swine, but we're talking about his grandchild, Maude, surely to God ...'

Maude shrugged. 'He was willing to have his grand-child adopted.'

'There's a great deal of difference between adoption and an orphanage.' Olivia was beginning to feel sick. Could her father really have given his own grandchild away to an institution? 'I need to speak to Ted.'

Maude nodded grimly. 'I think it's best you do. You can use the phone in the NAAFI. Come on, I'll show you where it is.'

Olivia followed her friend. Her father had always said that he had done what he thought best at the time, yet the last time she had seen him he had said he was sorry. She had assumed he was apologising for his rude behaviour at the hospital, but now she wasn't so sure. Could it be that finally his conscience was getting the better of him? She dismissed the thought. Her father didn't have a conscience, and she could hardly see him developing one after all these years, not unless ... If her father thought he was dying, could that be enough to make him see things in a different light? The common-sense side of her spoke up. Why be so evasive about where the baby was buried or cremated, unless it hadn't actually happened? The more she thought about it, the more Maude's explanation made sense.

She picked up the phone and spoke to the operator. There was a brief pause before a woman's voice came down the receiver from RAF Speke.

'Can I speak to Ted – I mean Corporal Edward Hewitt, please?'

Olivia waited patiently as the woman placed a hand over the receiver and called out for Ted.

Olivia crossed her fingers, praying that Ted wasn't too busy to come to the phone, then smiled when she heard his familiar voice.

'Is that you, Toff?'

Olivia opened her mouth to speak, but the enormity of what she was about to say rendered her temporarily speechless.

Ted's voice came again. 'Toff? Are you there?'

'I'm here,' she said, her voice barely above a whisper.

'What's happened?' Ted asked urgently. 'Have you had an accident? Is it one of the girls ...'

'I'm fine,' said Olivia, quickly adding, 'and so are the girls – it's not that.'

'Then what is it?' said Ted. 'Because you sound as though you've the weight of the world on your shoulders.'

Olivia was surprised that her voice had given so much away when she had hardly uttered a word; she supposed it was a reflection on her connection with Ted. She drew a deep breath. 'I was in the queue at the cookhouse with Maude and we were talking about Dad's red herring ...'

'I take it you're referring to our trip to Glasgow?'

'That's right,' said Olivia, feeling a flicker of annoyance at being interrupted when she was finding it so hard to tell him her thoughts. 'And as we were chatting I remembered the name my dad wrote down – it was Greystones. I told Maude, and one of the cooks overheard, and it turns out she knows it well.' She hesitated, gathering the courage to continue. 'Greystones is an orphanage in Glasgow, and it's on Edinburgh Road.' She held a hand to her forehead. 'It's too much of a coincidence, Ted, to get the name of the orphanage and the road right. I don't think Dad sent me off on a wild goose chase on purpose. I think he made a monumental error, inadvertently telling me the truth by accident.' There was a lengthy pause before she continued, 'Maude thinks Dad gave our baby to an orphanage, and I'm beginning to think she might be right.'

There was silence the other end. 'Ted? Are you still there?'

When he spoke, his tone was quiet, his voice heavy. 'I am.'

'Well, say something, Ted, because I feel like I'm losing the plot!'

'I'm not surprised, and if it's any consolation, I don't think I'm far behind you.' He paused, then went on, 'We both know what your father's capable of, but rather than guess, I reckon we give the orphanage a bell and see what they have to say on the matter.'

Olivia felt relief sweep over her. She was normally so good at taking charge, but this was like walking over stepping stones when you know that some are treacherous, and she was glad to have Ted holding her hand. 'Do you think they'd tell us?' she asked doubtfully. 'I always thought that sort of thing was confidential, a bit like adoption.'

'All we can do is try,' said Ted. 'So, who's going to ring Greystones? Me or you?'

Olivia knew this was something she had to do herself. It was her father, so her responsibility. 'I'll try them first thing in the morning, then let you know what's what.'

'I'm going off base for a couple of days from tomorrow,' Ted said, 'so I won't be around to answer your call, but I can ring you at Shirehampton when I get back, if that's OK?'

It was a shame she wouldn't be able to talk to him straight away, but it couldn't be helped. 'Of course. I hope to have more information by then.'

The operator's voice came down the receiver letting them know their time was up.

'Give my best to the girls,' said Ted.

'Will do. And Ted?'

'Yes?'

'Thanks for being so understanding.'

She could hear the warmth in his voice. 'I wish I could hold you.'

'Me too,' sighed Olivia.

'Love you, Toff.'

'Love you too, my darling ...'

There was a click as the operator ended the call.

Olivia replaced the receiver and relayed the conversation to Maude.

'Never mind waiting until morning – best to strike while the iron's hot. Besides, I'll be a bag of nerves till I know what's what, as will you, so get back on that phone quick before someone else wants to use it,' said Maude.

Olivia glanced at the clock on the wall and saw that it was seven o'clock. 'Don't you think it's a bit late to be calling?'

Maude shook her head. 'They don't shut up shop like a business – they're open round the clock.'

'But what will I say?'

'Tell them you're trying to trace a child that was brought in on Christmas Eve in 1923, then go from there.'

Olivia put her head in her hands. She had been about to ask Maude how she could be sure her father had taken the baby to the orphanage on the same day she had given birth, but she knew the answer: he would want to be rid of the child as soon as possible. She picked up the phone again and asked to be connected to the orphanage.

There was a moment's pause before the operator's voice came back down the line. 'Sorry, dear, but that number is no longer in use.'

Despite her worries over what to say, Olivia was disappointed to hear her attempts had been scuppered once more. She thanked the operator before hanging up and turning back to Maude.

'It's closed down,' she said simply.

'Oh, damn and blast,' said Maude, 'talk about dead ends.'

'I'm beginning to think I should leave well alone,' said Olivia miserably. 'I seem to hit a stumbling block at every turn.'

'We could always ask that cook, the one who told us about Greystones in the first place. She might know what happened to the children.'

'I don't know,' said Olivia, disheartened. 'I can't see she could tell us anything useful.'

'It's got to be worth a shot,' Maude urged. 'You never know what might crop up. Besides, what harm can it do?'

Olivia sighed. 'All right, but I'm not getting my hopes up. I'm sick and tired of having them repeatedly dashed.'

They went back to the cookhouse, but the cook in question was serving a long line of hungry customers. 'We can't talk to her now,' said Maude. 'How about we come back in an hour or so when things have calmed down a little?'

Olivia nodded. 'Sounds like a good idea. I don't fancy every Tom, Dick and Harry listening to my business.' She hesitated. 'On the other hand, how are we to know where she'll be in an hour? For all we know, she might finish her shift in five minutes and be off round town.'

'You're right. I'll nip over and see when she's available.' Without waiting to hear what Olivia thought, Maude trotted over to the queue and caught the cook's attention. Olivia saw the cook looking at the clock and saying something, then nodding as Maude repeated it back to her.

Maude came back to Olivia. 'She won't be able to talk until ten this evening.'

'Thanks, Maude. I'm sorry if I'm being a pain in the neck, because I daresay it wasn't what you had in mind for my visit.'

Maude waved a dismissive hand. 'I've always liked the idea of playing detective, and this is quite thrilling, especially if we find him or her ...' She looked inquisitively at Olivia who had let out a small gasp.

'I had a girl!' she said, her eyes growing round.

'How on earth do you know that?' asked Maude, astonished.

'Isn't it obvious?' said Olivia. 'The cook lived at Greystones – surely that must mean it was a home for girls?'

Maude shrugged. 'Maybe ...' She smiled at Olivia. 'I think we've just solved a piece of the puzzle!'

Maude and Olivia found a quiet table and tried to make sense of what they'd learned so far.

'I'm struggling to work out what was going through my dad's mind,' Olivia said. 'I'm guessing that he was so worried we'd discover the truth, he just fobbed us off with a tissue of lies. Trouble is, he couldn't remember what he'd said, which is why things kept changing, so he had to invent new lies to cover the old, and even he didn't know truth from fiction.' Her heart quickened with anticipatory excitement at the thought her child could still be alive, but then she imagined the hard truth behind the doors of an orphanage. She had never been in one herself, but if *Oliver Twist* was anything to go by, then her daughter would have lived a miserable existence with the poorest diet and filthiest living conditions, and not an ounce of love to be found within the cold walls. She thought of the name: Greystones. It sounded more like the name of a graveyard than an orphanage. How could her father, a man of means, give his only grandchild up to such a dreadful institution, purely because he didn't approve of her relationship with Ted? Fishing a hanky out of her pocket, Olivia dabbed her tears. 'I know my father's a businessman who puts his own needs before anyone else's, but this? He can't claim he was protecting me and Mum, because he didn't have to go this far. He's done this simply to ensure we never saw her again.'

'It would have worked, as well, had Ted not come calling.'

Olivia hung her head. 'How could I have been so lackadaisical over my own child?'

'Because you trusted your father, and there's nothing wrong with that. It's not your fault, Liv, you were fourteen and still a child yourself.'

'What a mess!' Olivia said miserably. 'How could I be related to someone so heartless?'

Maude shrugged. 'Maybe it's because he thinks with his head and not his heart?'

'Maybe,' Olivia agreed.

Maude shrugged. 'It's the only thing that makes sense. Either that or he's psychotic ...'

Olivia's mouth rounded. 'They do say people who are psychotic show no emotions, and that's Dad to a tee.'

Maude gave a short snort of laughter. 'I was being facetious! He's not *that* bad. Psychos go round murdering people for no reason, like Jack the Ripper. Your dad might be a bit of a Scrooge, but that doesn't make him psychotic.'

Olivia relented. 'All right then, maybe he's not that bad, but I don't think he's more than a stone's throw away ...' She stopped dead. 'Good God, Maude, you've hit the nail on the head! My father's exactly like Scrooge. Look how Scrooge treated Bob Cratchit! Dad's exactly the same with his workers, and couldn't you see Scrooge giving his grandchild away if he thought it would be better for his business?'

Maude nodded without hesitation. 'And you having a child with one of your dad's employees would have made him the topic of hot gossip in the industry. He'd lose respect, and possibly clients. His reputation could've been ruined.'

'And Scrooge gave up the love of his life because he devoted himself to his firm, just like Dad with Mum. Because he was loving once, Nana told me; it was when his father died and he had to take over the factory that he changed.'

Maude raised her brow. 'Suddenly everything falls into place, doesn't it?'

Olivia nodded. 'I never understood why, but I do now, although I'm not saying I approve and I certainly couldn't be like that ...'

'That's because you think with your heart not your head,' Maude interrupted.

Olivia glanced at the clock. 'We've got hours yet, which'll seem like days if we sit here waiting.'

Maude brightened. 'How about we go and see what they're playing at the cinema? We don't have to go far, they've got one on base.'

'A cinema on base!' moaned Olivia. 'You're spoilt, Maude Harris!'

Maude laughed. 'Funny how when we were on a base with a cinema all we wanted was to get our legs loose in the town!'

'True,' conceded Olivia, 'but you never appreciate what you've got until it's gone.'

The girls spent the rest of the evening watching the main feature, *A Day at the Races*, featuring the Marx brothers. As they left the cinema, Olivia turned to Maude. 'Thank you. That's just what I needed to help me unwind.'

'Good. And we're in perfect time to catch the cook coming off duty.'

They entered the cookhouse and waited for the cook, who had waved to them as they came in. She had already removed her overalls and was walking round to join them. She smiled curiously as she sat down. 'I'm Bonnie, by the way.'

Maude smiled. 'I'm Maude, and this is my pal, Olivia.'

'What can I do for you both? I expect it's something to do with Greystones?'

Olivia nodded. 'It's rather a long story, but I'm looking for someone who we think used to live there.'

'I guessed as much. What was her name?'

Olivia glanced at Maude before speaking. 'I'm not sure. We're not even certain that she was brought to Greystones – it was just something that was said in passing by a rather old relative. Of course we were intrigued to find out more when they hinted one of our relatives might have gone to Greystones.'

The cook raised her brows. 'Oooh, I love a mystery. Do you know how old she would be now?'

Olivia nodded. 'She'd be nineteen.'

The girl grimaced. 'I'm afraid it's not good news.'

Olivia's face fell. 'Why, what difference does her age make?'

'I was there when war broke out. They sent all the little kids to Glencoe away from the threat of bombs, but the ones who were fourteen or older were sent to Brownhill. It's a poorhouse.'

As far as Olivia knew, a poorhouse was about the same as an orphanage. 'But surely that's good news, because it means we can still trace her.'

Maude and the cook exchanged knowing glances. 'The poorhouse is your worst-case scenario, Liv, it's where the desperate and destitute end up.'

'And Brownhill was the worst of the worst,' the cook confirmed. 'In fact, it was so bad, I believe they were under investigation; it might even have closed down by now.'

Olivia regarded the girl tentatively. 'Is that where you went?'

Bonnie shook her head. 'I wasn't an orphan. My mother worked there, so it was different for me.'

'Do you think it's worth giving Brownhill a ring?' asked Maude.

Bonnie nodded. 'I should imagine things are very different there nowadays.'

Olivia looked at Bonnie. 'How bad did it use to be?'

'Bad as it can get,' Bonnie said. 'From what I heard, the inmates had to fight for their food.'

Olivia stood up so abruptly her chair toppled over behind her, causing the late diners to turn and stare. She stared at Maude, tears trickling down her cheeks, she struggled to find the words.

Bonnie looked at them in surprise. 'Sorry, I didn't realise that this was a close relative ...'

Olivia nodded, but instead of disclosing exactly who the relative was, she spoke directly to Maude. 'We need to ring Brownhill, now.'

Maude looked towards the telephone, which luckily for them was not in use. 'I'll wait here for you.' She turned to Bonnie. 'Thanks, you've been ever so helpful.'

Bonnie watched Olivia walk towards the phone. 'I would never have been so blunt, but I didn't think for a minute that she was looking for a close relative – she doesn't seem the type.'

Maude gave her a grim smile. 'You mean she seems well-to-do?'

'Exactly. Most people who wind up in care are poor or parentless. She doesn't strike me as either of those,

367

and I couldn't imagine anyone in her family fitting that description either.'

Crossing her fingers, Olivia picked up the phone and asked the operator to put her through to Brownhill. As the voice of a Scottish woman came down the receiver, Olivia's stomach somersaulted. She quickly explained who she was and asked about the girls brought over from Greystones just after the outbreak of war.

The woman spoke cautiously. 'We can't give out information over the telephone. If you'd like to call in …'

'I'm based in Shirehampton,' Olivia explained. 'You can't expect me to come all the way up to Glasgow.'

There was an impatient sigh on the other end of the phone. 'You say your daughter was brought to us on September the fourth, 1939, or thereabouts. Brownhill was under the old management back then.'

'You'll have their records, though,' said Olivia, determined to get answers.

'Well yes, but we didn't have anything to do with the old management, and we can't be held accountable for their actions, and …'

'I'm not ringing to have a go,' said Olivia, her patience beginning to wear thin. 'I just want to know the whereabouts of my daughter, and for your information, I'm not exactly cock-a-hoop over the fact that a child of mine entered the care system, which is why I want to find her. It could well be the case that she never came to Brownhill, but if I know that, it means I can continue my search elsewhere.' *Although goodness only knows where,* she added silently, knowing her options were shrinking.

'Hang on a minute …' The woman's voice faded as she turned away from the phone and it was a minute or two before she spoke again. 'I've spoken to my manager and we don't possess the records that go back prior to our taking over. Because of the allegations made against Brownhill at that time, they're still in the possession of the inspectors.'

Olivia gave a weary sigh. She didn't know why she had expected anything different. Thanking the woman for her help, she returned to Maude and Bonnie who were looking at her expectantly. 'No go,' said Olivia as she sat back down.

Bonnie nodded. 'I thought as much, that's why I waited. I know that they got into a lot of trouble for the treatment of their girls, but with your … relative going in so late on, it's highly likely that she would have been removed from the system and taken elsewhere.'

'But where?' sighed Olivia.

'Dunno,' said Bonnie. 'Haven't you anything else to go on? I know you don't know her name, but do you know her date of birth? Where she was born? Anything?'

Olivia, tired of trying to find her daughter without giving the full story, shrugged helplessly at Maude before turning appealingly to Bonnie. 'She's my daughter, and she was born on the twenty-fourth of December, 1923. The reason why I haven't looked for her any sooner is because my *darling* father told me she was stillborn, and that he'd had her cremated whilst I was recovering from the birth.'

'Crikey!' said Bonnie. 'Lovely father you've got there.'

Olivia nodded miserably as she relayed the tale of their fruitless trip to Glasgow Crematorium, and how when her father said he'd taken the baby to Greystones they had believed him to be confused by all the lies he had been telling, until Bonnie had put them right.

Bonnie listened to the story, deep in thought. 'I wasn't born in 1923, so I'm afraid I can't be ...' She paused. 'Did you say your daughter was born on Christmas Eve?'

Olivia nodded, and something in Bonnie's expression gave her cause for hope. 'That's right.'

Bonnie fixed Olivia with a stern look. 'Is your father a nasty old man with mutton chops and a cane with a silver-headed snake as the handle?'

Olivia stared back, open-mouthed. 'How the hell do you know that? You can't! You said you weren't born in 1923 ...'

'I wasn't,' replied Bonnie icily, 'but as I said before, my mother worked in the orphanage, and she had a run-in with a violent old man who left his ...' She stopped speaking as she locked eyes with Olivia.

'Go on,' said Olivia, gazing at Bonnie with hollow eyes. 'There's nothing you could say that would surprise me, not any more.'

'He left what my mother believed to be his daughter on the steps of the orphanage. She caught him red-handed and he tried to deny any connection to the baby, despite the fact that his were the only footprints in the snow, but she wasn't having any of it. She told him what she thought of him and said she would turn him in to the police – that's when he threatened to strike her with his cane.' She drew a

370

deep breath before continuing. 'He thought Mum was after money because she was pregnant with me, so he pushed a lot of cash into her arms before storming off into the night, never to be seen again.' She shook her head as she retold her mother's side of events. 'She nearly got the sack that night, because Mrs Ancrum, the woman who ran Greystones, accused her of trying to steal money your father left for the baby, but she wouldn't do that.'

Hardly able to believe what she was hearing, Olivia turned to Maude. 'It's him, Maude, and he did it. You thought he might and you were right, only he didn't want to be traced, so he left her, like a sack of spuds, just lying ...' She paused. Something that Bonnie had said was troubling her, but she couldn't think what. She ran the younger girl's words through her head before looking up sharply. 'You said his were the only footprints in the snow?'

'Yes, that's how Mum had him bang to rights.'

'Please tell me he didn't leave her in the snow?' asked Olivia, her tone incredulous.

'I'm afraid so. If my mother hadn't found her ...' Bonnie didn't feel it necessary to finish her sentence.

'So, what happened to her?' Olivia's mind raced as she tried to come to terms with what she had just learned.

Bonnie brightened. 'She's fine. Not only did she survive, but she didn't go to Brownhill. She ran away the night before they were due to send her.'

Olivia was reeling. Whilst she was pleased her daughter had managed to run away, how bad had things got that this seemed the only viable option?

'Well, I'm glad she escaped, but I don't know where she is, which means I'm no better off than I was …' She was looking at Bonnie, whose face was being split in two by a slow smile. 'Surely not …'

Bonnie nodded, her cheeks tingeing pink. 'I'm afraid I butted heads with your daughter quite often when she was at Greystones, and even though I know it was my fault, I'm still rather ashamed of the fact.'

'Do you know where she is?' said Olivia, struggling to hold on to her patience.

Bonnie nodded. 'I do, or at least I can find out where her boyfriend's stationed.'

Olivia clasped Maude's hand. 'What's her name?'

'Jessica Wilson, Jess for short,' said Bonnie, eager to help. 'To cut a long story short, I discovered Jess and Ruby – that's her best pal – were in the NAAFI, when the corporal in my battery …' She paused. 'I think it's best I start at the beginning.'

Bonnie explained how she had blamed Jess for a lot of her unhappiness in Greystones. 'If her father hadn't left that money, Mam would never have been accused of trying to steal it. Ancrum was rotten to her after that, and I blamed Jess. I thought I'd seen the last of her until I came across a letter belonging to Corporal Tom Durning – he was in charge of our battery – from his girlfriend Jess Wilson. It didn't take me long to work out it was the same Jess. I was jealous that she'd made a new life for herself, whilst me and Mam had been kicked out, so I'm afraid I did something rather childish. I reported Jess and her pals for joining up under age. I don't know what I was hoping to achieve, but it caused a lot of trouble.'

'Why? What happened to …' Olivia paused as she said her daughter's name for the first time, '… Jess?'

'Nothing. She and Ruby were considered old enough to be in the NAAFI. I got kicked out of my battery, as I had inadvertently given them the heads-up that I, too, was under age.' She shrugged. 'I guess you reap what you sow, and I deserved what I got.'

Olivia looked doubtful. 'I wouldn't say you deserved to get kicked out …'

Bonnie was shaking her head. 'I did. Because I reported George as well – he was a pal of theirs with whom I'd had a run-in. Only they didn't take kindly to George lying to them, and they sent him overseas under age.' She looked at them gravely. 'I would never have done it had I known those would be the consequences. I was being stupid and petty over something that happened when we were kids.'

'Does Jess know what you did?' said Olivia.

Bonnie nodded miserably. 'Tom told her, after giving me a right dressing-down. He wanted me to ring her and apologise directly, but I told him that after what I'd done, Jess deserved an apology in person. Tom, being part of an ack-ack battery, moved on shortly afterwards and I've not seen him since.'

'But you'd be able to get in contact with him if you really needed to?' Olivia said hopefully.

Bonnie smiled. 'I reckon I could, because I stayed in contact with some of the girls from my old battery.'

'How quickly can you get in touch with these girls?' Olivia asked.

'I'll try a couple of them tonight,' said Bonnie. 'It's a lot harder to contact people in batteries than it is if they're on a base like this, but I'll do my best, and with a bit of luck we might know where Tom is by tomorrow.'

Olivia gave her a grateful smile. 'Thanks, Bonnie, and if it's any consolation, the measure of a good person is knowing when they've done wrong, and that's what you've done, unlike my father who still refuses to tell the truth.'

Bonnie eyed her curiously. 'Is it too nosy for me to ask what happened? Only my mother said your father was rich, so he assumed that Jess was born out of wedlock – to his mistress or something similar – but obviously that wasn't the case.'

Olivia relayed the tale of her time in Glasgow.

Bonnie nodded slowly. 'So Mam was partly right. He was a rich Scouser, and Jess was born out of wedlock. She said he got angry when she accused him of being the father, so that'll be why.'

'It would have been too close for comfort,' Olivia agreed. 'The less you all knew, the better. That's why he chose to leave Jess on the doorstep. The last thing he wanted was for someone to record his details, because that way I might have found my daughter or she might have found me, and everything he had done would have been for naught.'

'Is it all right if I tell my mother?' said Bonnie. 'She'd be interested to hear the truth after all these years.'

'Only not before you speak to your friends,' said Olivia, giving an encouraging nod in the direction of the telephone.

Bonnie got to her feet. 'Back in a mo.'

Olivia stared at Maude. 'All this time and not a clue, then one chance conversation and boom! What are the odds?'

'Millions to one,' said Maude. 'When are you going to tell Ted?

'As soon as Bonnie's finished on the telephone.' Olivia shook her head in disbelief. 'I'd better make sure he's sitting down before I tell him everything.' She gave a mirthless chuckle. 'At least he can get his teddy back now.'

'The memorial!' said Maude. She eyed her friend cautiously. 'How do you feel about your father?'

Olivia's features clouded over. 'I don't know. Part of me wants to scream at him for lying to me all this time, but the more rational part thinks, why bother? He'll make excuses for his behaviour, saying that he did what he thought was right at the time, because that's all he ever says.'

Bonnie returned. 'I've put word out that I need to speak to Tom Durning as a matter of urgency.' She held up crossed fingers. 'Hopefully he won't ignore my pleas.'

Maude looked up in surprise. 'Do you think he's still annoyed with you?'

Bonnie shrugged. 'He knows I rued the day I opened my big gob, but my actions had huge consequences for George. If the worst has happened, and I pray it hasn't, I wouldn't blame Tom if he never wanted to speak to me again.'

Maude gave Olivia a grim smile. 'Time to phone Ted?'

Olivia walked towards the telephone, picked up the receiver and asked for Ted's base, her heart beating as though it were trying to escape her chest. How did you tell the father of your child that not only was his baby alive, but was serving in the NAAFI?

'Liv?' Ted's voice came down the receiver.

She hesitated.

'I thought you were ringing tomorrow?'

She could hear the note of dread in his voice; he was obviously anticipating bad news.

'I know, but I couldn't wait that long. I tried to ring Greystones, only they've closed due to the war, so I chatted to Bonnie – she's the cook – and ...' Olivia relayed the conversation to Ted, then paused, waiting for his response. When none came, she feared they had been cut off. 'Ted?'

'Jessica ...' His voice was hoarse with emotion. 'We have a daughter?'

Olivia bit back the tears. What she would give to be in Ted's arms right now. 'We certainly do, and she sounds just wonderful, Ted ... I could ruddy well swing for my father – all those lies, the wasted years ...'

'No point in dwelling on the past. I just thank God he inadvertently told the truth in the end, else we'd never have found her ...' Ted paused. 'She obviously hasn't got a clue about us?'

'Not an inkling. Not only that, but she thinks Dad's her father.'

Ted made a hissing noise between his teeth. 'We're going to have to find her as soon as possible, so that we can put her right on that score, because I'm not having my daughter think that ... that *man*,' his tone was filled with disgust, 'is her father.'

'I wish you'd been with me when Bonnie told us about Jess ...' Olivia's voice faded as she tried to hold on to her emotions. 'I hate this war. You should've been with me, we should be learning the news together, so that we could comfort each other.'

'I'm with you in principle, queen,' he said softly, 'but this war brought us back together. Not only that, but if it hadn't been for the war you'd never have met Bonnie, and then where would we be?'

Olivia let out a small gasp. 'We'd never have found Jessica, and she'd never have known the truth, because goodness only knows what she must be thinking of her family.'

'With your father being the only example she has to go on, then I'd say she probably hasn't a high opinion of any of us, which is why it's so important we find her.' His voice trembled. 'We can't have her thinking we knew anything about his callous behaviour; she needs to know the truth.'

'Bonnie's put out some feelers,' Olivia said, 'so hopefully we'll hear something soon. I wonder what she'll think when she hears that we're searching for her.'

'If she mistakes me for your father then she'll probably run a mile!' said Ted bitterly.

'That's where Bonnie can put her straight,' said Olivia. 'She can speak on our behalf.'

'Only didn't you say that Bonnie wasn't Jess's favourite person?'

'True,' Olivia conceded, 'but she says she's changed a lot since those days, and that Tom, Jess's boyfriend, knows how remorseful she is for her previous actions.'

'Then we have to place our faith in Bonnie's hands, and hope she comes up trumps.'

'She will,' said Olivia. 'I've a good feeling about this, Ted.'

'Caller, your three minutes is up …' interrupted the operator.

'Let me know what happens,' said Ted. 'Ta-ra, Toff, sending all my love.'

'I love you too, Ted.' Olivia heard the click as the operator terminated the call.

October 1943

It had been a couple of months since Olivia had visited Maude, and despite several attempts to get in touch with Tom Durning, Bonnie's search had drawn a blank.

'That's the trouble with the ack-acks,' Bonnie told Maude and Josie, as the girls took a seat at the table. 'They can move daily if necessary, so trying to track them down is virtually impossible, and because Tom was training the girls in my group they're not with him any more.' She shrugged helplessly. 'It's going to be like looking for a needle in a haystack.'

'What about getting in touch with Jess directly? Or what about her friend – Ruby, was it? Being in the NAAFI, they shouldn't move around so much,' Josie suggested.

Bonnie shook her head. 'Wouldn't even know where to begin. They could literally be anywhere in the country, and as they're not part of the forces …' She shrugged.

Maude heaved a sigh. She was not looking forward to breaking the news to Olivia, who had pinned her hopes on Bonnie's ability to trace her daughter. 'I can't think of anything we can do that we haven't already tried. Poor Liv's going to be dreadfully disappointed.'

'I'll keep asking,' Bonnie assured her, 'I'll not let them forget. Tom's bound to surface sooner or later.'

'If only we knew his home address,' said Josie. 'I always miss the big events – first Ralph, now this. Exciting things always happen to other people.'

'Are you saying your weekend with Clive wasn't exciting?' asked Maude with a mischievous grin.

Blushing to the roots of her hair, Josie aimed a playful swipe at Maude, who dodged out of her way. 'You know very well what I mean!' she said with a giggle. 'Besides, we're getting off topic – we're meant to be helping Bonnie find Tom.' She turned to Bonnie. 'I don't suppose you know where he lives?'

'One of his relatives used to own a house on Edinburgh Road in Glasgow, but that's been taken over by the military and they won't give out personal information, so I'm afraid that's another dead end.'

'You can only try your best,' said Josie. 'I'm sure summat'll crop up sooner or later.'

'You've been a great help,' Maude added. 'I'll let Liv know what you've found so far.'

'Or rather my lack of findings,' said Bonnie regretfully.

'I think you're just as disappointed as we are,' said Maude.

Bonnie nodded. 'I wanted to show Jess that I was sorry for opening my big gob, and I thought this could at least go part way to mending a few bridges.'

'We all do stupid things when we're young,' said Josie. 'I'm sure Jess will see that with time.'

'My biggest regret is George,' said Bonnie ruefully, 'because he's the one that suffered the most.'

Maude gave Bonnie what she hoped was a reassuring smile. 'You weren't to realise they'd try and make an example out of him.'

'Doesn't make any difference at the end of the day, though, does it?' sighed Bonnie. 'I don't blame Jess and the others for being angry at me; I deserve it.'

Maude opened her mouth to say something, then closed it again. It was silly to assure Bonnie that this young boy would come home safely, because no one could guarantee such a thing. 'Would've, could've, should've,' she said simply. 'George would have gone over sooner or later – you can't hold yourself responsible for his destiny, no matter what you might think.'

'She's right, you know,' Josie agreed.

'I will, though,' Bonnie said miserably. 'I can't help it. I was being vindictive, whether I knew the outcome or not. I didn't stop to think. I was more bothered about getting my own back, which is ridiculous because George didn't really do anything to me, bar stick up for Jess and Ruby when I was poking my nose in.' She shook her head. 'I've been doing a lot of thinking since bumping into you and Olivia, and I've come to the conclusion that I was angry at my own father for scarpering the moment he found out Mam was pregnant. He's the reason why I grew up in an orphanage even though I wasn't an orphan.' She sighed heavily. 'I couldn't fit in with everyone else, no matter how hard

I tried, and even though Mam did her best to let me know I was loved, it didn't stop me feeling like an outcast.' She shook her head sadly. 'I assumed the other girls hated me because I was lucky enough to have my mam, so I was nasty to them before they could be nasty to me.'

'You've got to stop carrying this burden around with you,' said Maude. 'In some respects it was nobody's fault – you're just the product of your circumstances – and those days are far behind you.' She placed a reassuring hand over Bonnie's. 'It's time for you to leave them there.'

Bonnie jutted out her chin in determination. 'You're right, and I'll help Olivia find her daughter if it's the last thing I do, because I'm not that girl any more.'

Spring 1944

Tom Durning lay in his bed, waiting for the bell signalling an attack to ring. The war had moved up a gear of late, and even though they weren't privy to the whispered conversations and secret meetings, they all knew something big was coming their way, which was confirmed when all leave was cancelled.

Tom jumped as a soldier rapped a brief tattoo on the door to his shared room. 'Phone call.'

A look of anxious anticipation swept over Tom as he got to his feet. 'Anyone I know?'

'Sally Durning.'

Tom raised his brow. Sally Durning used to serve on the same base as him. She was a nice enough girl, but because of their surnames people were forever getting their mail muddled. He couldn't think why she'd want to speak to him after such a long time. He made his way to the office and picked up the receiver. 'Hello, Sal, what can I do for you?'

'Hello, Tom. I'm afraid my reason for getting in touch is rather bitter-sweet.' She cleared her throat. 'Remember Bonnie McKinley?' She broke off as Tom's spluttered response came down the receiver.

'How can I forget?' he said bitterly. 'What's she done this time and how does it involve me?'

'I don't know. She wouldn't say anything, only that she needed to speak to you as a matter of urgency and that it involved a Jessica Wilson?'

Tom frowned. 'Jess?'

'That's what she said,' Sally confirmed. 'Do you have any ideas?'

Tom shook his head before remembering he was on the telephone. 'Not a clue. Jess is my fiancée. She does know Bonnie, but they've not seen each other for years, and as far as I know, Jess would like to keep it that way. I can't think what Bonnie could have to say that would be of interest to Jess.'

'I told Bonnie I'd try and get in touch with you and pass on the message. She's in RAF Ramsbury working in the cookhouse – unless you want me to pass on your details?'

'No!' said Tom hastily, causing Sally to giggle.

'Not keen to rekindle your friendship?' she asked.

'I'd like to hear what she has to say first,' said Tom slowly, 'and I'd like a chance to talk to Jess, see if she can shed any light on the matter.'

'Don't blame you,' said Sally. 'I seem to remember Bonnie being a bit of a troublemaker.'

'A bit! She ...' Tom paused. 'I'll give her a call after I've spoken to Jess.'

'OK. Good luck, Tom.'

'Thanks, Sal.'

He pressed the button to cut them off, then spoke hastily to the operator, asking her to put him through to Jess's NAAFI.

'How do, Tom. Jess isn't here at the minute, can I help?'

'Ruby! How's George?'

'Last time he wrote, most of his letter had been censored, which is annoying, but at least I know he's alive.'

'I wonder if he knows what's going on?' said Tom, temporarily sidetracked.

'I'd like to think they wouldn't leave the ground troops in the dark, but everything's so hush-hush, they may be just as clueless as us. How about you – how are things your end?'

'I've had a message from Bonnie McKinley,' Tom said. 'She wants to speak to me as a matter of urgency, and it's regarding Jess.'

'Bloomin' Nora,' breathed Ruby. 'There's a name I never expected to hear again. I wonder what she wants?'

Tom gave a disappointed sigh. 'I rather hoped you or Jess might know the answer to that.'

'Haven't the foggiest, and I know Jess won't either,' Ruby said simply.

'What do you think I should do?' said Tom. 'I don't particularly want to have anything to do with Bonnie, and I can't see why she needs to speak to me so urgently, but on the other hand if I don't ask, we'll never know.'

'I would give her a bell,' said Ruby. 'It might be something to do with Greystones – one of the girls maybe?'

'That's a thought,' said Tom. 'I'll give her a ring and let you know how I get on. Tell Jess I called, won't you?'

'She'd have my guts for garters if I didn't let her know you'd rung,' chuckled Ruby, 'and I daresay she'll be just as keen to know what Bonnie has to say, so make sure you ring back as soon as you've spoken to her.'

'Will do. Ta-ra, queen.'

'Ta-ra, Tom. Take care.'

Olivia held Ted's hand as they lowered her father's coffin into the grave.

Ted gave her a sidelong glance. 'Are you OK?'

She gave a feeble attempt at a smile. Her father's death had come out of the blue. When she had asked the doctors at Sefton General what the cause of death was, they had said pneumonia. She had spent the last few months being so angry at him for hiding the birth of her daughter, so to be told he had died knocked the wind out of her sails. She had gone from vowing that she would not waste her breath on asking him questions to wishing that she had. With all leave cancelled, she had been granted a forty-eight on compassionate grounds.

Now, as her eyes glazed over, she wrestled with her emotions. She had gone from grieving for the child she thought she had lost, to grieving for missing out on her daughter's life to date. It was all very well searching for Jess, but Olivia had no idea how she would be welcomed, and without her father's presence to prove Olivia's innocence in relation to abandoning her baby to an orphanage, Jess would have to take her word for it. She wouldn't be able to grant her daughter the answer as to why her grandfather had behaved the way he had. In short, he'd left her up that familiar creek without a boat, never mind a paddle. She looked to where her grandparents stood, hand in hand, as they each dropped soil on to the coffin lid. She saw her grandmother wipe a tear from her cheek.

Olivia wanted to tell her grandmother to spare her tears, because her father didn't deserve them, but to do so would be an act of petulance. Olivia wasn't just angry at her father for what he'd done, but for dying, leaving her all alone, with a business she had no desire to run, and a house which would stand empty, no doubt a mecca for thieves and vagabonds. He hadn't just left her with a whole heap of unanswered questions, but a mass of responsibility. Pops was running the factory, but she knew they were already experiencing losses, probably because his appearance had been an invitation for some of the workers to take advantage. For the first time in her life, Olivia empathised with her father. Unless you were prepared to spend all your time overseeing production, the business would suffer. She glanced guiltily at her grandfather. His face was grey, and a line which had not been on his forehead previously now ran deep between his brows. Unless they could get some real help soon, they would have to sell the factory at a knock-down price, because she would not see her grandfather run into the ground operating a business he had no wish to be involved in.

Ted nudged Olivia, bringing her back to the present. She looked up and saw that the vicar was holding the soil box before her. She took some dirt and threw it into the grave, then watched Ted do the same.

With the ceremony at an end, Olivia, Ted and the Barnhams left the churchyard.

'End of an era,' said Pops. 'I always thought him a real slave-driver when I worked for him, but I'd rather do my old job than his.'

Olivia gave him an apologetic smile. 'I'm so sorry you've been landed with this burden. I'm doing the best I can to get someone to help you run the factory.'

He waved a vague hand. 'I know you are, Liv, but your father's shoes are hard to fill, and I doubt you're going to find anyone as dedicated as him.'

Nana threaded her arm through the crook of her husband's elbow. 'It's not worth the hassle if you don't reap the rewards. You can't pay someone to do what he did.'

'That's because no one wants to be married to a business,' said Olivia, 'as my father was.'

Pops shot her a reproving glance. 'I dunno so much about that, Liv. Take it from one who's walked in his shoes, it's not a question about wanting to be married to it; you *have* to be married to it if you don't want to see it go under.'

Olivia eyed him doubtfully. 'Surely they can't all be crooks? He must have some loyal staff?'

Pops shrugged. 'Times are hard, Liv. If they can half-inch a bit of stock and make a bit of profit on the side, they're going to. And you have to have years of experience to run summat like that. I'm winging it at the moment, but that can't last. I don't really know what I'm doing, so I have to take everyone at face value. Unfortunately that means half of them are pilfering when my back's turned – or at least that's what it looks like according to the latest stock count.'

Olivia nodded her head decisively. 'Enough's enough. I shall put word out that the factory is up for sale ...' She held up a hand as her grandparents began to protest. 'I know I won't get its true value, but I'll not see you turn into my father, nor Nana turn into my mother, because of some stupid factory.'

Her grandmother raised an eyebrow. 'Beginning to see things from your father's point of view?'

Olivia gave a shrug. 'I don't know about that. After all, I'm choosing my family over the business.'

Pops nodded slowly as though deep in thought. 'True, but that's because of the way you're wired. The factory was in your father's bones, had been since the day he was born. His father took him out of school at a young age because he told the headmistress that the only training your father needed in life was how to run an empire, and he was the best tutor for that.'

Nana gave her granddaughter a small smile. 'Your father was what he was.' She looked repentant. 'I felt sorry for him, because it's not the life he had planned. We know that, because he was a marvel with your mother in the beginning – it was only after the death of his father that things changed.'

Pops held up a finger. 'He was a victim of circumstance.'

Nana nodded. 'Nail on the head, Ivor.'

Olivia stared at her grandfather. 'Just like you.' She shook her head sadly. 'Because you're the only one we can trust to run the factory, it's fallen on to your shoulders, but it's plain to see the toll it's taking on your health. Maybe you're right in saying that Dad had no choice but to pick up the gauntlet and run with it, but you don't have to, and I'm going to do everything I can to make sure you don't.'

But her grandfather was shaking his head. 'Never mind me, you concentrate on finding your daughter.'

They turned on to Aigburth Road. 'I've been searching for months. For all I know, it could take years, or maybe it'll never happen. I can't let you work yourself into the ground for something that might never come to fruition.' Olivia turned her head, pretending to look at the park to hide the tears that threatened. In the beginning, she had been certain they'd find Jessica, but months had passed by and still there was no news, and she was beginning to fear the worst. Operating an ack-ack battery was not without its dangers, and people died all the time. If Tom Durning's battery had been hit, then the trail would run cold.

The wake, such as it was, was held at her father's house – now her house – on Aigburth Drive. Ted glanced around the kitchen as they helped Annie to plate the sandwiches and brew the tea.

'What will you do with the house?' he asked.

'I'll give it up for the war effort until it's all over, then sell it.' She glanced around the room. 'This house holds no good memories for me, not any more.'

He raised an eyebrow. 'Not even your mother?'

'No. I only see her sick and dying when I enter her room, but when I think of the happy times, it's day trips to Brighton, or weekends in North Wales, just me, Mum, Nana and Pops.' She eyed Ted quizzically. 'Aren't you angry with him?'

He shrugged. 'What's the point?'

'Because we can't hold him accountable for his actions. He got away with all the lies, scot-free.'

'Did he, though?'

'You know he did! I didn't confront him, so he's no idea we know the truth behind his despicable act.'

'He lived with the guilt of what he did all his life, too caught up in the lie to tell the truth. He had to take it to the grave. We all make mistakes, Liv, but most of us get a chance to do something about them – but your father didn't because it was too late. Once he'd committed to the lies, there was no backing out. Or to put it another way, he'd dug himself a hole so deep, there was no hope of escape.'

'Do you really think he felt an ounce of guilt? Because I don't,' she said sharply. 'Dad was always manipulating people to get what he wanted; it never bothered him in the past.'

'I can't believe a fellow human being can live the way he did without ...'

Olivia pointed angrily outside the window. 'Hitler, Ted – Hitler is murdering thousands of innocent people because he wants to rule the world; Dad's no different to him. They both have a goal in mind, and they'd both do anything to achieve that goal. My father gave his own granddaughter away because he didn't like you, and yet you were a product of the workforce he created. The man had no scruples or conscience. You got in the way of his ambition by getting me pregnant, so he got rid of you and got rid of your baby.' She was staring at Ted, hot tears running down her cheeks.

'And does being angry make you feel any better?' Ted said calmly.

Olivia blinked. 'Of course not, but tearing a strip or two off him would.'

'Really? Because I don't think it would. Your grandmother was right. It's like being angry at a dog for being a dog.' He handed her a handkerchief.

'Being angry at Dad takes my mind off Jessica.'

Taking her in his arms, Ted smiled down at her. 'I thought as much. Your father might be a lot of things, but he's not Hitler!'

She eyed him curiously. 'Are you saying I should forget everything he's done and move forward with my life?'

'Do you enjoy mulling over the whys and wherefores?'

She shook her head miserably. 'No.'

'Then why do it?'

She smiled. 'You make things sound so simple.'

He gave a soft chuckle. 'Because they are, certainly compared to trying to change the past.'

She snuggled into his chest. 'I hope that one day soon, we get to show our daughter how lucky she is having you as a father.'

Bonnie took the receiver from the Waaf. 'Hello?'

'Bonnie?'

Bonnie's heart skipped a beat. 'Tom?'

'I got your message,' said Tom. 'What's up?'

Bonnie glanced around the cookhouse, but there was no sign of Maude. 'I need to get in touch with Jess. Do you have her details?'

'I do, but she asked if I wouldn't mind speaking to you on her behalf,' said Tom. He recalled Jess's words the day they discussed the matter.

'I don't give a monkey's what she wants. It's bound to be bad, but if you want to know, then by all means ring her, and on your head be it.'

Bonnie had suspected Jess would be reluctant to speak with her – not that it mattered. Either way she was determined to let Tom know her findings. 'I'll be brief as we won't have long before the operator cuts us off ...' She told Tom of her encounter with Olivia and Maude and the outcome of their discussion. Once she'd finished, she waited to hear his response. 'Tom?'

'Please tell me this isn't some kind of prank, Bonnie, because I don't think it's very funny if it is. Or if you're trying to get into Jess's good books ...'

'I'll admit I'd like to make amends with Jess,' said Bonnie, 'but I wouldn't conjure up a fictional person in order to do that.'

'Why doesn't she call Jess herself?' Tom asked guardedly.

'She doesn't know how to get in touch with her, and neither do I, which is why I'm coming to you, and believe you me, you take some finding.'

'So, this was a chance encounter and these women just happened to describe Jess's father ...'

'Grandfather ...' Bonnie corrected.

Tom heaved a sigh. 'Jess's grandfather whilst waiting for their spuds?'

'No!' Bonnie insisted. 'I told them Greystones was an orphanage whilst they were waiting for their spuds – it was when they sought me out later that Olivia described her father.' She sighed impatiently. She knew they couldn't have too much longer before the operator terminated the call. 'She got her date of birth right, and when I mentioned that rotten cane of his, we put two and two together. Tom, it *has* to be Jess's mother ...'

'Caller, your time is ...' came the operator's voice.

Bonnie interrupted without apology. 'Why would she lie? She knew everything ... Tom, if you don't believe me then I can't do anything about it, but promise me you'll tell Jess. Her mother's name is Olivia ...' She paused. She was sure she'd just heard the line go quiet. 'Tom?'

'Caller, please replace the handset.'

Bonnie could have screamed with frustration. She hadn't had a chance to tell Tom Olivia's surname or her base. Not only that, but Tom hadn't said where he was based so she couldn't return his call. She would have to tell Maude that she had made contact, but what else would she say? She had no idea what Tom thought, but his last words hadn't sounded too positive. She sighed heavily. She had done her bit. If Tom wanted to know more, he knew where to find her.

At the other end of the line, Tom chewed his lip thoughtfully. Bonnie had certainly sounded sincere, and it would seem a bit far-fetched for her to invent some woman claiming to be Jess's mother. He shrugged. He would tell Jess and let her make up her own mind.

*

Ruby skipped across the rain-puddled yard to the gate, waving frantically at Jess as she got out of the car.

'Wait!'

Jess furrowed her brow. 'Is everything all right?'

Ruby beckoned to the guard on gate duty to lower the gate so that the car could not pass through. The driver, who had been about to pull away, wound down his window. 'Hello, Ruby, what's up?'

'Hello, Lenny.' She looked past him to his passenger. 'Hello, Dana.' She glanced at Jess. 'Have you told Dana and Lenny about Bonnie?'

Jess pulled a face. 'Yes. Why, what's up?'

Ruby blinked as raindrops dripped from the peak of her cap. 'Can we go into the NAAFI?'

'I don't see why not,' Dana said, 'if we've got time?'

Lenny glanced at his watch. 'Ten minutes won't harm.' He turned to Ruby. 'We'll meet you inside.'

As soon as they were all inside, Jess turned to Dana and Lenny. 'Remember how I told you about Bonnie, the girl who was in the orphanage with me and Ruby?'

Dana nodded. 'The one who grassed you up?'

'That's the one,' said Jess. 'Well, she's been trying to find Tom, so that she could speak to me.' She glanced at Ruby. 'I take it Tom's spoken to her?'

Ruby nodded fervently. 'He certainly has, and you wouldn't believe what she had to say.'

'Can't see it has any importance to me, not after all these years, but fire away.'

Ruby urged them to take a seat. 'This affects you too, Dana.'

'*Me?*' said Dana, incredulously. 'But I've never even met the girl.'

Ruby nodded. 'Bonnie thinks she's found your mother. It's a long story, and Tom had to be quick because you know how eager some of these operators can be …' Ruby relayed Tom's words. When she finished she eyed them anxiously. 'What do you think?'

Jess and Dana exchanged glances. 'If it was anyone else I'd believe them without question, but *Bonnie*?' Jess said.

'I know,' Ruby agreed. 'The only thing she's got going for her is she can let Tom know where your mother is based, so you don't actually have to speak to Bonnie at all.'

'Oh, well, that's a bit different. Where is she based?'

'Ah well, she didn't manage to tell Tom this time because the operator cut them off, but he's certain she was trying to give him the information but thought he'd check with you first before calling her back.'

Jess shook her head. 'So, essentially, if we want to speak to our so-called mother, we have to contact Bonnie first?'

Ruby nodded. 'But I don't mind doing that, and neither does Tom, if you don't want to.'

'I don't trust her,' Jess said simply. 'You watch, she's doing all this so that we'll get back in contact, then, just as we're about to meet up with this woman, poof, she'll disappear without trace.'

Dana was looking doubtfully at Jess. 'I don't know. Bonnie must realise she'd be expected to tell you the base where you could reach her. One quick phone call would soon establish whether she was telling the truth or not; once you've done that, all we have to do is find out why this woman thinks she's our mother.'

'That's a thought.' Jess turned to Ruby. 'Bonnie doesn't know Dana's my twin, but our mother would know. Did she mention anything about twins?'

Ruby pulled a face. 'Tom was speaking so quickly, trying to get all the information across before we got disconnected, but I don't remember him mentioning twins.'

'Then it's simple,' said Dana. 'We contact Bonnie and find out exactly what the woman said to her. If she didn't mention twins, then it's obvious she's either making the whole thing up, or it's not our mother.'

Olivia squealed with delight, causing Maude to whip the phone away from her ear.

'Good old Bonnie! She said she'd try her best and she's certainly done that. Did she say anything else?'

'Only that she got disconnected before she could tell Tom where you were, but he knows where she's based so she's hoping he will back once he's spoken to Jess.'

Olivia's tummy fluttered with excitement. 'I really thought the trail had gone cold. I can't tell you what this means to me, Maude, and Ted'll be so pleased.'

Maude wound her finger around the telephone cord. 'On a more sombre note, how did the funeral go?'

'All right, I suppose. There were more people there than I thought there would be, as he was hardly what you'd call popular or well liked. Ted thinks they were possibly old business acquaintances who were sniffing around to see what could be gained from his passing.'

'Oh Liv, that's terrible,' said Maude.

'Birds of a feather,' Olivia said simply. 'He'd probably have gone to their funerals for the same reason if the shoe was on the other foot.'

'No love lost, eh?' said Maude.

'That's what they're like, Maude, only out for what they can get.'

'Well, at least you've got something to look forward to now, because I'm certain Jess'll get in touch with you.'

Olivia smiled. 'I hope so. It's maddening to be so close, yet so far away.' She mulled her words over. 'I don't think I'll tell Ted just yet. I want to wait until I hear more, because whilst it's lovely to know that Bonnie's made contact with Tom, we're still no closer to speaking to Jess.'

Maude snapped her fingers. 'Why don't you write to her? You could send it to Tom and he could pass it on. That way there's no awkwardness and you can tell her everything before you've met, so she'll get the whole story without interruption. You can get your side across, tell her the truth about her grandfather, so that she doesn't fear meeting him, and tell her about Ted.'

Olivia was beaming. 'That's a fantastic idea, Maude, I'll certainly do that.'

Maude could hear the smile in her friend's voice. 'I do have good ideas on occasion.'

'Well, this one's a corker!' said Olivia.

'I'll ask Bonnie to give me Tom's details.'

'Thanks, Maude.'

'Ta-ra, Liv.'

Olivia replaced the receiver and turned to Beth who was waiting patiently for her. 'Have you got any spare paper I can use?'

Beth nodded. 'Of course I have. Has this got anything to do with Maude's fantastic idea?'

Olivia grinned. 'I'm going to write to Jess and explain everything so that she knows what's what before I speak to her.'

Beth smiled approvingly. 'You're right, that is a good idea. Does that mean you know where she's based?'

'No, I'm going to send it to her boyfriend Tom, and ask him to pass it on.'

'Oh heck, I hope he doesn't move around too much. It took long enough to find him this time,' said Beth.

Lowering her voice, Olivia glanced around. 'I get the feeling that this is the calm before the storm. According to Bonnie, Tom's been at his new base for a few days now, and I know Josie said things seem to have settled down in Ramsbury. It reminds me of a game of chess, where you get all your pieces in position before you checkmate.'

Beth's tummy lurched unpleasantly. 'I hope to goodness that whatever they've got planned works and that this isn't another Dunkirk.'

Olivia nodded reassuringly. 'Course it will. We've got all the key players – you mark my words, we're approaching the beginning of the end. Oh, I do miss having Josie and Maude around, like the old days.'

Beth nodded. 'Me too. Fingers crossed we're all right and this wretched business really is coming to an end, because the sooner that happens the sooner we can all get together again.'

Tom looked at the address on the envelope, which read *Jessica Wilson, care of Tom Durning*. He turned the fat envelope over in his hands. During a brief conversation with Jess, it had been agreed that Tom should telephone Bonnie again, giving her his whereabouts should she need to make further contact. She had rung a few days later to say that Olivia was sending a letter to Jess via him, and he now assumed that this had to be that letter. He licked his lips nervously. He held in his hands what could prove to be the answer to the mystery surrounding the night of the girls' birth – or at least he hoped he did. It would be such a shame if it all came to naught. He wondered whether to ring Jess and let her know the letter had arrived, then thought better of it. This was Jess and Dana's life, not his. He would forward the letter post-haste. Jess had asked him whether Bonnie had mentioned Dana being her twin, but he felt certain she had not, although, as he told Jess, the conversation had been centred on Bonnie's interaction with Olivia and the role of Olivia's father, and not the whys and wherefores surrounding the girls themselves.

'I'll see what she has to say, and go from there,' Jess had said, 'but if this woman only mentions me, then we'll know straight away she's not our mother.'

He wrote Jess's address on the new envelope and kissed it for luck. Silly, he knew, because the girls were happy as they were.

All her life Jess had believed herself to be an only child, right up to the day she had found a photograph of Dana in someone else's scrapbook. It had been obvious to everyone that the resemblance between the girls wasn't just passing, but identical. They had done some digging and found out where Dana was based and

Tom had been present when Dana and Jess met for the first time. Jess had been uncertain as to the reaction she would receive, but after getting over the initial shock, Dana had proved to be both warm and welcoming. It turned out that she had been adopted by a family of travellers, and her earlier life had been far better than Jess's.

This meeting had happened in the spring of 1943, and the girls had formed a strong bond. When Tom had proposed to Jess on the eve of Christmas 1943, the girls had immediately talked Tom and Lenny into the idea of having a double wedding. Tom smiled as he recalled Jess and Dana's faces as they examined the pearl ring which Tom's Great-Aunt Edna had given him as an engagement ring for Jess.

'Just imagine the sight of us walking down the aisle with Mum in the middle,' Dana had said excitedly.

Dana's adoptive mother, Colleen, had taken Jess under her wing without question, treating her as she did Dana. 'It should save us a bob or two an' all,' agreed Jess, much to Dana's amusement.

Tom and Lenny had both agreed that it would be pretty special to have identical twins getting married on the same day, and they had begun to make the arrangements.

He wondered now how Colleen would take the news of their birth mother. A small smile tweaked the corner of his lips. Colleen would welcome her with open arms if it made the girls happy.

Tom very much wanted this woman to be his fiancée's mother. It would be the final piece in the jigsaw.

*

Jess read the letter aloud to Dana and her friend Patty.

'Well, I don't know who she is, but she's definitely not our mother,' sighed Dana.

Jess shook her head. 'Can't be.' She glanced up at her sister. 'I must say, I can't help but feel a little disappointed. It would have answered a lot of questions.'

'It certainly would,' agreed Dana, then she frowned. 'It's so odd, though – her father sounds just like ours. Surely there can't have been two men with matching canes of such an unusual nature in Glasgow that night?'

Jess rubbed her hand across her chin. 'I've been thinking about that one, and Olivia said he bought that cane when he was in Glasgow, so it's not out of the question that the shop which sold it to him had more than one in stock, and when it comes to his physical description …' she shrugged, '… old man, mutton chops … probably describes most old men. The only thing that differentiated him from the others was the cane with the cobra head detail.'

Dana looked uneasy. 'So, her daughter might really have died that night.'

Jess nodded. 'That poor woman's gone through such a lot. I hope our biological mother didn't endure something like that.'

'What are you going to say in your letter to Olivia?'

'Well, I'm certainly not going to suggest her father might have been telling the truth from the start, because that would banish all her hopes, and I'm not going to be the one who does that to her.' She mulled it over for a moment or so. 'Until we hear differently, we have to assume her father did bring her baby to Greystones, so perhaps ask around and see if anyone

400

remembers anyone who might fit the bill. After all, there were a lot of girls in Greystones, and her father might have taken her baby there several days after me for all we know.'

Dana nodded. 'Let me know if there's anything I can do to help. That poor woman deserves to find out the truth.'

Beth trotted into the billet and made a beeline for Olivia. 'You've got mail, and I don't recognise the writing ...'

Olivia's stomach performed a cartwheel as she held her hand up to receive the letter. She looked at the writing on the outside of the envelope, which was indeed unfamiliar. Slitting the envelope open with her knife, she glanced up at Beth, who was nibbling the corner of her thumbnail. 'Here goes ...'

She looked down at the letter, then began to read it aloud.

Dear Olivia,

Thank you so much for your lovely letter. It was nice to hear from you in person and Dana and I both read it with keen interest. However, after reading what you had to say, I was rather disappointed to learn that it appears there has been some kind of miscommunication and it looks like you're not our mother after all, even though the man who abandoned me at the orphanage sounds a dead ringer for your father. I'm a twin, and as you did not mention having twins, it looks as though there's been some remarkable coincidences surrounding the Christmas Eve of 1923.

Dana and I have discussed it at length and we would very much like it if you kept in touch. I'm still in contact with another girl who was in Greystones, and I shall ask her if she knows anything that could be of any interest to you.

Olivia scanned the rest of the letter before sighing heavily. 'Looks like another dead end.'

Beth took the letter from her unresisting fingers and quickly scanned the contents. 'Are you going to stay in touch?'

Olivia nodded. 'They're the closest I've come to finding my daughter, and their friend might know of someone who fits the bill.' She tutted beneath her breath. 'Why didn't Bonnie say that Jess was a twin? I'd never have bothered writing to her had I known that.'

Beth shrugged. 'It does seem a bit odd, especially as she never mentioned the man abandoning two babies, just one.'

Olivia drummed her fingers on the edge of her bed. 'None of this makes sense.'

'Are you going to tell her about this letter?'

'I'll tell Maude, and I daresay she'll pass the message on.' She took the letter from Beth. 'They sound like nice girls, though, because they could've wiped their hands of me.'

'Kindred spirits,' said Beth. 'You're looking for your daughter and they're looking for their mother.'

'I s'pose so,' she put the letter into her box of keepsakes, 'although no one's going to be doing anything whilst all leave has been cancelled.'

Beth pulled a face. 'I know. I thought whatever it is they've been planning would be over and done with by now.'

'Fingers crossed it's soon, because I'd really like to go and see Ted. Jess and Dana, too, for that matter, because those girls might just be the link to finding our daughter.'

'Are you going to tell Ted? About them being twins, I mean?'

Olivia nodded. 'I promised I'd keep him informed of any developments. He'll be disappointed because we'd got used to the idea that Jess was our daughter, but Ted's no quitter, and I know he won't give up until we've found our baby.'

Olivia rang Ted later on that evening, and just as she had anticipated, it came as a low blow.

'I was convinced,' he said. 'I knew I shouldn't have got my hopes up, but I couldn't help myself. I was positive Jess was ours – it all seemed to fit so perfectly into place.'

Olivia drew a deep breath. She hated having to break bad news over the telephone, but she couldn't have left Ted thinking Jess was theirs. 'We'll just have to keep looking,' she said. 'The girls have said they'll help in any way they can.'

'That's good to hear,' said Ted. 'They've got more connections than we have, so we'll find our baby faster with them helping out.'

Olivia smiled. She knew Ted wouldn't let her down.

The operator's voice instructed them to replace the receiver.

'Thanks for letting me know, Toff, and try to keep your chin up.'

'You too,' said Olivia. 'I love you, Ted.'

She could hear the smile in his voice. 'I love you too, my gorgeous girl.'

Chapter Eleven

With the air force deciding to stop using female balloon operators, Beth and Olivia had both retrained as drivers in the motor transport section, where they were transferred to RAF Stoney Cross in the New Forest.

It was on their second day at their new base that they awoke to the news of the Normandy invasion. 'Why's everyone running round like headless chickens?' yawned Beth.

Olivia held a newspaper towards her friend. 'See for yourself. I'm off for a wash, back in a mo.'

Beth read the headlines which dominated the front page: *Our armies in France. Over 4000 invasion ships cross the channel* ... She scanned the lines below. 'Blimey,' she said under her breath. She laid the newspaper on her bed, slung her greatcoat around her shoulders, picked up her washbag and joined Olivia in the ablutions.

'So that's what all the fuss was about,' she said to Olivia as she joined her by the sinks.

'You can see why they kept it so hush-hush now,' Olivia agreed. 'Did you read it all? It looks like it's been a huge success so far.'

Beth shook her head. 'I'm a slower reader than you. By the time I've read that lot, I'll have missed brekker.'

Olivia rinsed her toothbrush under the tap. 'Looks like we're finally giving the Nazis a run for their money!'

'About time too,' said Beth. 'Do you think they'll let us have leave now it's all over?'

Olivia gave her friend a reproving glance. 'I think you might be jumping the gun a bit there. It's far from over, but they've certainly got a good footing.'

'Perhaps I did put that badly,' Beth conceded. 'What I meant was, now that the cat's out of the bag and everything's no longer hush-hush, will they let us have leave again?'

Olivia blew her cheeks out. 'I'd like to think so, but I doubt it.'

A Waaf at the sink next to Olivia's spoke up. 'It depends on what else they've got planned, but if they've got Hitler by the short and curlies, I doubt they'll give us any time off until they've got the job done.'

'But that could be ages yet,' moaned Beth, 'and I so wanted to see Spencer. It's been yonks since I saw him last.'

'There's no harm in asking,' replied the Waaf.

Olivia glanced at her reflection in the mirror. If they really were allowing people to have leave again, she could make arrangements to go and see Ted. 'Let me know when you ask for leave, I'll come with you. Perhaps the success of the invasion will have put Officer Wendell in a good mood and he might say yes to both of us!'

After breakfast, the girls headed for their commanding officer's private office. 'You go first,' Olivia told Beth. 'I'll keep my fingers crossed for you.'

Smiling, Beth straightened her jacket, rapped on the door and waited for the order to enter. She headed into the room, only to reappear a few seconds later looking forlorn.

'Oh,' said Olivia dejectedly, 'I'm taking it the answer was still no?'

Beth nodded miserably. 'He laughed first, though, so at least his sense of humour's returning.'

'Oh heck,' said Olivia. 'I won't even try if that's the case.' She brightened a little. 'Perhaps Ted and Spencer might have better luck asking to come here?'

Beth brightened. 'Worth a shot, I suppose.'

The girls wasted no time in telephoning the relevant NAAFIs only to be told that there was no chance of the boys coming down to visit.

'Already asked,' said Ted, 'and his precise words were: "No one told me that hell had frozen over and I assume it must have, because that's the only way you'll be getting leave."' Ted sighed. 'He could've just said no.'

'At least he didn't laugh at you,' Olivia said.

'Looks like we'll have to make do with letters and phone calls for a bit longer yet,' said Ted. 'How're Nana and Pops?'

'Much better. Pops thinks he's found a buyer for the factory, one of Dad's old acquaintances, so that's good news. They were disappointed to hear that Jess wasn't our daughter but are keeping their fingers crossed that something turns up.'

'Have you heard from Jess recently?'

Olivia drew a deep breath. 'Only to say that she hadn't heard any more from her old friend, but that she would keep trying.'

'She's a good 'un,' said Ted. 'It's a shame things turned out the way they did.'

Olivia nodded to herself. She knew Jess couldn't be her daughter, but deep down she wished she was.

With the Normandy landings far behind them, the war had quickened its pace and Britain and her allies had gone from strength to strength. Victory over Germany was looking more and more likely and morale was at an all-time high.

Olivia had remained in contact with Jess and Dana despite their attempts to find her daughter drawing a blank. When receiving mail from either of the girls, she no longer expected to hear mention of her daughter, but they kept her posted as to how the war was progressing from their end. In their most recent epistle, Jess had written to tell Olivia of her and Dana's upcoming double wedding.

We had agreed to wait until the war was over, but goodness only knows when that will be, and what with them cancelling leave willy-nilly, we've booked the first free date in Brougham Terrace Register Office, which is August 14th. We'd both really like it if you could come to the wedding ...

Olivia felt a lump rise in her throat. She had become close to the girls and it was heart-warming to know they felt the same. So she had immediately telephoned Ted to ask if he could get the time off to attend the ceremony.

'I'll have to ask, but I can't see it being a problem,' he said cheerfully, 'especially with it being close to base.'

August 1944

Olivia waited outside Ted's barracks, her tummy fluttering with anticipation. She caught sight of him and waved as he approached the taxi. Smiling, Ted slid along the back seat towards her and kissed her softly. 'Hello, darling.'

Olivia felt her heart rise in her chest. 'Hello, Ted.' She spoke directly to the driver: 'Brougham Terrace, please.' As the cab pulled away, she turned her attention back to Ted. 'It's so good to see you. I've missed you so much, and I know we talk over the telephone two or three times a week, but it's not the same as seeing you in person.'

Ted cupped her face in his hands and kissed her again, only this time, the kiss lasted longer and was deeper than the first. 'Not as much as I've missed you,' he said quietly. 'How do you feel about the wedding?'

She smiled. 'Mixed emotions. I know I shouldn't have placed all my eggs in one basket when we thought Jess was our daughter, but I did, and even though I know it's not possible, I feel as though she's mine – her and Dana – which is ridiculous, I know.'

Ted ran the back of his fingers down her cheek. 'It's not ridiculous, sweetheart, or if it is then I'm just as guilty, because I was also certain that we'd found our baby girl.'

Olivia nodded. 'I feel like a ghost parent, if that makes sense?'

'If you mean you feel like you're a parent which no one else recognises, then yes, that does make sense. I feel so proud of them both, yet I've never met them.'

'Me too,' enthused Olivia. 'Those girls have really beaten the odds and are doing so incredibly well for themselves despite the hand that fate dealt them. I can only hope our daughter's done as well.'

He shrugged. 'Perhaps they feel the same way. You've an awful lot in common with them regarding nasty fathers.'

Olivia leaned her head against his chest. 'Two evil so-and-sos, both from Liverpool – I'd never have believed it.'

Ted frowned. 'I don't suppose your father had a twin?'

She laughed mirthlessly. 'No, Ted, he didn't, but a cousin of his did – but if you're suggesting his cousin's twin was in Glasgow the same time as us, with the same dilemma, I think that's even more far-fetched than some of the theories I've come up with.'

He smiled. One of Olivia's theories had been that she'd had twins and not been aware of the second baby. This, of course, had been dismissed straight away by Ted, who had asked her how anyone could have another baby without knowing.

Olivia thanked the taxi driver as Ted paid the fare and together they made their way into the register office. They asked where they might find Jessica Wilson and Dana Quinn, and the receptionist pointed them in the right direction. 'You'll have to be quiet,' she said, 'they've already started. We're actually running ahead of time for once.'

Olivia tutted beneath her breath. 'I really wanted to watch them get married,' she said to Ted as they hurried down the corridor. 'I hope we're not too late for the vows.'

They opened the door as quietly as they could and sat at the back of the room. Olivia was pleased to learn that they hadn't missed the exchanging of vows, and when it was Jess's turn to repeat the registrar's words she caught sight of Olivia and Ted and gave them a small acknowledging wave before nudging Dana, who did the same. An old woman at the front of the room turned in her wheelchair and glared accusingly at Olivia and Ted for causing a distraction.

Ted waited until the vows were complete before hissing, 'Don't think that old bat was too pleased to see us.'

Olivia grimaced. 'I'm not entirely sure I'm pleased to see her. I'm fairly certain she could be one of Dad's old associates because I seem to recognise her from somewhere.'

'She certainly looks miserable enough.' He stifled a chuckle. 'Mind she doesn't run over your foot with her wheelchair! I daresay that thing weighs a ton.'

But Olivia wasn't in the mood for laughing. She was very keen for her first meeting with the girls to go well, and even though they knew from what Olivia had told them that her father was a nasty piece of work, she didn't relish the idea of having a lecture in front of a room full of strangers about her father's shenanigans.

With the ceremony at an end, they waited for Jess and Tom, and Dana and Lenny to walk down the aisle followed by their closest friends and family, one of whom was the old woman in her wheelchair, with a middle-aged woman pushing her. As she wheeled past Olivia and Ted she cast them a disapproving glance but said nothing, much to Olivia's relief.

Ted jerked his head in the direction of the old lady. 'Do you know where you recognise her from yet?'

Olivia slid her arm through Ted's. 'I think so, and I'd like to know where before she recognises me. The last thing I need her doing is harping on about how my father diddled her in some way or other.'

'Diddled!' Ted sniggered. 'Is that what they're calling it nowadays?'

Olivia slapped him lightly across the arm. 'Don't be so crude!'

She was interrupted by Jess, who was calling for her and Ted to join them outside the building. 'I'm so pleased you could come to the wedding. We're having a bit of a tea at Lyons café as a kind of wedding breakfast, I hope you can join us?'

Olivia nodded enthusiastically. 'We'd love to, wouldn't we, Ted?'

Ted agreed heartily.

Jess smiled brightly. 'Good, it'll give us a chance to have a real chat.' She gazed into Olivia's eyes. A faint crease marked her brow, and she excused herself and joined her sister.

'Gosh, aren't they beautiful, Ted?' said Olivia, admiring the girls with their strawberry-blonde hair, rose petal mouths and large green eyes.

Ted nodded hesitantly.

'What?' said Olivia. 'Don't you agree?'

'I do, it's just …' He fell silent. He didn't want to put ideas into Olivia's head, but she and Jess had the same coloured eyes, something which he conceded could be coincidental as apart from that they looked very different. Olivia had dark hair, and the girls' hair colour was more like his. He smiled. 'Let's get to Lyons before they eat everything.'

Olivia laughed. 'Never turned down a meal in your life, have you, Ted?'

'Silly thing to do with a war on,' said Ted. 'You have to be grateful for every morsel.'

They followed the guests to the café. When they arrived, Olivia helped herself to a cup of tea and surveyed the room, her eyes unfortunately settling on the old woman in the wheelchair who was staring at her with a fixed glare. 'Oh heck,' Olivia muttered under her breath as the old lady instructed her companion to wheel her over to Olivia. 'Ted,' she hissed from the corner of her mouth, 'she's recognised me, but I've still not got a clue who she is.'

Ted watched the woman, who was eyeing Olivia with suspicious intrigue. As she drew to a halt, the woman who had pushed her over gave them an apologetic smile.

'Do I know you?' asked the old lady accusingly.

Olivia shook her head. 'I don't think so.'

Narrowing her eyes, the woman stared at Olivia intently. 'I never forget a face, and I've seen you somewhere before, I'd bet my life on it.'

Her companion leaned forward, her hand outstretched. 'Hello, dear, you'll have to excuse Auntie Edna. Once she gets an idea in her head she's like a dog with a bone.' She shook Olivia's hand. 'I'm Sylvie, Tom's mam.'

Olivia smiled pleasantly at Sylvie. 'Lovely to meet you, Sylvie. I'm Olivia, I'm a friend of the girls.'

Seeing realisation dawn on Sylvie's face, it was plain to see the older woman knew who Olivia was. 'How wonderful of you to come all this way! Our Jess talks highly of you, as does Dana.'

Olivia placed hand on Ted's elbow. 'This is my boyfriend, Ted Hewitt.'

Sylvie shook Ted's hand. 'You must go over and chat to the girls, they've been so excited about meeting you both.'

Grateful for any move that took Olivia away from the wheelchair-ridden woman, Ted led her over to where Jess and Dana were deep in conversation with a couple of girls around their own age.

'Dana,' said Jess, when she saw them, 'this is Olivia and Ted.'

Turning, Dana clasped Olivia's hand firmly in her own. 'I'm sorry we didn't have time to talk at the wedding. How are you both?'

Olivia smiled. 'We're very well, thanks, although we'll be a lot better when this war is over and we can get on with our search.'

'Have you had any more luck tracing your daughter?' said Dana.

Olivia shook her head. 'I've all but given up. I'm even beginning to think that Dad might have been telling the truth from the beginning.'

Jess and Dana instantly rallied. 'Oh no, you mustn't do that,' they said in unison.

414

'I'm sure you'll find her when the war's over. It'll help enormously when everything returns to normal and you can quiz the authorities responsible for taking orphans in. They might have taken your daughter from Greystones and rehomed her elsewhere,' Dana said encouragingly.

'There's an orphanage for boys, called Nazareth House, not far from Greystones,' Jess said. 'It might be an idea to give them a call.'

Olivia brightened; for the first time in a long while she felt hope return. She became aware that Sylvie had brought the old woman over to join them, and the old woman's head whipped up as she saw Olivia's eyes glisten with tears. 'I know you,' she said. 'I can't think where from, but I definitely know you.'

Olivia wanted to tell the old bat to go away and leave her alone, but of course she couldn't, so instead she smiled sweetly down at her, and to her surprise the woman smiled back, and this time, her eyes smiled too, in a kind and friendly fashion, the same as they had all those years ago. Olivia's mouth dropped open. She not only recognised the woman but she knew where she had seen her before.

'It's you,' she said, her voice barely above a whisper. 'I'd bet my life on it – you're the matron from the hospital that night.'

The smile faded from the old woman's lips and she quickly fished around the inside of her handbag for a pair of spectacles which she promptly placed on the bridge of her nose. Leaning forward, she peered up at Olivia who was now kneeling down beside her. 'Tell me I'm wrong,' Olivia said quietly.

The old woman dropped the spectacles into her lap. 'I said I never forget a face, and you're right, it was me.'

Ted looked around the sea of faces, all equally mystified by the conversation unfolding between the two women. He cleared his throat. 'Where do you know each other from?'

Olivia straightened up. Turning to face the girls, she stared at them, whilst speaking to the old woman. 'But how could I not know ...'

The old woman's eyes darted from side to side as she tried to think quickly. Eventually she took Olivia's hand in hers. 'None of us knew at first – Jess was a complete surprise. You were so young, and so exhausted from your experience, we thought you were having difficulty expelling the afterbirth, because of course it still hadn't come out, so when Jess appeared it was quite a shock.' She looked at Jess. 'The cord was wrapped around your neck, so we had to whisk you away in order to get you breathing.' She turned back to Olivia, her eyes now glistening with tears as well. 'I told your father that there was another baby on the way, but he didn't seem interested.' She blew her nose on the handkerchief Tom had handed her. 'So I got on with the job in hand. It didn't occur to me that he wouldn't hand the two of them over to the Quinns. When I asked the nurse looking after Dana to come and take Jess to join her sister, the poor girl was inconsolable because your father had already sent the Quinns on their way.' She shook her head as tears fell into her lap. 'How anyone could knowingly split the girls up was beyond us, but we'd already

416

been told to keep shtum and get on with things, so we did. We all made a pact that night to never speak of it again.' She glanced miserably at Jess. 'And I didn't, until Jess came into my life.'

Olivia stared at the girls, tears silently trickling down her cheeks. 'I don't know what to say, apart from I'm so sorry.'

The girls enveloped her in a tight embrace. 'There's nothing for you to apologise for,' said Dana, her voice barely above a whisper. 'None of this was your fault, you are just as much a victim in all this as we are.'

Jess beckoned Ted to join them. As he did, Olivia stared over their shoulders to a woman who was eyeing the girls with such deep-rooted affection, Olivia knew it had to be Colleen. She gave the other woman a wobbly smile. 'Thank you for loving my children.'

Colleen's bottom lip trembled. 'It was my honour.'

Ted kept his head lowered. 'All this because he thought I wasn't good enough for his daughter or his family,' he said quietly. 'He was so keen for me to never be part of his life, he made sure we couldn't come back and trace the girls.'

Auntie Edna spoke up. 'You say he didn't think you were good enough, but he suspected you'd try and find your girls, and only a loving father would go to that much trouble.'

Olivia nodded. 'She's right, you know. We only found our daughters because you came back and started asking questions which led to us discovering the truth. If Dad got anything right, it was the fact that he knew you would be a better father than he ever could be.'

Colleen stepped forward. 'I think we've spent enough time talking about the past.' She held up her cup of tea. 'I propose a toast, to new beginnings.'

The guests repeated the toast.

Dana wiped a tear from her eye. 'I would suggest we repeat those words one day with a glass of champagne in our hands instead of a cup of tea, but I can't stand the stuff.'

Jess looked at her sister in surprise. 'When did you taste champagne?'

'Well, I haven't,' she admitted, much to the amusement of those around her, 'but someone said it was like fizzy wine and I don't like wine at all.'

Olivia rested her head against Ted's shoulder. 'We've reached the end, Ted,' she said, smiling up at him.

Dana wrinkled her brow. 'Is it rude of me to ask why the two of you never married?'

Ted ran a hand around the back of his neck. 'I suppose we were too caught up in trying to find out what happened to our baby,' he grinned at the girls, 'or *babies*! We didn't have time to think about anything else.'

'Well, your search is over,' said Jess.

Dana's friend Patty came forward. 'You've obviously got a lot to catch up on. Is there any chance you can stay for a bit longer?'

Olivia shook her head sadly. 'No, I'd be for the high jump if I outstayed my leave, but I'll be straight over to see the girls next chance I get.'

The rest of the afternoon passed pleasantly with Colleen and Dana telling Olivia and Ted all about Dana's childhood, and the love and adoration Colleen and her late husband, Shane Quinn, had lavished on their adopted daughter. When it came to sharing what she knew about Jess's time in Greystones, everyone agreed that this would only cause pain and upset which no one wished to revisit, so it was best if they left it in the past, the same as they had with Olivia's father.

It was early evening when Olivia and Ted eventually said their goodbyes. Olivia clasped Dana and Jess's hands in her own. 'I shall miss you both terribly. We've such a lot to catch up on, so many birthdays and Christmases,' she waved her hands in the air, 'everything!'

Dana and Jess hugged Olivia goodbye. As Ted came forward for his turn, Colleen took Olivia in a warm embrace. 'You're a very special lady, Olivia Campbell, and I consider it a privilege having any part in looking after Dana, and Jess as well over the past year.'

Olivia's bottom lip trembled. 'I don't know about me being special. You took in a complete stranger's baby, and for that I can never thank you enough.'

Ted placed his hand in Olivia's. 'Time to go, Liv.'

Nodding, she hugged and kissed both girls, then hugged and kissed them again.

Waving goodbye as they ran down the street, they arrived at the station in the nick of time, for the guard was calling for people to board the train.

'Talk about cutting it fine,' said Olivia as she kissed Ted goodbye. 'I shall ... oh Ted, are you all right?'

Ted had dropped suddenly, landing on his knee. He pushed his hand into his pocket and pulled out a small box which he opened and turned towards

419

Olivia. 'Toff, Liv, Olivia Campbell, you're all these women to me, and I've been carrying this ring round for such a long time, just waiting for the day when I could finally ask you to be my wife. I wanted to wait until we found out what had happened to our baby. Little did I know when I got out of bed this morning that today would be the day that I could finally ask you.' He beamed hopefully up at her. 'Olivia Campbell, will you be my ...'

Olivia squealed with excitement, drowning his last words out. 'Yes!' she cried ecstatically.

There was a ripple of applause from passengers who had stopped to watch his proposal. She looked at the silver band with a tiny blue stone which encircled her finger. 'Where did you get it?'

'It was Mam's. Dad gave it to me when I told him we were back together,' said Ted.

'Your lovely father,' said Olivia. 'He'll be made up when he hears about Jess and Dana.'

He nodded. 'He certainly will.'

She smiled happily. 'My darling Ted, I think I must be the happiest woman in the world right now, and once again it's all down to you.'

He picked her up and swung her round before setting her down and kissing her softly. 'I can't wait to see you again, so that we can visit our daughters and spend some proper family time together.' He smiled blissfully. 'That's going to take some getting used to – "our daughters".'

She gazed into his eyes, which sparkled enticingly at her. 'I love you, Edward Hewitt.'

The guard began to close the train doors.

Ted picked Olivia up again and carried her over to one of the carriages. Still holding her in his arms, he kissed her softly. 'I love you too, my darling Toff!'

READ IT NOW

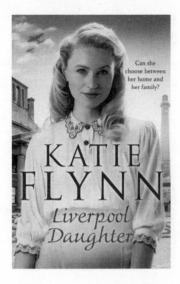

*'Home is where the heart is, and my heart belongs to Liverpool.
We wouldn't dream of leavin' our beloved city . . .'*

August 1940

As the Luftwaffe swarm over Liverpool, Shane Quinn
decides to move his family back to the safety of Ireland.
But his only child, the beautiful Dana, would rather stay
and serve her country than flee to a foreign land.

Determined to make it on her own, she joins the WAAF
with newfound pals Patty and Lucy. There's plenty of
excitement to be had on a RAF station, even a chance or
two at love . . .

But the stark reality of war begins to take its toll and the
three girls soon discover they need their friendship more
than ever. And when shocking news arrives from Ireland,
Dana will realise the true importance of family.

AVAILABLE IN PAPERBACK AND EBOOK

arrow books

READ IT NOW

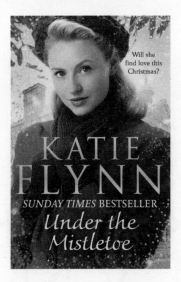

Liverpool, 1940

When war comes to Britain, Jessica Wilson and her friend
Ruby seize the opportunity to leave behind the orphanage
they grew up in and start new lives in the NAAFI. With
only forged papers as identification the girls expect to be
turned away but are delighted with an offer of work.

For the first time in their lives they experience real
independence and it isn't long before they're spending
their evenings enjoying the delights of Liverpool.

When Jessica meets the handsome Tom, she feels as
though her life is complete, but after a chance encounter
with a friend, she soon learns that not everything is as
it seems.

As Jessica begins to uncover the truth, she unravels a web
of lies, starting with the night of her birth . . .

AVAILABLE IN PAPERBACK AND EBOOK

arrow books

KATIE FLYNN

If you want to continue to hear from the
Flynn family, and to receive the latest news about
new Katie Flynn books and competitions,
sign up to the Katie Flynn newsletter.

Join today by visiting
www.penguin.co.uk/katieflynnnewsletter